DOWN from the SKIES

Spatterlight
Amstelveen 2024

DOWN from the SKIES

JOEL ANDERSON

A novel set in Jack Vance's Beyond

Published by Spatterlight, Amstelveen 2024

Cover art by M.J. ter Brughe

ISBN 978-1-61947-495-6

www.spatterlight.nl

Foreword

The name of Joel Anderson (1950 – 2024) should not be unfamiliar to those who have been reading Jack Vance's works since the early years of the new millennium and the start of the Vance Integral Edition project. Joel worked on the composition and typesetting of many VIE volumes and went on, in post-VIE years, to singlehandedly produce nearly all the paperbacks in the Spatterlight Press Signature Series, then the hardcovers, then the Integral Edition in Dutch, followed by a slew of Vance books in French, German and Italian. There has never been, nor will there ever likely be again, anyone who has typeset as many Jack Vance books as Joel Anderson. That's why, if you didn't know Joel Anderson before — you will now.

There is another reason, which you hold in your hands: Joel's personal labour of love, which he titled *Down from the Skies*. Joel had been a lifelong fan of Vance's books when in the late 1980's he began to plot a novel set in that grand Vancean setting, the galactic "Oikumene" and its lawless counterpart, the rough and tumble "Beyond". The novel came together gradually, over many years.

When interstellar travel was made possible by the invention of the Jarnell Intersplit, every religious sect, every political grouping — every minority that felt restricted or oppressed by the laws, rules or conventions of Earth society — packed their bags and left to find a new home in the vastness of the galaxy, free space where they could live according to their own devices. Even then, there was not enough room for the more troublesome sort to persist acceptably; and these folk went Beyond. With time, a vast volume of space — a perceptible fraction of the galaxy — was settled in relative peace and order. Within the Oikumene — renamed "the Gaean Reach" in later Vance work — travel and trade were protected by the Interworld Police Coordinating Company, while society and technology were monitored and (to an extent) controlled by The Institute. But in the Beyond, law and order had no reach. Anything could happen.

In a backwater of the Beyond lies Wennoc, a mostly rural world colonized hundreds of years earlier by refugees from Old Earth. Wennoc has witnessed turbulent times in the past but is now relatively quiet; scattered vestiges of old technology are poorly understood, in varying states of disrepair. When visitors come down from the skies, the question is whether they are benevolent, or have a more sinister plan for Wennoc and its inhabitants.

It is, after all — the Beyond.

This is Joel Anderson's literary legacy: a tribute to the worlds and works of Jack Vance, that goes well Beyond: *Down from the Skies* is an entertaining romp through a believable, idiosyncratic new world — an adventure which earns Joel a fitting place among the Paladins of Vance.

— Koen Vyverman
April, 2024

Contents

1. MORA OLD HALL

The old southern land route from the Harnish peninsula to the Eynnish mainland had long been impractical for conducting trade due to the expansion of the wetlands surrounding the ruins of Mellatuno, but ships crossed regularly to Hoiin and Parnala with cargoes of Harnish lumber for furniture and paper, medicinal herbs and fungi, tree oils and distilled spirits. Such exports provided the folk of Harna the hard currency with which they purchased manufactured goods from the mainland. Some Harnish farms exploited the possibilities for trade and prospered, while others kept to their old habits of isolation and self sufficiency.

Mora was a farm richer than some of its neighbors, poorer than places like Inboa or Marstoc. It kept the wildness of the mountains to its back, and was hidden from the southern end of windy Hoina Bay by forty miles of intervening hills and woods.

By early afternoon one spring day the farmers of Mora were setting potatoes on a flat piece of ground below the apple orchard. Others tended the pigs, chickens and oxen, or sharpened hoes. Those inside the house were washing up after the noon meal, reading, weaving, napping, kneading bread, preparing the wort for the week's brewing.

Above them Mora's slate-clad roofs wandered in their hips and gables, supporting look-outs, cupolas and sleeping porches, leaning on chimneys of many flues.

Under a sloping ceiling near the top of the west range, Micca pulled open a door, but Hennig called from somewhere behind.

"Micca! Tell Branna to cut us four yard-boards, for the finished wall then. Some of that yellow fir, tongue-and-groove one-by-fours. They don't need sanding, but we don't want any knots in them. We'll give them a bit of waxing when everything's up."

"Right," Micca hollered back. "I'll tell him." Saying 'us' and 'we' didn't' mean Hennig would be doing any of the work, of course. He spent much of his time drawing measured plans of Mora from the deepest cellar to the cupola on the water tower. He'd been at it since before Micca was born, and hadn't completely finished even the first floor yet.

But that was all right. It was a worthy project in Micca's opinion, and he wouldn't mind putting up Hessy's new pantry.

He clumped down a dogleg stair and took a meandering route through the house, avoiding places where there might be people who thought they should talk to him. He came to another stair with balusters carved to resemble running children, this one rising, entered the Mora's apartments, then went up another short stair and into his own room.

He examined a set of wooden knobs under a window seat, which were set as he had left them. These were the only visible parts of his grandfather's radio receiver, which he had disassembled and rebuilt into the wall after Priest Palmer's preaching on the danger of 'listening to the Eynnish voices' (a phrase equivalent to 'embracing subversive heresies' by the Invigorationists). If anyone had snooped in Micca's room they probably hadn't recognized the receiver's tuning knobs, now disguised as drawer pulls, and the earpieces lay undisturbed under the bed. But *The Voice of Hoiin* and *Parnala Speaks!* didn't come in very well until after dark. There had been talk in the newspaper of a party of investors defying Eynnish patents and establishing a broadcasting station in the Harnish city of Hannava, but nothing had come of that yet...

He didn't have time to play with it now. Micca left his room and moved on again, now through a series of dark, interconnected store-rooms, out and onto a high, open balcony, back into the house, down a storey and southward. The region he was now in was quiet, and smelled of old wood and bee's wax; its rooms had been empty for most of Micca's life, though they were sometimes put at the disposal of guests. The farm's population rose and fell generation to generation (there were eighty-two people living at Mora last time Micca had counted), not dramatically in either direction, but currently there was room for young people to move into their own rooms when they married, and a few to set aside for visitors from other farms. Priest Palmer had frowned sadly at the empty windows when taking up duties at the farm several years ago, and had recommended larger families during one of his homilies, hinting that the methods commonly used to prevent conception were both aesthetically repellent and displeasing to Wennoc. The Mora had countered that this smacked of mainland Eynnish teaching, and although ninety percent or more of Harnish religious practice was identical to that of the Eynnish, Palmer thanked the Mora for his insight and made no more pronouncements on the subject. But it was about that time that the new priest began to hold special devotional services one evening each week, attended at first by only a few.

Micca walked slowly down an empty corridor, thinking he might see if Merim and Danna were having supper in their apartment tonight. Merim always put something tasty on the table, and Micca didn't want to join the majority of his relatives in the big hall tonight. And Danna was famed for his doughnuts, the only thing he'd ever learned to cook. Sometimes he mixed in berries or nuts, or sprinkled them with caster sugar. Micca had caught a whiff of hot lard near there this morning…

A few yards on a glimmer of lamp light cut the increasing gloom. A door had opened, a hand visible clutching its stile. Then a face looked out, Ennesia's face.

"Micca!" she hissed, and looked both ways down the corridor. She came out, pulled the door closed behind her and examined Micca. He wore hide pants and boots and an old smock-like shirt of faded green. From the belt around his shirt hung a hammer, pry-bar and spooled measuring tape. A pair of glass lenses was set on his nose. Their thin silver bows were loose behind his ears, and to keep them from slipping off his face at inopportune times, he had fixed a length of cord to them and tied it behind his head. He could see things close at hand well enough without the lenses but had to squint at things far away. He had told Ennesia that his reason for acquiring them had been to make hunting easier, and he had reportedly become a better hunter, but he wore them most of the day now, and Ennesia hadn't heard the other people in the house mock him as having grown old before his time, as several had when she had been at Mora during Yule.

Micca approached her. "Who are you afraid will see you, Nessy?"

The smile she had shown when she caught sight of him became crooked. "Who do you think? My mother. I told her I had a headache so I wouldn't have to go stamp and dance with them in the church."

"You don't know how to dance?" Micca held his arms by his sides and shuffled his feet. "We could try it a bit up here, have some practice."

"As the old saying goes, if you want to dance, you need a little bit of grace." She raised her hands over her head and spun on her toes. "That's how it's done. Like a forest sprite, free but dignified. Or like this…"

She took his hands and swayed her hips as Micca had. He moved his hands to her waist, but she pushed him away.

"Not the kind they do in the church, anyway. They stamp their feet up and down like they're trying to kill mudrunner fry, and lately they've started throwing up their arms and lurching from side to side. It's ridiculous."

Micca laughed. "There might *be* a few mudrunners down there. Hennig said that when he was a kid they burned bricks to pave the floor, but even then a lot of people wanted the dirt floor to stay dirt so they could be closer to Wennoc."

"If that's what they want, they'd do better going outside!"

Micca looked at her bare feet. "Is that where you're going?"

"I don't know. Probably not. It's still fairly cool outside. I just don't like to confine my dainty little feet unless I have to, and your house is warm for this time of the year."

Her feet were for a fact dainty, certainly when seen next to Micca's. The dress she wore looked summery, calf-length ivory cotton spotted by tiny flowers of colored thread, belted by a length of blue cord, the same color as the one that secured her hair behind her neck… in repose her face was delicate, almost wistful, but her eyebrows were often lifted, her mouth wide in a toothy smile, showing strong white teeth, her eyes wide or squinting in turn…

They had started walking without apparent purpose, back in the general direction Micca had come. Ennesia caught him studying her. She looked back at him for a moment, then turned away and said, "It was a nice funeral, as far as funerals go."

"I guess it was. It was good so many people from the other farms came for it."

"Everyone liked your grandfather, or respected him, at least. His tricks and growls scared me when I was little, but he could be so funny. I suppose a child wasn't sophisticated enough to appreciate his kind of humor."

Micca and Ennesia walked on in silence, a companionable one, but bearing a certain tenseness. They ducked to pass under a low balk of carved oak. Micca swung an arm up to slap it, and caught Ennesia's hand in his as he dropped it again. "When are you going back to Topping? Your dad went already, didn't he?" Micca wondered why he had said that. She might think he wanted her gone...

But she said, "Yes, there's a lot to do this time of year, and I don't have to tell you he was getting tired of mother's friends here trying to Invigor him. She wants us to stay until Sunday, though. Apparently your priest's got some special service coming up." She rolled her eyes. "I can hardly wait."

"They'll make us holy or kill us trying."

Ennesia laughed. Micca laughed too. They grew quiet and smiled at each other, almost involuntarily. Then Ennesia laughed again.

"Don't we make a precious little scene! Anyone would think we were lovers, when we're actually just cousins."

Micca shook his head at the suggested folly on the part of these presumed observers, flushing at the same time. "Only third-cousins, once removed," he said.

Ennesia's hand was still in his, and he felt like he was on the shore of a sunlit lake, hot and sweaty, in dire need of a swim.

They wandered into the Mora's office. Ennesia stood over a large, wood-covered book lying open on a lectern, turning the pages. "You haven't recorded Mora Stennig's death in your house book yet."

"I'm leaving it for Sam. That's the new Mora's job."

She looked at another book, this from the shelves on the wall, illustrated with engravings of Eynnish churches. The next she looked at was written in Harnish. "'Something about bird houses?"

"'Sundry Hints Concerning Rightful Care of Domestic Fowl'," Micca read over her shoulder.

She re-shelved the book, then looked around the room. "Where is the Mora's radio set? Remember that pretty song we heard from

Parnala when I was here at Yule?" She sang, "Forever and always, I will love theeee..."

Micca continued,

"Until the bright stars wink out in the gloom..."

They joined voices, Ennesia in a croaking effort at baritone, Micca singing falsetto:

"And till the lamps fall into the sea;

"Yea, even then,

"I'll be loving thee!"

Ennesia stopped, coughing and laughing. "I think we missed a few lines. I love the melody, though."

"Parnala had somebody or other singing it almost every day for a while. Milli Incinen sang it last week on Hoiin's station with fiddles and horns."

"She's my favorite! Maybe they'll do it again — but where *is* the receiver? You didn't let your priest smash it, did you? I've heard he takes a dim view of radios."

"Come on, I'll show you."

In his room, Ennesia laughed, pleased and impressed with the way Micca had built the receiver in the wall, but she changed her mind about listening to it. "Somebody might catch us, and then you'd probably lose it."

"We could wait till after dark. It would come in better then. Or I can bolt the door."

Ennesia made no response. Micca closed the door and slid a locking bar into its slot in the casing. He noticed a slight trembling in his hand. Telling himself to grow up, he squatted down and retrieved the ear pieces from under the bed. "We can each use one, like before," he said. "The newer receivers come with something like a hat or a bonnet that you wear, not these crude loose ones."

"I've seen the advertisements. They look smart, but then only one person at a time could use it. And I'd think it would be confining."

Micca sat motionless for a moment, then tossed the ear pieces away. "Speaking of confining, isn't your dress a little tight? I'm concerned for your circulation."

Ennesia looked down, blushed, then undid a row of buttons over her breasts. "Yes. That's better. I suppose I ate too well last winter." She traced a line with her fingertip up the inside of Micca's thigh. "I think those leggings might be compromising your circulation, too."

Micca put a hand on the bow of his lenses, then said, "Take these off for me. Like before."

She carefully removed his eye-glasses and set them aside, then undid the rest of her buttons. Micca leaned backward, fumbled with laces and tried to pull off his pants and his boots at the same time. After a brief struggle he kicked them aside.

"How long has it been?" Ennesia asked as she helped him get off his shirt.

"Since the time we heard that song! If I remember right. I thought I was dreaming."

"Do you have a pen handy? Maybe you should take notes this time."

Laughing, Ennesia tried to avoid him as he lunged. He caught her and they rolled together in a tangled embrace. Micca put his mouth to her neck and kissed it.

"Micca," Ennesia whispered.

He raised his head, blinking at her.

She took his head in her hands and kissed his mouth.

Micca stared into her eyes, and after a moment reciprocated.

Their clothes lay on the floor or hung over the foot of the bedstead. The blankets and sheets were tangled. They lay on their backs, feet playing with each other at the end of the bed. Ennesia turned onto her side and pulled hanks of his hair this way and that. "Have you ever tried tying it up in back?"

"I don't know if it's long enough."

"It might look good on you. That's how the bravos in Hannava have it, or at least that's what Harlic says. Last month he came back from there with it tied up, and Priest Linto sneaked up behind him and cut it off with a shears."

"Priests are a sly bunch."

Ennesia lay down again, then raised herself and smiled at him. "I wondered if we'd have an opportunity for this. I was afraid the circumstances would make it difficult."

"We can talk about my hair any time you like."

Ennesia punched his shoulder. "You're an awful brute. But I thought maybe that with the funeral and all..."

"I think my grandfather would have been all for it. Us, I mean." He wanted to say something more, but couldn't find words.

Ennesia suddenly sat up and put her feet on the floor. "I have to go. If my mother finds out what's been going on she'll make us get married."

Micca sat quiet for a moment, then blurted, "Would that be so bad?"

She too hesitated, then began buttoning her dress. "Well, I'm certainly old enough. So are you. But there's more to marriage than bed play, and they don't always want you to marry whoever it is *you* want to."

"Oh, we're not that stodgy at Mora. People choose on their own unless they wait too long and the oldsters round up some other procrastinator for them."

Micca swung his legs over the side of the bed, stretched his arms and cracked his knuckles over his head. "We could just run off, go live somewhere else for a while. Marstoc, maybe."

"Where in the world did you get an idea like that?" Dressed now, Ennesia took up Micca's brush pulled it briskly through her hair. But she went on in a musing tone. "Not that Marstoc isn't a nice place. The gardens are wonderful."

"They'd probably want you to tend them. You've always been wild for plants and things...and they've only got an old-fashioned liturgist, no Invigorated priest."

"Well, that's a definite advantage! But I'm going before you lose your head and issue a formal proposal of wedlock!"

She fumbled at the door. Micca joined her and released the lock. She looked at him and smiled a little. "You look like someone just told you your pet chicken was in the soup pot."

"I never had a pet chicken."

She ran her fingers lightly along the line of his jaw. "Let's be sure to get together again before I go back to Topping. And put on your clothes! At least for now. Goodbye!"

2. AFTER SUPPER

icca flopped onto the bed and buried his face in the pillows. Then he sat up, got into his leggings and a clean shirt, put on house-shoes, straightened up the room. He sat on the edge of the bed, standing up a boot with his toe and tipping it over again. The sun hadn't set yet, but the light from the window was dim and brown. He warmed up the receiver and lay again on the bed, the speakers over his ears. He was able to raise the Voice of Hoiin, but after a few minutes it faded into chirps and sizzles.

A thought occurred to him, a vision of a cloud of bugs, a great bank of them hanging high over Hoina Bay, obstructing the waves of disembodied sound as they tried to make the leap from Hoiin to the wire that waited for their signal, strung between two of Mora's chimneys. Or maybe a storm was brewing. Clouds had been gathering all afternoon in the north and east. There might be lightning over the Bay, where the fishes swam and jumped…

Though he wasn't fond of oily sea fish, this made him think of food, and indeed his stomach felt empty. He secured the radio, washed his face in his grandfather's bathroom, then trotted down and through the west range.

Although Danna and Merim's place was surrounded on three sides, and had access to other regions of Mora by way of a couple of ground-floor doors, it felt like a separate house. Its parlor windows and a rarely used 'front' door faced the big hall across a courtyard. It had two floors, its own cellar and attic, several bedrooms and two bathrooms; and while many of the apartments used by married couples were equipped with a pantry and basic cooking facilities, Danna and Merim had a full kitchen.

As Micca had hoped, Merim was in it. Heavy, red-cheeked and usually cheery, she greeted Micca with a half-puzzled expression, but asked him to stay for supper. He sat down on a bench between the table and the wall.

Danna, younger brother of Micca's father, lumbered in, smelling of yeast and malt. He was bulkier than Merim, with a broad face and thick black hair. He sat down beside his nephew, propped his feet on the table.

"I wrote a letter for Sam," Danna said.

"Did you post it yet?"

"Not yet."

"I should write one too to put in with it."

"Yes. And think carefully before you write."

Micca wondered what there was to think about. Now that the old Mora was dead, Samma would come back from Hoiin and take up his grandfather's duties. Maybe not this week, depending on the weather over the Bay, but soon. Danna said nothing more.

Merim looked into a pot on the stove and said supper would be ready in a little while. Danna wordlessly pointed to a covered jar on the table, and Micca took out a doughnut, speckled with sugar. He propped his feet on the table (he had heard no complaint from Merim when Danna had done so), picked up last week's newspaper from the table and began reading.

Micca's cousin Westin came into the kitchen. He joined Micca and Danna on the bench and peered at the newspaper. "What's so interesting?" he asked Micca.

Micca grunted. Westin had preferred to do other things when kids his age were learning to read…The newspaper's title was worked out in old Eynnish glyphs, a system of syllabic writing originally impressed with styluses on clay tablets. The glyphs, their forms frozen by tradition, weren't well suited for the representation of Eynnish as it was spoken now, less so to Harnish, and to make them readable a tangle of phonological modifiers crawled over the words like parasitic ivy on a tree. The rest of the newspaper was printed using the thirty-two characters of the Harnish alphabet. In modern times everyone in Wennoc used these letters, but when a more imposing or ornamental effect was wanted the old glyphs were employed, even in Harna. Micca's grandfather had remarked once that it was ironic the only Harnish words in the newspaper, its title, 'Hernespela Hænnavæ', were disguised by Eynnish glyphs, while the rest was all in Eynnish, Wennoc's common tongue, but printed with Harnish letters.

His eyes fell at random on an advertisement for electric batteries. "Recharges for a single-pot battery are down to a tenth of a penny," he said. "You can buy the pots themselves for two... at least in Hannava."

Westin said, "The peddler who comes here gets a good bit more than that."

"You get quite a lot for your silver," Merim said as she added a measure of salt to the pot. "You can light sootless lamps with these things, and listen to the Voice of Hoiin, too."

Westin smiled slyly. "Listen to heretics?"

"*I* like to listen," said Danna and Merim's daughter Tuny. "The songs are so pretty."

Her brother Binta, a couple of years younger than Micca, sat opposite him at the table before a battered old copy of the Writs. Binta studied with Priest Palmer and did no farm work. He looked up with a serious expression. "The Eynnish voices pry us from Wennoc's Bosom."

Micca snorted. "If we're worried about Eynnish voices corrupting us, why do we *speak* Eynnish? We didn't always. We could go back to Harnish and after a couple of generations nobody'd understand Eynnish anymore. Then we could relax and enjoy the music."

A chuckle came from Danna. "And say rude things to the faces of those who didn't have their grandfathers' tongue."

Micca glanced at him with a smile. Danna was the only other person in the kitchen who understood Harnish.

Westin went to the door. "Thanks for the doughnuts, Danna. I'd better get on."

"You can stay for supper too."

"Thanks, Aunt Merry, but I told Branna I'd eat with him in the hall."

"Remember you've got chores in the morning, boy."

Westin assured his aunt he would be in bed early and sober. Micca heard him walk away. A door opened. Westin's voice echoed back, low and sullen. Micca looked up. Westin came back, shoulders slumping. Binta scrambled out of his chair and ran to the door.

Micca hid his face in the *Hernespela*. Westin fidgeted uncertainly near the table. Binta escorted Wudego Palmer, the farm's priest, into the kitchen. Merim made rote apologies for the mess.

"I haven't come on an inspection tour, my dear," Priest Palmer said cheerfully. He looked around the room, tall and thick under the beams, a middle-aged man with scant, straw colored hair, small features in a large, square face, eyes glinting behind a pair of pinch-nose lenses. The priest was wearing his long red coat and red hat, evidently just up from the church. "My concern is for your spirit, Merim, not your pots and pans!"

Westin chuckled obsequiously. Palmer smiled at Westin briefly, then became serious. "As I was saying, young man, I hope that the whispers I've heard about you and Lenia are unfounded; the two of you are neither affianced nor wed, and your alleged behavior would of course be illicit. You and Lenia will meet with me in my office tomorrow, together with your respective parents, and we'll have a frank discussion."

Now Palmer smiled at the others in the room. He clapped his hands together. "Ah, here's the girl Tuny! How smart you look in your little frock. Are you a good helper to your mother, darling?"

"Yes, priest."

Binta said, "A braggart is not pleasing to Wennoc."

"You lazy snot rag! You don't help her at *all*!" Tuny cried, outraged at her brother's slur.

Over the edge of the *Hernespela* Micca saw Palmer take Binta and Tuny by the backs of their collars. The priest pushed them together, faces inches apart. "Kiss each other and show your respect, just as you would to Wennoc," he said. "This is my earnest instruction."

When Palmer was satisfied the youngsters stood again in Wennoc's grace, he looked around the room again. His gaze fell upon Micca. Micca lowered his eyes and started slowly moving his lips, as Branna did when he read, but he couldn't hide. His legs were long, and his feet were still on the table.

Merim said, "You'll stay for supper, priest?"

"No, Merim, but thank you." He squinted through his lenses. "Is that Micca hiding yonder?"

Micca nodded, but didn't put down the paper.

Palmer's face softened. "Tell me, Micca. Are you feeling better now about your grandfather's passing? I know it was hurtful, but you must remember that his leave-taking was blessèd. He has achieved unity with Wennoc, our sacred parent. Saying this, I nonetheless understand how hurtful it was for you to see him laid to rest in the ossuary, so near the tombs of your own mother and father. The sad loss of Stennig, the twenty-eighth—"

"Twenty-sixth," Danna rumbled. He added something in Harnish but Micca didn't catch it.

"The departure of my dear friend Stennig, twenty-sixth in the line of Moras, has kept you, Micca, his already orphaned grandson, much in my mind these past days. In fact I came here looking for you. There's a matter some of us wish to speak with you about. Please come join us in the round parlor when you've had your supper."

Palmer nodded to the others. "Merim, Dannig, Tunia..." He clenched his fist and held it high. "Bindig! Study until your eyes are red, then study more! I'll expect you to have the first forty stanzas of The Dream in the Reeds word-perfect by Sunday week."

"Yes, priest!" Binta shouted.

"Westin, I'll see you tomorrow after breakfast."

When the priest had gone, Merim and Tuny, pushing Danna and Micca's legs to the floor, spread a cloth and set out pots, platters, cups, a jug of milk and another of beer. Plates and forks were passed around, and they ladled out portions of pork shoulder that had been well browned and then braised with cider, spiced bacon, onions and herbs. There were boiled dumplings to eat with the pot liquor, bread, and greens from the glass-house.

Micca ate with less appetite than the food deserved. Palmer couldn't have found out so soon, or at all, about his activity this afternoon with Ennesia, and if he knew of the few previous episodes, he'd have said something before. So why did the priest want to talk to him?

He looked sidelong at his Uncle Danna. Danna was pouring a cup of beer down his throat, but noticed Micca's glance. Danna put the cup down. After a moment he said, "You'd better think well before answering the priest."

"Answer him about what? And what am I supposed to think about before I write to Sam?"

"Haven't they spoken to you at all yet?"

Suddenly Binta came around the table and seized Micca's hand. "Oh, cousin!" he said, looking at Micca adoringly. "You'll fill us all with Vigor!"

Micca pulled away from Binta, repelled by the damp touch of his hand.

Danna pursed his lips, frowning briefly at his son Binta. "It might be better if you find out for yourself."

Micca thanked his aunt for supper and left before anyone spoke again, which they hadn't seemed likely to do. Danna could be notoriously taciturn. He was happy now he hadn't eaten too much. His stomach wasn't altogether easy. A good bath might help; he had only splashed himself earlier. Beer or something stronger would help more. He decided he had no intention of presenting himself before Palmer and whoever else planned to meet in the round parlor.

Maybe they only wanted him to make some decisions about late planting before Samma came back and took up the Mora's duties; there had been a lot of talk at breakfast about what to do this year with a field west of the mill pond. But that was a stupid supposition. He was a builder, a carpenter; he probably didn't know much more about crops than Binta did. There was no point in playing along with them.

Micca remembered he meant to talk to Branna. Branna generally had all the gossip around the house and was always ready for a jar of something. Micca skirted the rooms to the rear of the big hall and came out into the wagon yard. There was no rain yet but the air was heavy, and silent sheets of lightning flashed under clouds in the east. He ran up six worn stone steps, across an arcaded porch and into the house again.

Standing immediately before him was Westin, wearing a sly grin.

"Have you talked to the priest yet?"

"No."

"I think they're going to turn you into a deacon and dress you up in a red coat!"

"What are you talking about?"

Micca walked on and Westin kept up with him. "Something's going on. What is it? Is Sam on his way back from the University?"

"He's still in Hoiin. Danna's going to send a letter, but Sam doesn't know Stennig is dead yet."

"Micca!" The passage they were in widened to form little alcoves on either side. Micca hadn't noticed old Stalba sitting at the desk he kept in one of them. Stalba was ninety and had spells of lameness, but his ears were sharp. "Micca," the old man said again, struggling to gain his feet. "Weren't you counseled not to speak about certain things as yet?"

"I have no idea what you're talking about," Micca said. It looked as though Stalba meant to walk along with him and Westin. Micca tried to speed up, but Westin was in front of him.

"So you say," said Stalba. He glanced at Westin, then whispered to Micca as though Westin wouldn't hear him. "But you can tell old Stalba. Are you going to take them up on it? With some remedial training you might do, you know."

Micca's second-cousin Hessy was coming up a twisting stair with an arm load of table linen. "Do for what?"

"They're not telling," Westin said.

Hessy tossed her linen into a cupboard and hurried to catch up with them. "I'll bet it has something to do with all the 'special' meetings in the church lately. Isn't that right, Stalba? Some people around here seem to think they're dearer to Wennoc than the rest of us. Does that follow doctrine?"

"Wennoc knows its own," Stalba said grimly.

"Oh? And how do you know what Wennoc thinks, you desiccated old wreck? I suppose priest told you."

"You watch yourself, missy! You're not so old that I wouldn't take you over my knee and administer a good paddling if your behavior warrants."

Hessy and Westin laughed. Hessy was only fifteen years Stalba's junior, but very spry, and possessed of half again his bulk. Micca took the opportunity to walk ahead of the others. He was off course now and would have to double back to reach Branna's room.

He didn't get far, halted by a stink in his nose and a dirty hand on his arm.

"What's wrong with them two?" demanded Bacnod, a man who tended the pigs. Bacnod was originally from Marstoc, expelled by the Marling after some kind of trouble a couple of years ago, but he was Invigorated, and had been allowed residence at Mora on Priest Palmer's guarantee of his good behavior.

"I wasn't listening. They're making jokes or something," Micca said.

Bacnod, always on the watch for insult, assumed he was the subject of the joke. He shouldered past Micca and confronted the others. Upon learning the facts, Bacnod transferred his resentment to Stalba's cause, who had also come from another farm, though Stalba had long ago appended 'Mora' to his name. Bacnod told Westin he lacked Vigor, going around laughing like a girl when his elders were insulted.

Micca was almost around the corner, but Hessy called out to him. He turned reluctantly to see the whole group catching up with him.

"What do you say about it, Micca?" Hessy asked him. "Is Stalba right? Since when are women the only ones allowed to laugh? You're the Mora's son, and the Mora laughed all the time. What do *you* say about it?"

"Only the Mora's *grand*son," Stalba corrected.

"If his dad Robig hadn't got himself drowned, Micca would be the Mora's son," Hessy countered. "It's the same difference."

"Leave him have his say," Bacnod said. "Never mind little Westy. Better still let's hear what Micca thinks about when a 'Vigorated man should laugh, and when he shouldn't. It would be something new to hear Micca say anything at all about the Vigor."

Micca behaved as though he hadn't heard the calls for him to speak and walked on, eyes on the floor. To his dismay he found that he had walked into a room of tall oak panels and a bowed row of windows looking out on an interior yard. People called it the round parlor, though its only claim to roundness was the outward curve of its window bay. Henning referred to it as Mendith's Repose, since a lady of that name was supposed to have maintained a gazebo on this spot before the house had overwhelmed it. Mora's chief builder Henning was here himself, using a stick to poke at a loose brick in the chimney behind a tiled stove. Deaconess Wamod was also present, hunched over in a chair, her nose in a large book of Writs that lay open in her lap. A thin, hunched man with a shaved head stood beside her chair, dressed like Wamod in rusty wadmal. Micca didn't know him. Wamod and the stranger must have just come up from the church, since their feet were bare and dirty.

At least Palmer wasn't here. Maybe he had given up on Micca's arrival. Micca hesitated, mentally re-routing his path through the house. He eyed a door beside the tile stove. The spaces next to chimneys often presented convenient cavities for stairwells, and there was one here, but Henning stood near the door, and he'd be sure to stop Micca and start wittering on about the sad state of the round parlor's chimney.

Henning saw him now, but Hessy, Westin, Bacnod and Stalba were coming into the room behind him, and to Micca's relief Henning went to speak with Bacnod, who, when he could be separated from the pigs in his charge, did fair work as a mason. But before Micca could slip out, Wamod looked up from her Writs. "Micca!"

"Is this your candidate, then?" said the stranger, pointing at Micca. Westin also peered curiously at him. Hessy frowned.

Micca got by Bacnod and Henning and pulled open the door beside the stove.

Someone was behind it — Ennosa Topping, Ennesia's mother. She stared at Micca, who reflexively stood aside to let her enter the room. "Oh, Micca," she said with joyful solemnity. "You'll be such a blessing, such an example to your kin!"

"Come here, Micca," Wamod said. Micca complied, only because her chair was near the main exit from the parlor. As he approached Wamod continued, "I've just come up from the church, where some of us had a very Invigorated communion with Wennoc — oh, what glory! And with that fresh in mind —"

"Glory!" Ennosa interjected.

Westin's theory had horribly become real. They meant to make him a deacon. Wamod started to speak again, but Micca walked out of the room, not looking at her or anyone else.

Westin followed him, then Henning, and finally all eight of them, Wamod coming last, hopping as she struggled into a shoe, burdened by her heavy book.

Micca felt like he was a fishhook that had snagged a heavy hank of weeds. Would they follow him all the way to Branna's place? Westin trotted beside him with questions and speculations. The shaved-head stranger, striding on long legs, got ahead of them, turned and stood in front of Micca. "Is this the one, then?" he said, speaking over Micca's shoulder to Wamod.

"He's the one," Wamod confirmed, smiling somewhat grimly at Micca, who had moved away and found himself backed up against the wall. "Micael Robigæn of Mora: a rosy-cheeked youth of eighteen winters, pure, full of Vigor—at least potentially."

Hennig pushed forward. "Micca is nineteen. He carried his coals and put his token on the cairn up Greenfell."

"Huh," said Bacnod. "However old he is, he slumps and wilts like a sissy-boy."

"Vigor is as Vigor does," the bald stranger intoned mysteriously.

Hessy elbowed forward and put her face close to the stranger's. "Don't I know you? Yes! You're Smola, the Yarl's gasman over at Topping Farm."

Micca realized Hessy was right; he hadn't recognized Smola with his hairless head and more or less clean face.

The man frowned at the floor. "One time, so I was." Then he met Hessy's eyes. "But I have got the call, the call of Holy Wennoc!" He thrust up his arms, which trembled in the air over his head. Ennosa responded in kind, raising her arms, swaying like tall grass in the breeze. Some of the others imitated her, perhaps embarrassed to be doing so outside the church.

Wamod put her book carefully on the floor, took the newcomer's hand and patted it. "Since not all of you know him, I should introduce the Monitor Smolic—he's an associate of our own Priest Palmer, and Visiting Member of the County Commission on Invigoration."

Ennosa smiled. "Yes, Smolic comes from my home place. He used to tend the sumps and excrement crypts there, and I'm sure he'd tell us his idle hours were spent in sin and despair." She gave Smolic a little hug. "But now he witnesses to the glory of Wennoc, and it shines through him as he goes about alerting folks to their need for an ever more Vigorous Holiness."

Smolic responded stiffly to Ennosa's hug. "Glory," he said. "But I'm not the one we're concerned with. Let's have us a look-see at the candidate. As Monitor, I might want to set him a few questions."

"What do they mean, 'candidate'?" Westin asked Micca.

"I don't know and I don't care." The narrow passage had trapped him in the middle of the group. He was no longer leader of the promenade, and somehow the group had reversed direction and worked its way back into the round parlor, taking him with it. Westin and Henning had taken up positions before and after Micca, like they were his wings on the ball field. Annoyed with them though he was, the presence of these two made him feel a little better.

"So just what is it they want you for?" Westin asked.

Henning said, "Yes. What's all this about?"

"Micca will shortly be entering into a new and important career," Wamod said solemnly.

Henning scowled. "Micca is my apprentice. He's Mora's Deputy Builder. I have something to say before he takes up another profession."

"Not to mention *me*!" said Micca. "Yes, I'm a builder, and I'm not going to be anything else."

Westin stared at Wamod. "You want him to be the new Mora! That's it, isn't it? But *Samma's* the new Mora. *He's* the first-born, he's the heir."

Micca had his hand on the latch of the door beside the chimney, but he had to turn back. "The Mora?"

"Samma may not want to cut short his schooling in Hoiin," Ennosa said with a sour smile. "I suppose you'd tell us that if we were as wise and learnèd as your brother with his yellow Eynnish hair, we wouldn't need our Vigor, or correct doctrine."

Some of Mora's most Invigorated residents, including Priest Palmer, had yellow hair, but before Micca could work his outrage into words, Westin said, "But that's why he's *at* the University, to get schooling so he can be the Mora. All the Moras go to the University for a spell, and the Marlings down at Marstoc, too."

Stalba ignored Westin. He told Henning, "That's just it, according to Wudego Palmer. Priest says Sammy's more'n likely to have got corrupted by those Heresiarchs in Hoiin."

The Heresiarchs had all been drowned by the Eynnish hundreds of years ago. Was everybody insane? Micca was angry and disgusted, and frightened. What was happening?

"I am not going to be the Mora!" he shouted. He wiped his mouth with the back of his hand. "What's the matter with you people? Samma's the Mora. I'm only his brother, but it's obvious I've got more wits and authority to talk about this than any of you halfwits."

Ennosa gasped. Bacnod stepped forward with an ugly face. Wamod waved them back with her hand. She prepared a smile, then faced Micca. "You're going to be something a little different than an ordinary Mora, my boy. Or let us say, something more than head of the farm. Much more."

"Micca's right," Westin said hotly. "You're halfwits — no, you're *outlaws*, that's what! You should be put off the farm."

Ennosa hustled up to Westin and slapped him. "What a wicked speech! And what disrespect to your elders!"

Westin touched a red spot on his face. Ennosa interpreted his expression as a further sign of wickedness, grabbed his upper arms and tried to shake him. Bacnod jerked Westin away from Ennosa, gave him a brutal back-handed blow to the face. "Get out of here and mind your own business!"

Micca watched in horror as Westin retreated, his nose and lip bleeding. Hessy went with him, arm around him, smoothing his hair. She glared back at the others in shock and anger.

Wamod, face now working in distress, raised her hands. "Oh, friends and kin!" she cried. "Let us come together in harmony! Westin's folks and a few others haven't been visited yet by the inner glory, but let violence be shunned! Peace and serenity are Wennoc's holy watchwords. Come, let us smile and rejoice at the glory coming to our farm."

Bacnod sullenly lifted his feet up and down. "Glory, glory."

Wamod and Ennosa showed more spirit. They kicked aside a small rug and began to dance a quick pattern on the planks of the floor.

"Glory, glory; we'll see glory!" they sang.

"Vigor, vigor; we've got vigor!"

Smolic and old Stalba joined them, waving their hands, eyes on the ceiling. Wamod cried out to the earth she worshiped in a strange, keening voice. Henning backed away and joined Micca, who stood paralyzed beside the stove.

The party of Invigorationists reformed and stamped toward them, swaying in unison. Wamod and Smolic closed in on Micca, grinning, beckoning for him to join them. Micca was used to turning his eyes away from such people, used to ignoring this kind of embarrassing behavior. Now he had no choice but to witness it up close, smell the musty fabric of their red coats, see the sweat stains on Monitor Smolic's hat and the pit-like pores on his nose. Wamod pushed her face close and winked moistly at him.

Micca edged backwards. He thought he might have been smiling, his face as mad as theirs, but he retained enough presence of mind to reach behind, grab the latch of the door beside the chimney.

Ennosa understood his intention. She compressed her lips, leaned in and gave him a vicious pinch on the butt. Micca jumped with a startled shout.

Wamod ceased her stamping and stared raptly at him "Glory! He's finally got the Vigor in him!"

Stalba shuffled up and shook both Micca's hands, nodding and grinning toothily. "You'll make your farm a fine Husband after all, yes sir!"

Micca pulled free, drove through the crowd and out the door.

Henning brandished his measuring stick at the others in the round parlor. "Just because somebody jumps and carries on—the boy doesn't know what you're planning! And so far as that goes, neither do I. What's this 'husband' business?"

"Keep out of it, old man," said Bacnod.

"The theory for the rite we're going to perform is well informed by Invigorated precepts," Wamod said primly. "Our sistren and brethren at Topping are committing a youth to Wennoc in the same manner."

"And what manner is that?" Henning asked.

3. IN THE DARK

Almost immediately Mica regretted not taking the stair beside the chimney. Here came Priest Palmer strolling down the passage toward him, hands clasped behind his back. Now he threw them out to either side.

"Micca!" he called. "I suppose you'd given up on me. I'm sorry. We had such energetic devotions in the church this evening that I went outdoors for a breath of air, and I seem to have forgotten the time."

Micca hadn't gotten more than a couple of yards from the round parlor, and now someone called his name from there...

Palmer performed a sleek maneuver, slipping past Micca and grasping the handle of the parlor's door. Wamod and Bacnod, both speaking at once, tried to come through. Palmer said, "Please return to the church. Sing numbers Eleven and One-eighteen. We'll join you presently."

He closed the door on them and turned to Micca. "I think after all we can have a more productive discussion without a lot of other people involved. Come, let's walk."

Micca walked on, more quickly than Palmer, but turned back. "They're crazy. They want me to be the Mora instead of Sam. Was that *your* idea?"

He had said it, plain and simple. Did the priest look chagrined, embarrassed? Micca thought so.

Palmer pulled out a handkerchief to polish his lenses. "I can imagine what they told you, and how they put it...

"Micca, you've lived here all your life, and you must know that some of the people in this house are not as sophisticated in their outlook or as capable of complex thought as others. Sometimes I have to frame subtle theological themes in picturesque language so they can understand them. Unfortunately, some of those who hear these colorful descriptions still miss the point, and embroider them in their own minds, sometimes with odd, even grotesque results. Another problem is that some of them are naturally dull and resentful. You could probably name of a few of them yourself."

'Odd'? 'Grotesque'? Micca began to wonder if he hadn't heard as much as the priest seemed to think.

Palmer sighed. Micca was afraid the priest was going to put his arm around his shoulder or commit some other supposedly friendly display, but he continued walking.

"It's a real struggle sometimes to keep them on a sensible path," Palmer continued. "The Harnish people have a long and sorry history of mimicking the errors of the Eynnish, forgetting or looking down on our own culture and its unique and innate appreciation of Wennoc. But we Harnish have a spiritual core, a feeling for and understanding of our world's soul. It might be this that prompts some to over-react. They get over-excited, to put it in plain words."

Palmer turned to look at Micca. "What I had intended to ask you to do is this: to stand up as a beacon to your less enlightened kinfolk; become a leader, show them the way, with strength and dignity. The office of Mora might have been part of this, but if you feel your brother really will return to Mora, that he'd be offended or regard you as a usurper, I withdraw that suggestion here and now. There are other ways a young man like you can help your kinsmen recognize the spiritual food present in their own culture."

"What's this husband business?"

"That! Well, it's more important than who becomes the next Mora. I'm sure Wamod, the Monitor, Bacnod — good people, but as I said, possibly lacking a full understanding of these matters — I'm sure whatever they said may have sounded a bit strange to you, or even unpleasant. What is actually intended that you — and you are the ideal candidate! — will enter into a ritual marriage with the earth, with Wennoc. You'll become your farm's Husband, a living, visible link between the people, their history, and the divine. Everyone will participate in the rite, and so become more closely knit, gain more than a blood or social kinship with each other. The office itself, as I see it, is essentially an honorary one, requiring only a few light duties on holy days, but the spiritual benefits will be immense, simply immense, for all involved!"

Micca was speechless. They had climbed a short flight of steps that gave onto a gallery over the big hall. The only light in the space came from doorways below, but Micca could make out the wooden heads (likenesses of long-gone Moras, or so Hennig said), forming the capitals of the posts that supported the roof framing. Neither Micca nor Palmer had chosen their route, but had drifted along as the priest spoke. Palmer grasped the gallery's railing and stared into the dark.

"I haven't been here such a long time, Micca, but I confess I feel a special closeness to your family, or more specifically, to you and your orphaned brother."

Before Micca could think what to say, Palmer spoke on. "You see, I too have lost a loved one to the sea, as you did your parents. My wife, my dear Signy...we had been joined only a few months. We had been living at a seminary in the south, and were to return home to Palma in the spring; Signia had fallen pregnant and we wanted our first child to be born in its homeland. But there was a storm. Our boat foundered. Signy...she was gone. I clung to the broken mast, I witnessed her go down, and I wanted to die too. But I swam to shore. Something told me my life wasn't finished. Afterward I asked myself many times why I deserved to live while she didn't. Finally, as I lay on my pallet one sleepless night, it seemed that Signy spoke with a quiet voice to my soul, and she told me to go out and try to improve the lives of others who lived, but lived for no reason, without hope or joy. This became my purpose."

Micca was impressed, but he felt no new camaraderie with the priest, and was afraid Palmer would now tell him he felt like his foster-father. Micca looked up at the wooden faces. All of them had been carved long ago; there were no places for his grandfather or Samma. Micca had felt in the last hour that Mora wasn't his home anymore, that it was gone with his grandfather and brother. Like Palmer had felt when he lost his wife? But that wasn't true. There was much of Stennig, of Micca's dimly remembered mother and father, all the ancestors he'd never seen, and Micca himself, in the house and its fields and woods; not so much in the things his family had built and used, but the emotions, memories and experiences of their lives. They had been preserved in the house, become as much a part of its fabric as its wood and brick and stone. He could often feel them, as well as people he supposed had died long ago: remnants, fleeting emanations, atmospheres as varied, as warm or cold, as crude or complex, as the people who had lived and died here.

Micca glanced at the priest. Palmer had nothing to do with this, though. He might not be a devil, he might even have good intentions, but the priest didn't fit Mora's long pattern of years, and Micca wanted nothing to do with his schemes.

He cleared his throat. "I guess you mean well, priest, but I don't want to get involved with what you're talking about...sorry to hear about your poor wife, though." He raised his hand in what he thought was a respectful salute and walked away down the gallery. He didn't look back until he reached a door that gave access to the south range. Palmer was still at the railing. He stared at Micca with an enigmatic expression, then turned away.

Micca realized he had gotten off easily. People generally treated the priest, or anyone elder to themselves, with more courtesy. He hadn't even told him 'good night'.

And he felt a little shame now, after Palmer had opened up to him that way. But at least it wasn't likely the priest would bother him again with his notions. Despite his usually cheerful demeanor, the priest had never shown tolerance for rebellion or his own embarrassment, and he'd be sure to suffer some of that if Micca turned him down again, and in public.

Nélimy, Branna's mother, was the sister of Micca's mother, and had come with her from Marstoc to Mora when Micca's parents were married. A year afterward Nélimy herself married Hadoc of Notop and brought him to Mora too. Micca and Branna had been born within hours of each other and Branna was, most of the time, Micca's best friend. Branna was another Harnishman with yellow, 'Eynnish' hair, and he had grown up strong and deep-voiced, bigger than his father by the time he was fifteen.

Branna's room wasn't directly attached to his parents' apartments, but was nearby, a long space under a sloping roof near the top of the east range, with three square windows looking over the home wood. There was a stove at one end, a table and a cushioned bench under the windows, and a bed was built into a cupboard opposite. The bed wasn't large and when the weather was warm enough Branna slept on the bench.

He had been sitting on it now, and got up to pour Micca a cup of brown beer. "So what did you tell them?"

"So you knew about it? I told them they were outlaws and ought to be put off the farm...well, actually it was Westin who said that."

"I saw Westin a bit ago. Bacnod is a mean customer."

"Ennosa Topping hit Westin first."

"I wonder if they'll take after you like that?"

"They'd better not. I told Palmer to forget about involving me in any of this, just a few minutes ago."

Branna emptied his cup and filled it again. Rain began to knock on the windows. He said, "I heard all about it this afternoon. Scrucru Topping stopped down at the mill before he went home. He's in with some of Priest Linto's crowd over at Topping."

"I don't want to hear about it."

Branna drank. "Yes you do. The Mora stuff is just a trick to get you interested. I knew you wouldn't go against Sam, and anyway you're not smart enough for that job —"

Micca punched Branna's arm. Branna pushed him halfway down the bench, then poured him another cup of beer as Micca slid himself back...the spot where Ennosa had pinched him was sore.

"But it's the Husband thing they're really after," Branna went on, picking something out of his cup. "Scrucru told us about it. Some of the priests decided that every farm is going to marry somebody to Wennoc. It'll prove his farm's Vigor. Nobody's actually done it yet, but he said Harlic's supposed to be the Husband over at Topping. You remember Harla, long skinny kid, good stickman on the field?"

"More lucky than good."

"But Palmer wants Mora to be the first. I think Sam being gone and your Grandpa Stennig up and dying all of a sudden made him think he could get away with it if he was quick. And they were ready. Scrucru says Wamod and them have been out divining for Mora's holy locus since last fall, using forked sticks, eating mushrooms, all that. Scrucru says that Palmer told Linto they found it a week ago, down in the stream bottoms a little past the mill. They're still looking for one at Topping. But they found Mora's."

"So what? What's a 'locus'?"

Branna widened his eyes. "It's Wennoc's holy wedding bed. You're going to marry Wennoc, and to do that you have to go down in the earth. You're going to be buried an hour before sunrise, about a foot down, Scrucru said, covered up with dry hedge-tangle and dirt, and after an hour you sit up again and greet the new sun."

Micca frowned in surprise and horror. "That's too weird to be true."

"Think so? You never know what the 'Vigorationists might get up to. That's what my dad says about them anyhow."

Micca drank some beer. "There are mudrunners down by the mill, and wispins." He looked up. "And they can't mean to actually bury… this Husband, or whatever. He'd suffocate, even a foot down. He couldn't sit up. They'd dig out a dead body."

"You'd think so, but supposedly Harla lived through a test run. Scrucru said they changed Harla somehow, mutated him. They said he looked sort of like a mudrunner. Scrucru admitted he didn't actually *see* any of that, but still."

Branna tasted his beer. "It's supposed to happen this coming Sunday. You're supposed to be the bridegroom."

Micca stared at him. Branna looked genuinely concerned. "Are you making any of this up?"

Branna slowly shook his head.

"Why didn't you tell me before?"

"I more or less just heard it. In fact I was looking around for you earlier."

Micca's head swam. Had Palmer's talk to him been intended to lull him into an easy mood, to allay his sense of self preservation? He emptied his cup and moved it to prevent Branna from pouring more.

"What about everybody else? The ones who aren't Invigored?"

"You know my mother would take out the eyes of anybody who'd do anything to you or Sam," Branna said. "And there are others, too. But I don't think normal people know enough about this, or if they heard, they don't believe it. I mean, it could be *murder*!"

Micca remembered Danna and Merim's odd comments at supper. How much did they know about this? What had Binta told them? Would they stand up for him like Nélimy would? He thought so, but both of them were phlegmatic and not likely to take peremptory action. Things, whatever things they were, were happening too fast. Again he felt a sense of dislocation. The sorrow, loss and confusion brought on by his grandfather's death strengthened. Something had broken, a branch had snapped. This place was no longer his.

Micca reached for the beer, then changed his mind and stood up.

"That's it. I'm getting out of here. It's too crazy."

"Out of where? The house? The farm?"

"I could go to Marstoc. Or maybe Grandma and Grandpa Reddinge's place? But right away, tonight. If I'm not here maybe it'll spoil their plans. And I've got to get Samma back here."

"Grandma and Grandpa's is a good part of the way to Stoard…" Branna looked at the windows. "And it's raining."

"Marstoc then. It's only a few miles—but I should go find Ennesia first."

"You want to take Nessy with?"

"Yes! Yes. She might well go. We're pretty good friends lately."

"You mean you've been sleeping with her again?"

"Not sleeping, no…what do you mean, 'again'? Did you know about it?"

"How couldn't I, the way you float around when she's here? So I'd better go along. You two might be too distracted to watch out for yourselves."

Micca smiled weakly. Not everyone was against him. He slapped Branna's shoulder. "Can you be ready inside of an hour, say? I'll go get some stuff, find Nessy. Meet you by the old orchard door?"

Branna glanced again at the windows. "Bring your rain gear."

Halfway to the room in which Ennesia and her mother were staying (Ennosa would certainly be in the church), Micca encountered Bacnod and Incseth coming up a stair. Incseth was a plumber and chicken-man who lived in a small hut of his own. He was unmarried and unbathed, as bad-tempered as Bacnod, though not as big.

"And here's our Micky now!" said Incseth.

"We was just talking about you, Glass-Eye," said Bacnod with an uncharacteristic grin. "You're wanted in the church. They sent us to tell you."

Incseth looked Micca up and down. "So where's your jumping clothes, young boar?"

"They might've forgot to give them to him," Bacnod said. He smiled again, something that didn't come without effort. "You can wear your ball-playing togs for now. Mora's Husband-to-be's going to join us ones for some good sweaty leaps and stamps tonight."

"I told Palmer I'm not going along with that. Just an hour ago. Go ask him."

"Priest is too easy. There's others here that'll see you do your duty."

Micca nodded wisely and twitched out a grin. "Well, if that's the case I'll change clothes and be right down."

He jogged off and didn't look back.

Watching him go, Bacnod asked Incseth, "Think he's really got the Vigor? He did give out a good holler earlier."

Incseth shrugged. "If not, priest can probably dose him with something."

"Glory," said Bacnod, and they went back down the steps. "We better send somebody to go check after him though."

Micca went quickly through the house, meeting few people and speaking to none. Once in his room he tore off his clothes, put on outdoor gear, slung a hat around his neck by its cord and stuffed some house clothes into a pack-bag. He went to the door, turned back again and put his entire cache of silver pennies into a purse, which he strapped around his waist. He shouldered his pack, took up a closed lamp and left his room.

"Who's that?" Loísa demanded, tilting the lenses before her eyes.

Her husband put down his book and leaned forward on the settee. "It's one of those Topping girls, isn't it?"

Ennesia closed the door, as softly as she could. Mora was too big, too old and poorly laid out; the rooms were arranged more sensibly at Topping. She had been to the room she wanted only a few hours ago, but things in the house seemed different at night. Down the passage she tried another door. There seemed to be a draft coming from under it, maybe promising a way back to Mora's lower floors. She went through and found herself on an open porch. Roofs above and beside her, roofs spread out below. The rain had almost stopped. Wind blew through the porch's weathered balusters, the cracks and raised grain of the railing lit by the diffuse light of the waxing moon, just visible again, getting ready to set behind flying clouds.

Someone at Mora had once told her about Lost Betty, an old woman who had wandered off in the delirium of fever two hundred years ago. She was said to wander the Mora's house still, wailing on dark nights from an inaccessible attic or behind a wall, crying out for help that would never reach her…Ennesia shivered and found another door at the far end of the porch.

She negotiated a downward-twisting stair and entered a series of small, well-paneled rooms. She held up her lamp. Openings in their short walls connected them, but the only door she came upon that looked as if it would give access to a larger apartment was locked. In one of the rooms was a bath tub made of fragrant cedar, and another had a desk and walls lined with paper-filled compartments; in the next, several long, formal coats and old hunting clothes hung from pegs. Hats and folded linen lay on shelves. There was something vaguely familiar about them. Was she near the Mora's rooms? The old man might have worn that shirt. He was dead now, lying in his tomb —

Something caught her elbow. Heavy and flopping, it swooped down on her. She struggled in its arms, smothered by an earthy odor.

Ennesia fought it off and sat panting on the floor. She stared at the coat beside her, possibly the very one the old Mora had been wearing the morning he dropped dead. Ennesia picked up her lamp, which luckily remained lit. She went on, leaving the coat where it lay. At least she was probably on the right track now. In the last room she climbed fourteen steep steps, ducking to avoid a slanting ceiling under the roof.

A face hovered before her. She took two halting steps back, startled by an old portrait made with imaging-salts on glass. Holding her lamp to it, a reflection of her own face was superimposed on the one in the glass: a wizened, white-haired old woman with Ennesia's features. Ennesia as Lost Betty… She could go back to the porch, crawl down the roof, maybe find a patch of ivy she could use as a ladder to the earth.

But there was a closed door beyond the picture, almost invisible in the paneling. Ennesia opened it. Something was in there, and it wasn't a picture. A man's body, but only the parts from the waist down. Did the legs move? No, the thing was only a pair of old leather leggings, molded by wear to their owner's shape. She looked more closely at them and held her lamp to a shirt and waistcoat hanging from a peg. The clothes were Micca's, she was sure of it. In the sidewall was a further door, standing open a crack. Through it came a light.

She entered Micca's room. There was Smolic, bent over, rooting through a chest in the corner. Various articles of clothing and a few books lay scattered on the floor. Ennesia turned to retreat, but changed her mind and crept along the shadowed side of the room toward an open door, where she was less likely to get lost again.

Deaconess Wamod's voice came through the further door. "Hurry on now, Binta. Don't take No for an answer. And find Ennosa's girl, too."

Before Ennesia could move, Wamod came through the door and into the room. She and Ennesia stared at each other.

Smolic hadn't seen Ennesia, and was pulling the blankets from Micca's bed. "Why did you tell the boy to fetch Ennesia along, Wamod? The girl is headstrong and spoilt rotten, in spite of her mother. She's like to make a fuss and spoil the spirit. Takes more after her dad, a bad lot if ever—but no! Lookee here!"

Wamod was still staring at Ennesia, mouth pinched. Ennesia crossed her arms over her breast and said the only thing she could think of. "Well? What are you doing here, you house-breakers!"

"House-breakers!" said Wamod. "I think that would apply more to you, young woman, sneaking around in the night, coming by sly ways into someone's private rooms."

Monitor Smolic jerked upright and gaped at Ennesia. Then he held out the length of blue linen he'd found in Micca's bed. "O Wennoc, look away!" he groaned. "All is clear now. I saw her wearing this here riband at breakfast, so she's been here before. Likely she and the boy committed a fornication!"

"You're crazy!" said Ennesia, nearly shouting. "Besides, what business is it of yours?"

Wamod's face was grim. "We'll discuss it with the priest, and your poor mother, too. Monitor, come here and help me with her—quick now, before she tries to run off!"

It was important now that no one stop or question him, since his clothing made it obvious that he intended to leave the shelter of the house. Micca descended ladder-like steps to a cellar, climbed again, high into a dusty string of attics, trying to keep the layout of the house below clear in his head. At one point the straps of his pack got tangled in the antlers of a stuffed elk's head hanging from the rafters, and he had to open his lamp to free it. He felt rather proud that this was the first light he had needed.

Eventually he came down near the guest rooms by way of a stair that opened in the planking beside the tub in a small bathroom, the very tub Ennesia had probably used this morning. Luckily it wasn't in use. He dropped his pack in the bathroom in case someone should see him, then slowly pushed open the door. The passage outside Ennesia's room was quiet and empty, dimly lit by a gas-burning standard at the far end. Micca put an ear to the door, heard nothing. "Nessy," he hissed.

At a tentative push the door swung in. All was dark and quiet. But he could smell the fumes of a recently extinguished lamp. Someone had been here not long ago.

Where had she gone? Not to have a bath, he knew that much.

He couldn't wait, he couldn't look for her. She'd be going back to Topping soon. Maybe he could send a message from Marstoc, or even go to Topping for her.

"What are you doing up *here*?" came a whining voice from behind.

Micca spun, almost falling. A slight figure stood two yards down the passage. Eyes blinked behind two holes in a tall, sharply peaked red hood on its head. Hanging by their laces around its neck were the shoes Micca wore when he played ball, and draped over its arm was an embroidered red tunic. Micca strode forward and pulled away the hood. The boy Binta looked up at him.

"What are you doing with my shoes?" Micca demanded, trying not to shout. "If you've been in my room—"

"It wasn't me in your room, and you're *supposed* to be in the *church*, Micky, not up *here*. Deaconess Wamod said you're going to lead the special devotions, and you have to wear your Husband's raiments... you've already got the hat."

Binta held out the red tunic. Micca knocked it out of his hand and threw the hood down after it.

Binta stared at them where they lay on the floor as though he felt sorry for them. He looked at Micca with resentment and a little fear, but then he smiled. "Well, if you thought you were going to pitch woo to Nessy tonight instead, you were wrong. I'm supposed to find her, too. She has to learn how to trot the steps before Sunday."

Trying to sidle by Micca to Ennesia's door, Binta called out, "Cousin Ennesia! Are you in there?" He stopped, now noticing Micca's outdoor clothes. "Where were you going?"

Micca looked left and right. There was no one in sight. He took the boy's arm and pulled him away from Ennesia's room.

"I've been outside, Binta. I went for mushrooms. I found some saint's toes. They're in here, in the basin, didn't want them to dry out."

Binta tried to resist Micca's lead, but became more cooperative when he thought about the rare fungi, valued by some for their psychotropic effects and pleasant flavor when fried in butter. They could be found only for a short time in the spring and were a special favorite of Priest Palmer.

Binta peered into the bathroom. "Where are they?"

Micca pushed him roughly inside, leaning in himself to grab his pack. "I forgot—they're here, in my bag."

"If you've been outside, why are your boots dry? They say it's been raining."

Micca stepped into the passage, threw the door shut and leaned against it. Binta started thumping on the door and yelling. Unfortunately the jail he had picked for Binta locked from the inside...but the door swung out. Keeping the toe of one boot on the door, Micca reached for a chair set against the opposite wall. He caught it, dragged it across the floor and wedged it under the door's handle.

"Let me out, cousin! It's *dark* in here!"

Micca shouldered his pack. Now the nearest path to the attics was lost to him. After a moment of sickening paralysis, he leapt down a stair at the end of the passage. There was a sitting room just off the landing, appropriated a few years ago by Elbret as a quiet place to weave rugs, and it was empty now but for the loom. He hadn't considered this route before, and luck was with him as long as he met no one else. From here he had a more or less direct path to the orchard door.

After a relatively short trip, nearly running, he took a quick look both ways down a room used to store apple ladders and pruning equipment. Nobody there. Beyond was a broad set of stone steps. Someone was sitting on the bottom step inside a huge hooded oilskin, knees high, a big green pack on his back.

Micca went down softly, but the man heard him and leapt up. Branna's face stared out from the hood.

"What took you so long?"

"I just had a run-in with Binta, and Bacnod and Incseth before him."

"Where's Nessy?"

"I couldn't find her."

He pushed his hat down, opened the door. Branna followed him out of the house and into the night.

4. IN THE GARDEN

A cross the Bay and up the shore to the north was the port of Hin Hoina, or Hoiin, the modern, collapsed form of the name. At sunset the sky was clear over the city, but the weather diviner on the Voice had predicted the likelihood of rain before morning. Neypo Odé didn't know how long he'd be out, so he left his old double-trotter at home and rode downtown in his new sedan, which used four porters and had a roof and glazed windows.

He visited his shop to see how the day's work had gone there, then stopped at the Strivers' Lodge to see if any news for the Special Investigatory Committee had been delivered. As he had expected, there was no sign that either his of colleagues on the committee, Woitap and Micsin, had been there today. Caihar Olinom, a seventh-degree Striver, had suggested setting up such an office when a consistory held to look into Hoiin's odd party of visitors had resulted in no action taken against them. Caihar said a new commotio would be a way to continue the investigation, and give those involved an air of authority. Until now, Neypo hadn't been to the office today either, but he'd been occupied with a number of pressing business meetings. Woitap and Micsin lived off their respective families' incomes and had no such excuse.

The committee's secretary had a packet of papers for him. Neypo glanced through them, eyebrows arching, then sat down and went back to the first page. After a few minutes he remembered himself and looked at the clock. He stuffed the papers into his business bag and hurried downstairs to his waiting sedan.

"To the Olinom manse, double quick!"

Neypo's porters lit the running lights, then carried him through the narrow streets of Hoiin's commercial district, swerving around ox- and pig-drawn drays, passenger carts and other sedans. Neypo tried to look at the papers again, but the light was poor. He'd have to install a lamp inside the sedan. It should have come with one, considering what he had paid for the thing.

The day had been stuffy, and Neypo pulled open a window. The walls of the buildings were massive at street level downtown, sometimes enclosing arcades and secondary service lanes within their bulk. Their brick piles stepped back as they rose, creating spaces for terraces and narrow gardens. Wires had been hung over the streets in recent decades, and as the day failed Neypo saw electric lamps wink to life on street corners and behind windows. Otherwise the city almost seemed a natural part of the coastal landscape. Its brick had been eased to contours that reflected the patterns of the rains that blew in from the Bay, and shrubs and small trees grew on roofs and upper terraces. At the bottom of the canyon-like street, colorful patterns of glazed tile set into the walls passed Neypo's window like strata of glowing ore exposed by the passage of a vanished river.

The porters left the core of the old city, carrying Neypo into the hills east of the Bay. Walled villas, flowering hedges and devotional arbories replaced ancient brickwork in his sedan's windows, and they entered the suburb of Rose Pond. Neypo lived in Rose Pond himself, but the houses in his neighborhood weren't as large and old as the one he intended to visit.

The sedan finally thumped to the pavement. Neypo made sure he had his bag, got out and put his red hat on his head.

By the light of a welcome-lamp he studied the tiled glyphs over the gate, which were set in a curious old style. Eventually a servant responded to the bell.

Neypo told him his name and rank. The servant said, "The Family Olinom offers its welcome, your Honor. The Striver awaits you."

Neypo followed him through the manse's garden, past ranks of glazed doors.

From a balcony above came a sudden, anguished cry. Caihar's servant turned back to Neypo, who had paused in alarm. "Only a daughter of the house," said the servant, frowning discreetly.

Neypo nodded, though he had no idea what was wrong with Caihar's daughter.

They walked by the service wing and through the kitchen garden. Beyond was a brick arch hung with vines. Through it Neypo saw Caihar, pacing over a back garden of clipped grass, surrounded by dense shrubbery, black in the shadows. Neypo inhaled the heavy scent of lilacs.

Lamps on pedestals of carved stone lit the secluded spot. Neypo walked into their light, casting a long shadow behind him.

"Neypo Odé!" said Caihar, halting his progress. "You're late."

Neypo put his palms together and drew them down. "Unavoidably detained, I'm afraid."

Caihar waved his hand. "So goes the life of the commercial man, I suppose." He spoke to the servant. "Bring us a selection of spirits, Cullup... include a flask of the Lilac, and the new one too."

The butler lifted an eyebrow. "The one from Nessahógabugattan, Honorable?"

Caihar fished in his pocket and tossed the man a key. Cullup bowed and left the garden.

Neypo began an explanation of his tardiness, but was interrupted by a muffled cry from the house.

Caihar led Neypo deeper into the garden. "I apologize for the disturbance," he said. "My daughter is upset this evening... Swannet's made a friend of your Gillensa, hasn't she?"

"Indeed yes. She and Swannet are great chums."

"Of course. In any case, Swannet thinks she's in love with a certain Cadet. Tonight she apparently overheard a conversation between her mother and myself. We had been discussing our doubts as to her readiness for marriage, and I'm afraid Swannet was upset by what she heard. She's rather highly strung."

"Gillensa has once or twice used the term 'artistic' in describing your daughter's temperament," Neypo said.

Caihar frowned. "Swannet says she'd die for this lad, but then sulks for days over some trivial insult she imagines he's made her. It's true the Hunsacup lad is a little coarse, but he's no fool, and his family is good. Swannet is too fastidious."

Neypo shook his head sympathetically, flattered to be trusted with such intimate details of the senior Striver's family life.

"It must please you that Swannet has chosen a Cadet. My Gillensa has been stepping out with an outlander, if you can believe it!"

Neypo closed his mouth. Caihar had spoken of the Harnish in an enlightened manner at the consistory last week, but even so, the conservative old guard of Hoiin's wealthier class might not smile on the potential inclusion of a foreigner in the family of a Lodge member.

Caihar only nodded. "The son of a citrus merchant from the south? An ambitious Harnish grandee?"

"The lad is a Harnishman," Neypo admitted. "Heir to the chieftain of a plantation south of Hannava. He attends lectures with Gillensa at the University."

Caihar nodded again, gravely. "Well, times change. Despite the prejudices of people like brother Riino, common sense dictates an enlightened attitude...Gillensa's chap has given up wearing his animal skins and so forth?"

"I've never seen him in Harnish folk-dress, though I have my doubts as to whether the faddish costumes affected by students these days are any great improvement."

Caihar chuckled. "You speak the truth, Neypo, though it's not only the youngsters who are taken in by fads — but here's Cullup again. Will you take essence, Neypo Odé?"

Neypo put his palms together. The butler rumbled a small wheeled cart over the turf, and Caihar chose three or four small bottles from it. The Strivers seated themselves on a stone bench. The butler arranged several thin porcelain cups on a table beside them and retired.

No more cries came from the house, and the garden was silent but for the cheeping of insects. Caihar poured and they tasted the liquor. The odor of lilacs from some previous spring competed with that of the blossoms in the garden.

Neypo took another sip and rolled the liquid around in his mouth. "This is excellent, Striver. I've been told that lilacs are poisonous, but the Harnish are apparently able to transform them into something altogether delightful. Where, might I ask, did you find it?"

Caihar waved his cup in a modest gesture. "I know a factor in

Hannava who buys a few cases each year for his own cellar. Supposedly the blooms required for this drink grow only in a remote district where the Harnishmen hardly know how to speak, and where the lilacs have only a few days before they wither. This short spring is what gives the flowers their fervent odor, they tell me, much like the Harnishmen themselves — excepting your daughter's friend, I'm sure."

Neypo laughed. "As a matter of fact, Gillensa's Harnishman is so keen on bathing that he considers it a daily necessity!"

Caihar smiled benignly when he saw his guest hadn't been offended. "Let's have another taste, Neypo."

Neypo held out his cup. "A delightful liquor, excellently served. I must say this is a pleasurable end to a stressful day. If I might speak frankly..."

"By all means! I'd be offended if you thought otherwise. I suppose you want to talk about what we're going to do about these so-called visitors and their ridiculous pronouncements in the newspaper."

Neypo nodded seriously. He thought of the documents in his bag, but decided to put first things first. "Indeed, the matter concerns me greatly." Neypo broke a lilac blossom from the bushes behind him and sniffed thoughtfully at it. "We know what a commotion their most recent statements have caused."

"Yes. Every man and woman gainfully employed, living without crime or sloth, all blissfully content; no one poor, no one wealthy. Can you believe it, Neypo? They paint a sad, feeble vision of perfection, as man in his inadequacy would imagine it. Wennoc's sublime and transcendent perfection is what the orthodox hope for, and will one day attain if they're faithful. As if these unlettered trouble-makers could produce even one of the crassly materialistic improvements they boast of!" Caihar sat back to catch his breath.

"Wildly improbable, yes," said Neypo. "As for the visitors being 'unlettered' — but we can come back to that. I agree with you that the strangers seem to define divinity in man's base terms. But the credulous, those jealous of their betters, the mentally infirm — that sort will always listen wide-eyed to such ravings, and we have our share of such people in Hoiin. Rumors are running wild downtown. Many otherwise steady men in the 'Change are remembering the corn riots during the tenure of the Grand Fellow Heinimystap. They're worried about the effect the visitors' stories might have on the market."

Caihar started to speak, but Neypo was determined to show his colors. He threw back his spirits and leaned toward his host.

"But unlike some fainter hearts, I am steadfast in my confidence of the market, in particular regarding radio broadcasting. In fact this kind of gossip will bolster people's desire to own receivers, so that they can keep up on the latest developments as announced over the aether. You may be aware, Caihar, that my firm is just ready to sell our own receivers. Valves and windings of our own manufacture, a dainty lemonwood case, polished brass fittings; a handsome and up-to-date set in every respect, capable of excellent reception. I anticipate so many orders, in fact, that I'm considering taking on a partner or two, just to make sure additional capital is on hand in case the demand forces me to expand my works suddenly."

"Very interesting!" said Caihar. "But I'm afraid I have only the sketchiest understanding of the mercantile processes. Wennoc has ordained sterner duty for some of us, and I have a good manager to keep track of my sea-coal yard. But you were talking about radio receivers, Neypo? And the visitors speaking on them? Thankfully they haven't spoken through yours nor anyone else's yet! We can't allow *that*!"

"No, certainly not," Neypo said dully. He seemed to have overestimated Caihar's interest in opportunities for investment.

Caihar busied himself opening another bottle. "So tell me, what news do you have of them?"

"The visitors?" Neypo unslung his business bag. "A minor revelation or two. But first I must mention my fellow member of the investigatory committee, Woitap Halanoi."

"What about him?" said Caihar. He poured a trickle of yellow-green liquid into a fresh cup and gave it to Neypo.

Neypo sipped. An astonishingly bright herbal pungency overwhelmed his mouth and nasal passages. "Magnificent!" he gasped when able to speak. "Blenaglellan's Number-two Tincture?"

Caihar smiled. "I knew this one would fool you. You're drinking a nameless spring tonic from Nessahógabugattan, whether a village or plantation, I don't know. Thirty years old, and it's said to increase vitality in all respects. Now, what was that about Micsin?"

"It was Woitap I spoke of, Striver," said Neypo, sipping again with careful appreciation. "He's been worse than useless this past week, and in fact has become a detriment to the investigatory committee's work. Couldn't you intercede with the Grand Fellow and have him replaced? Or perhaps yet join the committee yourself?"

Caihar shook his head grimly. "The Fellow and I are still on the outs. Go on with your news."

Neypo dug in his bag and handed Caihar his papers. "I have these from Narnet, the Guest Hall's housekeeper."

Caihar took out a lens on a stick and peered through it at the papers. "I thought the visitors had sent the servants away."

"So they had. But Narnet was quite peeved at paying a temporary but unfairly high rent to her opportunistic son-in-law, who has a tenement on Hostimeniaisenen. She took her complaint to the committee office. I happened to be on hand and saw merit in her case. Narnet's quarters at the Hall are in the annex at the end of its garden. It was clear the old woman would be no bother to our visitors back there, so I told her she could return ... and suggested she keep her eyes and ears open."

"You enlisted her as your spy?" said Caihar, lowering his lens with a smile of surprise.

"An unpleasant choice of words, colleague. But Narnet, though she's nearly ninety, likes to keep herself busy, and she's so fastidious that she feels compelled to inspect the service runs and scuttles in the place's walls on a regular basis, checking to see if her staff have kept them clean and free of vermin. The visitors are apparently unconcerned about her return, although I suppose they may not have noticed it. Her tread is as light as a bird's, and the walls are thick."

"Well done, Neypo!" Caihar laughed, refilling both their cups. "I'm glad you're on my side in this matter."

"I feel somewhat soiled by the affair."

"The situation demanded such action."

"Well, in any case, we have here the first fruits of Narnet's observations. In your hand is —"

"Yes, the housekeeper's report," said Caihar, holding one of the papers to the light of the garden lamps. "Descriptions of the visitors' physical likenesses, their eating and lavatory habits, rather incoherently set down..." Caihar picked up another sheet. "Ah. This looks interesting... it seems our agent caught sight of a tablet lying under a serving hatch in the Hall's breakfast room, from which she copied several lines of writing. Hm. She mentions pains in her finger joints afterward..."

"We should grant Narnet a retirement pension."

Caihar studied the facsimile from a variety of orientations. "What does it say?"

"I examined it only briefly downtown, but it must be a cipher of some kind."

"Ha!" said Caihar triumphantly, laying down the paper and pouring again. "Definite proof the visitors have something they want to hide from us."

"So it would seem, yes. Did you notice how all the letters are drawn separately from their fellows, each standing alone? From this we can infer that they were set down slowly and carefully, as if the scrivener was perhaps referring to a schedule of letter substitutions; Mim for Bit, Hac for Wa, and so on."

"Will you be able to decipher this, Neypo?"

Neypo sat back and knit his fingers over his belly. "I'll consult certain texts in my library. Grammatology is something of a hobby with me, you know. I'm rather proud of my collection of Mennelian Writs. One of them, in fact, which I believe to be an early version of the Dream in the Reeds, was written in a sort of cipher in order to confound the Heresiarchs' saint-catchers."

"I don't think you'll find any spiritual inspiration in this paper here." Caihar stared down at the grass for a moment. "And speaking of papers, the visitors cannot be allowed to put their words into print again. Or worse, broadcast them over the Voice of Hoiin."

"No, definitely not. But how will we stop them? Are there grounds for imposing an Edict of Official Secrets on the newsmen?"

Caihar glared at his cup. "Grounds could be found if the Lodge was of one mind, as it should be. But it isn't, and the Grand Fellow seems well on his way to dotage."

"Couldn't you, or Riino, or even I, arrange to give a talk over the Voice and set things right?"

"Thereby dignifying the visitors with official recognition? Treat them as equals to be debated with in public?"

Caihar leaned forward. "Think about it, Neypo. That would be worse than giving them residence in the Hall. No, I'm afraid I'll have to pull a few strings of my own. I fault myself now for hesitating last week! But the visitors must be silenced, disgraced publicly if possible. When they've been taken care of, we'll write up an article discrediting them and place it in the Word."

"Which by then they'll be unable to answer. This sounds like a wise and prudent plan."

"Prudence for a day or two, but if they continue to intrude themselves in our affairs other action will have to be taken."

"What sort of action?"

"Whatever sort is necessary."

"I see." Using his influence with the Word and the Voice was well and fine, but Neypo wondered how far Caihar was willing to go.

Caihar noticed Neypo's troubled expression. "I suppose you think I've become a bit radical in my feelings about this, colleague, but Strivers of the fifth degree and above have access to certain little-visited chambers in the Lodge, certain archives. The information found there, read correctly, imposes a sense of urgency upon us."

Neypo forgot his doubts and leaned forward eagerly.

"But I won't tell you about it just now," Caihar decided. "It might be useful to preserve your objective opinion for the time being."

Neypo was disappointed. He knew of the locked rooms in the Lodge, which were supposed to contain texts and tablets of great antiquity. In the east, where the strictest kind of orthodoxy had persisted well into the modern age, this sort of collection had been destroyed long ago due to their heretical associations. The few strange, curvilinear old glyphs Neypo had seen, so unlike the modern variety, had always fascinated him. And entering the secret archives conferred an automatic rise in status to a Lodge member for reasons of security, whatever the circumstance; Neypo had read the Striving Rule carefully before his initiation.

"Are you sure I shouldn't be brought up to date immediately?" he asked Caihar.

"We'll see how things develop. In the meantime you'll have at your disposal the judgment of advisors with more experience in matters of state than you've had time as yet to acquire. I've arranged to meet tomorrow with a few responsible citizens who share our concerns: Riino; Lemwulin Litu; Merta and Carin, the doughty Neyrman sisters; Commander Cwentoi of the Office of Public Assistance. With their help we'll put down these subversives."

Neypo waited for an invitation to this meeting, but Caihar looked glumly to the house. "Well, I suppose I should go in and see whether my lady wife has settled Swannet."

Neypo got out of his chair to bow. His sleeve caught one of the bottles on the table and a few drops of tincture were absorbed by the grass. At the same moment a wail issued from the house.

"No matter! No matter!" said Caihar, grimacing at the sound and waving off Neypo's apologies for the spilled liquor. He picked up another bottle, apparently changing his mind about going inside. "Look what else Cullup's set out for us: Cornamun's Amber Nectar, made of wild vineberries. A boon for us in our time of need."

Caihar poured into fresh cups, and he and Neypo discussed the qualities of the Cornamun.

Finally Neypo heaved himself erect. "Striver, I must thank you for a genial and most enlightening evening."

Caihar also stood and called to the house. "Cullup! Fetch a fresh bottle of the lilac, and order a cart for the Striver."

"No need, brother Caihar! My porters are waiting for me at the gate."

Caihar bowed. "Well, good night to you then. We'll keep in touch about our mutual concerns."

Cullup brought a bottle wrapped in blue paper, which Neypo accepted with pleasure.

"Add a little good grain liquor to the lilac when you taste it again and let me know what you think," Caihar suggested. "It would lessen the initial impact, but it may well reveal a host of subtle aromas over-whelmed by the fervency of the unalloyed product."

"I will certainly do so! Sleep well, you and all your family."

Neypo walked slowly through the garden, protectively cradling the bottle in his arms. Cullup closed the gate behind him, and rain suddenly spotted the road. Neypo got into his sedan. The sky over the Bay to the west was heavy, undershot with lightening.

He hung out the window as his porters raised the sedan. Neypo inhaled the odors of new rain on the pavement. The air also carried a hint of coal smoke from Hoiin's manufactories, the night smells of Rose Pond's trees and gardens, and over all its lilacs.

The meeting had gone well, Neypo decided. Caihar had been impressed with his initiative, and if he wasn't to be shown the secret archives or invited to the meeting of 'responsible citizens', well, Neypo didn't have the time anyway. He patted the bottle of rare Harnish liquor in his lap. It was clear Caihar thought well of him.

Neypo leaned out the window again, savoring another taste of spring. Inspired, he quoted from the Writs: "'Our poor lives are short and swift!'"

His porters huffed the response: "'But Wennoc is ever young.'"

"'And in its grace we ever live,'" finished Neypo, shaking rain from his hat and settling back for the ride home.

5. MARSTOC

The rain had gone and it was clear now, the moon riding west behind retreating clouds.

Branna threw back his hood, walking beside Micca. The south side of the house straggled along beside them, walls of squared gray timbers. The land fell as they walked, exposing the stone of the ground floor and cellars, splotched by moss in places, patched and amended with brick. Chimneys fumed from night fires, adding a tang to the damp scents of spring.

A high, ivy-hung bay swam out of the dark. One of its windows swung open, emitting a yellow glow and pelting Micca and Branna with drops of water from the disturbed vines. Micca stopped and tried to dry his eye-glasses on his cloak. He couldn't see anyone in the window from where he was and knew they couldn't see him, but he could feel something's attention turned his way, as though the house were aware of him leaving.

Where was Ennesia now? He should have left a message with someone for her, or a note. She could read a little Harnish. That would have been as good as a cipher for most of the people in the house.

It was too late now. He couldn't go back the way things stood. And Ennesia wouldn't necessarily have been willing to take off like this anyway, not so abruptly. She thought of herself as being adventurous, but in practice she was usually pretty conservative. Micca wondered with a dull pang of horror what he was doing. He had never been adventurous at all.

Branna, a loping black shape under a silhouette of apple and pear boughs, was five yards ahead. When Micca caught up, his cousin tossed a doughnut at him. "One of Danna's," he said. "I swiped a few this morning. He always makes lots."

Micca chewed it as the last outshots of the house and its barns, granaries and sheds fell behind. He turned to the north, and could see irregular lines of roofs straggling away, a few glowing lit windows scattered in the dark. Beyond the squat bulk of the water tower was the peak of the church's cupola, and its tiny round windows also showed light. The sawmill was invisible from here, but Micca felt a perverse curiosity; he would have liked to see the site the Invigorationists had chosen for their Husband's burial.

But it was better to imagine Palmer and his gang paying the price for what they'd meant to do. The situation made him think of a book in his grandfather's library, *Tales of Brave Beyalmer*. Beyalmer was supposed to have been one of the first adventurers to come out of the sea and establish a farm in Harna. Beyalmer always carried a sword or pike and wore his war-suit day and night. From this Micca assumed the heads of farms in those days did little work in the fields or barn, which remained the case today, though now a leader kept accounts, planned the work and settled disagreements peaceably rather than carrying on vendettas and murdering those who insulted him. Once a man had stolen Beyalmer's cattle while he was away capturing Eynnish thralls, and on his return Beyalmer hadn't hesitated to break the villain's head. Micca hoped Samma would do the modern equivalent with Palmer, which he supposed would mean sending him to trial before the law-court.

They passed through the orchards, walking uphill for a while, then down, climbing occasional stiles, using paths bounded on one side by trees, on the other by open fields and pastures. Finally they left tilled lands behind and heard Mora's stream again. Ahead was a short bridge of arched stone. They crossed it and left the farm.

They trotted down a slope and entered rolling woodland. Micca found the path they wanted. The wagon road to Marstoc would have been their usual route and easier walking, but the lane from Mora that met it required a mile's detour to the north and east. Micca thought it was about an hour past midnight when the woods opened and they saw cultivated land again.

The clouds flew off, uncovering a field of stars, but the moon had set and the house at Marstoc was an uneven black mound as they approached it. Branna pointed to a few windows that were still lit. Micca looked into a peddler's way-hut on the lane that gave Marstoc access to the North Road. Branna didn't argue about sleeping there, and Micca needed some time to figure out what he was going to tell the Marling.

The hut's single window opened on the east, and the sun crept up and shone on Micca's face. He grimaced and sat up on a broad bench that served the hut as a bed. Branna yawned beside him, got up, went to the door and hailed the day with a yodel.

"Don't do that," Micca told him.

"What kind of breakfast do you suppose they'll give us?" Branna asked.

"I want a bath first," said Micca. He still didn't know just what he'd say to the Marling.

There was no bath in the hut but they took turns washing their faces and hands at a basin in an alcove, then left the hut.

The main house at Marstoc stepped back in sections as it climbed to surround a mound of rising land to the west. The barns and other farm buildings occupied lower land to the south. Shouts and animal noises came from the barns and Micca and Branna passed several people who were on their way to the fields. Branna exchanged greetings with a man who had come here from Mora a few years ago. The lane from the road ran beside the barns, then curled up to a broad portal giving entrance to a yard between the gardens and the upper levels of the house.

A thin old woman sweeping a stone terrace cocked her head at the visitors. "Branna, Hadoc's oldest?" she said. "And Micca, Samma's little brother—or not so little, I see." She put her broom aside and shook their hands. "I'm sorry I didn't come to see Stennig laid away, but my legs aren't so good anymore," she told Micca. "Still, they make me earn my keep here, such as it is."

Micca didn't remember her name, but thought she was some relation to Red Sten, a fieldman at Mora. He asked her if the Marling was about. The woman seemed in no hurry to get back to her sweeping and took them into the house. "You two go down to the hall. I'll toddle off and see if I can find him."

Marstoc's hall was wider and longer than Mora's, but not as lofty. Banners hung from the beams and galleries, and on the end walls were stuffed heads of elk and wild pigs. Branna stopped to admire a table whose top had been sliced from one gigantic candlewood root. They walked by the tall skeleton of a bog-elk, a collection of knives in a glass-fronted cabinet, a fan of clubs on the wall, an arrangement of pikes in a brass pot, and a row of lifeless figures wearing armor and closed helmets, some arranged in heroic poses. Other than bows for hunting, there weren't many war-like implements left at Mora. The tenets of both the old In-Dwelling and recent Invigoration encouraged an attitude of pacifism, and they had been taken to more strongly at Mora than at Marstoc.

Micca and Branna sat down on an upholstered bench. "Maybe we should wait in the kitchen," Branna suggested.

Micca shook his head. "We're not here on a casual visit."

"Maybe so, but we ate all of Danna's doughnuts."

After a while they got bored and began looking around the hall again. Branna hefted a pike and stood admiring a suit of armor. "If we borrowed some of this stuff and went back in it, Palmer and Bacnod would run for the woods."

Micca lifted a helmet from one of the armored suits. He took off his lenses and his hat, pushed the helmet over his head and turned to Branna. "How do I look?"

"I can't hardly hear you," Branna said, examining another helmet. It was made of boiled leather and sported the remains of a feathered crest. The padding inside was stiff and dry. Eye-slots and holes to let in air pierced the face parts. Buckles on either side had rusted, and the mask couldn't be raised. "I don't think I could get it over my head."

"I think there's spiders in here," came Micca's muffled voice. He put his hands to either side of the helmet, then bent over, pulling and grunting.

The Marling walked into the hall, a gaunt man of medium height with a beaked nose and a small beard on his chin. He wore a long black house coat and brimless black hat with a tassel hanging from its crown.

Branna looked at the Marling with an embarrassed smile. "He can't get it off."

The Marling supported an elbow in one hand, and used the other to rub his whiskers. Finally Micca pulled the helmet off and replaced it atop its display. He looked sheepishly at the Marling, rubbing scraped ears.

The Marling clasped his hands behind his back. "Those suits haven't been worn for many years. I'm surprised the helm didn't fall to pieces when you touched it."

Micca put on his lenses again. "I'm sorry, Marling."

"No harm done, apparently. But welcome to Marstoc, Micael. And Brannoc, tell your mother to visit me more often! It shouldn't take a funeral to bring us together… I suppose you two are looking for Voling. But didn't he tell you at the funeral? He set out for Hannava an hour ago. He and my brother Ingram are going to take care of some business with the lumber factors up there."

"Actually, Marling, it was you I wanted to talk to."

"Do you have something to take up, on Samael's behalf?"

What an excellent way to put it, thought Micca. "That's it exactly. It's pretty important."

The Marling nodded and said they would talk in his office. As they walked he paused at a display of chest and shoulder armor set in a recess. "I know you've always been interested in our heirlooms, Micca, and it's sad so many of Mora's old things have been lost over the years. Such stuff contains many lessons for us. But warlike gear like this can be dangerous, as you've just learned."

He continued reflectively as they walked on. "According to the house-book, we once had a set of very fine head-to-toe armor at Marstoc, all made of crystal; the ice-man, they called it. One of my ancestors donned this suit before going out to deal with a bully who had offended him. It's unclear how the fight went, but Rimmanædnoc, who was fifth in my line, found when he came home that his armorer's recollection of the trick necessary to open the suit again was faulty. It seemed that it was easy to get into, but that getting out was another thing. The armorer was pent in an empty cistern to prompt a return of his memory, and it's possible he's there yet, since Rimmanædnoc is said to have spent the rest of his days in the armor. When he died they boiled him in a great cauldron until the armor opened, and the resulting broth was poured out and interred. They thought laying him to rest while still in the armor might prevent him joining with Wennoc, you see. We don't know what became of the suit itself. Possibly buried somewhere to prevent further accidents."

They entered the Marling's office, a modest room paneled with planks of figured maple, a tiny open fireplace in one wall. Micca and Branna sat on spindly chairs, and the Marling behind a polished desk. The Marling arranged some papers, then peered inquisitively at Micca.

"I think I can speak for Samael," Micca began. He cleared his throat. "First off, he doesn't know grandfather is dead yet. Danna wrote a letter but hasn't posted it yet."

"That's not good. A carrier was by here just yesterday, and probably won't be back for another week."

It looked as though the Marling was taking him seriously, and Micca felt a little more confident. "It's worse than that. He has to get back as soon as possible. The thing is that Priest Palmer and the Invigorated people at home don't want him to become the Mora, and—"

"What?" the Marling said, half standing.

Branna spoke. "They want Micca to be the new Mora."

The Marling stared dangerously at Micca.

"He wouldn't do it," Branna said. "He told them they were outlaws and should be put off the farm."

The Marling settled in his chair. After a moment he said, "You did well bringing this to my attention, Micca. This so-called Invigoration has gotten far out of hand. Damned nuisance, and Stennig just laughed it off. The Mora, the Yarl, the Hengest, all have been eldest sons, or even daughters, for time out of mind, but always firstborn! It ain't proper to do otherwise."

Micca almost relaxed. The Marling was an important man, influential.

Branna spoke again. "It's even worse than that, sir. They've got a scheme—the Invigorationists do—to kill him!"

"Kill Samma?" the Marling exclaimed.

"No, Micca. Besides the Mora, they want him to be this Husband,

Husband to Wennoc—don't look at me, Marling, it wasn't *my* idea. But they want to bury him, bury him alive. I'm not joking. They carried around twigs, they sang and stamped, and they found a grave for him down by the mill—and they mean to do it to Harlic at Topping, too."

"Your story is absurd…But I wonder. I've heard rumors of some kind of barbaric new practices in the south. The Invigorationists…but it won't do. It just won't."

The Marling rearranged his papers, got up and began pacing. After two turns around the room he stopped and faced Micca.

"There's no sense in dawdling or being over-delicate in regard to the feelings of some of your household, Micca. I'm going to take your word that things are as you and Branna describe and dispense with any corroboration. Action must be taken, and at once; better to overreact than sit in confusion. The mail is slow and sometimes unsure…

"Is that travel luggage you have with you? Good. You looked ahead and didn't simply flee Mora in a panic. This is what you'll do. Go to the North Road. Ingram and Voling won't have gotten very far; my brother is rather short of wind these days, and no longer the hill-runner of his youth. If you don't dawdle you should overtake them by noon.

"Tell Ingram to return home, and you and Branna can accompany Voling to Hannava in his place. Once there, Fola can introduce you to Timminen Numo, a friend of mine who holds a seat on the City Directorate. You'll present the case to Numo and he'll take care of this matter in an official and unequivocal way. County Wendum has no exemption from the rule of law!"

The Marling sat down, set eye-glasses on his nose, and began writing. Micca opened his mouth, but the Marling spoke on. "I'm going to send this letter with you." He looked over his lenses. "And some silver, since I don't suppose you anticipated a trip like this—no, don't worry about it. The new Mora can reimburse me in due time."

He sanded and folded the letter, put it into an envelope. Then he took a box from his desk, slowly counted out nine silver pennies, pursed his lips, added one more, then put them into the envelope too and handed it to Micca.

"That should cover the hire of board and respectable lodgings for you and Branna for a few days. In Hannava the townsman hardly speaks to his neighbor, much less thinks to offer him common hospitality. You must also write to Samma while in Hannava. Tell him everything, and mention your discussion with me. There's at least one boat to Hoiin every day, so he should receive your letter much more quickly than one sent from down here. Find a ship's master and hand it to him personally. Include a gratuity; five coppers wouldn't be too much in a case like this."

Micca took the envelope and muttered his thanks. He looked up and said, "Couldn't you send some of your people over to our place and clear things up right away?"

Branna said, "The priest might send somebody after us. Some of his people are pretty ugly."

The Marling shook his head with a grim smile. "I don't doubt they're ugly, but when Wudego Palmer learns Micca has taken things into his own hands he'll think again. But I'll keep both ears open, and my eyes too. If he tries any more tricks, I'll pay him a personal visit. For now I'd prefer he think himself secure. I'd hate to see him scurry back to Palma before Samma summons him to Mora's Doom Stone. If Numo doesn't deal with him first, of course. The City Directorate has been rather more active in recent years."

Micca didn't remind him that Mora's Doom Stone had been used in the foundations of the new mill ninety years ago. They went down to the pantries. Food for the road, in case Fola wasn't carrying enough for the three of them — crisp bread and a disk of cheese, part of a cured ham, preserved peaches, a jar of pickled cucumbers — was brought out. Micca and Branna packed it all into their bags.

The Marling shook their hands and waved them off.

6. THE NORTH ROAD

The sky began to cloud as they walked down to the road. There were people working in Marstoc's fields, too far off for them to do more than wave.

Micca was still getting used to the idea of going to Hannava. He and Branna, often with Fola, had been down to Stoard a number of times, but neither had been to port town in the north before. Fola had mentioned his intended trip to him at Stennig's funeral and Micca hadn't really registered it at the time. Going north with someone who knew the place, and presumably this Directorate friend of the Marling too, should make things easier.

They ate preserved peaches out of the bottle and some of the bread as they walked. Micca knew his hair was greasy, and now his fingers were sticky from the peaches. The Marling said Fola was to stop at Rudescoa that night; Micca had been there, and remembered that it had a good bath. It would be cold yet, but a swim in the lake might feel good too.

A pair of weathered, man-high stones, both graven near their tops with 'Marstoc' in squared letters, stood on either side of the lane where it joined the North Road. Where Marstoc's lane had been sand and gravel, the road was paved with cut stone along much of its course. Where it passed near a farm the stones had often been carried away and used for other things, cement or hard-packed gravel used to replace it. It was still mostly straight, making broad, tipping curves as required by the terrain. There were places hills appeared to have been cut away, or valleys filled to make its route more direct. Its serene evenness made smaller lanes look like drunks as they staggered out of the woods and hills to join or cross it.

They were better than half-way to the lane that led from Mora to the North Road when they caught up with Fola and his uncle. Ingram was sitting on a low stone wall, almost hidden in a cloud of smoke from a pipe with a stem so long it almost reached his knees. Fola sat on the ground, back against the wall, writing something on a paper supported by a small board.

They looked up at Branna's greeting yodel.

"Branna Mora... Micca!" Fola said.

Ingram saluted them from his cloud. "Good morning. What sends you lads out? No boards to saw or hammer at Mora today?"

Micca held up his arm. "Good morning. The Marling sent us."

Voling, or Fola as he was usually called, looked in most ways like a younger version of the Marling, with an out-thrusting nose, lanky frame and narrow shoulders. His hair was long and brown, tied in a queue. He wore a plaid shirt under his coat, and the black hide trousers typical of Marstoc. Fola was a year older than Samma and had already taken a degree at the University in Hoiin. His uncle was obviously his kin, though shorter and greyer. He wore unremarkable traveling clothes other than his hat, which had a very narrow brim and was bright yellow.

Ingram wasn't offended, and didn't seem surprised, when Micca relayed the Marling's instructions that he go back home. "I enjoy your company well enough, nephew, but not so much these road trips, and I wasn't looking forward to camping out at the lake tonight either. Bound to be damp and unaired, and nobody there yet to cook for us! That said, I'm sure you'll do well for Marstoc in your dealings with the factors in Hannava."

Ingram coughed for a minute or so, then relit his pipe, hefted his travel bag, wished the others successful trips, and started off down the road with a light step.

Fola put away whatever he'd been writing and they began walking north. "So what's up? Obviously you hadn't intended to go to the city, at least not before you talked to my father. What's going on? What kind of business does Mora have that Samma couldn't take care of on his way home? He is coming home, correct?"

"Danna intends to send a letter, but he hasn't yet so Sam doesn't know grandpa is dead yet."

Micca shot Branna a warning glance. "You might as well know, you'll hear sooner or later. We're having some trouble with the Invigorationists."

"They don't want Samma to be the Mora," Branna said.

"Do they think he's been corrupted by the Eynnish?" Fola said, smiling.

"Worse," said Branna.

"Your father said I should talk to Timminen Numo. I guess it's a matter of law."

"I know Numo by reputation," Fola said slowly. "But is it that serious? Why do you care what the Invigorationists think?"

Micca shook his head. "You don't know how much influence they have at Mora. Or Topping, or a lot of other places, probably. You're sitting on a happy little island at Marstoc and you can't see the water around you."

"Pshaw," said Fola.

"It's more than that," said Branna, and ignoring Micca's black looks, he described Invigorationists' plans for Micca as Mora's Husband. "I wouldn't wonder that they'll feed him a lot of mushrooms until he thinks there's really a woman down there in the grave. But he'll put out his horn and probably run into a mudrunner's nest."

"Sometimes I don't know about you, Branna," Micca said in disgust, and stumbled on a hole in the road.

Fola skirted the same hole. "Don't be so quick, Micca. I've read about primitive rites somewhere or other, and your cousin's perverse fantasy might not be so fantastic."

"It wasn't *my* idea!" Branna protested.

"Ah, the whole thing makes me sick," Micca spat.

The sky had cleared again and sun was near the middle of the sky when Mora's gate posts came into view. A brass box was attached to one of them for the use of the mail carrier. The little yellow-painted flag was down, so Danna hadn't posted his letter to Samma yet. The narrow dirt road twisted up the hill, trees close on either side. Nothing could be seen of the farm from here, not even any of its fields, the woods coming right down to the road.

He hadn't been gone even a day, but Micca felt a rush of longing and despair. Probably mostly to do with Ennesia and his grandfather's death, he thought, and there was nothing he could do about it until he got Samma back home.

He had been trying not to think of Ennesia. And why was he thinking so much about her today? He hadn't really after Yule, or last midsummer, wonderful as those visits had been. What was different about this time? Maybe just that Stennig had died too. In any case he could see her face, looking at him from under her lashes with that half-sly smile...

"You've got a pen and paper, Fola. Can I use them?"

Fola rummaged in his bag and produced a pot of brown ink, a pen and a sheet of paper.

"And a wrapping paper?"

"We shouldn't hang around here too long," said Branna, staring up the lane.

"I'll just be a minute." Micca squatted at the side of the road, paper on his knee. He decided not to put the date on his letter, then wrote in careful, simple Harnish:

> *Had to leave suddenly. Ask your mother if you do not know why.*
> *Have talked to important man at farm we talked of yesterday and will consult another man of high status.*
> *Pr P & others will face hard judgment.*

He paused, then added,

> *I tried to find you last night. I miss you.*

Then, at the bottom, since he didn't want to put down his name, he drew a carpenter's rule and a compass. That could be his signature. She'd think it was clever if she figured it out what it was supposed to be.

Branna was looking unabashedly over his shoulder, but although he could speak hunter's Harnish well enough he couldn't read it, and that would be true of most others who might see the note. If they could, he hoped his vagueness would baffle them.

He folded the paper, wrote 'For the eyes of Ennesia Topping and hers alone' on the blank outer surface, pushed it into the envelope, and wrote in large script,

> to the Hand of
> Dannig Mora
> Mora Farm
> WENDUM

Danna could read Harnish, but he probably wouldn't open the letter the way it was addressed. Micca put it into the post box. With luck Danna would come down here today with Samma's letter and find it.

"Are you two done then?" Branna called, already walking down the road. "Let's get going."

"We should get to Rudescoa in time for a swim," said Fola, putting his pen and ink away. "It probably would be midnight if Ingram was still with me."

Micca stood looking up the lane for a minute, looking at the trees he knew, then trotted after them.

They walked another half hour, talking about this and that, then fell silent. Branna suddenly growled, moaned…Micca didn't know what was wrong with him. Branna moaned again, apparently trying to sing the bass line of the *All's Well in Wennoc*. He found the right place to start and got into tune. Fola blinked at him in shock, then smiled, threw his arms out and began singing the tenor part. When Micca had controlled his laughter he took the counterpart baritone, dodging up and down between the other two. Alarmed by the noise, birds jumped up from the trees beside the road.

They sang through that, then *O Blessèd Orb* and *Evening's Dusk Does Fall*, and afterwards all the verses Branna could remember of *When Lindy Lost Her Darling Love*, Branna booming out the lead, Micca and Fola doing the choruses in harmony.

A beck passed through a culvert under the road, and they went down to drink. They got out food for a late lunch, took off their boots and stockings and dangled their feet in the water as they ate a late lunch.

※

Once in a while a hare or a tree-hen crossed the road, and they saw a pair of wild pigs trot out of the woods, inspect them briefly, cross the road and nose into the brush on the other side. The three walked on through the increasingly balmy afternoon. Two men and three women from Ofstuna came down the road from the north, on their way to visit relations at Stengad, and the two parties chatted for fifteen or twenty minutes before going on. These were the first other travelers the three had met. The North Road must have been busier at some time in the past, but now most of the north-south traffic used another one nearer the coast of the Bay.

The sun started to sink, and skikers ground out their rhythms in the undergrowth. There were several lakes nearby, and huge, white, long-necked water birds flew over from time to time. Micca, Branna and Fola walked down a long hill, crossed a wooden bridge over a splashing stream. Ahead was another grade, unusually steep, built more recently than most of the road. They were near Rudescoa now and Branna yelled challenges to Micca and Fola and ran up the slope. The disk of the sun was now half hidden by the trees on the western hills. The road was in shadow, but the sun lit Branna as he reached the top and dropped to a squat under a tree.

Micca and Fola climbed more slowly after him. Branna stood again and looked out on the far hills behind them.

Micca neared the top of the hill, Fola some way behind him. Branna was facing Micca, but he stared past him. To the south the road rose like a dusky ribbon up to a narrow slot where the road cut over the hill they had just descended. A stick-like figure could be seen in the cleft, indistinct in the waning light.

Branna pointed. "It looks like there's somebody else out walking our way."

The stick shortened and seemed to vanish, blending into the shadows as it came down the far hill. Another stick appeared in the gap, then two more, who followed the first down toward the bridge.

Micca heard a distant shout. Fola stood a little below him, raising his arms to the other travelers. He panted up beside Micca. "Who do you suppose they are?"

"I don't know. Quit waving."

Branna looked out from under his hand. "A couple of them have tan leather, like ours or Topping's. They're walking faster now... I think one of them's wearing a red hat."

"Micky!" came a thin wail.

Micca dropped to the ground like he had taken an arrow. "That's Binta or I'm pig's bastard!" he said, somewhat hysterically. "I recognize his voice. Palmer must be with him."

"No. It's Binta, Bacnod, Incseth, Wamod I think... and Delwinc Topping?" Branna said. He turned to Fola. "What side of Rudescoa is your place on? North, right?"

Fola was surprised at Branna's low, serious tone. "Yes, the north shore."

"I know this country," Branna interrupted. "It's two miles or more till we even get to the turn-off."

Then they both looked north, hearing a strange shout, a bark of fear or laughter. Micca was already some way off, and disappeared behind a bend in the road.

He breathed heavily, running head down, feeling soft and sluggish after the winter. Sweat trickled under his arms. The road was ancient masonry here, but its surface began to tip precariously to the right, and the land on that side fell steeply into a green slough. Big old trees bordered the road's left side, a rising hillside.

Micca clambered over a pile of tree limbs and brush, but the way ended beyond it. He saw that he was standing on a thin tongue of gravelly concrete. It curled down slightly, like a wood shaving, high above mossy masonry stumps of the pillars that must have once supported it. Further on, the pavement had crumbled into a rushing water course.

He bent down slowly and crept back on his hands and knees. The surface under him quaked and he heard splashes below. When he thought the way was solid he stood, ran, fought through the brush pile and threw himself off the road altogether.

He fell into a thicket of blackberries. Micca got to his knees and carefully pulled away prickly branches. From this vantage he saw that at some time the road had been redirected, veering downhill to follow the stream.

Micca heard a low, dismal call: "Mic-caw!"

Branna and Fola were nowhere in sight. There was another call, a shrill piping: *"Mic-ky! Mic-ky!"*

Binta's voice was unmistakable. The low call was repeated. This was Bacnod, Micca was sure.

He struggled out of the blackberries. Rather than make for the lower road below, which the Invigorationists from Mora were sure to follow, Micca crawled upward, into thick woods.

The slope lessened and he was able to stand and jog. The trees were younger away from the road, but the undergrowth wasn't as dense as he would have expected in such new growth. After a few minutes he stopped. Where was he going? Where were Branna and Fola?

From behind a big hand seized his wrist. Micca leaned sideways and snatched up a thick branch from the earth. His captor released him as Micca spun around, brandishing his weapon.

Branna backed away, holding his up hands, palms out. "Remind me not to surprise you again," he hissed.

Fola was nearby, leaning back on a tree, panting. "He probably thought…you were a fierce buin of the forest…ready to cut out his heart and eat it for supper."

"Be quiet!" Branna whispered harshly.

"Where are they?" Micca whispered back.

"Me and Fola ran off just after you did, thought we lost you."

"How'd they know to follow us this way?"

Branna shrugged. "Maybe they sent some north and some south. Maybe the Marling told them where we're headed."

"He did not!" said Fola. "I don't think he would anyway, not if you told him what you did me."

Branna glanced over his shoulder. "Doesn't matter now. It could have been anybody at Marstoc, or even those folks from Ofstuna. Let's go a bit farther—they strung themselves out up and down the road, and Bacnod's probably not far away."

"I'm glad we all took the same side of the road," Micca said as they walked softly north. He caught a glimpse of the road between dark tree trunks, but could see no walkers on it.

"We'll have to get ahead of them and go across quick, hopefully just where the lake lane meets it."

"I'm getting tired of behaving like an outlaw," Fola said petulantly. "Why don't you stand up to these louts and tell them you have business elsewhere? What are they going to do, truss you up like a dead boar and carry you back on a pole?"

"I wouldn't put it past them," Branna muttered. "Why else would they send the biggest goons after us? Not counting Wamod and Binta, there's three of them, three of us. Could we deal with them? Be honest now."

Fola sobered, now more frightened than offended.

Micca shook his head. "I'd rather be a live coward than a dead hero, or a maimed hero. They could be anxious we don't get away and tell other people about this. Once I was — if they were able to pull off this Husband plot, somebody would be dead and afterwards everybody at the farm would be involved, guilty, and they wouldn't dare to make a fuss. Nobody else would even know where to look for the…corpse."

Fola spoke quietly. "Let's make sure we avoid them, then."

Somewhere behind them a branch snapped. They all stood frozen. A fluting call came through the trees: "Glory! Come, Husband! Your bride awaits you, near Mora Farm!"

Deaconess Wamod. She and Binta might have been meant to try to sweet-talk Micca into conversation, the others would jump him and tie him up…

He had a premonition. Fola would run like a hare and get lost in the woods; Incseth and the others would beat Branna bloody; they'd catch Micca, maybe break his legs, carry him back and force him to eat mushrooms. Sunday they'd put the red hat on him, throw him in a hole. There'd be a crowd of glassy-eyed farmers above, waving their arms and stamping their feet as he felt the clods of earth hit him —

He lowered his head and crashed through the undergrowth. There were indistinct shouts behind him, rapidly fading.

He ran out of breath and slowed. Someone grabbed his arm and almost pulled off his shirt.

Branna again. "Back!" his cousin hissed as they ran on. "Other way! We'll be safe on the road now, if I can find it."

Micca saw Fola two yards off, running beside them in the dark woods. Branna thudded off between the trees. They halted in a small clearing. Branna stood motionless now, studying a little wood-cased compass in the light of the rising moon. Fola joined them and argued in whispers with Branna over which direction the road lay. They came to an agreement and soon stumbled back onto the North Road, both Branna and Fola surprised at the success of their compromise.

They didn't seem to have come far beyond the bridge where the Invigorationists had appeared, and they hurried north, down the newer track.

"I don't know whether you planned it or not, but we seem to have gotten our pursuers lost in the forest," Fola panted.

"Ha! We lost them good," said Branna. "You don't have to whisper any more, Fola!" He gave out a low yodel as they came around a bend.

Something rustled under a bush ahead. It jumped up, flew down the road, and Branna found a pair of thin arms clamped around his waist.

"O cousin, you've come to save me!" sobbed the boy Binta. Leaves and twigs were stuck in his hair, and his coat was torn. He peered through the gloom and recognized Micca.

"Micca! You have to come home!"

Branna peeled off Binta's arms. Binta whipped around and attached himself to Micca. "They left me here to watch. I got frightened. It's getting so dark, and all the eery noises—but now you have to come back and do your duty!"

Micca wrenched himself free. "Leave me alone! Go back!"

Binta staggered aside. "Oh, Micky, how can you be so wicked? But you won't be wicked once you're the Husband, and then I'll forgive you for your cruel trick last night—

"But who's *that*?" he said, looking at Fola. "One of those Marstoc toughs? He looks like an Eynnishman with that nasty tail of hair…"

Branna and Fola ran on. Micca sprinted after them.

Binta stumbled pathetically behind them for a few yards, then dropped to the side of the road. "I can't walk so far in the dark all alone! The others will forget me! Wild pigs will chase me down! I'm *tired*, Micca," came a receding whine. "The priest will be cross with me…"

From where he was Micca could no longer see Binta, but something moved under the trees, and a small figure ran the other way down the road, away from Micca.

It met a number of other dark shapes. Arms waved and pointed, and then all of them started north, toward Micca.

Micca ran as fast as he ever had. He met Branna, who'd been waiting. They both ran and caught up with Fola.

Branna told him, "They'll find us for sure if we go to your house now. Even if they don't see us turn onto its lane one of them's bound to know about it and where it is."

"Hide…in the woods?" Fola gasped.

"No," Branna said softly. "I know a way to deal with them. Follow me." He trotted off, veered to the east side of the road. A mossy brick pillar stood crookedly under a tree. Branna slapped it as he ran by and disappeared into the woods.

Their pursuers were behind a turn in the road, invisible for the moment. Micca followed Branna past the brick pillar, down a narrow, grass-grown lane. Fola staggered behind.

The lane wound between huge old firs and fragrant waxwoods, rising in a twisting path for a hundred yards, then dropping to a more or less straight run between great banks of ferns. Micca smelled stagnant water and heard mudrunners buzzing somewhere. The lane climbed a stony, washed-out hill, curved south, or maybe west, Micca was no longer sure, and the way became mossy and slick under a solid canopy of tree branches.

The lane twisted again. Micca caught up with Branna, who was standing at the foot of a long hill. The path mounted the hill in a straight line, fenced closely on either side by trees. At the top Micca saw a small patch of star-pierced sky and three black gables. "Whose house is that?" Micca asked.

Branna had made no move to start up the hill. "It's Goranstura."

"Goranstura!" Micca echoed.

Fola trotted slowly up to them. He looked at the house on the hill. "Come on, then," he wheezed.

Branna took Fola's arm to stop him from starting up the hill. "No. We're going this way."

Branna made a brief search, then ducked under the low branches of a waxwood to the side of the lane.

"We could ask the people up there if we could stay the night," Fola complained to Micca. "Tell them…bandits are after us."

"There's no bandits around here and nobody lives there," said Micca, starting after Branna.

"Somebody does. I see a light."

"A light?" Micca looked to where Fola pointed. There was a glimmer in a window under one of the gables now, greenish-blue and wavering. It hadn't been there a minute ago. Micca stood frozen.

"What's the matter with you?" said Fola impatiently. Then they both turned. Somewhere behind them an indistinct voice called out.

Micca and Fola followed Branna down a nearly invisible branching path, quietly as they could. After what seemed like a mile of stumbling over unseen stones and ducking under branches, the path ended before a dark hut.

The place was hardly more than a shake-covered roof over a trench in the ground, but there was dry fuel inside and a hearth under a smoke-hole. Micca stood looking through a crack in the door for a while before he'd let Branna light a fire, but there was no sign the party from Mora had followed them here.

They sat on benches on either side of the fire, smoke stinging their eyes, and ate supper. Afterwards they drank from a bottle of tonic Fola had in his bag, but even when the bottle was half empty Branna was unwilling to answer Fola's questions about the big house on the hill; "It's bad luck to talk about it," was all he would say.

Micca didn't know much about Goranstura and Branna had never mentioned it before. But Micca had once heard his grandfather talking to some visitor or other about it. Goranstura had been a hunting lodge used by the people of the farm one of Branna's grandfathers had come from. The lodge had been in use for six generations, then was suddenly abandoned during the excavation of a new cellar. Men and women of sound mind had seen something that had sent them running into the woods. One of Branna's great-uncles had his hair fall out after catching a glimpse of whatever had been loosed beneath the old lodge, and so far as anyone knew, remained there yet. Micca didn't tell Fola this, agreeing silently with Branna that it would be unwise to tell such stories here. Neither did he tell Branna about the flickering blue-green light.

They finished the bottle. Fola complained about having to sleep on the hut's hard benches, but both he and Branna were asleep in minutes.

Micca took off his lenses and lay awake, watching embers pop on the hearth. He felt a dull ache centered on his memory of Ennesia, and of his lost home, but the liquor he had drunk made his mind fuzzy, and he could neither worry over nor dismiss his longing.

He slipped into a half-dreaming state. Branna snorted in his sleep. Micca blinked back to awareness. There was a hoot outside, a bird. He reached to the floor and tossed another stick of wood onto the coals. It kindled with a wholesome yellow flame. He wondered if Binta and the others from Mora had found their way up to Goranstura, as Branna had apparently intended them to. Maybe they'd find out who had lit the flickering lamp he and Fola had seen. The Invigorationists would go home with white hair and trembling hands, if they went home at all. Maybe they'd learn to mind their own business.

7. A TALK WITH PRIEST PALMER

At Mora, the evening's routine had been upset. The more Vigorous of its residents sat glumly at a table of their own in the hall at supper, having heard that Sunday's Wedding might have to be postponed. Due to Deaconess Wamod's absence, no choir practice had been held. Hulda had said she would play the string-organ and a few singers had gathered, but no one could be found to pedal the organ's drive mechanism and the rehearsal was uninspired.

Old Stalba, conscripted that morning by Priest Palmer as his in-house messenger, puffed crankily along several paces behind Ennosa and Ennesia Topping.

Ennesia had just been released from her room, and had had neither dinner nor supper. She walked briskly anyway, ignoring her chaperon, while her mother trotted beside her, whispering fretfully.

The three of them stepped onto the landing near the bottom of a longer staircase. A gaggle of youngsters sat on the steps above, whispering, eating apples and doughnuts. The youngsters had been unruly all day, sensing something unusual in the house. There was no Mora in the house, and the priest seemed to have lost something of his authority too. One boy, when Stalba had directed him earlier to take the saddle behind the organ, told Stalba that he could pedal it himself. Stalba quoted the Writs, a passage concerning the duty owed by children to their elders, but Budro, the child in question, had laughed at him and run off. Now Budro sat on the steps with his siblings and cousins, laughing again, most probably at Stalba. Nor did his parents correct his behavior. They and other adults, none of them known for their Vigor, loitered in a nearby sitting room.

Stalba guided Ennosa and Ennesia to a door at the side of the landing. The door opened, and a farmer and his wife came out. The woman smiled in an unfriendly way at Ennosa before joining the group in the sitting room. Stalba nodded to Ennosa.

She entered the room, hand grasping Ennesia's wrist. Within, Priest Palmer was studying a sheet of paper lying on his desk.

"How nice to see our guests from Topping this evening," the priest said, eyes still on the paper. He signaled with his hand. Stalba left the room, closing the door behind him.

Ennosa freed Ennesia and sat on the edge of a chair. Ennesia went to examine a shelf of books. After a moment the priest looked up at Ennosa. There were dark circles under his eyes. "'I've been in communication with my associate, Priest Linto of your home farm. He sends you greetings and urges that you aid me in my duties here, perhaps for a day, perhaps for several days; we shall see."

Ennosa produced a fragile smile. "Yes, priest, gladly."

Palmer dipped a pen and began scratching notes on the paper he had been reading. Ennesia took a book from the shelf: a manual on the symbology of cloud formations. The book proved to be uninteresting. Ennesia walked softly to the priest's desk. She inspected the paper he was so intent upon, but Palmer's script was difficult to read upside down. Among the books and papers on the desk was a bowl containing a pool of congealed gravy and a few bits of meat and vegetables. Palmer absently explored the bowl with his left hand, pulled out a small onion and popped it into his mouth.

Ennesia clucked her tongue disdainfully. "Don't they use knives and forks where you come from?"

"Daughter!" cried Ennosa.

Palmer adjusted his lenses and found the young woman staring at him. "Give me your hand, my dear," the priest said in a weary tone.

Ennesia stood motionless. Her mother hissed something unintelligible.

"Please be quiet, Ennosa," Palmer said. Then he craftily caught

Ennesia's hand and gave it a smart slap. Ennesia cried out in astonishment and tried to slap him back.

Palmer dodged her blow. He sat back and sighed. "I'm sorry, my dear. Forgive me. Beside Micca going missing, evidently his cousin Brannoc has, too. I've had a hard day, trying to hold this madhouse together."

"Who made it a madhouse?"

Palmer pursed his lips. "I may have played a somewhat destabilizing role here, I admit it. I overestimated its people's intelligence. But I think you can help me sort things out…

"I asked you earlier where Micca was hiding, and I ask you now again. It's known that the two of you were close — indeed, possibly too close for two people who have not been wed, if certain speculations prove true."

Ennosa had heard the rumors, too, but to hear the priest speak of them was too much. She let out a high-pitched cry.

Stalba's head appeared in the door, and a murmuring from the people outside drifted into the room. Palmer impatiently waved Stalba away and the door closed.

Ennesia said, "You mean the story Binta told about finding Micca sneaking into my room? Binta is one of your madmen. He's infatuated with me, and probably wants to discredit someone he sees as his rival."

Palmer leaned back, his chair creaking, clasped his hands over his stomach and stared at her. "That's a clever accusation. It sounds plausible. But no, I had discounted Binta's tale. What I did not discount was a certain item found in Micca's room. Under the bedclothes, to be precise."

He held a bit of blue linen cord between his fingers. Palmer said, "I remember you wearing something quite like this in your hair yesterday morning at breakfast, Ennesia."

Ennosa gasped. After a moment Ennesia spoke. "Well, what of it? I may have given it to him as a remembrance, before he became Wennoc's Husband — yes, are you surprised? I finally heard about your sick plan, you criminal…you heretic!"

Ennosa leapt up and slapped her daughter.

"Ennosa, please!" said Palmer. "This isn't helping. Why don't you go and lie down for a while?"

Ennesia's mother shuffled out, walking like a tired old woman.

Her daughter looked after her sorrowfully. "You people have driven my mother nearly mad...What are you going to do to me?"

"Nothing!" Palmer folded his hands on the desk and leaned forward. "An hour ago Haralt returned with the news from Marstoc. The Marling showed our deacon little hospitality, but he did convince him that Micca wasn't there. Others have gone out to help him in case he loses himself in the forests. But after all, I think you and I know it's more likely that Micca is still here at Mora, hiding in some unused outshot or remote attic. He knows this place like a rat, and that would certainly be his first instinct."

"I don't know my way around this house. I can't tell you where he'd be."

"Nor do I!" Palmer said. "And Henning says there are no builder's plans, charts or maps."

He stood and clasped his hands behind his back. "What I want you to do, Ennesia, is walk around, inside and outside the house, softly calling out his name, perhaps adding a few endearments. One or two steady hands will follow discreetly behind you, ready to help him when he emerges. Don't you want to see him? Aren't you, too, concerned for him?"

"I won't help you."

Palmer leaned forward. "Why are you so intent on preventing his participation in our ritual? I really don't understand."

"You *are* insane then!" Ennesia cried. "You mean to murder him!"

Palmer looked genuinely dismayed. "Where did you get that idea?"

Ennesia threw up her hands. "That's what everyone says! My mother and Binta, at least. You're going to bury him in a hole down by the mill, leave him there to suffocate under the earth!"

Palmer leaned back and sighed. "As I said, this is a madhouse. People get a fragment of a story and it's distorted more with each telling. I told Micca as much. Sit down, Ennesia. I want to show you something."

Ennesia remained standing. Palmer told Stalba bring in one of the youngsters outside.

Stalba brought in Rasling, a cousin of Micca's several times removed and about his age, a stocky youth known for his energetic stamping in the church.

Palmer took something out of a cabinet near his desk. "Watch now," he told Ennesia.

Palmer stretched a bag of green gum over the uneasy Rasling's head and let it snap home. A snout covered Rasling's face, and his eyes blinked behind two oblate bulbs of glass. A pipe curved from the snout to well above his head, and there was a ragged, hollow sound as Rasling breathed.

"You see?" Palmer asked Ennesia. "If he were to lie under the earth, this head covering would prevent soil from entering his mouth and nose, and yet air could do so, fed to him from this hollow tube. The device was invented by eel-catchers in the south, probably inspired by the tubule the mudrunner extends from the bog while he lies in wait for prey."

Palmer lightly slapped the side of Rasling's head. "Outfitted so, the Husband will easily survive the ritual." He looked at Ennesia. "So, what do you think now, my girl? Let's have no more talk of murder."

Rasling tore off the bag. "I ain't going to be no husband down in the dirt!" He tossed the bag aside, ran to the door, crashed into it, picked himself up, flung it open and scrambled out of the room. The door remained open, and from outside came voices raised in alarm and dismay.

Ennesia gave the priest a long look, then shook her head. "And you call the people at Mora mad? Are you sure you're not talking about yourself?"

Palmer sat back and tapped his fingertips together. Suddenly he stood, hands flat on the top of his desk. "That's enough! I've had my fill and more of this barnfull of ungrateful fools. I'm more weary than I can say of explaining things three times and soothing people's delicate feelings. My only concern has been their welfare — but to Hinnioc with them! There will be no ritual, no Husband. Go tell them. Tell them they don't deserve what I've offered them."

He pointed to the door. "Now get out."

Ennesia opened the door, looked back at him, and left the room.

Palmer sat down. After a moment he said, "Stalba, any word from Wamod and her group?"

"Not yet... but priest, you don't really mean to cancel —"

"When they return tell them not to go out again. If they do have Micca with them, bring him to me at once. And a cold meal and some drink. We'll need to talk. Now go away. I need to rest."

Stalba paused at the door. "What about our devotions? It's almost time to go down to the church."

"Do what you like. Just don't bother me with it."

8. LUNCH IN HOIIN

Neypo Odé's father, Ipsin Hinto Odé, had come to Hoiin from the eastern seaboard of Eynna when he was sixteen, walking the whole distance. After eight years of apprenticeship to a glass blower he had established a shop of his own in which he made fancy bottles, used mostly as containers for scents and expensive cordials and spirits. Ipsin Odé (originally 'Odéghilisypa', which Ipsin shortened in an effort to present himself as more modern and western), though he never rose above the rank of First-degree Hustler in the Lodge, prospered in trade, and made enough money to live well. His wife, Hylial Laula of the Hollata Laulas, was also an easterner. Neypo's parents sent him and his sisters to Saint Rimini's, a small but prestigious college north of Mennedal. Ten years ago the elder Odés had retired to a villa on Lake Ornii, and Neypo had taken over management of the family business.

The Odé shops were still located on the ground floor of a commercial building in downtown Hoiin, but Neypo had also taken over part of a warehouse next-door and built another furnace in the courtyard. He no longer sold bottles, and only five of his thirty full-time employees were still engaged in blowing glass. Those who did so made bulbs to house electronic valves used in radios, small transparent onions much like electric light bulbs in appearance. Using tweezers, other workers assembled little bits of wire and metal that went into the bulbs, which were then fixed to ceramic bases stamped with the Odé glyphs. In the cellar men worked pumps which drew the air from the bulbs, and after this operation they were sealed, tested, and packed in boxes bearing the inscription, Odé's Precision Electrical Essence Valves,

H'HOINA & H'PARNALA. Neypo didn't actually have a shop in Parnala, but he did have an agent there.

Four years ago he had hired an old Harnish émigré to make shipping boxes for him. The fellow had thought himself something of an artist and spent far more time than necessary over the boxes. It had been his suggestion that Neypo also produce cabinets for the increasingly popular radio receivers in which the Odé valves were used, and Neypo had decided to give the idea a try.

Through an agent Neypo found a cheap source of furniture-grade hardwood in Hannava. The radio cabinets sold well to a couple of the local makers, and one thing led to another. A year ago Neypo had paid over an honorarium to Humwei Ohímpala, grandson of the antiquary who had discovered the method by which voices could be transmitted through the aether. (Those transmissions included items of public interest, such as the arrival and departure of ships, weather divinations and official proclamations, as well as music, light entertainment and paid announcements for various commercial products. By the time the impious and frivolous potentials of the new technology had penetrated the attention of the dour Preceptors in Mennedal, it had become too valuable to men of business to make any meaningful restrictions on its content tolerable.) With the honorarium and two percent of the price he received for the finished sets, Neypo was granted license to manufacture complete radio receivers.

The coil winding, wiring and so on were done downtown, but Neypo had set up a temporary final assembly shop at the back of his own garden to save costs. Every part of his receiver was made by him but the listening bonnet, and these were made to his specification by a subcontractor. Four dozen sets had been completed so far, their cases ready for the final coat of varnish, or so the foreman of his garden shop had promised this morning. The Spring Fair was to begin that weekend, and Neypo had rented a booth there in which to display his new receivers. There were already four or five other makes of receivers available, but those that were sold with their own cabinet were heavier and bulkier than Neypo thought necessary, substantial pieces of furniture in their own right. Odé's Improved Heavenly Ear could be set on a table, and was also somewhat cheaper to own than the others. Every year it seemed that another town was establishing a broadcasting station, and the market was booming. Other manufacturers would soon realize the advantages of a more reasonable price and ease of shipping offered by a compact unit. It was essential Neypo have as many of his receivers as possible crated and ready for buyers at the Fair, establishing his firm as an innovator ready to put a radio within the reach of anyone with some discretionary income.

But he hadn't been able to inspect the first fruits of his new enterprise that morning. A runner had come to Rose Pond from downtown before Neypo had even finished his breakfast. One of the men who pedaled the vacuum pump had gone home sick. Other workers, insisting upon retaining the dignity of their trades, had refused to take the malingerer's place. Neypo had brought his son Tympo, who was fourteen now, downtown and set him to pedaling. Tympo had complained stridently of the menial nature of the work and the constant exertion it demanded, but since Tympo had planned to march with the Junior Cadets that afternoon, certainly an energetic undertaking, Neypo had been unsympathetic. The family business was more important than tramping around challenging long-dead Heresiarchs.

By the time Neypo had corrected the technique of a newly hired cathode-setter and dealt with a number of other problems at the shop, it was past the middle of the morning. He reluctantly made a stop at his investigatory committee's office in the Lodge building. As usual neither Micsin nor Woitap were there, but a dozen or more citizens possessing varying degrees of sanity waited in the receiving room, all demanding interviews with the controversial visitors. Among the more respectable were a newspaper correspondent from Slivotuno and several out-of-town dignitaries who thought the Strivers of Hoiin were hiding a party of celebrities from Mennedal, come to bless the Fair. A hobbling old woman attended by two brutish lackeys claimed she was a high official in the Office of Antiquities, and insisted that she had urgent business with the visiting strangers. Neypo was briefly intrigued, but put her off with a promise to see what he could do to arrange an interview. He refused to talk to any of the others and returned to the street; there would just be time before lunch to inspect his receivers if he hurried home.

Neypo found his sedan where he had left it. He saw his porters

sitting on a raised terrace on the other side of the street taking a lei-
surely cup of tea. Neypo shouted over the traffic and waved his hands
to attract their attention. Eventually they acknowledged his signals.

Before they had come across Neypo heard someone call his name.
The Striver Caihar Olinom skipped down a flight of steps on the side
of the next block and skillfully dodged a grocery cart as he crossed the
street. He approached Neypo with long strides. "How lucky to find you
downtown, colleague!" he called, still four yards off.

"Good morning, Striver," Neypo replied, watching for his porters.

"Morning! It's nothing like morning," Caihar said, though it wasn't
quite noon yet. "I'm just going to lunch, and you'll come with me."

Caihar wouldn't listen to Neypo's excuses. He took his arm and led
him away. Neypo hung back and shouted orders to his porters, who
were climbing up to the sidewalk from the street. He told them to go
home and come back for him at two.

Caihar took Neypo down the block, around the corner and over
a bridge. They entered an arcade lined with shops and eating places.
Caihar guided Neypo into the vestibule of a restaurant Neypo considered beyond his means.

An attendant bowed to them obsequiously. "We'd like a private parlor,"
Caihar said, looking into the dining room to see if he recognized anyone.

The attendant became agitated. He turned the pages of a large book.
"I am so sorry, Striving sirs! The only reservation I find placed by the
Lodge is for a party of four, at an hour past noon! Our mistake, I'm
sure! But I have a nice table in a quiet corner…?"

Caihar agreed to this. The corner was not quiet. Five boisterous
Mendicants, from the Lodge at Ettei to judge by their accents and
jauntily askew hats, probably in town for the Spring Fair, sat at the
next table. They politely touched their hands together when they saw
the plaid of the Strivers' coats, then went back to their jokes and back-
slapping.

Neypo and Caihar ate dishes of watercorn with onions and sharps,
seababies poached in the Peaceful Garden's own Arrangement of
Twelve Spices, a small pike that had been boned, marinated, stuffed
with tree-ears and broiled, with bowls of soused greens and orange seg-
ments on the side. The attendant returned with inquiries concerning

the Strivers' intentions as to after-lunch sweets. Caihar ordered two cups of Glinting's Fragrant Rain and waved him away.

Neypo's finger was still in the air as the attendant scurried off. He had been set for a pastry, or maybe a dish of strawberries.

Caihar hunched down over the table, folding his long arms. "What have you learned, Striver?"

"What have I learned?" said Neypo absently, trying to get the attendant back. "Oh—about the visitors."

"Of course."

Neypo faced him and smiled wryly. "Well, the fellow who calls himself Tæfel Adinnegram stopped by the committee's office yesterday on his own, without being summoned. It seems he and his party have taken a booth at the Fair!"

Caihar flipped a hand in the air. "To give out tracts and provide sympathy to abused servants, I suppose. Well, not as bad as what they've been doing elsewhere. What else?"

"Let me see…apparently not all of the visitors are here with us in town. Adinnegram said something in passing about another one of them who's camped out somewhere up on the north coast, digging up some sort of ruins. I'll write to the local authorities at once, advising they arrest him for trespass and the disturbing of antiquities. But Caihar, this is the best bit: they plan to leave us soon." Neypo leaned forward, smiling with satisfaction. "We'll be rid of them."

"When? Where are they going? Parnala? Midoi? Even Mennedal, perhaps?"

Neypo waited a moment, having hoped the news of the visitors' intended departure would please Caihar. "Adinnegram mentioned no itinerary," Neypo said. "He simply said that things were going well and that they'd soon no longer be needed in Hoiin."

Caihar shook his head. "It won't do. We can't have them bothering our neighbors. It would make Hoiin's Lodge look bad, very lax. What else did he say?"

"Oh, more of their usual tripe. He was quite chatty, actually. Somehow he must have discovered that I manufacture radio receivers, and told me that one day we'd carry such instruments in our pockets, or even in our ears! Then he waxed philosophical and said that the most important of us will receive—and the fellow said this with a straight face—a new conscience, fresh and pure, to make our saintly behavior more easily achieved!" Neypo laughed and shook his head. "He's an engaging chap in his own way, but clearly deranged."

Caihar didn't laugh. "What rubbish!"

"Yes, of course. He invited me to take beverages tonight with him and what he called some of his new friends, whoever they might be, at a townhouse near the University. Unfortunately I neglected to ask the address, since these 'friends' should be investigated. In any case, I told him I had another engagement...he didn't say much else, other than to confirm that it was, in fact, Reimi Rytalla who arranged the opportunity for his little speech on the Voice the other night. He was quite open about it."

"We suspected it was Rytalla all along. That idiot will soon see that he's gotten himself into some very serious trouble. Anything else?"

"Well, let me see. Ah yes. I regret to say that Micsin has become as useless as Woitap. He can't do anything but repeat the words of his new mentor, the Emeritus Uho, who advises quiet contemplation and submission to Wennoc's peace."

"Micsin? Taken in by Uho's pablum?"

Neypo nodded. "So now Micsin doesn't want to confront the visitors with questions that might make them feel 'unwelcome' or 'ill at ease'. Meanwhile Woitap pesters me to visit the Guest Hall with him. 'We may profit by speaking with them in a relaxed, informal setting,' Woitap says, but otherwise he has shown little interest in conducting the investigation since his visit to them that night after our consistory; you remember, when he'd sworn to throw them out of the Guest Hall? So anyway, I'm left by myself to deal with the throngs of curiosity seekers and madmen who present themselves at the committee's office—" The attendant bent over the next table, completely oblivious to Neypo's hisses and gestures.

He gave it up. "But Caihar, did you see the absurd story the Word printed about the visitor's speech on the radio?"

Caihar grimaced. "'Mystic Philosopher Addresses City Over the Aether'." Speak of tripe! I hear the papers in other towns have picked it up too, spreading the damage to our reputation. And then Rytalla had the gall to hint, on his news program, that the Lodge was actually studying the visitors' proposals! Proposals!"

"I think it's time to put the censors to work; past time, probably. A general consistory should be called to sort this out. We need more of the Lodge involved."

"The censors, yes, if we could get the Grand Fellow to agree as to their instructions," Caihar said bitterly. "And a consistory might make things worse, spin this whole business out for months."

The attendant appeared with a bottle of spirits. "Bring us also a half-dozen strawberry pastries," Neypo told him quickly.

He settled back and spoke carefully as Caihar poured. "It seems the political situation is messier than ever. Might it not be best to say good riddance to the visitors and let them go?"

"By no means," said Caihar. "They've got to be stopped, and right here in Hoiin."

"I see. And as to the strings you told me you were going to pull in order to keep the visitors silent... did they change their minds?"

"No," Caihar sighed. "My 'strings' did what they could. Not enough, it seems." He tasted his spirits.

"How much damage do you think has been done?"

Caihar shrugged. "Who knows? Whatever damage there was already, it's certainly been compounded. Even the street sweepers and porters are speculating about the nature of the visitors' supposed gifts and wondering which government office they'll land. Others cry Heresy, but not loudly enough. I almost wish a mob would storm the Hall and show some of the boldness they found in themselves nine hundred-odd years ago, when they weighted the last Heresiarch with his treasures and jeweled skulls and gave him to the sea."

Caihar drank again and refilled both their cups. "Pay no attention to my babbling," he said to Neypo's alarmed expression. "We aren't such savages in this day and age. But tell me about the visitors' cipher. Have you had any luck with it? If we had proof of something unmistakably dangerous, things would be a lot easier."

The attendant set a plate of biscuits on the table. Neypo offered the plate to Caihar, who shook his head.

"The script itself was no real problem once I had familiarized myself with it," Neypo said. "But otherwise I've drawn a blank. I have a new theory about the situation, however."

Caihar drummed his fingers on the table, then suddenly jerked upright. "I've been evolving a theory, too, Neypo. Quite a wild notion, I thought at first. You'll say I'm mad, of course...' He pursed his lips and looked at the table.

Neypo tasted a pastry. It was particularly good, with an unctuous, flaky shell and a cream filling speckled with finely minced, fresh red strawberries. Neypo glanced up, licking his lips, but Caihar had apparently decided not to reveal his theory just now.

"Perhaps things aren't so bad," Neypo said, pouring for them this time. "I have an experiment in mind that should at least clarify a certain aspect of the case."

"Well, go on," said Caihar, sniffing at his cup.

"I should explain the inspiration behind it first, which is this: my daughter's Harnishman sometimes uses unfamiliar words, very peculiar words in fact. He becomes embarrassed when I catch him at it; most of them are agricultural or geographic terms, or so he says, and he's anxious to be thought of as a scholar rather than a farmer."

Neypo warmed to his subject. "These words were no surprise to me at first, given the variety of dialects out east. I thought the explanation was that some obscure, locally specialized word might drop out of one style of speech, only to survive in another. And what's so surprising about having two or even three or four ways to say the same thing? It fits in with the fragmented way in which man, with all his flaws, looks at and reacts to the world. It seems to him, by the evidence of his eyes, that all the little items of which Wennoc is composed are unique in themselves. It's only when each of us is spiritually united with our earth that we'll have a full understanding of transcendent Totality."

"But Neypo, what—"

Neypo had leaned forward. "I see Wennoc—Wennoc as it should be and the way we all trust it some day will be—as a perfect whole, harmonious in all its parts. But for better or worse, we can't throw off our present corruption simply because we wish it gone. Nor is it possible to impose perfection on man, no, nor even upon the simpler of the world's creations."

Caihar put up his finger, but Neypo took a quick swallow from his cup and continued. "Can we command the stoat to go about his ways free of error? Does the cherry tree put forth its branches with absolute symmetry?" Neypo waved his cup. "Hardly. A cold spring stunts the tree in its youth; any sort of random incident might influence the actions of the stoat."

Caihar held up his hand. "Your theology is sound and insightful, but I didn't mean to elicit a dissertation. Just what is this theory of yours?"

"Yes, of course," said Neypo, selecting another biscuit. "Well, here it is. Since there's such a variety of life in Wennoc, I believe there might have arisen a completely separate way to speak among some of its people; not merely an odd accent, or something like the Old Tongue, akin to modern speech but more or less unintelligible to the uneducated. An *unintentional* cipher, so to speak. Such an independent set of words may have been used at one time by the Harnish when they were more isolated from the mainstream of Wennish life. If it should turn out that my daughter's Harnish friend is able to understand some of the words the Hall's housekeeper copied out, it might be proved that the visitors are after all only a troupe of surprisingly sophisticated evangelists from some remote Harnish valley on the other side of the mountains. This isolation would also go a long way in explaining their...but you appear skeptical, Striver."

Caihar tried to hide his smile, turning to order another bottle of spirits from the attendant. He faced Neypo and said, "So you've come up with your own version of Riino's Harnish connection, hey? But Neypo, do you realize how many words are necessary for even the most rudimentary human communication? I should think that all possible combinations of sounds have already been used. With this in mind, how can you expect me to accept the existence of another complete language?" Caihar sighed. "Granted, your notion is clever, but I'm afraid it's time to leave off theorizing. We must act."

The elder Striver looked around the dining room and went on in a whisper. "The group of dedicated citizens I mentioned to you the other day is ready to act, and act now. You're already involved, and can be of valuable help. I want you to be included in our activities."

"Activities? Activities directed against the visitors, I suppose."

"Yes! We can't stand motionless like your cherry tree and let an intemperate breeze determine the outcome. Wennoc's given us limbs to walk about and hands to work with. We are Wennoc's tools. As such we have responsibilities. We must Strive for Wennoc in the best way we can discover!"

"I bow to your wisdom, Striver...'

"Sit down, Neypo!" Caihar hissed. "People will think you're drunk." Caihar looked around fretfully. "Now, since you're already in the mood to make fun of me, I'll tell you about my wild notion after all."

"I wasn't making fun, no!"

"Never mind." Caihar bent forward and clutched the edge of the table, speaking rapidly. "Listen to me now. What if our uninvited guests are not of Wennoc at all? What if they're monsters from the supernatural realm of Hinnioc, utterly opposed to Wennoc and everything we hold sacred?"

Neypo was astonished. "But they're human beings, Caihar, and Wennoc is the author of all men! If you're correct in your theory, what could it mean?"

Caihar looked him in the eye. "Come, Neypo! There are challenges for us in Wennoc's design. The world tests us and proves us. On another scale, Wennoc has made creatures so small that only the most cleverly arranged set of lenses will reveal them. The beneficial of these animalcules go unnoticed and unthanked, but what about the wicked ones? What happens when they find entrance to your body? You become ill, of course. And your corporeal self has to employ all its resources to fight these intruding creatures. You grow hot and fevered; you toss and sweat in the turmoil of the battle. But finally, if Wennoc is satisfied of your resolve to live, it helps your body to destroy the invader...or in its mercy, Wennoc takes you to itself.

"That is what the saints tell us in the Writs. But rather than our individual bodies being infected, it's the entire world, or at least our city! We may have come to such a state that Wennoc is testing us, as it did when it afflicted us with the Heresiarchs." Caihar sucked in a breath and leaned back in his chair.

Neypo sat back too, and sipped from his cup. "An interesting and frightening theory, Caihar; very frightening indeed. But respectfully, I think we should perform my linguistic test. If the visitors *do* merely turn out to be some type of Harnishmen, we risk offending their cousins if we molest them too severely. We may lose the valuable market for our goods in Harna, not to mention our source of life-preserving medicines, fine spirits and cheap timber for building and making charcoal."

"Wennoc's children, and not so long ago, found it repugnant to burn their world's beautiful trees, especially when Wennoc freely offers us its sea-coal!"

"Indeed, indeed," Neypo admitted absently, then put both his hands on the table. "But I have to admit, colleague, that I've been plagued by a wild notion too, one you don't seem to have considered. If there was only a fragment of truth in the visitors' fantastic promises, I'd be drunk with excitement over the miracles of progress and profits we could realize."

Caihar stared at Neypo. "Wicked temptations!" he shouted.

Several other patrons of the restaurant turned to look at him curiously. Caihar glanced nervously side to side and reduced his voice to a whisper. "Temptations, Neypo, false promises! Don't the Writs warn of such things? Merely being born into the world at all is the greatest of gifts. What more should we ask of Wennoc than the plain and simple things of life, given to us naturally as integral parts of our wonderful world? Anything more can be a danger, a dangerous test. Even the ability to hear voices and music from far away is a corrupting pleasure, one we haven't earned and certainly don't need! People used to make their own music, have conversation with their family and neighbors."

Neypo observed the tables near them, but the other diners had gone back to their food and conversation. "What does your group mean to do then, Caihar? Will you kill them?"

"Neypo!" Caihar hissed. "Do you think us capable of murder?"

So Caihar was still willing to entertain the possibility that the visitors were human beings, Neypo thought with relief, since murder necessarily involved humans. "Certainly not, no!" he said. "But you did make reference to the subaqueation of the Heresiarch Mylly a moment ago."

Caihar whispered earnestly. "All we intend is that the visitors be prevented from further endangering the harmony of our lives. We're going to initiate a small police action. If they cooperate, they'll be free to go back to wherever it is they came from; they can take a boat to Harna, or disappear in a cloud of sparks. And if they refuse to leave Eynna, we'll shut them up somewhere so they won't contaminate other cities."

"I suppose I can see the theoretical need for such a scheme," said Neypo. "But if there is any violence, won't certain factions within the Lodge be wildly upset? Micsin and the Emeritus Uho won't believe that a few oddly dressed foreigners represent so urgent a threat to require such what is essentially a private action."

"Reinitap Uho should take up holy orders and find himself a tree to sit in. He was always an impractical utopian. And as to how harmless 'a few foreigners' can be, look to your Writs, Neypo. Do you remember? 'From an acorn did Nimi's great oak spring.' But enough of this argument."

Caihar leaned over the table, eyes narrow. "Remember the archives I mentioned last week? I think you should take a look at them this afternoon, and afterward I can virtually guarantee you'll sing a different song."

Neypo's eyes opened wide. "I had intended to go home, but in light of what you've said..."

Caihar wasn't listening. He had half risen, hands on the table, staring toward the door.

"Neypo," he hissed, dropping quickly back to his chair. "Look again to the Writs — 'Who comes in farmer's smock, but to ravage the corn?' — and then look to the door."

Neypo swung around. Into the restaurant came three of the visitors, their identity made obvious to Neypo by their height, their dark, artlessly cropped hair and peculiar clothing. And Neypo started to see Micsin Ompito follow them into the dining room. His coat was of Striving plaid, but under it Neypo could see that Micsin wore a snug gray jumper and pantaloons identical to those of the visitors.

The restaurant's host was unsure of the visitors' status, but he saw that they were in the company of a Striver. The host darted forward with a smile and led them to a table.

Neypo wondered if he should go over and speak to Micsin, but his fellow committee member apparently hadn't seen him, nor anyone else in the restaurant. He hung on the visitors' words as though each one were precious. Such fawning wouldn't have been out of character for Woitap if he thought he could profit by it, but a sour old crank like Micsin?

9. HANNAVA

The North Road had swung east, headed toward Hoina Bay and Hannava. The afternoon before, Micca, Branna and Fola had reached a small farm of thirty souls called Nessahógabugattan, whose head had been a fishing friend of the Mora. They were treated with hospitality, and Micca finally got a bath. Since Fola had said they'd reach Hannava today, they had all put on fresh clothes from their bags. Micca wore a white shirt embroidered with fir trees around its hem, and he had oiled his boots. Branna's shirt was stitched with a pattern of vines bearing green, red and orange berries, and his codpiece was padded like a bridegroom's. There were dandelions in the roadside grass, and Branna fastened a bunch of them to his hat. The clothes Fola had reserved for the city were more restrained. He wore a coat of dark blue and green plaid, black knee-pants, white stockings and low, buckled shoes, all consistent with the manner in which a man must outfit himself if he didn't want to be taken for a rustic from the woods, as he had said in reply to Branna's ridicule.

By the middle of the morning the road came alongside the banks of the Silma, a rapidly flowing river formed by the joining of several others flowing out of the low green mountains to the west. At one point a stone bridge arched over it, but there were no longer roads at either end, and a few trees had taken root near the middle of its span; Micca saw a small timber house under them.

They walked on. There were houses, corn bins, chicken coops and stinking piggeries along the road now. People were out working in gardens, small farmers who grew produce for the town. After another mile the houses grew taller and closer together, interspersed with shops.

Finally the walkers could see the tall brick blocks and colorfully domed churches of Hannava's inner core. It was said the Eynnish had built the older parts of Hannava, but Micca thought there were many Harnish qualities to the city's architecture, translated from timber into brick.

They walked up to what Fola described as Hannava's western gates, though now they seemed to be well inside the town. Two towers of vine-covered brick rose among the surrounding houses. A pair of tall, bronze-bound doors stood to either side, held permanently open by the pavement that had risen around them.

Beyond the gates was a large square. At first Micca felt at home again, surrounded by throngs of people, but he quickly understood that most of them probably wouldn't even know each other's names. The only Eynnishmen Micca had seen before were a few peddlers and spirits buyers, but to judge by their long, tied-up hair and strange accents, a lot of the people here had come from over the Bay. They called from their booths, boasting about the quality of their merchandise. Little yellow-haired children ran in the streets chasing down potential customers. Branna laughed and compared them to the dandelions in his hat.

The majority of the people here appeared to be Harnish, though, and Micca wondered if there were a lot of fights in the market; here and there he saw uniformed men, carrying clubs and wearing shin-guards and helmets with flared brims. One pair seemed to be sorting out a dispute between a shopkeeper and her customer. Fola said these men were employed by the City Directorate. Micca wondered if some of them would go down to Mora to seize Priest Palmer when he brought his complaint. But the guards didn't seem very serious about their business. Most of them lounged against walls, chatting with each other and smoking pipes of sotweed. Branna wondered if their shin-guards were meant to protect them from the bites of the Eynnish children.

In front of a fountain they saw three young women. The women had painted their faces and their breasts were barely covered; one of them ostentatiously adjusted her clothing, and a nipple winked out at Micca. Branna whispered that these must be the women who sold their favors for money. Micca stared at them. Branna didn't know how much they charged.

But many of Hannava's citizens seemed more respectable, and

wealthy. They strolled casually by the booths of the merchandisers with faintly amused expressions, walking with the aid of carved sticks, warding off flies with fans of colorfully printed paper. Now and then they'd stop to examine some piece of fancy-work or buy a paper cup of early strawberries. A party of grandees languidly climbed a flight of steps and entered a long, canvas-covered terrace set into the wall above the street, a place where food was cooked to order to judge by the smells wafting down from it. On the terrace a troop of smartly liveried servers hurried up to the diners, bowing and smiling, pulling out chairs for them. Micca wondered what a meal in such a place would cost; as much as a hired woman, probably.

They entered a district of narrow old brick mansions, carved doors in their portals, bays of windows with colored glass fronting their upper stories, fanciful dormers, belvederes and teremocs popping out of roof-tops. Micca lagged behind for a minute to look down a lane where he thought he could see the water of the Bay; he could smell salt water, but the gleam was only the sun striking the dome of a church.

Someone tapped him on the shoulder. He moved aside and a fancily dressed man strode by, turning back to inspect him through a lens on a stick. Micca ran to catch up with his friends.

Fola and Branna stood by a fountain in the intersection of three streets. "Here we are," said Fola.

He led them down an alley, then went to a door that was flanked by windows on either side. A spider's web of worked iron was set over the door, and from it hung a board on which a square maze of letters had been painted. With some difficulty Micca read, 'The Resort of…Gracious and Somnolent Repose', and under it in normal script, 'Dinners and Lodging to be Had'.

"Is this an Eynnish place?" Micca asked Fola. "What's the cobweb for?"

"The best inns are owned by Eynnishmen. They all have a spider's web outside because at one time the liturgists warned against drinking beer and liquor; technically it's still against the law here! Let's go in and see how dangerous their drink is."

"They probably don't have anything to eat but boiled fish heads," Branna muttered, ducking behind the others under a low arch.

At the near end of a long room was a counter set with casks, stone jars and bottles. Tables and benches filled the rest of the room. A pretty young Harnishwoman with a long brown braid stepped out from behind the counter and gave all three cups of thin beer before anyone could speak. "Will you have meat?" she asked, and described what food might be had as she led them to a table.

"You have to admit they're pretty hospitable so far," Micca told Branna as they sat down.

Fola told the woman he'd have the Estimable Chicken Composition, the day's special. Micca fretted and delayed, but finally ordered the same dish. Branna asked for boiled potatoes and sausages.

The chicken had been cut up and fried with candlenuts, fresh green sharps, nobble shoots and pepper pods. Micca sputtered, mouth burning, but he ate it, rapidly consuming his beer as he did so. When they had finished, a stout little Eynnishman appeared.

"Mister Voling!" he said with a bow. "It's been a while since we've seen you."

"I'm happy to be back, Mister Toivo. Do you have lodgings available for myself and two associates?"

"Most certainly."

They climbed the stairs. It had been bright outside, but the one window in the room Toivo showed them looked out on a narrow courtyard and admitted little but a smell of saltwater and fish. The landlord lit the gas so they could see the fresco of lakes and trees on the wall. A saint smiled down from the branches of one of the painted trees.

Branna whispered to Micca. "Look at this little gopher's den, all plastered like a cellar, even the ceiling. Can't we go to the Directorate this afternoon and get it done with?"

"Remember that Fola has business here too, and I think it'll take him more than half an hour."

The landlord had politely ignored their conversation, but now he inquired, "May I ask you young gentlemen what business brings you to the city? Do I presume correctly that you will represent your plantation's interests in town, Mister Voling?"

Fola nodded. "I have some hardwood options to sell at the lumber exchange, and my friends have a matter to discuss with the City Directorate."

"You should receive some good offers. The market over the Bay is said to be booming."

Then the landlord made a sort of salute to Micca and Branna, and turned again to Fola. "If your friends are to be inducted, you're wise to bring them here for a night or two first. This part of town offers many enjoyable diversions for young chaps from the south such as yourselves. They would have pleasant memories to take with them."

"Take where?" said Branna.

"What do you mean, 'inducted'?" said Micca.

The landlord peered at them. "I had assumed you'd been conscripted into the City's Service, although I admit you're the first I've seen to present themselves so willingly."

"No one's presenting themselves for anything," said Fola. "Mister Micael here is brother to his plantation's chief, and will bring certain legal concerns to the attention of the Directors."

"I understand perfectly," the landlord said with a doubtful bow.

He and Fola came to an agreement over the price of the room. "And as you'll recall, Mister Voling, an old-fashioned Eynnish breakfast is included in the tariff. It would also be my pleasure to provide you gentlemen with a beverage, courtesy of the house."

They returned to the lower room. At Mora two types of beer were brewed, 'lunch beer', light and effervescent when fresh, and 'supper beer', darker and still; the Somnolent Repose offered a choice of seven kinds, including two in the Eynnish style, rich and almost black, with brown, foaming heads, which Micca came to enjoy, though Branna wondered if he didn't want a spoon to sup it. After the first cups Fola bought the landlord one, who suggested they try the 'Welcoming Strand Bitter', then stood for the next round. Soon the young woman who had served them lunch had to take over management of the bar.

By late afternoon both Branna and Micca felt at home. The barroom had filled with cheerful people, all laughing and talking. Three additional waiters had come to work, carrying pitchers of beer or cider and bottles of distilled spirits to the tables. Toivo had been dosed with strong tea by his wife and now they both worked behind the bar, tapping casks and counting money. From the kitchen came sounds of clattering pans and sizzling food.

At suppertime Fola convinced Branna to try a dish of Harnish food cooked in the Eynnish manner: loin of pork, crisp green and white cabbage, fragrant brown mushrooms and onions, all of it sliced up, fried together and tossed with a piquant gravy, served over plates of steaming watercorn. Later they tried pipes of sotweed, and after they had stopped coughing they joined the company in a sing-song.

In the morning Micca woke with a headache. He got out of bed and walked around until he found the inn's bathroom. Two more of the inn's guests joined him in the big stone tub and Micca cut his bath short, although he felt better for the short soak.

In their room Branna was still snoring, but Fola was awake. Eventually they all went downstairs where a boy gave them tea and fried sugar-dusted bread. Micca and Branna waited for the rest of their breakfast, but it never came, and Fola wouldn't allow them to embarrass themselves by asking for hen's eggs or fruit. "This is all I ate before noon during my years in Hoiin," he told them. "On the mainland it's considered unhealthy to gorge yourself first thing in the morning."

"We're not on the mainland and it's not the first thing in the morning," Branna pointed out glumly.

They went up to their room again. Fola said Micca should put on a clean shirt and comb his hair. Fola dug in his bag and found another Eynnish-style coat. "When you speak to the Honorable Timminen at the Directorate you want to look like the Mora's representative."

"And not some fugitive brush-cutter, I suppose," Micca added.

But he tried on the coat. Branna shook his head and laughed. Doing his best to ignore Branna, Micca said, "I'd look stupid with just the coat. It would be better to have some of those knee-pants, too. But then my boots would look stupid."

Fola looked him up and down. "I don't think what I have in that line will fit you; the coat is a bit tight as it is. But what we can do is go to the tailors' shops and get you some new clothes. Then we'll have lunch in the square before we go to the Directorate. Afterwards I'll make some appointments at the Lumber Exchange."

The streets were noisy and full of people again. When they came to the market Branna asked Micca if he was really going into the booths of the pomaded clothiers with their measuring strings and condescending smiles. Micca hesitated, but Fola pushed him in.

Micca was impressed by the variety of garments for sale, all more or less ready to wear. He tried on three different coats, finally deciding on a black one with a narrow collar. He also bought a new white shirt and a neckband. Fola suggested dark green pants that tied at the knees, long stockings and black shoes. The tailor suggested a new hat with a pinched crown and a brim only a finger wide. Micca didn't like it, though Fola said clothes like this were the last word in stylishness. As it was, Micca was uneasy spending one and seven-eighths silver pennies when clothes cost him nothing at home, but looking at himself in the clothier's mirror he decided the effect was rather striking. He looked like a different man. Maybe he'd wear these new clothes at Samma's Seating as the Mora and alarm the Invigorationists. The man who took his money offered him a ribbon free of charge. Micca used it to fasten his hair into a short tail behind his neck.

Fola was impressed with him. Branna said Micca looked like a lich-layer, but he no longer seemed so flattered when people stared at his country finery.

Fola decided it was still too early for lunch, so they went to the City Directorate. They registered Micca's name with a doorman and waited with a crowd of other people on cold stone benches in an echoing hall. The place was ancient, a little shabby, but still grand. Micca's mouth felt dry. He tried to loosen his tongue by talking to Branna, but his cousin had lost his normal good humor and made only short, noncommittal replies.

From time to time someone would shout from a window up under a tiled vault for one of those waiting. After half an hour the voice called out: "The citizen from Mora Plantation, County Wendum! Stand for tallying!"

Fola pulled Micca after him. They walked to the wall and bent their heads back. Fola pushed Micca forward and called up, "This is Micael of Mora, representing the Mora of County Wendum. We wish to speak with the Honorable Timminen Numo, who is known to my father, the—"

"You will receive your confirmation call presently," the woman in the window said. "When you do, enter the Petitioner's Door under the second transept on your left. Give the secretary the information he requires. Thereafter, proceed as directed."

The woman left her window. Micca sat down nervously. Branna and Fola stood a little way off, talking together.

Fola approached Micca. "Be sure you talk directly with Timminen Numo, and don't call him Timma or something like that. Remember to tell him you know my father."

Micca stood up. Fola went on. "We should be back soon. If not, we'll meet you at the Somnolent Repose."

Micca jumped up, following them half way to the outer door. They looked back and waved. Micca stood with his mouth open for a moment, then went back to the bench, his old clothes in a bundle on his lap.

The streets of Hannava were as busy that afternoon as they had been in the morning. Micca walked up a street that led from the harbor back into the central part of the town, looking frequently behind him, still carrying his package of old clothes.

Ahead was the Bay. He'd seen it before, but here it seemed wider and grander. It stretched east and met the sky with no other land in sight, though he knew Hoiin was almost directly across the Bay, forty miles east.

He couldn't see Hoiin, but he could make out the sails of a boat far out on the water, and even a sailor climbing its mast. The new lenses he wore improved his vision better than the old ones had. The optical shop he had visited let him try a dozen different grindings, where the peddler who visited Mora with such things had carried only three. His store of silver had shrunk substantially today, but he hadn't touched the Marling's contribution yet and probably wouldn't have to.

Micca searched for the Somnolent Repose, carefully avoiding a man in a uniform on the corner. After asking his way from a talkative old woman, he found the right street.

Micca opened the inn's door. He was welcomed by a rush of noise and sotweed smoke. Toivo the landlord saw him and drew a cup of Sunset Cellar-brew for him. Micca gulped it down and asked for another. Toivo complied, and pointed to where Fola was sitting.

Micca made his way across the crowded room. He sat down, glancing at Fola's companion, wondering where Branna was, then swung his head back.

Branna sat next to Fola. His yellow hair was pulled back and away from his face, tied behind his head with a length of stiff white ribbon. He wore a coat of cerulean blue, a darker blue waistcoat, yellow knee-pants, and a broad grin.

"Pretty fancy, huh?" said Branna.

Micca studied him for a moment longer, nodded and tried to smile, then sat down next to Fola. "Why are there so many people here?"

Fola said, "It's a holiday tomorrow. Nimoi Tuvimat, as they say in Eynna. Some like to start celebrating early. It's the same as our May Day, actually."

"That was two weeks ago," Micca said.

"The Strivers reformed the calendar a hundred and fifty years ago. Most of the Harnish wouldn't go along with it, and they recognize two holidays in Hannava."

Micca looked at Branna again as Fola poured him a cup of liquor. "Is that why you're wearing that costume?"

Branna frowned. "Costume?"

"Tell us, Micca," said Fola. "What took you so long? What have you been up to this afternoon? Did Timminen Numo give you lunch? And is that new glass in front of your eyes? Rather smarter than your old lenses, I think."

Micca drew a breath. "I've been doing a lot of things — or two things, actually. One because of the other, or partly because of it, anyway. You shouldn't have left me there, you know. Then again, you couldn't have done much good."

"Slow down," said Branna.

"Your Timminen wasn't there," Micca told Fola. "They said he wasn't even a Director anymore. He was deposed, voted out by the others."

Fola poured Micca another cup. "That's a surprise. Did you find another Director to talk to?"

Micca drank. "No, they're too important to talk to me. You don't know Hannava so well as you think you do, Fola. We don't want to hang around here. It's dangerous."

Fola smiled sympathetically. "You're just suffering a reaction against city ways. It's all brought on by homesickness and the unfamiliar situation. The people here are more friendly than you might imagine, and after another day or—"

"You're wrong. They want to put us in the City Service, Fola—all of us! Anybody the right age. They let me talk for about two minutes, then all they did was ask questions that had nothing to do with Palmer or Samma or Mora or anything. They couldn't care less about who's the Mora. 'Local problem', they said, none of their business. What they do say is their business is that Mora—or any of the farms down south, including yours, Fola—hasn't sent anybody to join the City's Service. They made a law five years ago that says if you live anywhere in Harna, you have to be a guard or help build roads or whatever for two years when you're old enough."

"I don't—" Fola began.

"I said I never heard of this Service thing. 'You have now', they said, and 'Ignorance is no excuse'. Then they said I was dressed above my station, that I was an idle fop, and that I was away from my plantation without a permit or an exemption from service. Then they put me in a room and made me take off all my clothes. An old man with bad breath came in and pinched me and poked me and looked at my teeth like I was an ox for sale. They took my eye-glasses too. 'Too young for such crutches,' the old man said. Said I was wearing them so I'd seem like a cripple and get out of duty. I sneaked into a place on the way back here and got new ones."

"I'd've pounded him," Branna said faintly.

"You wouldn't have pounded dozens of guards with clubs. They were all over the place. But I overheard another man say, 'No exemption papers, and it looks like we're going to need new recruits. Put him in a ready squad.' So I said I *had* exemption papers. I said you two were keeping them for me, here at the inn."

"You told them where we were *staying*?" Branna said.

"I lied. Brave Beyalmer was in a situation like this once. I remembered the name of another place I saw by the market and told them that. They sent a big old slobbery guard with me to get the papers, but I ran off quick down a twisty road. The guard was out of shape and I lost him."

"Quite an adventure!" Fola said as Micca paused to drain his cup.

Micca spoke to Branna. "I went down to the harbor and talked to the boat people. There's one that leaves for Hoiin three hours after candlelight, the *Spry Foam-Rider*, I think he called it. I know what dock it's at anyway. We should take it; Fola, do you want to go too?"

Branna looked at Micca doubtfully. "To Hoiin?"

"I thought you were going to send word to Samma by the post," said Fola. "There's no need to leave town. You're just upset right now. The City Directorate can't really conscript you. They're bluffing. You're with me, and I have papers, lots of papers. My father's stamp is on all of them. Why, we'll go back to the Directorate first thing in the morning and demand an apology! And your eye-glasses. They can't push us around. Whatever governing we need we take care of ourselves at the Stoard Fair. There must be a few members of the Directorate who are totally out of contact with modern day realities."

Micca said, "Branna, I don't want to go alone. Don't you want to go see Sam?"

Branna pressed his lips together. "I don't know, Micca. Shouldn't we wait until we hear from him? And I heard stories at the clothes shop. There's supposed to be trouble over in Hoiin."

Micca stared at him.

Fola filled his cup. "We're safe here," he promised. "We're not men to be ordered around by impotent functionaries. Samma will come to Hannava as soon as he hears from you—have you written your letter yet? We can stay at Toivo's until he comes and all go back together."

Until this afternoon this would have sounded like an excellent suggestion. Micca thought his silver would hold out for a while, even if he paid for Branna's room and board. And of course Fola had his business concerns to look after. But didn't they understand they were risking two years of slavery?

"Didn't you hear me?" Micca said, getting desperate. "They're going to shave your heads and put you in guard suits!"

"Don't take this the wrong way," Fola said, "but I'm afraid you're a little naive, Micca, and you're overreacting. I've been in Hannava five or six times, and I can assure you it's as safe here, probably safer, than it is anywhere. And Branna was right—people are saying there's some kind of political upset in Hoiin."

"Then it's all the more important to get Sam away!"

Fola spoke patiently. "Samma will certainly know much more about whatever's going on there than we do. He knows the city, and he'll know what to do. I can imagine him making sensible, careful plans, only to have you throw everything into confusion by appearing at his door unexpectedly. You'd be a burden to him."

Fola signaled a waiter, who came back with a black stone jar. "Empty your cups," Fola told Micca and Branna. "Here's the real thing—Hronda's Old Acme!"

Micca tasted it doubtfully. He was going to be riding on a boat, and he still had to convince Branna to come…

The Old Acme belonged to a class of essences called hundred-herbals. It was very good, and so well distilled that much of it was absorbed by the skin inside his mouth before he could swallow it. His head swam, trying to sort out the subtle patterns of flavor.

Fola poured them each another dram of the Acme. "Besides that, you'd get lost two streets from the harbor on your own over there! Hoiin is probably five times the size of Hannava. Bigger, even."

Micca sullenly swished the green liquid around in his cup. A young woman approached their table. She was tall and buxom, almost skipping along in flounced skirts. Fola sprang to his feet, took one of her hands and placed a lingering kiss on it.

"I'm *sorry* I'm so late, Foly," she said. "My accountancy class at the Lyceum ran late."

Fola held her hand to his cheek and whispered, "I'd wait all night for just a glimpse of your sweet face."

"Introduce me to your handsome friends, Foly."

He blushed and smiled foolishly. "Of course, Carny. This fine big fellow is Brannoc of Mora Plantation, and the dark-haired, flashing-eyed gentleman is the brother of his chief, Micael of—"

"And I'm Carny Toivo," the woman said. She waved her hand high in the air. "Daddy! Yes, over here! Can we have a little jar of Rosy Dreamland, please?" Then she turned back to the table, smiling shyly at Branna and Micca. "My father's the landlord. I take terrible advantage of him."

Toivo himself brought a colorfully labeled glass bottle. "With my compliments," he said, beaming. He bowed to the table and took himself off.

Carny invited a friend to their table, a pert young woman called Maristella, who found room to sit next to Branna. "Oh good! I'd love a cup of Dreamland," she exclaimed.

Fola poured for everyone. Micca had a small taste: raw corn spirits steeped with raspberries and probably carmine, and well sugared. He saw that the others' lips already showed red stains. Fola must have been completely smitten by this Carny if he was willing to drink something like this. Her presence explained why Fola hadn't come home at last year's Yule; he probably wasn't studying for his exams in Hoiin, the announced reason, but instead spent the holiday at Hannava.

A woman styling herself Abrinda, the Harnish Songbird, sat down at a portable string-organ, one of Toivo's sons ready at the crank. She began to sing, and Branna ordered pipes for everyone.

Micca got to his feet, struggled to get by the others's chairs. He found the landlord at the bar.

"I know you're busy, Mister Toivo, but—"

"Ah, one of Mister Voling's friends! Micco, wasn't it? What can I do for you? Another bottle? Let me warn you, Maristella is a real handful!"

"Can I talk to you for a minute? It's serious. I just want to—"

"Of course, of course," Toivo said, noting Micca's drawn face. "Through here."

He led him to a little office and threw open a window. "I need a break anyway," Toivo said. "It gets awfully smoky in there of an evening."

Micca cleared his throat. "You were telling us about the Directorate, how they're doing this conscripting. I had a run-in with them today."

"No! Sorry to hear that! But I see you came back with your hair still on your head and without a uniform."

"Only just barely. How likely do you think they are to find me again?"

Toivo sat down at a cluttered desk, pointing Micca to a chair. "If you stay away from the main market and out of disreputable taverns, you'll probably be all right. They can't expect much voluntary compliance with this new levy, and they'll probably take most of the recruits they want with press gangs. They usually do their dirty work under the cover of night."

"What's this talk about trouble in Hin Hoina?"

"You heard about that, hey? Well, I don't know quite what to think. I doubt there's been any violence. A piece in the *Private Tattler* said that Hoiin's Strivers have welcomed a cabal of seditious lunatics to the city, while the *Evening Bell* calls the same group a party of reformers who will remedy the long years of shocking misrule by Hoiin's Lodge. But both the *Bell* and the *Tattler* are published in Parnala, and Parnala and Hoiin, as you are no doubt aware, are traditional rivals. Still, there was an odd article in the *Word of Hoiin*, too…that was more along the 'valiant reformer' line."

"So Hoiin's probably not very dangerous for an innocent foreign visitor?"

Toivo shrugged. "He may slip on a pile of pig droppings and break his head on the curb—if he had had more drink than was good for him, let's say. Or again, he may buy a lucky lottery ticket while there, that will finance a membership in the Lodge. Who can say?"

He leaned over the desk and looked keenly at Micca. "But do you know what? I think the best course for an innocent visitor would be to forget going to Hoiin for now, leave Hannava early in the morning, and go back to his home farm as quickly as his feet or cart will take him."

Micca heaved himself up, blinked blearily and shook Toivo's hands. "Thanks for your advice."

Toivo followed him. "Wait here for a moment. I think you could benefit from a taste of bean-brew…no liquor in it, but quite refreshing, and I think you could use some refreshing."

The barroom was more crowded than ever. Micca leaned on the counter-top and sipped Toivo's brew, which though rather bitter and steaming hot was in fact refreshing. After a second cup he looked around. Where were Fola and Branna? He squinted through the smoke, but saw no one he recognized, not even the landlord's daughter Carny.

He went up to their room. It was dark, but he couldn't seem to operate the lighter attached to the gaslight. Why had he drunk so much tonight? Stumbling, he took off his new shoes and knee-pants; he didn't think such clothes were the thing for a sea voyage. He dropped to the bed and pulled on the hide pants from home.

Micca looked up at a sound from across the room. Maybe his eyes had adjusted to the darkness, or maybe he just hadn't noticed before, but dim light from the window illuminated the back of a slowly heaving torso on one of the other beds. Small hands rose to clutch it. "Oh, Branny!" moaned a voice, soon joined by deep grunts.

"That didn't take him long," Micca muttered. He put on a boot, grabbed the other, but it fell from his hand with a thump.

"What's that?" came a voice from the other bed.

"Just me, honey flower," came Branna's whisper.

The noises across the room became more urgent. Micca got his boots on. He stood, knocking his pack-bag to the floor.

Someone jumped out of the bed. There was a scratch, a spark, and the gas sprang to flame. Branna stood with a sheet around him. "Micca!"

"I'm going to Hoiin. Are you coming?"

"Who is it Branny? Oh, make him go away!"

Branna turned the valve and the room went dark. Blinking at the after-image of the flame, Micca heard him say, "We'll talk about it in the morning. Now get out of here."

10. IN THE ATTIC

igh up in the south range at Mora, Ennesia walked back and forth across dusty planks.

A lamp she had grabbed on the way here flickered on the floor. Ennesia went to a small window and looked out. The moon shone in a cloudless sky, but it would do little to light her hiding place when the oil in her lamp was gone. She went to a low door at the end of the room, cautiously opened it a few inches: beyond was the same loft, black and full of eery potential.

She closed the door and sat under the window beside the lamp. The adjoining room hadn't seemed as threatening when she had come up from a hatch in its floor during the bright noon. But even then it had been mysterious, full of old furniture and chests, heavy with shadows. Who could tell what might be in those old trunks, or hiding under that table with the carvings of laughing faces and scampering animals? But it was the only way in or out of the refuge she'd chosen.

Through the window Ennesia could see a patch of moonlit grass, far below. The roofs she could see were still too steep to climb... If Micca was still here she was sure he would have found a more congenial place to hide.

Something creaked. Ennesia turned. She couldn't see anything that hadn't been there before. But on the other side of the room, a panel was coming away from the wall.

It shuddered, caught at its bottom, then swung out all at once. Light glimmered up from below. A hooded form rose in the cavity behind the panel and pushed a closed wicker basket into the room.

The figure stooped to enter the room, holding up a lamp, and threw back its hood.

"Marfa!" Ennesia said.

The old woman nodded cordially. "Good evening, my dear. Oh, look how dusty my skirts are. Nobody bothers to clean in these parts up here."

"How did you find me?"

"Hey?"

Ennesia spoke more loudly.

"I saw the light from the window whilst I was out taking the air. And I know the house better than anybody, including Henning. I thought you'd more likely be up in these parts than the cellars, and didn't think you'd left the house." The old woman patted Ennesia's wrist. "We know where your place is now, don't we?"

Ennesia smiled uncertainly.

Marfa said, "Anyway, I brought some supper for you," pushing the hamper toward Ennesia with her foot. "Merim said you'd been at their place, and then you'd disappeared. She and Danna were afraid the Vigorists had got you…they had their boy Binta to deal with, too. He was in bed, all atremble over something he saw in the woods."

"Really? I wonder what he saw? But yes, I thought it would be a good idea to keep out of sight for a while after I told off Palmer night before last. I thought I could risk sneaking up to see my mother—she wasn't mad at me anymore, but then some of her insane friends came while I was there. They said they were going to cut off my hair, make me do the 'Dance of Penance', whatever that is. They said I had *violated* their would-be Husband to Wennoc! So I ran away and got myself lost…lost on purpose, but still lost."

Marfa shook her head. "They've stamped themselves mad, that lot. Winsy Wamod's been odder than usual too, since she and Binta and that lot came back from their expedition."

"Expedition?"

Marfa didn't hear her. She tapped the basket with her foot. "Merim fixed this up. There's oil for your light, too."

"Thank you, Marfa," Ennesia said earnestly, "and please give Merim and Danna my thanks."

"Think nothing of it, my dear. I'll be back tomorrow with more, but I don't expect you'll have to stay too long. Sooner rather than later people will come to their senses...you should be able to find some comfy blankets in the chest over yonder in the loft. Be sure to shake them out well."

The old woman disappeared into the cavity in the wall. Ennesia ran after her and looked down. Bobbing lamp light shone up, making shadows on wooden steps, then vanished.

Ennesia closed the door in the paneling. She remembered how hungry she was and opened the basket. There was a smoked sausage, a loaf and a lump of butter wrapped in paper, several apples, a pot of stew, still warm and smelling of herbs and chicken, a jar of peary, six doughnuts, even a linen napkin. And under the napkin, an envelope.

She recognized Micca's handwriting. Ennesia pulled out the paper inside and moved her lips, following the Harnish words...

She didn't know whether to laugh or cry. But the message was clear enough: he'd gone to Marstoc to talk to the Marling. The little drawing made her smile.

Ennesia wiped her eyes, found a spoon and started in on the stew. She ate all of it. Chewing a piece of bread, she sat down under the window. Finally she told herself, "Well, there's nothing else for it."

Ennesia topped up her lamp. She braved a few steps into the haunted room next door and found a heavy old shawl decorated with a tasseled fringe. Wrapping herself in it, she took up the lamp and the basket, and pulled open the panel Aunt Marfa had come through. After winding her way down the flue-like stair, Ennesia pushed open another panel and found herself in a region of Mora that seemed familiar. She heard voices, but moved quickly and found an exterior door before she met anyone.

The moon was still behind the trees. A few stars dusted the high dome of the sky, and the heavenly lamps hung bright among them. The lights of Mora fell behind as she walked south over the fields.

11. MIDNIGHT

The mariners furled the sails and the *Spry Foam-Rider* coasted, losing speed. Micca gripped the rail and squinted blearily at the lights of Hoiin.

To him it seemed a miracle that the tub-like boat, pitching and heaving in the wind (and his stomach with it) had been able to make it across the Bay. He was sure he had seen huge fish jumping and snapping after it, following them all the way. Micca was the only passenger who remained on deck, and the boat's master, growing talkative, had told him that the big fish cruised this side of the Bay during the windy hours. This was also the best time for sailing, though smaller boats did so at their own risk.

During the first hour of the voyage Micca had been occupied in emptying his stomach into Hoina Bay. The taste in his mouth reminded him regretfully of the paper of fried potatoes and onions he had bought from a vendor at the harbor. Otherwise he had had no supper but liquor and Tovio's bean-brew.

His physical discomfort helped keep other things out of his mind, at least partially. There was dull pain connected with the thought that Branna had abandoned him. Worse was a nagging worry. What would happen to Branna and Fola in Hannava? The memory of his experience at the Directorate was still sharp. If he hadn't been drunk he doubted he would have had the courage to go out into the dark streets and risk meeting one of the press gangs Toivo the landlord had warned against.

The lights of Hin Hoina, hundreds and hundreds of them, grew closer and a little less blurry. He had lost his fine new lenses to the sea along with the contents of his stomach. Their bows had seemed more secure than the old ones, but they had failed him.

But Micca began to feel a sense of adventure. New horizons opened before him (he couldn't actually see any horizons, but the thought seemed appropriate). He was entering a new city, a new land. He felt like Brave Beyalmer must have, who had traveled all over Eynna looking for his wife Nansil after Siglat had stolen her. But Micca didn't have a wife yet, and the girl he wanted was far away. At least he'd see his brother soon, who must be somewhere among the lights of the hill-like town ahead.

The boat entered the harbor and coasted toward a pair of stone towers. They had been worked to resemble men; Strivers, Micca supposed. The giants stood knee-deep in the water, gazing blindly out on the Bay. Each stretched out an arm to the other, and their hands joined high in the air to make a sort of gateway. Micca watched, head thrown back, as the boat passed under them. They might be so old it was possible they weren't Strivers at all, but ancient Heresiarchs. Ages of wind and rain might have softened their stone faces into human semblance.

Ahead he could see deep, spark-lined avenues, wide at their tops, narrowing as they reached down between buildings, cloven like cracks in a great cliff. From the widest of them flowed a black river, bridged by lamp-lit arches. It was amazing that so many lights burned so late, but Micca reasoned that people who didn't have to farm probably stayed up far into the night, and the city's dynamo, driven by its river, was said to be the largest in the world. He had also read somewhere that in old times electrical power had fallen from the sky and was caught in a large field near Hoiin. He'd have to ask an Eynnishman, who would know about such things.

The boat's master steered them toward the tongues of stone sticking into the Bay. He shouted, calling the hands to their docking positions. Lines were flung down to one of the piers. The boat was secured and a landing plank extended. Micca walked down and into the land of Eynna.

As he set foot on the pier he realized the land was rolling under him. Micca's stomach jerked. The boat's master hauled him to his feet. He touched his hands together in front of his face, wished Micca a pleasant visit and disappeared into a warehouse.

Micca wiped his mouth with the back of his hand. A few deep breaths made him feel better. He reviewed the directions the master had given him and walked down the shore. Three hundred yards up from the harbor he found tiles set into the corner of a wall, making up a set of glyphs. Micca thought he knew all the common Eynnish glyphs, but he didn't recognize these. A man hurrying by stopped for a moment to read them for him.

"Concourse of the Sunny Reed Beds," he said.

"Can you tell me where to find the Avenue of Excellent Virtue?" Micca asked.

"Going to the University? Follow Reed here about six furlongs west, then turn right into River Street and keep an eye out for three round towers, the one to your left taller than the others, all with peaked roofs. Think you can find it? Fine, and good night to you!"

Micca nodded gratefully and walked on. Despite all the lights visible from the harbor, at its lowest level the road was dark. Eventually Micca discovered that the heaps of dirt he'd been stepping over were in fact pig shit. Narrow alleys like the mouths of caves opened here and there under bridges and railed upper ways. He heard an occasional voice from high windows, but saw few other people out walking.

He found the Avenue of Excellent Virtue, which was set with yellow tiles in recognizable glyphs. Micca kept to the lower level, thinking he'd get lost on the raised ways and arcades above him. He paused to look at two stone men, not nearly so big as the giants in the harbor, but more realistically carved, supporting the lintel of a tall two-leaved door with their arms and shoulders. Deep within the portal a light burned behind windowed doors, illuminating frost-like patterns in them. Micca realized the patterns were etched in the form of decorated glyphs. He was able to recognize one of the glyphs as 'strive'; there could well be Strivers inside this very house. The stone men holding up the lintel might represent the way the Strivers saw themselves, bearing the weight of the world on their shoulders. He wondered if the real Strivers were so muscular.

On the other side of the road even grander buildings rose to the stars...

There was suddenly a clatter on the paving stones behind him, a grunting and panting. Micca looked over his shoulder. Some kind of wagon came careening around the corner, rolling on a pair of nearly man-high spoked wheels. A rider's compartment was mounted to the front with a third, smaller wheel before it that seemed to be steering the thing. Between the rear wheels several hulking shapes hunched on saddles, pushing their legs up and down, working pedals. On the rider's compartment was a glyph drawn in an eccentric style, another one Micca didn't recognize. He jumped out of its way as it rattled past, flattening himself against a damp wall. He heard a gasping voice from a window in the rider's box: "Careless Eynnish beast!"

Micca stared after the strange vehicle as it tore off down the street. Was this a sign of the troubles in Hoiin Branna had mentioned? But Toivo had downplayed that, and if it had been Strivers rushing around on one of their midnight revels, they wouldn't have called him an 'Eynnish beast'. Besides, it had sounded like a woman's voice, and he didn't think the Strivers took women into their Lodge.

He walked on, keeping a lookout to all sides. The buildings became smaller, a little less crowded. He saw treetops and three cone-topped towers in the distance. Now there were couples and small groups of young people with him on the street.

Samma Mora and Gillensa Odé climbed arm in arm up a staircase inside Uhilen Residential Hall. They found Samma's room. Gillensa put a finger on Samma's ribs. He lurched into his room giggling.

"Shush!" hissed Gillensa. "You act like a drunkard!"

"Nonsense," said Samma. "You only let me have two pints." Then he took the young woman into his arms and whispered, "Gillensa, that dancing got me a little excited."

Gillensa put her arms around his neck and tipped up her head, smiling. "Only a little?"

Samma smiled broadly.

"I'd think you'd be very excited by the praise your agile dance steps won from the crowd," Gillensa added.

"You're making fun of me again."

They moved across Samma's little room and sat down on his bed. After a while Gillensa said, "Well, besides the dancing, what did you think of the Unimpeachable Aesthetic? It's a very exclusive place, you know."

"I couldn't understand what the musicians were yowling about."

"They were singing folk songs, you idiot. Morose lovers, wicked robbers and so on. They used an old eastern dialect. Very pretty and expressive, I thought."

"Oy noy, oy na-noy, na-noy, na-noy. That's all I heard."

"You have ears of wood and a tongue of stone — Samma, stop that!" Gillensa tried to push him away, laughing again.

"I'll show you what my tongue —"

Samma sat up and looked at the door.

The knock came again. Gillensa sat up, smoothing her hair. Samma buttoned his shirt and went to the door.

Outside was a young man clad in a stylish black coat and incongruous leather leggings and boots. His hair stuck out under his hat, though in back it was still tied with a ribbon.

"Micca?" Samma said, gaping at him.

"A little Eynnishman downstairs let me in," Micca said. He squinted as Gillensa switched on an electric bulb and came up to have a look at him.

Neypo stumbled in the dark. Ahead of him Caihar turned, gesturing anxiously for silence.

Rearranging the skirts of his coat, Neypo went on. He followed Caihar and eighteen members of the Office of Public Assistance through a tunnel under the streets. The Striver Lemwulin Litu, Office-Chief Cwentoi Macwei and another squad of Officers were entering the Strivers' Guest Hall by a more direct route. The visitors were sure to be surprised by one group or the other.

Neypo was still not entirely convinced the expedition was necessary. He felt like a fool in his bronze casque, but Sergeant Hyvva and Caihar had insisted he wear it. They had given Neypo a combination club and bodkin as well. "You never know," Hyvva had warned. "They may resist the law."

Neypo doubted that, and he doubted the necessity of sending forty men to arrest a mere handful of foreigners. But Lemwulin had gone to the Grand Fellow's manse that afternoon and somehow convinced him to issue a secret edict declaring the visitors Public Nuisances, so at least the operation was legal. Neypo wondered what Micsin, Uho and the other more pacific members of the Lodge would say tomorrow morning.

Even so, Neypo had to admit to himself that he was excited. He hadn't been on such an outing for years, not since his days as a Cadet. The 'Lodge secrets' Caihar had shown him after lunch that afternoon added further excitement to the project, and he could hardly stop himself from rubbing his hands in glee when he remembered that the fact that he had seen such Secrets automatically raised his rank within the Lodge by several degrees, and with no increase in his quarterly dues, either.

And what he had discovered browsing the dusty volumes and tablets in the vault might be far more important than his rise in status. Caihar had shown him texts he claimed were proof that the visitors were dangerous creatures of some kind, but the ancient scriveners had used a highly symbolic style of language, and Neypo knew that the significance of certain words had shifted over time; Caihar's proofs could be interpreted in a number of ways.

Neypo had found much more interesting information on his own, while Caihar was occupied in another alcove. There were just three tablets and fragments of two more, but they confirmed certain old stories concerning the lamps in the sky, and also made an astonishing connection between them and the ancient city of Mellatuno. A few sheets of paper, dated only twelve years ago and efficiently filed in the same section, gave the stories a shockingly modern significance. He hadn't told Caihar what he had discovered yet. In his present state of mind Neypo was afraid the elder Striver might be given rash ideas.

And he probably wouldn't have believed Neypo anyway. What he'd found was fantastic, but in theory no less likely than Ohímpala's discovery of the means by which voices could be broadcast over the aether, something Caihar seemed to consider the next thing to evil magic. Neypo wished now that he had taken time to interview the peculiar old woman from the Office of Antiquities who had appeared at his committee's office the day he had lunched with Caihar. Considering she had come from Mellatuno, she might have been able to cast some light on the tablets in the archives and what they said about the ancients' machines; indeed, she may have had a hand in preparing the modern report herself. Someone from the Lodge would have to make a trip to Mellatuno as soon as the visitors' case was settled.

And tonight the questions about the visitors' origins and true intentions would be settled. Decorum and cordiality would be lacking, but Caihar's worries would be put to rest, and Neypo hoped too that there would be an honorable explanation for the change in behavior exhibited by Woitap, Micsin, and certain other Lodge members in recent days.

Sergeant Hyvva turned and motioned them to a halt. Neypo watched him climb a ladder and disappear. The other Officers should by now be in the Hall's basement, somewhere above Neypo, entering from a scuttle in the garden. Neypo slumped down and sat on his heels, thankful for a rest. Caihar crouched tensely beside him, shoulders hunched.

Water dripped from the vaulted brickwork over Neypo's head, making an echoing plinking on the floor of the cellar. Neypo fingered his bodkin, recalling an ancient subterranean temple he had once visited in the east, and the Heresiarch's ghost he thought he had seen…

A hissing whisper came from the hatch in the ceiling. Caihar jumped up and signaled the assembled Officers. Everyone climbed up the ladder, Neypo coming last.

Neypo found himself in a dark cellar. It seemed Hyvva hadn't located Lemwulin and his group. "They must already be in the Hall itself," the sergeant whispered, and waved them up a stair.

They found themselves in a dark service room. A short passage led to the Hall's entrance chamber. Caihar fumbled with his Order of Deportation, which would officially expel the strangers from Hoiin, and by implication, all of Eynna.

Before them were the street doors, behind a richly furnished reception room lit by a chandelier of a hundred electric globes. To the side a narrow but elaborate wooden staircase led to the upper chambers. Between the flights of steps Neypo glimpsed a glass roof, five storeys above. Everything was silent, and all the lamps in the place seemed to be lit. There was no sign of Lemwulin, Cwentoi and his men, nor any of the visitors.

Neypo started at a touch on his shoulder. Old Narnet, the Hall's housekeeper, stood behind him.

"What are you rascals doing here, treading all over the rugs with your great dirty feet?" Narnet demanded.

Neypo made silencing motions with his hands. "Where are the tenants?" he whispered. "Have they seen you?"

"You told me to keep out of sight, your Honor, and so I have. Your outlanders are gone just now."

"Gone?" Caihar hissed in alarm. "Gone where?"

"You ought to know, Striving sirs. Someone came to collect them, not an hour ago, and I heard him say he was from the Lodge. Then someone else called not long after, sounded like a woman; funny accent, too. I never heard such a petulance when no one answered her knocks. But where your visitors went, I don't know. They don't confide in me; after all, I'm nothing but a ghost in the walls to them." The old woman smiled craftily at Neypo.

"Who called first for them?" Neypo asked her. "Was it a Striver, a Hustler?"

"I wouldn't know, Honorable. I was listening at an air shaft in the buttery, just under the portal here."

"It couldn't have been Lemwulin," Caihar said perplexedly.

"Ah!" said Neypo. "You remember I told you the other day that Adinnegram said he was going out to visit some local people? Maybe that's where—"

There was a thumping of boots somewhere below. Lemwulin Litu, Cwentoi and a group of helmeted men pushed out of a door under the staircase. "The men had to break in the garden door," Lemwulin panted, "which is not easy to do silently! Someone had locked it!"

Neypo and Caihar looked at Narnet. The housekeeper's expression was defiant. "You didn't alert her to our plans?" Caihar asked Neypo.

"Well, considering all the oaths and vows you made me swear, I hardly thought that would be wise. But this may all work out for the better." Neypo held up a finger. "We can wait in the reception room, out of sight, until they return, then serve them with the Order of Deportation. Faced by our numbers, they'll have no option but to humbly—"

Neypo stopped, seeing a shadow move on one of the landings above. Lemwulin Litu saw it too.

"One of the scoundrels must have remained behind!" he shouted. "We'll capture him before he slips out to warn his friends!" Litu ran up the staircase, borrowed club raised high.

Hyvva told his squad to stay below. He, Cwentoi and his Officers went after Litu. Neypo told the house-keeper to conceal herself, then joined Caihar on the stair, bringing up the rear again.

The next floor appeared tenantless. Somewhere above was a shout. At the top of the next flight of stairs Lemwulin Litu reappeared. He glanced quickly behind, then ran down, pushing by the Officers. "It was terrifying!"

"Where? How many?" Cwentoi shouted.

Lemwulin just pointed back the way he had come, his arm trembling.

Cwentoi, Hyvva and their men pounded up the stairs. Lemwulin pressed himself against the railing as they passed and cried out, "Come back! They cracked the floor under my feet without touching it! There's something unholy here!"

An awful, wavering scream sounded somewhere above. Lemwulin Litu, eyes starting from his head, clapped his hands over his ears and hurried down the stairs. The rest of Cwentoi's men rushed up. Neypo and Caihar followed them.

There was a another terrible scream. Up ahead a man flew across the gallery surrounding the stair well, arms and legs sticking out from the path of his flight, blood and ropes of intestines trailing out of his torn belly. He crashed backwards into the balusters of the railing, breaking several, and slumped to the floor.

Neypo stared at him, eyes wide. Caihar took Neypo's arm, and somehow they went on to the open door. Beyond the press of Officers Neypo saw a room furnished with cushioned benches along the walls, upholstered chairs and a divan, a large desk, several tables. Behind the desk stood a woman, strangely swaddled and bulky, trying to push her hair up to the top of her head. When she saw them she lunged to grab a small black tube from the desk. Nearer the door was a nearly naked man, his garments in a tangle around his ankles. He looked ridiculous, but his expression was crazed and he brandished another black tube at the Officers. "Haven't you learned?" the man yelled in a shrill, accented voice. "I'll do it again! I'll do it again!"

Had the two been surprised in the midst of a sexual encounter? Neypo thought not. The Officers surged forward. Neypo's line of sight was cut off, but he heard a low buzz and more screams. Three Officers in rapid succession were knocked back, as if by the fist of a monstrously powerful ghost. One lay near the door, twitching and bleeding, and the others looked dead.

A few of the Officers quailed, but the rest of them pushed by their fallen comrades, clubs in hand. Neypo struggled between them, not knowing whether he was trying to fight or escape. In a moment he found himself inside the room, surrounded by shouts and screams. "Monsters, devils!" he heard Caihar yell from somewhere ahead.

An almost soundless concussion sent Neypo reeling. Another one caught the Officer to his side. The back of the man's helmet split with a squeal and ragged strips of bronze petaled out. Neypo's coat was spattered with blood, brains and bits of splintered bone.

Neypo steadied himself, clutching a table. The naked man he had seen from outside had fallen over his clothing, and now crouched just in front of him. He pointed his black tube at Neypo.

Neypo dropped behind a table as the tube buzzed. The air twisted. Neypo felt brief, shivering pain in his left shoulder.

Without conscious intent he threw his club at the naked man. It hit the man's hand and his black tube fell to the floor. An Officer pushed forward and broke the man's skull.

Shouts, bellows and screams filled the room. Neypo started to get up, then threw himself to the floor again. A quivering transparency corrupted the air over his head. The chest of an Officer beside him shuddered to a blur and imploded.

Neypo pressed himself to the carpet. There was another scream, and then the scuffling and cries died away. Someone said, "The subjects have been subdued."

Neypo got up slowly and peered slowly around, full of shock and dread. Several Officers stood nearby, panting, hands still tight on their clubs. How long had the fighting lasted? A minute? Two minutes? The room Neypo was in, a long salon with windows opening to the Hall's back garden, looked relatively untouched except for some overturned furniture and patches on the wall where the plaster had been knocked off the underlying brick.

Neypo stooped to examine the naked man who had threatened him. He looked young. His eyes were still open, but his hair was pasted to his head with blood; he was certainly dead.

Neypo's legs failed him. He knelt on the floor and crawled away. Another dead man confronted him, one of the Officers. There was a foot-wide cavity in his chest. Neypo could see the back of his rib cage. He scuttled backward on his knees, choked, opened his mouth and emptied his stomach on the dead man's leg.

Someone helped him up; Hyvva, it seemed. Neypo wiped his mouth on his sleeve and threw off his helmet.

He saw Cwentoi lying near the door, his jaw and some of his neck gone. His hand twitched. One of his men took it. Blood foamed from Cwentoi's throat, and he died.

Neypo clapped a hand over his mouth and jerked away from Hyvva, bent over and vomited again. He saw Caihar perched on an embroidered chair in the middle of the room, holding his head with his hands.

"What happened?" Neypo gasped, trembling before him.

Caihar looked up. The surviving Officers were moving slowly around the room. They stared at the visitors' possessions, knelt over their maimed friends. Caihar hugged his elbows and rapidly shook his head.

"I don't know. I don't know. If it weren't for our numbers, we'd all be dead. Torn apart like poor Cwentoi. And Elmo and Soibin and Tappei…What happened? Has Wennoc sent devils to punish us?"

Neypo drew in his breath. "I think not. If you consider—"

Caihar's eyes were wild. "No! My wild notion has been proven true!"

"Well, I admit what has happened is beyond my—"

"It's beyond your understanding, and mine! Who but the Heresiarchs have done such things, or wished to do them?" Caihar shouted. He hugged his arms together and shook. His eyes darted back and forth, finally noticing Neypo again. "Striver—what's happened to your arm?"

Neypo twisted his head and looked at his shoulder with a queasy return of memory. Fine Undoi plaid hung in shreds. The flesh under it was so bruised it looked burned. He touched it and was staggered by pain. And then sick again, seeing the splatters of blood and organ on his coat. He tore it off, feeling a new stab of pain from his shoulder.

"You must have it seen to." Caihar called, "Hyvva! Has someone gone for the physicians?"

"Yes, Striver."

Caihar looked through the windows, but saw only the night sky. He seemed a little calmer, muttering the names of the gleaming lamps, and Neypo guided him back to his chair.

"In my house my wife and children are sleeping," Caihar said, "dreaming of going to the Fair tomorrow, planning a fine holiday. But here am I, having become a murderer. Lemwulin was wise to flee. What have we done, Neypo? What are these people?"

"I don't know," Neypo muttered, looking around the room, trying to ignore the pain in his shoulder, gathering his wits. He spoke with more certainty. "But in spite of their terrible miracles, if they can be killed like men, they must be men. And you're not a murderer, Caihar; none of us are. We didn't actually attack them — they attacked us! Wennoc itself gave us the instinct and duty of self-preservation."

A smile jerked Caihar's lips. "You're right. Of course you're right. And we have to do something. What?"

"What about the others? The Adinnegram person, for one, and the other woman at the least — Solalie or whatever she was called? They weren't all here."

"Yes, we have to capture those we missed. How many were here? Two, only two? Six more then. But how? How will we subdue them? Will they kill everyone sent against them?"

Neypo looked at one of the black tubes, lying nearby on the floor. "If Wennoc is with us — let's pray they took none of these… weapons with them. We should gather the tubes here and make some experiments, see if iron or some other shield will thwart their shattering effect."

"No! If we use them we'll be devils too. They must be drowned in the sea at once."

The housekeeper showed two medical men into the room, then clapped her hands to her mouth and disappeared. The medical men looked around in horror. Hyvva swore them to secrecy and they set about treating those who had survived the unseen force. One of them applied a strong unguent and bandaged Neypo's shoulder.

Where had Caihar gone? The senior Striver's face suddenly thrust itself in front of Neypo's. Caihar seemed a little more like his old self, though his eyes blinked rapidly.

"Neypo! We may be able to learn whether the missing monsters have weapons, or discover a way to fight them off—Hyvva tells me we have a prisoner."

Caihar strode across the room. Neypo followed him, pausing to examine a thin tablet on a table, covered with writing. "Caihar, look here. It must have been something like this the housekeeper saw."

"Never mind! Come."

Neypo slipped the tablet into his pocket. Caihar pulled him past the large desk. On the floor in the shadows behind it was the corpse of the woman Neypo had glimpsed as the fight began. Her head was pathetic and bloody, hair spread in a tangle on the floor. The rest of her body looked as though it had been dipped in wax, so that she was coated in a thick, translucent cocoon. What other horrors were they to discover tonight?

Caihar tugged at Neypo's sleeve. "Come, come!"

Neypo went with him to a divan which faced the rear windows. On it lay a glassy man.

Before Neypo's shop had begun making radios and the electrical valves used in them, his father had produced bottles for scent and expensive essences. Some of those were novelties, representations of country maids, herdsmen, bravos, even Strivers, with corks in their heads. This thing reminded him of them, though it was huge, life-sized, a stylized version of a man, but inhuman, grotesque. It was a suit clearly intended for utility rather than beauty. For a suit it must be, Neypo decided with a slight feeling of relief. The fact that someone had bound this one's wrists and ankles indicated the presence of a living man inside it. Not a monster or wraith.

"We found him hiding back here, Strivers," said Hyvva, who had followed them. "I don't think this one actually killed anyone, or at least he didn't have one of those black tubes. Geill said he was talking to himself, shouting almost, like he was praying for help, though Geill couldn't understand him."

Hyvva held out a little round box, glossy black. A tiny blue light flickered at one end. "Geill took this from him," Hyvva said. "He was holding it to his…casque, mask, whatever it is."

Caihar snatched it away, threw it down and stamped his foot on it. The box didn't break, but gave a brief squeak and a final spark of light. Hyvva took off his Officer's scarf and carefully wrapped it around the box.

"Drown that with the rest of their demonic stuff!" Caihar ordered.

Neypo bent to study the glass man on the divan, who suddenly twisted. Neypo backed off, startled.

Caihar knelt beside him. "Talk to us, monster! Where did your friends go? Where are they?"

No sound came from the glass head.

Caihar rapped on it with his knuckles. "Can you hear me? Can you smell the blood you've spilled? Speak!" Caihar hit the prisoner's head with more force.

He stood up and sucked his knuckles. "Hyvva!" he shouted. "Get this creature out of his shell by whatever means necessary, but don't let him die!"

Two Officers gingerly rolled the glass man from the divan to the floor, where he landed with a heavy thump. They tried without effect to twist the helmet, and poked their bodkins at the neck, but their points found no purchase.

The Eynnishmen stood away from the prisoner. Caihar shook his head. "I wonder how we were able to capture him? The others gave up only in death."

Neypo had gone to examine several man-shaped, translucent husks in an alcove at the side of the room, where they were piled like cord wood; they had the wax-like look of the dead woman's, but must be similar to the prisoner's glass suit, though slightly soft rather than hard and glossy. They were empty, but when he prodded one of them with his toe it responded with a movement of its own.

Neypo retreated and spoke to Caihar. "I presume the trio here were unaware of our presence until Lemwulin stormed up here shouting and waving his bodkin. They became alarmed, and clearly part of their response to the perceived threat was to dress themselves in these strange suits. We interrupted them before all were clad. You recall that when we arrived one was in the process of removing his ordinary clothes, and the woman hadn't yet covered her head. Only our prisoner here managed to complete his costume. Evidently he has less taste for slaughter than his companions, or didn't have time to find a black tube."

Caihar nodded absently. He and Neypo watched as the Officers began beating the glass man with their bronze clubs, which made clacking, clunking sounds. No cracks showed in the glass he wore, if it were indeed glass, and the man inside lay silent under their blows.

Caihar pursed his lips and fluttered his hands. He summoned Officers and told them to cordon off the street and then carry the dead across to the Lodge. Another group had been searching the other rooms of the Guest Hall, and reported finding a chair fitted with bonds which may have been used while torturing the visitors' victims, presuming they had indeed harmed someone before tonight. Caihar ordered them to gather the visitors' tube-weapons and throw it into the waters of Bay. Neypo made sure the tablet he had found was still in his pocket and tried to persuade Caihar that the weapons should be examined. Caihar wouldn't hear of it. He told Hyvva to lock the prisoner up in the cellars of the Lodge.

"He'll get a proper interrogation in the morning," Caihar muttered, and shuffled out of the room.

The Officers removed most of the visitors' surprisingly meager possessions. All that remained were the empty suits in the alcove of the upper room. Neypo intercepted Hyvva at the door and told him to take the suits to the cellars along with the corpses, rather than throw them into the sea. "We'll want to put the bodies of any visitors who may die into them before disposal... it will prevent contamination of Wennoc's water and soil."

Hyvva nodded wearily, then turned and remembered to salute. "Very good, Striver."

12. DINNER
AT ROSE POND

"City on top, country on the bottom," Samma said, examining his brother. "It's like you aren't sure whether you're coming or going. I expect I know why you forgot your pack if you were with Branna and Fola Marstoc. A good rule to follow with those two would be to drink one jar for every three of theirs."

Micca agreed but didn't say so. "I was in a hurry to catch the boat. I didn't have time to finish changing."

"We could still go back and get you some of my pants."

"Well, I don't fit in your shoes, and it would look weird to have those short pants tied off an inch over the tops of my boots. But I appreciate the clean shirt. At least I'm not a complete yahoo."

Samma smiled. "The trip to Hannava got you keen on fashion, hey?"

"Oh, shut up."

They approached an intersection, and Samma caught Micca's arm. "Watch out! Those carts don't stop once they get going. You're not supposed to cross until the signalman holds his flags up."

"Where are all these people going?"

"To the Fair, I suppose."

In the sunlight Micca found Hoiin less intimidating than it had seemed the previous night. The fabric of the city was still hard and unfriendly, lacking wooden surfaces or many windows at street level, but Hoiin's ubiquitous bricks were far from monotonous. They had been set in a variety of patterns and bonds, molded in many shapes and sizes; and their color varied from smoky red, pale rose or glaring orange to every shade of umber, ocher and rust. Micca didn't know if this was because the bricks were made of clay from a number of quarries, if they had been burned differently, or if they had just been exposed to the weather for differing lengths of time. Samma couldn't tell him and didn't seem very interested in the matter. Whatever the reason, Micca thought the result was pleasant. And although the walls that faced the streets rose flat and plain and had no over-hanging eaves, their tops were decorated by complicated patterns — saw-teeth, brackets, sockets, blind crenellations — as if the masons had become playful as they finished their work. And Micca saw glazed tiles here and there, sheathing domes or set into the bricks in zigzags or keyed patterns of blue, green or yellow, sometimes outlining a door with a pattern of glyphs spelling out Eynnish names.

The Eynnish themselves were interesting too. Only about half of them were blond, contrary to Micca's expectations, but most were short. Micca speculated that this might be because they preferred accompanying their greens and roots with a little bit of fish or a dish of beans rather than good meat and cheese, and so grew up undernourished. But he decided there wasn't a lot of difference between the Harnish and Eynnish after all. It was more like the averages were weighted a little in one direction in Harna, and in the other on the mainland.

Micca studied Samma from the corner of his eye. A half-inch or so taller than Micca, he was also thinner than he had been at home, though still well knit. His hair, yellower from the sun he supposed, had gotten long and was tied up in back. At times he tried to speak like the announcers on the Voice of Hoiin, without as much success as Fola. He wore knee-length pants and a long coat, with colored bands around its sleeves that indicated his scholastic standing at the University. Samma had no hat, but wore horizontal rectangles of blue glass before his eyes.

"Where did you get those smoked lenses?" Micca asked. "Was it near here?"

Samma looked at him. "I thought maybe you'd given up yours as part of your new look. I suppose you left them in Hannava, too."

"They fell off when I was puking my guts out on the boat over here.

Are the ones you've got just to keep the sun out, or did you damage your eyes reading books all night under electric lamps?"

"Just for the sun."

"And fashion? They're too small to be very efficient."

"In any case, there are a lot of optical shops downtown. We can go there tomorrow...or you know, there'll probably be some at the Fair, too. Won't be cheap, though."

"I don't suppose so." Micca was glad Samma had gotten over his pique at his interrupting what might have been a pleasant adventure with the young Eynnishwoman last night. Micca had had trouble keeping his eyes off her. She wasn't as plump as some Harnish girls, but soft and round and perfectly proportioned. Her hair was fine and almost transparent, waving around her ears. Her face was delicate as a sprite's. Micca had almost expected her to speak in verse.

Gillensa Odé had had plenty to say, and it wasn't verse. When Micca tried to tell his brother about Priest Palmer's plans for Wennoc's Husband (referring to only a generic 'Husband', and not mentioning his intended involvement), Gillensa took out paper and pen and began interrogating Micca in depth about the Invigoration.

Samma had interceded, telling her that Micca needed to sleep. Gillensa gave up and called for a hired sedan, but before she left she told Micca and Samma to come to dinner at her house today. She said that her father, like her, had an interest in antique survivals and cultural oddities, and would want to interview Micca.

"Miss Odé's father is in the Striving Lodge then?"

"He hasn't been in it very long, but he's kind of intimidating."

"But he's still a Striver. Maybe he could do something about the Invigorationists at home. I told you the only thing about Mora the Directorate was interested in was putting me in the City Service."

Samma shook his head, frowning. "Palmer and his bunch wouldn't have listened to the Directors, and they sure wouldn't have sent anybody down there anyway. And a Striver from Eynna? They'd do exactly the opposite of what the Lodge wanted. I think the only practical legal solution would be from the law court at Stoard. Hannava doesn't care about us, I don't care what the Marling says."

Samma sighed. "But I suppose I'll have to do something before that.

Try to put things in order. I'll have to try to figure out what Grandpa would tell them. I wish my voice was as loud as his."

"When are we going back?"

"I don't know. The sooner the better, though I don't have enough merits for a degree yet. Maybe I could come back for a while once things have settled down. Somebody could stand in for me for as —"

"Not me."

"Maybe Danna, then."

They walked through Rose Pond, a quiet neighborhood of two- and three-storey houses, most with walled gardens, not so crowded as the jammed-together rows of narrow houses near the University. Micca wondered how there could be a pond on a hill. Samma said he had never seen one, but that there were a lot of roses.

There was more light and air here than there had been downtown. Flowering trees and bushes framed views of the Bay below. Spring seemed well advanced here. The Eynnish lilacs were nearly gone; at Mora they'd just be opening.

Samma stopped near the end of a long brick wall. Micca followed him through a tile-bordered portal and into a vestibule where Samma pulled on a cord. Somewhere a bell rang.

A crabby looking old man carrying a hammer appeared and led them into a garden. He looked Micca over curiously, then turned and left them there. Micca didn't think the old man could have been the Striver.

Two children, a little girl with ribbons in her hair and a sullen boy wearing a stiffly embroidered tabard, came down a flower-bordered path. They, too, stared at Micca. Samma said hello to them, calling them Winnet and Tympo. The children took them down the path, deeper into the garden.

A stout man with a thin blond mustache rose from a wicker chair. His hat was embroidered with leaves and ears of corn; he wore a neck-cloth of starched white linen, and his red and black plaid coat fell to the tops of polished black shoes.

The Striver put his palms together in front of his face, drawing them downward as he nodded. Samma repeated the motion and nudged Micca. Micca started to imitate him, but the Striver took his hands and shook them Harnish-style, with a smile Micca decided was con-descending.

Samma made introductions. "Thank you very much for having us, Striver," he said. "I hope we're not putting you out with such short notice. If Gillensa hadn't —"

"No trouble at all. We're very happy you could come."

The Striver had the most elegant accent Micca had yet heard, and made the radio announcers sound like yokels. They stood there, all smiling, for a few moments. Did the Striver sniff? Micca had taken a bath at Samma's residence hall, without any kind of privacy, just an hour ago. He felt lost. He stupidly thought of Brave Beyalmer, whose example was no use here. When Beyalmer met Eynnishmen, he struck off their heads with his axe as often as not.

The Striver waved them to chairs beside a fountain. The old man who had let them in reappeared with a glass pitcher and poured cups of iced punch.

"How goes the crating, Teimo?" the Striver asked.

"Well enough, for a holiday!" the old man muttered.

The Striver frowned as the old man walked away, then turned and smiled at his guests. "We should be eating soon," he said.

They sat and sipped their ices. The fountain beside them bubbled and splashed. The Striver gazed off into the bushes with a distracted expression. Micca cleared his throat.

"His Excellency has a nice garden," he said to Samma, hoping his brother would say something in turn.

The Striver spoke to Micca. "Thank you, Farmer. It's a pleasant place to relax when the weather is fine."

Micca watched the Striver's face from the corner of his eye. Was he making fun of him with the old Harnish honorific?

But the Striver seemed to be smiling only at the taste of the drink. "Are you familiar with the distillations of Notop Plantation, Farmer?" he asked Micca. "This punch is based on their apricot tonic."

"My name is Micca, your Excellency, and yes. Notop's not that far from our farm. They've always had good luck with tree fruit."

"They can't grow much else," Samma said, smiling for no reason apparent to Micca.

"It's a small farm," Micca explained. "What kind of crops do you grow around here—" Micca suddenly remembered the correct form of address "—Honorable? You've got such good weather that your corn must be knee-high already." He couldn't think of anything to say but what he was used to saying to old men he didn't know very well.

The Striver nodded, looking over a hedge where men were carrying wooden boxes by. Then he took off his hat and smoothed his hair. "You may address me as Odé, or better, simply as Neypo. We don't bother with ceremonial niceties in the garden. I can't tell you much about our local agriculture, but I doubt that anything is knee-high yet. They've probably just planted the first crop of watercorn in the meadows, a week or two ago, perhaps. My own business is manufacturing; essence valves in particular, if you're acquainted with such instruments—"

Neypo stood up suddenly and called to one of the box carriers, telling him to not to pile his load so high.

"We have a radio receiver at our plantation," Samma said as the Striver sat down again.

"Oh? What make is it?"

"I'm not sure."

Micca leaned forward. "It's a Sennecon Wave-Catcher. But you make essence valves, Honorable? Do you make receiver sets too?"

The Striver looked directly at him for the first time. "A Sennecon, hey? Somewhat outdated but not a bad set. But yes, I certainly do make receivers. The fellow who just went by was carrying one of them. I have plans to market a reasonably priced annunciator as well."

"You mean so you can hear it without wearing a bonnet clamped to your head?"

"Exactly. If we have time after dinner I'll have you audition one of my Heavenly Ears. But just now I'd like to get to know you, both of you, better. I've been so preoccupied lately that my head is often in the clouds. Eh-Samael, of course, I know, but I—"

"You only put 'e-' in front of somebody's name when you're talking directly to him, Honorable, like calling him," Micca corrected.

Samma rolled his eyes.

"Oh?" said Neypo, ignoring Samma and staring owlishly at Micca. "You seem to refer to a vocative inflection. But nowadays that's used only in the counties north of Mennedal, and it requires a suffix, not a prefix."

Neypo leaned forward. "I've asked Samma about this before, but tell me, boys...do you ever speak, ah, differently from the everyday fashion at your plantation?"

"Not much anymore," Samma assured the Striver. "Most of our people have a good command of cultivated speech."

Gillensa must have mentioned the antique survival, the cultural oddity she had found last night, Micca thought. He found Neypo looking expectantly at him. "I can understand Harnish pretty well," Micca admitted. "It's not so hard to read. There are a lot of stories written in it. In County Wendum we mostly use it when we're out hunting...kind of a tradition, I guess. Otherwise mostly it's the old folks or people from the high farms or over the mountains who talk that way."

The Striver was still peering at him.

"There are ways to say things in Harnish that you can't say at all otherwise," Micca stated with some defiance. "And our alphabet has it all over the old glyphs. Everybody knows that."

Neypo pulled his head back. "*Your* alphabet. Well, tell me this. Are any of the words in this Harnish way of speaking at all similar to the everyday ones?"

"I don't think so. I guess some of the names of trees and flowers are more or less the same."

"Some of the trees and flowers..."

The Striver stood up and beckoned to Micca. "Come with me, Farmer. Eh-Micca. I have something I'd like you to look at."

Neypo was interrupted by Gillensa, her younger brother and sister in tow. She told them that they were expected immediately at the table.

Two huge trout had been broiled over vine trimmings and laid in a pool of spicy green sauce, decorated with sprigs and flower buds to represent a little garden. There was a pot of brown watercorn, a plate heaped with a fragrant fried vegetable Micca had never tasted before, dishes of thick mushroom soup, raw greens with fruit dressing, all served as separate courses. Rather than beer or cider, a watered mead was served to drink.

They passed around trays of fruit-filled pastries and honeyed nuts afterwards. As the diners chose their sweets, the Odés' cook shuffled into the dining room and everyone clapped their hands. Neypo's wife Winetra stood up from her cushion and received congratulations for the fish, which she had attended to personally.

Neypo patted his belly. "I love to eat," he said. "There's nothing like a good feed to relax a man."

"Or an over-dosing of spirits," said Winetra grimly. "Sometimes spirits can relax a man so much that he forgets how to walk properly and injures himself on the way home from his Lodge meeting!"

Neypo gave his wife a strained smile. He touched the bandages under the shoulder of his coat and turned away from her, nodding to their guests. "I noticed that our Harnishmen appreciate the arts of the table, too."

Samma stood up and formally thanked Neypo and Winetra for their hospitality. Micca stood with him. "I really enjoyed your dinner," he told Winetra, with whom he was beginning to feel quite comfortable. She reminded him of his Aunt Hessy. "At Mora all we usually have at noon is sausage or soup and bread. Supper is when we have the big meal."

Winetra leaned over the table and asked Micca what they liked to eat at their feasts on the peninsula. She told him not to be shy about describing dishes made of animal flesh. He shouldn't assume that just because her family was a Striving one it was overly orthodox; the Odés sometimes ate doves and even chickens. "Birds have some similarities to the fishes, after all." She couldn't hold with eating pigs or oxen, though, since they were the friends and servants of mankind and deserved to die a natural death when their days of service were over.

Micca explained that in Harna they didn't often eat oxen, but that there were wild pigs in the woods that could be quite dangerous.

"If they chase after you in the forests, I suppose you have no choice but to punish them and take compensation," Winetra conceded, glancing at Micca's hide pants. "But tell me how you people over there roast a fowl; you know, all in one piece. They're all the rage up in Lindenwood."

Micca said that he was no cook, but he described how at Mora hens were stuffed with bread, nuts, herbs and onions before being put into a hot brick oven, and how a sauce was made of the drippings combined with cider or undistilled grape-must. Samma corrected him on a few points, and Winetra called for pen and paper, eager to take down the particulars so that she could serve such an exotic dish herself.

Neypo stood up and suggested they all go into the garden. Everyone agreed that the dining room was becoming stuffy in the heat of the day, and they strolled outside, talking and laughing.

Gillensa pinned disks bearing the glyphs for Hoiin and Nimoi Tuvimat to Micca and Samma's sleeves. These would give them admission to the Fair, but they would wait an hour or two before going and avoid most of the speeches. Neypo had been to the fairgrounds earlier in the day and was more or less satisfied as to the fixings of his booth there.

A breeze came up from the Bay and cooled the garden. They sat on the grass and sipped ices. Gillensa brought out the sketches she had done in the eastern mountains last summer.

Micca moved closer to admire the detail of her drawings. He thought they were quite good...

He started at a tap on his shoulder. The Striver stood behind him. He gestured, indicating Micca should follow him.

Micca got up from the grass. The others remained outside. The Striver led him through a pair of doors into a small room outfitted as a study or library, then busied himself at a cabinet.

Micca saw a gleaming wooden case on a table, its face studded with dials. A small bulb glowed, showing the receiver was receiving power. Micca took off his hat and replaced it with the one wired to the receiver. A polished voice spoke in his ears. "...all of them tripping over the tangle of wires your roving correspondent, Reimi Rytalla, is forced to drag behind him! But I have with me now the Honorable Woitap Halanoi, formerly of the Striving Lodge, who only this morning announced that he would resign his office, saying that until..."

Neypo smiled up at him and Micca removed the receiver's bonnet. "A fine set, isn't it?" Neypo said.

The Striver guided Micca to a chair behind a desk. He set down two glazed jars, one blue and one yellow, and a pair of small cups.

The liquor from the blue jar was a respectable lilac, but done no favor when Neypo diluted it with mediocre corn spirits from the other. He praised it politely, following Neypo's lead. The Striver then dug into another cabinet and laid something on the desk. It looked like a panel of black glass.

"What do you make of this?" Neypo asked Micca, clasping his hands behind his back. "Have you ever seen anything like it?"

Micca shook his head.

"I didn't really think you had," Neypo said. "Touch it."

The Striver had handled the thing gingerly, but its edges were smoothed, not sharp at all…

The tablet turned from black to milky white. Micca removed his finger. Fifteen or twenty horizontal lines of small, very clear words materialized on its surface. When Micca recovered from his amazement, he recognized the writing to be something like that in some of Mora's books, in style like handwriting, but very neatly done, as though printed from type. But many of the words were spelled wrong, incomplete, or in the wrong place.

But it was Harnish. Micca started reading aloud, trying to correct the text. "I don't know this word 'trid', but it must mean tryget…'hrenðu tryget o nim inni shinoæsin evde, veymecre shadaðæ nahring…'"

Neypo leaned over Micca's shoulder. "You can read it? Do you understand the words?"

Micca shrugged. "More or less."

Neypo backed away, seeming to want some distance between himself and Micca. "Translate some of it for me."

Micca bent his head. "Let's see — 'And if the receiving of the, uh, the wee guiders? to the fresh helpers of that there project is after being of, ah, good quit?' — or 'successful', maybe. Something like that. Seems like nonsense to me. Maybe it's poetry."

He read on. When he neared the bottom of the tablet fresh lines of text rolled up from nowhere, driving off what was above.

"Holy—" He looked up at the Striver. "It's like it was watching my eyes."

Neypo slowly shook his head. "You may see things more incredible before the day is out."

Micca carefully shoved the tablet aside. What was written on it made little sense, but Neypo was excited. "What we'll do first, Micca, is this: we'll set down a list of the words you know, first the names of things, just basic, everyday things, and after that words which denote some action..."

Neypo's wife Winetra entered the room and held out a folded piece of paper. "A man just came with this, from the Lodge, or so I suppose. He was so hot and tired! I sent him to the back-house for a refreshment."

Neypo unfolded the paper. His eyebrows rose.

"What is it?" said Winetra.

Neypo quickly refolded the paper and put it into his pocket. "I must go downtown at once."

Winetra pursed her lips. "I told you your rise in status wouldn't come free. Nevertheless it's a holiday, and you should be with your family! Don't loiter down there all afternoon. Where will we meet? The ice booth near the main stage, I think. We'll check for you at four."

She kissed Neypo and left the room, clapping her hands and telling the children to get out of the fountain and put on their shoes.

Micca rose from his chair. The Striver's interest in the old language was surprising and gratifying, but he didn't want to spend a day as fine as this bent over pen and paper. He heard Samma's laughter outside and moved to the doors.

"Once we get back home we could probably send you a few of our books," he told Neypo. "Some of them have Eynnish written in under the Harnish lines. Then you could see it all at once."

Neypo had been staring at the floor. He looked up. "Would you like to go downtown and see the Lodge rooms?"

Micca blinked solemnly. "I was planning to go to the Fair."

Neypo became animated. He took Micca's arm and hustled him toward an interior door. Micca reached out to the desk and grabbed his hat.

"We'll go downtown first. I'll get you to the Fair in time for the Grand Banquet. I have to visit my booth again when the rest of the receivers get there, anyway—the first batch was entirely sold out by midmorning, you know—but just now you'll come with me. Come on, lad! Pick up your feet!"

Micca looked back and saw the others through the dining room doors, talking and laughing in the sunny garden.

Neypo led him outside to a narrow path between the house's

windowless north side and the garden wall of the house next door. Eight porters trotted down the alley with a sedan, apparently alerted to Neypo's wishes by his wife. The porters set the sedan down before Neypo and Micca, grumbling about having to work on a holiday and the probable weight of Neypo's lanky guest.

"I don't know what you think you're being paid for," Neypo snapped at them. "You're not even wearing your livery."

He pushed Micca into the sedan, got in and pulled the door shut with a bang. The sedan tilted, jerked up. "The Lodge, double-quick!" Neypo shouted from the window.

13. DOWNTOWN

Micca sat pressed against the right-hand window of the sedan. He took off his hat and tried to keep his head from bumping the ceiling. The rider's compartment was small, and the Striver, short as he was, took up much of the room inside it.

Micca glanced several times at Neypo. "What are we going to do at your Lodge, Honorable?" he said finally. "Why are we in such a hurry?"

Neypo took a moment to answer. "I mean to have you help us in a certain investigation. As to the hurry, you'll have to ask my colleague about that." He took out the message his wife had brought him and looked at it again.

Micca said, "When I was in Hannava there were stories about some kind of trouble over here."

Neypo looked hard at him. "So they talk about them even in Hannava. I suppose they're delighted with Mister Adinnegram's speech on the Voice, too. Hannava loves to hear about our troubles. The Directorate owes the city of Hoiin huge sums of money, you know, and they're resentful of certain trade restrictions."

"I didn't know that, Honorable. There are a lot of things about Hannava I didn't know."

The Striver stared for a moment out the window. When he turned back, his face was grim, almost frightened. "Or Hin Hoina. You'd have stayed in Harna if you had. There's a gang of miscreants, murderers, running loose in the city."

'Miscreants', Micca thought. The same things as heretics, as far as he knew. Had some ambitious priest sent Invigorated missionaries to

Hoiin? Had they already buried an Eynnish Husband? If so he must have died. Miscreants *and* murderers.

He found Neypo staring at him again. "You're soon going to find yourself in a position in which you can be of aid to the Lodge, Micca Mora. You may help us resolve a certain mystery, and you may also shock the world with your words. I mean that quite seriously."

Micca tried to smile, but felt only sick. Neypo sat back again, then suddenly grabbed Micca's arm.

"I must tell you more. You should be prepared. There was serious trouble in Hoiin last night — a number of men died, died horribly."

He didn't seem to notice Micca's alarm, but released his arm and frowned. "But Caihar would say I was speaking out of turn," he muttered, and fell silent.

'A number of men had died'? Micca stared out the window, mouth dry. Were they planning to use him to interrogate some evangelizing Invigorationists?

Gillensa must already have told him what she'd heard about Palmer's plan. The Strivers would think he was an Invigorationist too, which he was, in name at least! And here he was wearing animal skin, anathema to the Eynnish. The Striver could probably smell it in this close space. Micca's pants creaked accusingly as he pressed himself into the corner of the sedan. At the Striver's house he had been talking about eating warm-blooded animals too, and he'd probably missed all kinds of orthodox rituals expected of you in Eynna. Hadn't everybody, even Samma, made a sign with their fingers as they sat down to eat?

Micca could tell them he wasn't an Invigorationist, but it wouldn't help. After they'd finished using him to condemn the Harnish missionaries, they'd put *him* to the question and torture a confession of heresy out of him.

What would Brave Beyalmer have done? The unbidden thought made him sick with disgust at himself. This was real, not some story.

They emerged suddenly into the Avenue of the Second Virtue. The sedan tipped as the Striver leaned out the window to shout an order.

The porters dropped the sedan, panting. Neypo jumped out. "Come!" he called to Micca.

Micca looked out at him from inside the sedan.

Neypo stood impatiently. "What's the matter? Did dinner disagree with you? Bruho—help him out!"

One of the sweating men who had carried them downtown peered into the sedan. Micca crawled out the other side.

He looked all around. On the other side of the street were the same doors with the stone men he had seen last night. On this side was a much larger and older looking building of tan stone, carved and figured with vines, flowers and grotesque stone faces. What windows were visible were high up on the façade. Looking left and right, Micca followed Neypo up a broad, worn, stair.

Another Striver sat on a shallow step at the base of a cluster of squat, eroded columns, fanning himself with his hat. The sight was out of place, ludicrous, but it did nothing to calm Micca. When the Striver saw Neypo, he got to his feet. "What took you so long?" the new Striver said.

"I came the moment I had your message. What's happened now, Caihar? You have me very uneasy."

So this was the Caihar the Striver had spoken of, Micca thought. He was older than Neypo Odé, nearly white hair cut into a brush, and looked capable of cruelty.

"I've just returned from the harbor," Caihar told Neypo. "You'll see it too, though you won't believe your eyes. But first we'll ask our guest what he knows about his friends' apparition."

Micca swallowed. He had no friends here other than Samma, but they wouldn't believe him.

"What do you mean, 'apparition'?" said Neypo.

Caihar didn't reply. Rather than go up the steps to a pair of enormous bronze doors that looked like they hadn't been opened in a hundred years, Caihar led them to a small door at street level. Neypo and Micca followed him in. They passed an empty office, then ascended a long stair to a cheerfully frescoed meeting room, went out the other end, down a passage and into a cool, vaulted hall. Their reflections walked with them, up-side-down in the polished black stone of the floor. Past the foot of another staircase and through a pillar-flanked arch, tall doors hung open, giving Micca a glimpse of a cavernous space under lofty barrel vaults. Everywhere were dimly colorful mosaics and glimmers of gold leaf. What light there was came from a ring of windows under a central dome, high overhead. There seemed to be ranks of high-backed chairs arranged around a distant stage or altar. Micca remembered engravings he had seen of the great mainland churches, but the chairs were out of place (even the Eynnish stood in church, he understood). The place had a mysterious, secretive atmosphere about it, not like a place where people met to sing and hear the liturgy read. He could smell ancient stone and something strange and perfumey.

Neypo tugged on his sleeve. Caihar led them through a low door between a pair of columns. "I see you've decked yourself out in your party clothes for the Fair, Neypo. Frankly, it's beyond me how you can think of something so trivial when our very world…"

He seemed to notice Micca for the first time and stopped in the middle of the passage. "Who's this?"

Micca felt a degree of relief. Unless they were playing some kind of game, he wasn't the 'guest' the Striver had mentioned earlier.

"Do you remember that paper Narnet copied out in the Guest Hall?" Neypo said.

He pushed Micca forward. "I've found someone who can translate the cipher. This is my linguistic expert, Micca of Mora Plantation, recently arrived in town. Eh-Micca, I introduce the Striver Caihar Olinom, of Hin Hoina and Tinteneien."

"Surely this can't be your daughter's Harnishman. He looks like he just crept out of a forest. And I thought we had agreed, Neypo of Hin Hoina and Tamanello, not to discuss these matters in front of the uninitiated. You say the fellow claims to be a linguist?" Caihar glared at Micca.

"I think he'll be able to help us, although he's currently a bit confounded by his first visit to the city," Neypo replied. "But what did you see at the harbor? The missing visitors?"

Caihar shook his head, no longer concerned with Neypo's Harnishman. "No. No news at all of them. Clearly they got word of our raid somehow and have gone to ground. As to what's at the harbor, you can see that soon enough."

Caihar strode on. "But we're going downstairs first. Are the Grand Fellow and the others being kept busy?"

"Yes," said Neypo, hurrying behind. "Lemwulin Litu called on me this morning. He was humiliated about his flight from the Guest Hall last night, but he had gotten your message and he's keeping his eye on the others at the Fair. They'll be making speeches for some while yet. Micsin and Woitap are supposed to be there as well, though I haven't had answers to the messages I sent them. Will Riino be joining us here?"

"He's turned out to be more spineless than Lemwulin," Caihar muttered bitterly. "As have the others I was able to contact; and of course poor Cwentoi was murdered. It's up to us now, Neypo."

Neypo shook his head. Caihar opened a door and started down a long, shallow stair. Neypo followed, urging Micca ahead of him.

The descent must have brought them well below street level. At the bottom of the stair was a low tunnel. Its ancient bricks displayed as many variations in color as had those of noon-time Hoiin, but in stains of gray, black, and murky green rather than the warm tones of the upper earth. Micca shuffled ahead of Neypo, ducking under the electric bulbs that hung on wires from the apex of the vaulting.

Caihar opened a heavy door in the side of the passage. Micca hung back. Neypo clucked his tongue and went in first. Micca stooped under an arch, looking into the chamber. Caihar pushed him in and closed the door behind them.

Dampness and mold were strong in the air. The heavy ribs of the ceiling curved down almost to the floor. A single bulb shone from inside a niche, its light broken into shafts by a metal grate. A stocky, uniformed man stood opposite the door, holding something that looked like a large, malformed melon made of glass or glazed ceramic.

"Sergeant Hyvva," said Caihar. "It he talking yet?"

"Not a word, Striver," the man said.

There was someone else in the room, certainly the Strivers' prisoner. He slumped on the floor against the wall, arms bound behind him. What could be seen of his face in the gloom was thin and young, but he was heavily built and powerful looking. Micca realized he was wearing what must be a suit of armor. It was more like a smoothly polished statue with a small, naked head stuck on top than a Harnish armoring of boiled leather, but Micca remembered the Marling's story of his ancestor and his crystal armor. Was this something like it?

"But you got his casque off without drowning him," Neypo said, observing a large trough to the side of the room, the floor near it splashed with water.

Caihar nodded. "We held his head under water for nearly ten minutes, to no apparent effect. The monster hardly even struggled…he must be very hardy despite his wan appearance. Then Hyvva hit upon something that worked."

The Officer nodded modestly. "If vinegar won't finish the sauce, use honey. So my good wife says."

Caihar went on, "Hyvva, who puts duty before all, had missed his breakfast, which provided the inspiration. He sent word to the kitchens and laid out a luxurious breakfast: corn pudding with molasses; strawberries glistening with dew; a fried hash of potatoes, onions and pepper pods; hen's eggs and fillets of pike smoking from the skillet; hot black tea fortified for the morning with cane liquor. We sat the creature down before it. After a night of ignoring all threats and arguments, he made us understand he wanted to remove his helm. So we loosed his hands. He mumbled some prayer, then simply pulled it off."

Neypo turned to look at a plank set between two barrels, covered with greasy plates and empty bowls and cups. "It was kind of you to let him eat."

Caihar smiled sourly. "Our trusty Officer was ready, and bound his hands again as soon as his helm was off. Hyvva and I did the eating."

Neypo took the melon-thing from Hyvva and turned it gingerly over in his hands.

Micca came closer to look at it. Neypo looked at Caihar, who shrugged, and Neypo handed it to Micca.

The Strivers stood before their prisoner, putting questions to him. Micca went to the light and held the melon up to it. It must be a helmet, vaguely like those he had seen in Marstoc's hall, but both simpler and baffling, apparently cast or blown glass. A flattened prow or mask, obviously meant to accommodate the wearer's nose and chin, pushed down and out at one end, which he could move a little, as though it were hinged or jointed. It looked as though it should be transparent, but Micca couldn't see through it. He turned it over and peered into the neck hole. There wasn't sufficient light to make out the interior.

There were no slots or gaps to let in air, and what good would they have done its wearer under water? But around the inside of the neck hole were a few tiny holes … meant to connect with the suit? Was a supply of air stored inside the suit? Micca remembered reading how Siglat had once hidden Beyalmer's magic pike, and how Beyalmer in his warsuit had walked under Lake Findhamin to find it.

"He must have been able to take air from the water, like a fish does," Micca said aloud.

"An interesting notion," Neypo said doubtfully.

Caihar scowled, then turned back to the man on the floor. "You'd better make up your mind to answer our questions! Your face is bare now, soft and vulnerable. Can you imagine the things we might do to it?"

Behind them, Hyvva pricked his finger with the point of his bodkin, wincing dramatically. The prisoner said nothing.

Neypo whispered to Caihar. "Wait a moment, before you commit us to something ugly. You forget my linguist. What I intended is to have the lad attempt an experiment, the nature of which I have carefully—"

"Strivers!" called Hyvva. "Is it permissible he do this?"

Still holding the helmet, Micca was squatting near the prisoner. Fantastic notions jostled in his head like bees caught in a bottle. Maybe thinking of Beyalmer's days was no longer so inappropriate. He spoke as he would have to Beyalmer. "Cwænu scanas?"

Hyvva stifled a belch, but otherwise the cell was silent.

Micca looked at the prisoner's dark hair and pale skin. His face was angular, narrow, underfed. He couldn't have been any older than Micca.

"A-it Indedutam, a-Sumaritem," the prisoner said in a surprisingly deep voice. Then he looked up at Micca with a startled expression and rapped out a long speech.

"What's he saying?" the Strivers shouted in unison.

"Slower," Micca said in Harnish. "Not so fast. My name is Micca. I'm from Mora. Where's Sumarit? Who are you?"

The prisoner's face showed a mixture of surprise and hope. He repeated part of his statement more slowly.

Caihar and Hyvva frowned and bent closer. Neypo plucked at Micca's sleeve. "What's he saying?"

Micca turned briefly to the Striver. "I'm not sure yet, Honorable. He has a funny way of talking."

"A funny way of—!" Neypo gripped Caihar's arm. "But you see, they understand each other!"

"But this creature is a devil out of Hinnioc!" Caihar exclaimed.

"Then so are the Harnish. Or so, rather, were their ancestors. Wennoc has, as you said then, only one language — one *native* language. From what we have just witnessed we may posit people living in the moon, perhaps, or even other worlds attending other suns. The Harnish were born in Wennoc. The visitors were *not*."

Caihar shook his head wearily. "It's too fantastic, Neypo, but I'm beginning to believe it. You recall Riino's initial suggestions as to these creatures' background, his observations of their appearance? I can't see how we didn't credit them immediately. 'Gangling limbs, inky hair, popping eyes'? And look at these two..."

"You're right," Micca said, looking up at the Strivers. "He's not from Wennoc. He just said so. They came from somewhere else, to help us."

Caihar made a strangled laugh. "Help us, yes, so they claimed. Where did he come from then? And where are his friends hiding?"

"He says he's from Indeduit, or Sumarit. I'm not sure which is what. But out there somewhere I guess, up behind the stars... and he said that last night you killed his friends."

"Only two of them, and after *they* killed almost a dozen of our Officers!" Neypo exclaimed.

A dozen Officers. Micca was horrified and impressed. He returned his attention to the prisoner. The man didn't look like a murderer, but Micca had never seen a murderer before, and there were other things on his mind now.

"That's some fine looking armor you've got on," he said in Harnish. "I suppose they couldn't kill *you* because you were wearing it."

The prisoner's face looked lost and guilty. "Yes... I was the only one who had time to get all suited up," he said in a roughly pronounced and poorly arranged version of the same language. "But they can kill me now. My head's bare."

Micca looked at the helmet again, turning it over in his hands. "I don't think they'll kill you outright, but I thought they were going to torture me, and they probably will if I gave you your helmet back." He glanced at the Strivers. They looked back at him anxiously, waiting for a translation.

"Why did you kill Eynnishmen?" Micca asked the prisoner.

The prisoner shook his head. He looked exhausted and confused, but he spoke so rapidly Micca had to tell him to slow down again.

"We didn't mean to kill anybody," the prisoner said. "A gang of them broke in, screaming and yelling. We were afraid and tried to put on bodycasings, but it was too late—there were only three of us at the quarters and there were so many of them! They came at us with clubs and big needles. They stood in front of Cortina and Munzie's thrashers like suicides! I tried to call the lighter to come and get us, but they broke the avefactor before it was set in."

As Micca tried to sort this out, the alien stopped, then said, "But who are you? How can you speak Indeduits?"

"What's he telling you?" Caihar demanded.

"I'm getting a lot of information. Give me a few minutes."

Micca turned back to the prisoner. "I'm from Mora. That's across the water from here, and I'm not speaking Indeduish; you're speaking bad Harnish. You must have something to do with me and my people, or we do with you. We must have come from the same place!"

"If you're from another party, where's your ship? We didn't see any other ships from orbit."

Micca understood him imperfectly. He said that he was a builder by trade, not a sailor, that he had no ship of his own.

"They're plotting, making plans!" Caihar said. He grabbed the club from Hyvva's hand and advanced on them. Micca scrambled to his feet and held the prisoner's helmet out in front of him, ready to ward off a blow. Neypo took Caihar's arm and convinced him to stand away.

Glancing at them, the prisoner spoke carefully to Micca, trying to do it slowly. "If you lost your ship, then you're stuck here too. Last night most of my comrades went out to see some friendly locals. They thought things were going well, they didn't take avefactors. They must have been killed, too. But I did try to call our lighter last night. It might have come, it could be waiting."

'Us'? Micca thought. "What's a lighter?" he said.

"The ship's boat, the lander! The big ship can't land. It's in orbit, and we came down in the lighter," the prisoner said, impatient again.

He looked into Micca's eyes now. "Untie me and give me my head-casing. You run after me. We'll make a break for it. I have to at least try!"

Micca gaped at him. The idea that this man had come from outside Wennoc, had *flown* here, was finally sinking in. The ship he talked about, and the 'lighter'—both these things must necessarily *fly*. And he'd said 'we'—

Neypo suddenly grabbed his arm. "That's enough! Listen to me, Micca. Ask him where his friends went, ask him whether Adinnegram—perdition, boy! You can have his casque as a souvenir if you wish, but do as I say!"

Micca looked at the helmet with new interest. Then he said, "So he's not the only one left? Some of his people are still alive?"

"Why, yes. At least five of them, so far as we—"

Caihar almost leapt into the air, shaking his head and waving his hands at Neypo.

Neypo understood. "Micca, you will not, under any circumstances, tell the prisoner that his friends are alive."

Caihar whispered harshly, "If the creature thinks he's the only one of them left he'll be more likely to answer our questions. If he finds out otherwise, he might possess, or discover, some way to communicate with his fellows—"

Caihar spun to face Micca. "Young man! Prepare yourself for induction into the Lodge."

Micca's eyebrows rose, and Neypo blinked in astonishment, but Caihar pulled Micca forward. The Strivers made signs over his head. Hyvva stood by solemnly. The prisoner watched the ritual, puzzled. Neypo and Caihar muttered oaths and made Micca repeat them, then taught him a sign to make with his fingers and a certain way to shake hands. They touched his forehead and chest with dollops of their spittle, and Micca was created an Adjunct-Military to the Holy Striving Lodge of Hin Hoina by the Bay.

Caihar immediately placed him under a Class-Three Vow of Secrecy and asked, "Does the prisoner indeed believe his companions to be dead?"

Micca wiped his face with his sleeve. Samma and Fola would be impressed with him now. He wondered what the Invigorationists at Mora would say about him joining the Eynnish Lodge. But Micca wasn't pleased. Horrifying penalties had been mentioned concerning disloyalty. He was in a worse spot than before.

"Yes, he thinks they're dead," he told Caihar.

Caihar expelled his breath and criticized Neypo for not swearing Micca to secrecy earlier, but Neypo smiled with relief. "I think things are beginning to go our way."

"That's what you think, is it?" Caihar said. "Just wait till we go to the harbor."

"You keep going on about the harbor," Neypo said. "Just what is this frightful thing you're going to show me?"

Caihar leaned close. "I've never seen anything more eerie, Neypo. It seems to have appeared sometime last night. It looks like a great slab of slate, but floats in the water like a chip of dry wood. If it hasn't been thrust up from Hinnioc, it must to belong to the outlanders. What if the monsters who escaped should manage to take this new thing? Who knows what it might do, or what might be inside it!"

"Has anyone been seen aboard this floating stone, Caihar?"

"The Officers I sent saw no evidence of anyone, nor any sign of a cabin within," Caihar said, eyes shifting. "But it might contain a great charge of explosive powder. The survivors might return to set it off and destroy our harbor in vengeance."

"We'll open its hatches and sink it," said Neypo.

Hyvva shook his head. "Our men didn't find any hatches. No openings of any kind."

"Hidden, disguised perhaps? It must be at least partially hollow if it can float. Perhaps it's made of glass, as is their protective gear. A floating bottle."

Neypo turned to Micca, nervously smoothing his mustache. "Ask the outlander if he has a raft or a boat, Micca, one down here in Wennoc."

Micca debated with himself, but they already knew more than he did. "Yes, it sounded that way."

Caihar jerked forward. "Ask him what's inside it!" he barked. "And do not think to withhold any more information!"

"And ask him how to open it," Neypo added. "There must be some trick. Ask him that, Micca."

Micca looked back to the prisoner. The Strivers wanted access to his boat, and they knew where it was. If they were willing to take him and the prisoner there, something might be done.

"They're saying your boat, your lighter, is nearby," Micca said in Harnish. Harna was just across the Bay. If somehow they could get access to this boat and leave the Strivers behind, they could sail off—or *fly* off—across the Bay to Marstoc, or even to the hut in the woods near Goranstura, and stay out of sight until things had settled down. But what was he thinking? He had come here to bring Samma back.

"Untie me," the prisoner said urgently.

"You can see I can't do that right now! Come on. I've got to satisfy the Strivers before I can do anything. Tell me how to open the lighter."

"Untie me and give me my headpiece."

Micca was increasingly nervous, and he was losing his patience. "Shut up with that! If you don't cooperate with me, it's going to be bad news for both us!" he shouted.

Though they didn't understand his words, the Strivers were impressed by his tone of voice. Neypo nodded to Caihar.

The prisoner wilted. "I don't have an avefactor, but broadcasting through my headpiece should work—but tell them not to get any ideas. I'm sure Sula won't open for any these natives."

"Is Sula its name? But you can get us into it?"

"Of course! Sulawan will let me in. Just make sure to get my headpiece on."

Micca stood away from him, confused and excited. Was he to put the helmet on the prisoner's head, or on his own? The prisoner's grammar was garbled. But how was he going to get away from the Strivers? They wanted to sink the thing, something he couldn't be a part of…a flying boat!

Neypo and Caihar were clamoring for a translation.

"He can open it," Micca told them. "But it won't open unless it hears an Indeduish man tell it to. It can tell the difference…it's got radio equipment on it."

Neypo nodded rapidly. "We must sink it."

Caihar nodded too. "Unlicensed broadcasters! What luck we got the alien's casque off. It sounds as though there might be a miniature broadcaster inside *that*! It wouldn't surprise me. In spite of our losses I think we've been lucky so far, very lucky—" Caihar's head jerked up. He told Hyvva to take the helmet and keep it out of the prisoner's reach. Micca gave it up reluctantly, the prisoner eyeing him desperately.

The elder Striver stared at his fingers, meshing them tightly together. "But quite likely this raft thing is the greatest threat to us now. There may be worse things than explosives aboard. It may hold more tube-weapons, more of these man-bottles! A handful of men equipped with them could probably overawe our whole force of guards and Cadets. Even now the surviving devils may be creeping by back ways down to the harbor while everyone else, including most of the guard, is at the Fair—

"Your Harnishman says the raft's door is locked. We must make him open it, immediately. I don't want to commit any further—but no, in this case the ends will just have to justify the means."

He raised his head and looked at the prisoner. "I'm sorry, young man, or devil, or whatever you are." Caihar turned to Hyvva. "You should be able to get him out of his shell now."

Hyvva spoke slowly. "One of my men used to work for a disreputable money-lender. He's familiar with a number of methods for inducing keen but non-lethal discomfort. He's on guard at the harbor, so he can be here quickly."

"Micca Mora," said Caihar, "tell the prisoner what you've heard."

Neypo looked sorrowfully at the prisoner, his face as pale as Micca's. Perceiving a threat, the prisoner stood up, bent forward by his bonds.

"Wait!" Micca said quickly. When the torturer had finished with the outlander, he'd take Micca, too, cut out his tongue and break his fingers so he couldn't tell tales. He spoke rapidly to the alien. "Are there weapons or more armored suits on your lighter?"

The prisoner looked surprised. "I doubt it, don't know why there would be… Sula might have kept a 'casing in it."

"There's no weapons, no suits, no bombs on the raft," Micca told the Strivers. "He'll be able to open it up for us, but we have to be out there right next to it… it's a real short radio signal…"

He added another quick improvisation: "And he told me earlier that they're all trained to pass out, or even die! At the least little bit of pain, so torture won't do any good."

Neypo took Caihar into a corner. The Strivers whispered together. Finally Caihar took out pen and paper, scribbled briefly, and gave the paper to Hyvva.

Hyvva checked the prisoner's bonds, fixed a rope with a slipknot to his neck, handed the rope to Caihar. Neypo asked Hyvva something, who nodded and pointed in response. Before he left the cell, Hyvva handed the alien's helmet to Neypo.

Micca cleared his throat. "If we take him out there…"

Neypo was at the door. "Come with me, Micca. You and I are going to conduct a little experiment first."

Frightened and suspicious, Micca went with Neypo, out into the passage. They went down a few steps, around a turn and came upon another door, lower and deeper than the other one.

"Yes," said Neypo, looking in, "here we are."

Micca hung back. Was there someone inside, waiting for them? Would he be punished now for his less than accurate translations?

Neypo called to him.

Micca peeked in. Neypo had set three or four bulbs glowing. It was cold, but better lit than the prison room. There was a strong odor of fish. The far wall was hidden by blocks of ice, dripping slowly into a gutter in the floor.

Shelves lined the other walls. On two of them, one above the other, two forms were hidden by a black sheets. From under one of them hung a glass arm. Micca almost touched it, then jerked his hand away.

Neypo said, "These are the—"

"The dead outlanders," said Micca. "You didn't have to show me. I believed you."

"That's not why we're here. From what the outlander's told you, for the raft to open, it must receive orders orally transmitted by radio. Yes?"

Neypo expressed it better than Micca had. He nodded.

Neypo returned the nod. "Not surprisingly, the outlander mistrusts us, and it's unlikely he'll willingly help us. He may try to trick us. So what we need is an imitation of him, someone who can speak as he does. This person can expect to earn the lasting gratitude of the Lodge of Hin Hoina, and all true children of Wennoc. Do you understand what I want you to do?"

"I think so."

Neypo handed him the alien's helmet. Micca carefully pushed it over his head, again recalling the helmet in the Marling's hall.

It rubbed his ears going on, but seemed too large for him, and it rocked a little when he moved his head. There was no odor inside, nothing to tell him someone else had worn it. What he could see through it was murky and slightly distorted. He couldn't see any sort of switches inside it, and how would the wearer operate them if there were any? Was it possible you could simply speak inside it, tell it what to do, rather than manually adjust knobs and switches? He licked his lips, then said in Harnish, "Turn on. Send my words. Send." He tried Harnish words he thought could be taken as 'broadcast' and 'open' and 'start'...

Neypo leaned close, hand to his ear. "Your voice is muffled, but it doesn't sound like it's coming through a broadcaster."

"I can't hear you too well either." The helmet came off easily enough. He handed it back to the Striver, who examined it under the light, inside and out.

Neypo tugged his mustache. "I see no switches, nothing that looks like a voice-taker."

"I didn't either," Micca said, looking now behind the Striver. Something had caught his eye: a whole wall of shelves supporting covered, manlike shapes. He glanced at Neypo, went to the shelves and lifted one of the sheets. An empty glass suit, or something much like one.

"For one of *our* radios to work," Micca said, "you have to have the receiver, the antenna, the battery, all of them hooked up together."

Neypo nodded slowly. "That's so. It may prove a far-fetched theory, but given the exigencies of the situation we ought to test it. As a member of the committee investigating these affairs, I'll take responsibility for allowing a volunteer to place himself inside this artifact for a brief period."

Micca pulled the suit from the shelf. It was all of one piece and less rigid than it looked, more like a thick molding of cloudy varnish than glass. Another kind of suit? And how were you supposed to get into it? You could hardly enter through the neck-hole. He found a pair of raised tabs at the front of the collar, where they'd probably be hidden under the helmet. He pushed at them, then tried pinching them together. There was a pop, a hollow, almost moist sound, and the suit moved in his arms.

Neypo drew in his breath. Micca looked at the back of the suit. It had opened down the spine, from collar to tailbone. The edges of the rib-cage flaps or doors showed barely discernible layers. The innermost surface was soft. Micca tentatively stuck his arm into one of its arms. His sleeve bunched and snagged.

Neypo said, "The outlanders removed their clothing before donning these suits."

Somehow the Striver's mild encouragement to take the thing made Micca more uneasy. He shook caution out of his mind and quickly pulled off his coat and shirt. Neypo took them and laid them on the shelf. Micca unstrapped his purse and handed it to Neypo. "Don't run away with my money," he said weakly.

"Ah! Too bad. I had thought it might be a down-payment on one of my receiver sets."

Micca managed to return Neypo's smile. He took off the rest of his clothes, sat down on a shelf, shivering, and arranged the empty casing in front of him. One leg went in, then the other, and his feet slid easily enough into the boots. He stood up awkwardly. The thing was cold and clammy. Neypo held up the top for him. Micca reached into hollow tubes and watched a vague solidity come into them. He stood up, looked down at himself, then fumbled behind and pushed the flaps home.

Air hissed out from Micca's armpits and crotch. The suit expanded, contracted, lengthened and shortened in various places, conforming itself to his shape. Most of its exterior became rigid, more like glass. He felt urged into a more upright posture.

Micca exhaled shakily. What was he doing? Too late to think about it now. Now the gauntlets, the boots, all of it fit perfectly. Neypo handed him the helmet. Micca looked at the ceiling for a second, then ducked his head into it.

The collar of the suit crawled further up his neck to meet the helmet and caught it. The portion in front of his face ratcheted in and snugged up under his chin. What hair was left hanging outside was sheared off and fell in a little shower onto his shoulders. His field of view cleared and widened as the interior parts of the helmet closed in. At the same time whatever air was left between him and the body of the armor was expelled. He felt things inside it begin to wriggle and probe —

Micca jumped. He scrabbled with thick fingers at the helmet, twisting his shoulders and hips, shuffling rapidly backwards as though trying to run away from the suit. He stumbled into a crate behind him. His legs flew out and he sat down abruptly on the crate, splintering it to sticks.

"Are you quite all right?" Neypo said, approaching cautiously.

Micca looked up. Though he still felt a horrible flutter of claustrophobia, the fall had broken his first panic. He tried again, but the helmet seemed married to the suit now and didn't want to come off. It seemed to be doing something…his view outside further brightened, and its edges disappeared. Then everything blurred and distorted; a pattern of tiny sparks spun around in his eyes for a moment, and then everything abruptly snapped into a wonderful sharpness. He could see better now than with his lost eye-glasses, far better.

A line of illuminated numbers and nonsensical words appeared under the Striver's face. Micca could hear the Striver breathing through whatever had crawled into his ears; his own breath came easily, the air soft in his nose with nothing of the room's dampness or fishy smell. The suit wasn't cold anymore, either. Micca's fear subsided. He'd find a way to get out of it sooner or later, even if the Marling's ancestor hadn't gotten out of his — the Indeduish man could tell him how.

Neypo helped him to his feet. Micca looked down at himself, or a thickened semblance of himself molded in glass. His musculature was exaggerated, and his shoulders, elbows, crotch and knees were covered by thick bosses. A faint film of mirroring swam under the surface of the colorless glass.

He twisted at the waist, cautiously squatted up and down and flexed his arms. His movements weren't at all constrained, though he had to stand with his legs farther apart than seemed normal, his arms hung out a bit, and he felt a little heavier.

The last bits of claustrophobia vanished. Micca raised a gauntlet and tapped the prow of the helmet before his mouth. "Can you hear me now?"

"I hear you very well!" Neypo answered, stepping back. "But are you all right? You cried out, you know. Did the thing pinch you, or shock you with electricity? You may take it off again if you're experiencing serious discomfort."

"I'm fine," he said. He still had troubles, but now no one was going to bloody him or break his bones, or cut out his tongue to keep him silent.

Neypo nodded. "Well, your voice is loud and quite different, so it's sure I'm hearing you by way of whatever processes are hidden inside the suit. Perhaps an automatic switch is triggered when the suit's casque is attached. We'll go back, then, and carry out our plan."

Micca looked at the shelves. "Since you've got some more suits, should we take one of the helmets along for your prisoner?"

"No."

Micca followed Neypo in long, clumping strides and they came back into the prison room. Caihar was squatting on the floor beside the alien, speaking slowly to him, as to a child, tapping his shoulder with a bodkin from time to time for emphasis.

"You cannot defeat Wennoc's essential intent; this was founded before the Dawn and will persist even through the Night. You may inflict suffering upon Wennoc's children, but whatever seeming success you —"

"Colleague," said Neypo.

Caihar looked to the door, then flew up and flattened his back against the wall.

The prisoner struggled to his feet, hunched over by his bonds. "Who are you?" he said.

Micca felt himself smiling inside the helmet. "It's me, Micca, from Mora."

The prisoner slumped. "Why are you in a bodycasing?"

Neypo went to Caihar and took his arm, leading him away from the wall. "I thought you understood my intentions, colleague."

"I'm sorry I scared you, Honorable," Micca said, amplification making his voice harsh.

Neypo helped his colleague to a bench at the improvised breakfast table. Caihar sat but pushed him away, staring at Micca. "You gave me a fright, Harnishman! You look so ghastly pressed into that bottle. I thought you were a ghost, or the first of a new legion of devils…" He turned to Neypo. "And I thought you were going to extract a broadcaster from the thing, not put your linguist into it. I told you Hyvva's volunteer Cadet nearly shat himself this morning when trying one. He didn't even get as far as donning the helm."

"An innovative course of action seemed called for. And perhaps a robust farmer from the peninsula has more gumption than our city-bred lads. But are you all right, colleague? Let me test your rhythm." He took Caihar's wrist between his fingers, and Caihar quickly jerked away.

"Your pulses seemed very rapid," said Neypo. "You'd better have a lie-down upstairs."

"Do you think I'm a dodderer now, Neypo? Do you want me out of the way so you can experiment with further 'innovations'?" Caihar looked at Micca. "And can we trust this farmer of yours? Look at him coddle up to his brother monster!"

Neypo glanced doubtfully at Micca and the prisoner. "Micca has sworn himself to the Lodge. Your mind is uneasy, colleague. You need rest."

Caihar took a flask from his pocket and drank. "This tonic extinguishes the need for sleep; already I feel more alert. Now, let's go out and put and end to that thing in the harbor!" He looked around, picked up a bronze club from the floor and stuck it into his belt.

Neypo stood up. "The prisoner should be no problem with that halter around his neck… Micca, please remain inside the outlanders' armor for a little while longer, and come with us."

"Right," said Micca.

14. AT THE FAIR

At one time the city of Hin Hoina had occupied only the north side of the River Entenen, well up from the Bay, hugging the walls of a now-vanished citadel and protected by a belt of cedars from storms on the Bay, which were said to have been more violent in former years. In those years people ferried over the Entenen to a meadow on the south bank of the river for the Nimoi Tuvimat Fair and other important gatherings. After the ruin of Mellatuno, Hoiin had become the major port on the Bay. The city grew, throwing bridges over the river, and a basilica was established on the site of the old fairgrounds.

Historians differed in their opinions as to where the Fairs had taken place during this period, but later the basilica's dome collapsed, probably due either to its over-ambitious span or to poorly burned bricks, though at the time it was believed to be a sign Wennoc was not satisfied with its location. The basilica was rebuilt on a more carefully divined site upriver (with a more modest dome) and the Fair returned to its ancient grounds for a while, although the mounds of bricks under the turf made it difficult to create level fields for dances and athletic displays, and occasionally an unlucky visitor was taken by ghosts into forgotten subterranean chambers, never to be seen again. But Hoiin continued to prosper, and eventually both the ruins of the basilica and the old fairgrounds were hidden under warehouses and manufactories.

In recent centuries the Fair had been held on a flat circle of land to the north and east of the city. The area was a huge lawn of grass, turned to dust or mud each year by thousands of feet, depending on the weather, enclosed by a belt of trees under which stood the booths and tents where the Fair-goers were presented the opportunity to purchase the goods provided by Hoiin's craftsmen, as well as food, drink and various services and entertainments.

Throngs of people walked over the great lawn, past booths and displays, now and then stopping to buy trinkets or listen to someone try to convince them to have a fountain built, or a mosaic walk laid in their garden. They talked to and about their neighbors, ate pastries stuffed with minced seababies and herbs, drank cups of punch and iced spirits. They watched as the Daughters of Eynna, dressed all in green, performed the traditional postures. At noon Strivers and Mendicants from other cities were borne around the lawn, displaying their batons of office, followed by squads of marching Cadets, flag-spinning gonfaloniers and nodding Centenarians in their wheeled baskets.

The First Liturgist of Hoiin came to the front of the grandstand and sang an invocation. The Grand Fellow of Hoiin's Lodge stood at the back of the stage with other local notables, including important merchants, a popular elocutionist and several choral groups.

Grand Fellow Westo heard himself announced by the Liturgist. He arranged his hat's ribbons and made sure of his Fair button, squared his shoulders and marched out to the front of the grandstand.

Westo stepped up to a podium decorated with ropes of flowers and an antependium bearing Hoiin's insignia. A man from the Voice of Hoiin adjusted the stand of a voice-taker before him.

The Grand Fellow saluted the crowd. The people cheered and clapped their hands.

"I greet you!" the Grand Fellow called. "Greetings all! A hearty welcome to our honored guests and neighbors from the people and Lodge of Hin Hoina by the Bay!"

More cheers.

"I thank our speakers and entertainers, together with artists, artisans, cooks and brewers…"

The crowd cheered again.

"…and everyone else for joining us today, all who have come to ensure that our Fair is the most successful, happy and jubilant yet! I know," continued the Grand Fellow, shouting to the throng of upturned faces, "I know for certain, that tonight, tonight, our fireworks display will be the most wonderful ever!"

Happy cheers, then pounding drums from the stage. Twenty-four trumpeters came forward and blew a fanfare. A chorus of double-basses and sopranos sang,

"Long...flourish...the city...and county of...Hoina!"

When Westo could make himself heard again he declared Hoiin's Fair of the Nimoi Tuvimat officially in progress and retired to let the Liturgist sing thanks to Wennoc and announce the events of the day.

Visiting dignitaries began making their speeches. Many fairgoers remained near the grandstand, waiting to hear Milli Incinen sing, a favorite on the Voice, while others sauntered among the tents and booths.

Near the fairground's main gates, a man wearing the simple plaid of a Striver's Aide was talking to an Officer who had just gotten out of a sedan. "It was amazing, Sergeant Hyvva. I'd never seen this man before today, but he told me all about my past and predicted wonderful things to come."

"Sounds interesting, Hattala, but I have a message for the Grand Fellow. I don't have time for fun today, Fair or no Fair."

The Aide looked toward the grandstand, but from here it was hidden by the crowd. "No rest for some, eh? But you're in luck, Sergeant. The Fellow himself just went in to see this spiritualist fellow. Oh yes, lots of word-of-mouth about him going around today!" He pulled open the flap of a canvas-shrouded booth and stuck his head inside. "Ahoy! Have you seen—oh, there you are, sir. Sergeant Hyvva is here with a message for you."

Hyvva entered the tent, Hattala coming behind.

A little while later two commercial men, up from Hynnysoi without their wives, paused outside the same booth. It had neither banners nor ribbons, only a card over the entrance:

YOUR GLORIOUS FUTURE REVEALED!
Welcome All: Enter to Learn More.

"Do you think there are fancy-women at work in there, Mitti?" said one of them, hand to his ear.

His companion listened. "It rather sounds like it, Rosco. But if they don't advertise their prices I won't go in. These city sharpers will get the better of you every time."

"Well," said Rosco, "they can't demand silver for a simple inquiry."

Mitti said he'd wait outside. In a minute Rosco came blundering out of the tent, eyes wide. "Mitti! Call the polis, call the guard! They're cutting someone's throat in there!"

A man came running out of the tent after Rosco. "No need for that, sir," he said, seizing Rosco's arm. "There are Officers here already."

Another man came out of the tent and went after Mitti. Mitti took to his heels, yelling for help.

15. THE BOAT

The prisoner's leash in his hand, Caihar led the others along an elevated walkway. From nearby terraces a few people gawked at the Strivers and the strange figures that accompanied them, but no traffic hindered their progress after they descended to the lower level of the street again. Everyone must be at the Fair.

They walked toward the harbor, Micca taking slow (so as not to overtake companions with short legs), purposeful strides. His scope of movement was a little constrained by the armor, but he expected he'd move more freely when he'd become accustomed to wearing it. Though it clutched at him a bit in the crotch and arm pits, he wouldn't call it uncomfortable. He was still pleased by how well he could see now; out here in the daylight his eyes seemed even sharper. He was new and clean, like something made rather than grown. Micca dragged his gauntlet along a wall. He could feel the contours of the bricks almost as though he touched them with his bare fingertips. He drew his arm back and knocked the wall hard with his fist. He felt the impact, but there was no pain, and a little crumble of masonry rattled to the pavement. Micca grinned at the alien, who maintained his blank stare. He might be resentful that Micca, who was no soldier, was using his people's military equipment, or more likely he was simply worried about his situation... and he couldn't see Micca's smile anyway.

The great stone Strivers out in the harbor came into view. They weren't as impressive as Micca had thought them last night. Birds were perched on their shoulders and outspread arms, leaving the ancient figures streaked with white.

Other birds swung over the windy sea, occasionally dropping out of the sky to take a fish, or be taken by a fish. Nearer to land were ships' masts, hung with lines and flapping sailcloth. Among the freighters were smaller fishing craft, rolling on the swells that came in from the Bay. There were clouds in the southwest that looked like thunderheads.

Micca thought he recognized the pier where he had landed. The fat little cog was gone, probably returned to Hannava on the morning wind, but there was an oddly plain and unrigged raft floating at the end of the otherwise untenanted stretch of stone.

Caihar gave Neypo the prisoner's rope and trotted rapidly down the embankment. He stopped and spoke to two men in Officer's uniforms who were standing at the land-end raft's pier. When the others caught up with him, Caihar was less anxious.

"No one, outlanders or anyone else, has tried to approach the thing since I was here earlier," he told Neypo.

"So Adinnegram and the others who were absent from the Hall last night must yet be ignorant of its presence."

"Let's hope so." Caihar strode out onto the pier, Neypo coming behind with the prisoner. Micca followed, walking carefully; the stone was wet from spray, and while the soles of the armor's boots were deeply ridged he didn't know how well they'd grip. The Strivers' prisoner tried to run forward, stopped not by slippery boots but by Neypo's hand on his rope.

They approached the raft slowly. The strange thing was stranger still up close. If it hadn't been rocking a little in the water Micca might have thought it was the top of a shaft of stone rising from seabed. Its color was hard to pin down; it seemed unsteady, undecided—the sky, water, grass—the color of a rainy day? It was flat, a wave-washed rectangle, maybe four by five or six yards, rising only a couple of feet above the surface of the water. There were no railings or any other fittings visible. Several bollards rose nearby, but none had been used to secure the raft. Was it pinned in place by an unseen anchor?

Micca put his helmet close to the alien's face. "How does it work? How can it fly? Does it use electricity to make a magnetic field, like a powerful compass?"

"Yes, Micca!" Neypo said. "Convince him to tell you how to open it!"

The alien backed away from Micca. "How should I know how it works? Ask Sula. Give me your headcasing so I can call in."

"Be reasonable. The headcasing is mine now and that's that. You tell me what to do."

"What are you saying?" Caihar asked Micca. He turned to Neypo. "They sound like they're plotting something again."

The alien stared at Micca for a few seconds. "All right. I guess I have to take a chance on you. Untie my arms and give me your left arm — you're right-handed?"

"Yes. What do you want it for?"

"Please, just do it. I won't try any tricks!"

Micca turned to Neypo. "I have to untie his hands — he has to get a key or something."

Neypo and Caihar looked at each other. Caihar nodded reluctantly, and Neypo tightened his grip on the rope tied to the alien's neck.

Micca squatted behind the alien and clumsily managed to loosen the cord securing his wrists. The alien shook his arms and sent the cord flying off in the wind, which was gusting strongly now. Immediately he grabbed Micca's arm and fingered out a dancing pattern on underside of his wrist.

The Strivers' alarmed shouts went unheeded. "Are there two green dots under your left eye now?" the alien asked.

'Yes."

"Good. You're on." He spoke a phrase in Harnish. "Say that, just as I did."

Micca silently rehearsed the phrase. "Neffafinnegal? Is that your name then?"

"Yes! Now say what I told you!"

"Shouldn't it go something like 'needs immediate entry' instead of—"

"Just say it!"

Micca turned to tell the Strivers the boat was about to open, but something on the shore had taken their attention. Half a dozen new-comers stood at the other end of the pier, talking to the Officers who had been assigned to watch the aliens' boat.

Neypo squinted. "I believe I see Westo's man, Cresslu Tulio. But if

Micca gets the thing open and we have no difficulty sinking it, we won't need reinforcements after all."

Caihar clucked his tongue. "We'll need to tow it out to where the water is deep first. But you're right, we want as few involved in this as is humanly possible. We were premature to contact the Grand Fellow. I'll send Cresslu away with some story or other for him. In the meantime deal quickly with the monster and your translator and get that thing open!"

Micca watched Caihar go off down the pier. Things seemed urgent again. He stood beside the raft and shouted out what the alien told him: "Hallo the lighter! Neffafinnegal wants in! Quick as, ah...quick as boiled asparagus!"

Hearing Micca's words, Neypo rejoined him. The alien bit his lip, eyes fixed on the raft, which was nearly black now under the hurrying clouds.

The craft's surface dulled and flattened, losing a floating transparent layer Micca hadn't been aware of before. Silvery hairlines defining a neat rectangle appeared on the raft's deck. The outlined section of stone separated itself, lifted, then tilted up at one end. Glass hands, then a glass helmet emerged.

Micca sucked in his breath. Neypo gasped.

"Sula? Nial Sulawan!" the alien cried. "Help! Get me out of here!"

Micca recoiled from the man on the boat as he would at seeing a mudrunner crawl out from under a rock, though he supposed he looked just like this. As the armored man boosted himself out of the newly revealed hatchway, Neypo took several backwards steps. He dropped the prisoner's leash, turned and made a horn of his hands. "Caihar! Caihar! Call all the Officers out here! Hurry!"

Caihar was halfway between them and shore. He turned, stood frozen for a moment, then began running back to the end of the pier.

The new armored man had boosted himself onto the pier. He put a thin black line over a stone bollard and threw another to Micca. Micca stared dumbly at it, then hung its loop over a further bollard. The man from the boat must be afraid it would drift off now that he was out of it.

"What are you idiots up to?" Micca understood the man to say. "If you're in trouble, Finnegal, where's your headcasing? Why didn't you all answer me last night? I flew around for an hour after your first call. If that's Adinnegram with you—"

Neypo stood to the side, and Caihar came panting up. He took the club from his belt and flung it at the man from the raft. It glanced off his helmet with a 'bonk' and splashed into the water. "What the hell is going on here?" he said.

"They killed everybody else!" the prisoner yelled. "Get me out of here!"

"Who's the other guy in the 'fitting, then?"

"I don't know! Micca-something. He's from another expedition." Neffafinnegal moved to the edge of the pier.

"Another expedition?" the new glass man said suspiciously.

"Who cares! Get us out of here!" Neffafinnegal yelled, preparing to drop onto the deck of the stone boat.

Neypo unthawed, jumped forward and grabbed the end of the alien's leash. Gagging, Neffafinnegal scrabbled with his hands under his chin. Micca clamped his hand over the middle of the rope, trying to stop Neypo from choking Neffafinnegal.

The man from the boat must have misinterpreted Micca's action. He pushed between him and Neffafinnegal and slammed a heavy fist into the prow of Micca's helmet. Micca crashed down, landing on his back.

The Strivers backed away, staring at the armored men in dread. Sulawan stood over Micca. "Think you're going to steal my find?" he shouted. "You won't find me as easy to deal with as Adinnegram and his dilettantes!"

Micca tried to get up, but his suit was stiff, frozen. The man from the boat—Sulawan, Neffafinnegal had called him—prepared to kick him, but now Micca's armor let him move again. He leapt up, lurched forward and pushed the man back with both hands. Sulawan staggered and sat down heavily. He rose to a crouch, and Micca guessed from the way Sulawan held himself he was going to throw himself at his midsection. Did he think a carpenter, a farmer, was so stupid? Micca raised his fists in the formal manner, as though waiting for his opponent to stand straight. He remained in his crouch.

Micca advanced. Neypo was muttering prayers. Caihar raised his fist, giving Micca a Striving salute. When Micca saw Sulawan tense, ready to lunge, he brought up his right boot. The man took it with a loud clack under his glass mask.

His opponent flopped backward, propelled by the momentum of Micca's kick. The man lay on his back, head and shoulders hanging over the edge of the pier, evidently frozen after the blow as Micca had been. When he was able to move he began to rise, but his elbow slipped on the stone of the pier. He tried again, then kicked his legs wildly. Micca caught a glimpse of the backs of his boots, and he vanished. In an instant came a great splash.

Micca went forward, put his hands on his knees and looked over the edge of the pier. All he saw was wind-whipped water. The armored man must have gone down like a stone. In that suit he'd never swim.

Micca straightened slowly. The glass suit felt cold and alien around him. What had he done?

Neypo stood beside him. "There's no hope for the fellow. The water must be three or four fathoms here."

"By an act of manslaughter the Harnishman has saved us, and given us the raft," said Caihar. He faced Micca with a frightening grimace. "Welcome to the Holy Striving Lodge, fellow killer. May Wennoc forgive you for joining us."

Neypo took Micca's hand and gingerly patted his arm. "Pay no attention to my colleague. You did what you had to."

The wind was blowing harder. A few drops of rain blotted the pier. "Assuage the boy's conscience as well as you can, Neypo," Caihar said. "I'll get on with the business at hand. We'll get a good rowing boat and tow the thing out to the deeps. The waves should swamp it quickly now that it's open." He walked off slowly, waving to the Officers gathered at the landward end of the pier, who had started coming toward them, though with no great hurry. Maybe they had paused to watch the brief fight, or to avoid attracting the attention of the monsters at the end of the pier.

Micca looked over his shoulder at the Strivers' prisoner (or not exactly a prisoner anymore, since the rope tied to his neck had been abandoned again). The alien was far from happy, but neither did he look like he was grieving the loss of the boat's pilot. He was busy undoing the loop of rope around his neck.

And recalling a capability of the glass helmets he had presumed, one the Strivers had ignored or hadn't believed, Micca realized that this Sulawan probably hadn't drowned. Likely he was walking under the water toward shore right now, his helmet giving him air just as Neffafinnegal's must have done while Hyvva held his head under water in the Lodge's cell...just as Brave Beyalmer's must have if he really had walked under Lake Findhamin. Micca enjoyed a moment of relief upon deciding he wasn't guilty of manslaughter after all.

At the other end of the pier Caihar was waving his hands. He and the Officers seemed to be having a disagreement. Raised voices came over the water.

Neypo had already started down the pier. "Stay here and watch the outlander," he shouted back to Micca.

Neffafinnegal stood near Micca. "What are they doing?"

"I don't know," he said. But something was certainly happening at the other end of the pier. It looked as though one Officer struck another, and three others joined the fight. Arms swung and flailed.

Two figures fell and struggled with each other on the pier. They both rolled over the edge. A pale arm rose briefly from the water. Red and black plaid swirled in the slapping waves and disappeared.

Neypo turned and raced back toward the boat, wind flapping his coat.

"What's happening?" Micca shouted as Neypo approached.

"They've killed Caihar!" he gasped. "They've thrown him into the sea!"

Neypo looked back to land. A man was trying to swim to shore, the man Caihar had been fighting with? The struggle was still going on, and more men ran from shore onto the pier. Their clubs swung over the heads of the Officers who had been guarding the boat. Two of the newcomers bypassed the fighting and started down the pier.

Neypo snatched at Micca's arm and pointed to the alien. "Tell him they're—tell them this! These people want vengeance for their comrades who were slain by the outlanders last night. They're mad for blood and they'll kill us all!"

Neypo stared for a second at the Bay and swallowed hard. "We'll have to take refuge, refuge inside the raft, Micca—quickly now!"

Micca rapidly repeated what Neypo had said in Harnish. Neffafinnegal glanced landward in fear, then dropped to the deck of the boat. Micca jumped after him, Neypo following.

Neffafinnegal grabbed the edge of the hatch and swung himself feet-first into the dark cavity.

Neypo crouched on the boat's deck below the edge of the pier, hanging on to one of the smooth black lines that secured it to the pier. Micca put his legs into the hole. "Come on, Striver!" he called, and dropped into the boat.

Neypo waved in acknowledgment. One of the advancing men was a uniformed Officer, the other was Cresslu Tulio: a rebel, he now knew, one who had joined in the assault on the posted guards. And he was just as sure that the renegades' motivation was far worse than what he'd told Micca. There had been clues, hints, all week, but…

The rain suddenly increased and hammered the boat's deck. Over its noise Neypo heard another shout from the pier. Steadying himself again on the boat's line, he peeped over the edge of the pier.

Two more men were walking rapidly from shore to meet Cresslu… another Officer, and a tall, oddly dressed man — Tæfel Adinnegram.

Neypo reached up and lifted one of the boat's lines over the knob of stone that had secured it, then moved like a crab across the boat's deck. The waves were already pulling one end of it away from the pier. Neypo stretched over the water and plucked at the second line.

Yells came from the pier. They had seen him. Neypo got the second line free and tossed it into the water.

His shoes skittered over the wet, pitching deck. He fell on his side. The deck heaved again and Neypo slid toward the waves. A bodkin came spinning down from the pier and clattered on the deck.

Neypo flopped onto his stomach, arms and legs working as though he were swimming. His fingers caught the edge of the hatch. He dragged himself forward, reached the hole in the alien craft and tumbled into it headfirst.

Micca, who had just gathered courage to look out of the hatch again, saw the Striver coming and quickly got out of the way.

Neypo landed with a grunt of expelled breath. He sat up, holding his shoulder. "Where's the outlander?" he gasped. "Tell him to close the door!"

Before Micca could relay this the hatch swung to and sank into its socket. There was a hiss, and a sealing squeak. All light and sound from outside was gone.

Micca sat in a cramped space about as long as the boat's exterior, but not as wide. What light there was — warm, almost like candle-light — seemed to have its source somewhere forward of the hatch. To his left was an assemblage of complicated machinery — or not machin-ery, but something meant to sit in. Neffafinnegal was just crawling from where he had closed the hatch and now dropped himself into the couch-like space. Directly behind, Neypo crept cautiously into another similar cavity.

Ahead, at the end of the narrow aisle and a foot or two lower, there were two more of the couches, side by side. Micca crawled between them and eased himself in the one directly in front of the alien's.

The forward couches occupied a space surrounded by slanted, light-specked panels. Padded depressions or sockets cradled Micca's helmet and torso; he fumbled his legs into another set under one of the panels. He supposed the couch and the reclining posture it dictated were more comfortable than the slatted wooden bench on the cog he had taken to Hoiin, but the builders of this boat must have regarded its passengers more as cargo to be stuffed into the craft as compactly as possible than people who might like to walk around a little and enjoy their voyage.

Micca frowned. This was no time for such stupid observations. They weren't flying yet, or even sailing, and there were people after their blood outside — or the outlander's blood at least, and they'd take Micca for one now, too…even so, he thanked Wennoc for the windfall of the armored suit. He twisted his head and spoke in Harnish. "What are we waiting for? Let's go!"

"I'm not a pilot," Neffafinnegal said.

"So what? Nobody here is going to ask you for a certificate or license! There's people on the dock who are ready to kill us!"

"I don't think they can get in. Not unless they've got a radio or a 'cas-ing and know what to say."

Micca scowled in nervous frustration. "Striver!" he called, leaning out of his couch. "Would the people outside have any of the outlanders' machines?"

"Why do you ask?" Neypo said, also leaning into the aisle.

Didn't either of these idiots realize how desperate the situation was? "Neffafinnegal, the outlander, he says they can open the boat if they've got a broadcaster or they're wearing armor! What if they find the other suits at the Lodge?"

"I think we'll be all right for the time being," Neypo answered. "I have reason to believe we're no longer near the pier."

"Did you untie us before you came down?" Micca asked.

"I did. Afternoon storms always retreat to the north. Bottled inscriptions praising Wennoc's oceanic aspect that are cast into the sea here are commonly found as far up coast as Entapora."

Micca felt a little better. But he told the alien, "The Striver says we're drifting out to sea. We should fly this thing up the air a little, see where we are."

"We should wait for Sulawan to come back," Neffafinnegal said. Micca thought he sounded like a petulant child.

"Didn't you hear me? We're out on the sea! He's not coming!" Micca's helmet swiveled. "Can't you open a window or porthole or something? I want to see what's going on."

A snort from the alien was all the reply he got.

Micca fizzed with wrath and frustration. He twisted in the couch. The glass suit seemed more confining now that he wasn't walking around. The other Striver had said he'd been squeezed into a bottle. He had once seen the body of a baby pig that had been pickled in a jar of spirits, little snout and dead eyes pressed up against the glass.

"How do I get it off?" Micca asked the alien, trying to keep his hands still on his couch's armrests. "I want to take off the helmet, the headcasing."

A snort. "Tell it to let you go."

Micca tried not to gulp in his breaths too quickly. "Let go of my head," he whispered in Harnish, feeling foolish and panicky. He put his hands to the helmet, twisted and pulled.

"It won't come off!"

The alien got up and took the empty couch beside Micca's.

"Micca, what's the matter?" Neypo called.

Neffafinnegal observed him curiously. Micca breathed out. "Nothing," he said hopefully.

Neypo got out of his couch and took the one the outlander had left. He looked over Micca's headrest, staring at them suspiciously. Neffafinnegal was looking at Micca. "Your expedition didn't have any bodycasings, right?"

Micca's helmet shook.

"Do you know how to deal with any kind of machinery?"

"I know about electricity and radios. And water mills for sawing and grinding, and stills..."

"I guess I don't need to ask whether you've been initialized." Neffafinnegal reached out and tapped a pattern on Micca's wrist, then tapped another.

The armor froze as it had when Sulawan knocked him down. Before he could complain something pushed back his lips and worked itself between his teeth.

Pain like a burning wire sliced through his head. Micca squeezed his eyes shut and tried to bite his lip, but couldn't.

"What's happening?" Neypo called in alarm.

Micca suffered another, lesser spark of agony. Then a pleasant warmth washed from his scalp to his toes, and faded. His mouth was cleared and the armor relaxed.

"Everything's fine, Striver," he croaked doubtfully.

New lights appeared inside Micca's faceplate. A voice in his ears said something he didn't understand.

"That really hurt," he told the alien. "I feel like punching your face."

"The 'casing did it, not me," Neffafinnegal said innocently. "Mechanicals have to do that. It's their way of getting familiar so they can understand you better. Everybody has to be initialized if they're going to use machines. The 'casing you're wearing knows you now."

Micca thought the suit had gotten pretty familiar with him already. But his 'initialization' wasn't complete. He listened as the alien told him to think in a certain style, to put himself in a particular mood. Micca thought it sounded weird, like something Priest Palmer might do as he embarked on his meditations.

"What are you two doing?" the Striver demanded.

"He's teaching me about the boat," Micca said.

After three or four frustrating trials, an illuminated word appeared before Micca's eyes, telling him he had achieved the state of mind Neffafinnegal had described and that the suit had recognized him.

Then he memorized sound values for the fingers on his right hand (or left if so inclined, said Neffafinnegal), three or four for each, a chore made easier by the names the alien gave them. There were two rows of four spots on his wrist, not apparent except from the user's headcasing, each capable of reading a unique value from a finger; rolling his thumb over a patch to the side at the same time modified the basic value to give others. By skipping his fingers around, he was able to make enough letters to spell words in Harnish, if most of the vowels were left out. He saw it would take some practice to become easy with the method, but Neffafinnegal seemed to regard this tapping as the ordinary way to write, something any child would be familiar with. (Micca wondered how the alien would manage if given pen and paper and asked to write something.) He practiced the finger-words as his helmet spoke in response to his taps.

"If you people have such clever machines, why can't you just *talk* to them and say to Hinnioc to all this finger poking?"

Neffafinnegal shook his head. "That would be immoral, and dangerous too. We do talk to them a little bit, just simple things, or kids when they're learning, but you have to be careful not to break the fence between machines and people. There are a couple of old places where they didn't care about that, and now nobody goes there, and those who live there can't leave. Their machines don't remember that they're machines, and the people aren't real people anymore."

Micca sat still for a moment. He said, "So anyway, I finger out 'Head—Release', thinking 'Do It Thus', right?"

"Yes. Say it out loud if that helps at first; you'll be talking to yourself, not the 'casing."

Micca tapped out the word, thinking 'inpoa'. The body of the armor remained attached to him, but he felt his ears clear, and a mask he hadn't really been aware of before pulled away from his nose and lower face. The seal around his neck let go with a gasp, the collar loosened, and he pulled off the helmet.

Neypo exclaimed, "Micca! Don't give it to him!"

"I won't," Micca said in Eynnish. He drew in a breath. The odors inside the boat were unfamiliar, not necessarily pleasant, but interesting.

"I couldn't smell anything when I was wearing the helmet."

"So?" said the alien. "Sometimes things in the air can kill you or make you sick."

"What poison could there be in the air?"

"It can happen. And people can put it there."

"But how can you tell where you are if you can't smell? How would you know what kind of trees or crops are around, or what the food's like, or whether the people you meet are clean?"

The alien made an odd face. "Are you a dog?"

"A what?"

The alien shook his head and Micca gave it up. "Now what do we do?"

Neffafinnegal leaned over Micca to tap on the panel in front of him. "You wanted to look outside. Put your head back on."

"What? Why?"

"Or you can watch without it, but the view inside the 'casing is better."

Micca decided to leave his head uncovered for a while longer. Neffafinnegal fingered the console between their couches, then clucked his tongue.

"I can't raise a view," he said. "Ah, shit. I should have known. It's too quiet in here. Sulawan must have shut things down. That's why he tied us up to the dock. I'll have to turn on the engine. Warn that fellow back there. He might be surprised."

"We're going to open a window, Striver," Micca said over his shoulder in Eynnish. "Something's going to happen, but it'll be all right." So he hoped.

"What do you mean? What will happen?"

The alien tapped on the console. Evidently you didn't need a whole set of armor to do things, some things anyway, if you'd been initiated —

Neypo cried out. So did Micca. Long pads zipped out of slots over his shoulders and looped down under his armpits. Others appeared between his legs and curled over his hips. Micca took a deep breath, testing the straps.

Neypo called breathlessly, "Micca, Micca! I'm—you, too! We're all bound up!"

Micca felt foolish. The Striver had more reason to be startled than he did. "I'm fine," he said. "I think the boat means to keep us from falling out of our chairs."

"But Micca! Make sure he doesn't try to use a radio set—ask him if there is one!"

"Is there a radio in here? An...*avefactor*?" Micca quickly asked Neffafinnegal.

Neffafinnegal looked at him, brightened, and reached out to the panel over their knees.

Micca grabbed his arm. "Don't turn it on! The Eynnish, the killers, they'll take your Sulawan when he comes out of the water. They'll force him to tell them how to get at us. They'll follow us, they'll come out in boats and make him open the door, and then they'll torture us and murder us."

Neffafinnegal rapidly scanned the panel and found a glowing green bar. He tapped with his finger. The bar went red, and he expelled his breath.

"What's happening!" Neypo yelled behind him.

"What did you do?" Micca asked Neffafinnegal.

"I cut off the radio's guest reception."

"So nobody can broadcast to us?"

"They can try, but the lighter won't hear it. Nothing specifically addressed to us."

Micca turned. "The radio's dead, Striver. Neffafinnegal disabled it."

"Ah, excellent."

"So let's look outside now," Micca told Neffafinnegal.

Neffafinnegal worked his fingers on the panel. A low humming came from the wall to the right—where the boat's engine must be. Neffafinnegal tapped again.

Before the two couches, a broad oval cloud of pale light swam into existence, wrapping out and filling the forward part of the space. Images began to form, then cleared and sharpened. Waves lapped all around them; nearby, a big fish leapt into the air and submerged again.

Neypo and Micca shouted in unison, but the waves didn't soak them, and there was enough left visible of the boat's interior that they calmed down again.

The alien smiled at Micca. "I did it."

Micca slapped his arm in congratulations. "It looks like we've drifted out of the harbor," he told Neypo.

"As I had prayed," said Neypo. "And what a marvelous window—if you can call it a window!'

Neffafinnegal tapped. The image reformed and they saw what must be another area of water. Through the rain Micca made out the giant stone Strivers that guarded the harbor, not so large from here. But his warning to Neffafinnegal about boats had been prescient. Between the outlanders' boat and the stone Strivers came two long craft, oars on either side of them rising and falling.

"We didn't drift far enough, Striver! There's boats coming after us!"

"Yes, yes, I see them!"

A man stood up in the nearer one and waved both his arms.

Neypo reached ahead and grabbed Micca's arm. "It's Cresslu Tulio, I'm sure of it. They mean to tow us back and murder us all!"

Micca said quickly in Harnish, "You have to get us out of here!"

"I suppose I do," Neffafinnegal reluctantly agreed.

"What does he say?" Neypo shouted at the back of Micca's helmet.

"We're going to try and move the boat!"

Neypo wiped his forehead with his sleeve. "Good. Make for Siricu, or better, Parnala. Do you know where that is, Hin Parnala? Sail north of northeast, and keep a sharp eye out for the rocks at the Knees of Saimpu." The Striver pulled a surprisingly large flask from his coat, took a drink and offered it to Micca. "A tonic in our time of need."

Micca accepted it and took a good swallow…a basic but good corn. He passed the flask to the alien.

"Your 'casing has storage cells and an intake for liquids, you know," Neffafinnegal said nervously as he put Neypo's flask to his lips. "Just open your mouth and—"

The alien made a strange sound, sat up and sprayed his knees with spirits. He shoved the flask at Micca. "Take this away," he gasped.

"Then get up. We have to change places." He told Micca how to release his bindings.

But Neffafinnegal didn't move.

"What's the matter?" said Micca.

"I can't," he said faintly. "I'm not rated."

"What's the matter? Do you need my helmet to do it?"

"No, that's not it. I told you before, I'm not rated, not certified. It would be wrong. And if I think about it any more I think I'll vomit.'"

"Micca, they're getting closer by the minute! Tell him we must move!" Neypo called.

Head spinning, Micca wet his lips. "It turns out he can't drive it without a helmet."

And before Neypo could react he said in Harnish, "Tell *me* how to do it!"

Neffafinnegal immediately became calmer. "All right. You're right. *Somebody* has to. Put on your head. It'll be easier for the lighter to sort us out since we've both been interacting with it."

Micca couldn't believe it. He put on his helmet, waited a moment as it connected itself, sucked in a deep breath. He took hold of the grips at the ends of his armrests. Neffafinnegal told him what words to tap that would let the boat hear him and respond. "You tilt both for direction, push or pull that one for elevation," he said. "Twist that one for pitch and cant, this one for thrust, for speed. Use the lines of dots on the receptor panel instead of your wrist. That's how Sulawan does it. The layout is the same."

Micca's helmet bobbed. Neffafinnegal said three words, and Micca carefully tapped them on the receptor between their couches. His helmet showed two blue dots. The engine's humming rose in pitch.

Neypo said breathlessly, "Can you do it, Micca? It's now or never! One of Tulio's thugs is climbing aboard with a heavy cable!"

"I see him…" The view in Micca's helmet was even more realistic than the boat's 'window'.'"

"Are you ready?" said Neffafinnegal. "Lift now, slowly at first."

Micca pulled back on the left-hand rod.

The water fell away slowly and smoothly. Micca blew out a heavy breath. He glanced at the alien, who was smiling like an idiot.

Outside, the Officers in the boats jumped up at the sight, upsetting their oars. Micca saw the man who had climbed onto the boat, just a few feet away from him, rendered by the helmet as hanging unsupported in midair. The man opened his mouth in a scream and pressed himself down, groping for something to hold on to.

"Start on a horizontal path," said Neffafinnegal.

Micca moved the rod and the boat slipped ahead. The man above seemed to stare directly down at him, eyes horrible with fear.

"Why doesn't he jump off?" Micca said. "Striver, we've got to tell him to jump off." Micca switched to Harnish and started to ask the alien if he could send his voice outside.

Neypo leaned forward, grabbed Micca's arm and cried, "No! We must not speak to them or listen to their words!"

Micca jerked away from Neypo's hand, and his grip on the control rods changed.

They were all pushed back into their couches. The man outside went flying, tumbling through the ten yards of air that now separated them from the sea.

In an instant ten yards were a hundred, a thousand. Micca worked the rods, trying to steady the boat. It dipped forward, then dropped like an arrow loosed at the sea. Red numbers raced under his nose and the boat jabbered a flood of words into Micca's ears. Pitching images of sky and water skidded before his eyes, blurring, dipping, jumping up again, and then there was a quick glimpse of the brick hills and tiled domes of Hoiin. He pulled the rods. A line of trees swung up and hurtled toward them.

Neypo groaned. Neffafinnegal shouted. Micca desperately twisted the rods.

The boat spun. The trees returned to their proper places, then vanished as the boat popped up, too fast, too far, into a sky stained too early with darkness.

Micca pushed the rods. The sky brightened. Wennoc's blue and green face rose before him and bloated to fill his vision. Tree tops, leaves—

There was a brief, grinding roar. A deep silence fell.

Someone croaked in the darkness. Micca tried to reach the control panel, but his armor was frozen.

16. THE WATER-MEADOW

Winetra Odé and her younger children, Winnet and Tympo, were just visible through the press of people, huddled at the back of the barge. The narrow craft already rode low in the water of the canal, and the guards directing the evacuation were forced to threaten the anxious crowd with their batons. "Be calm!" one of them shouted. "There's no immediate danger for you here! I'm sure more boats will be coming!"

On the bank a young woman, small and well formed, fretfully twisted the handle of her parasol. She wore her pale hair in two gathered braids on either side of her head. Her face was often, though not always, pleasant. It had been very pleasant for the hour or two she strolled through the fairgrounds, stopping to chat with friends and admirers, tasting ices and sampling the fare at the food booths. She had worn her best spring frock, a wide-brimmed beribboned hat, and little slippers that were both comfortable and the height of style.

"No danger!" she cried, and took Gillensa's hand. "I myself saw that man hit the Mendicant with the end of his bodkin. He was bleeding! I'm not panicking for the fun of it. What an awful day."

Gillensa patted her friend's hand. "You're right, it's been dreadful. But we're out of it now."

Swannet wasn't convinced. "We're hardly more than a mile from the fairgrounds. The countryside is probably teeming with these insurgents or whatever they are."

Noler Hunsacup, Swannet's chief admirer, came up, elbowing a man out of his way. As a Cadet, he had worn his uniform to the Fair: a stiff, high-collared jacket of military twill, a red kilt, greaves and nailed boots; a bronze club hung from his belt. He nodded to the women. As he did, the visor of his ceremonial helmet snapped down, showing a snarling bronze face. He yanked the helmet from a head of tight curls.

"Why don't you simply get rid of that ugly thing?" Swannet said impatiently. "It's been doing that to you all day."

"It's official equipment. I'm responsible for it."

"Is there any news, Noler?" Gillensa asked.

Noler settled the helmet back onto his head. "Mostly rumors. One of my colleagues heard that there were murderers cutting people's throats in a booth near the grandstand. Officers went to investigate and supposedly there was quite a fight. All the trouble makers are supposed to be from Hoiin, though. Henso swears he saw one of our own Officers club the Grand Fellow—called old Westo a heretic, if you can feature that."

Gillensa said, "I hope this doesn't set off some kind of confrontation between the cities, wherever the trouble makers are from. The last time that—"

"What about the barges going to Parhutni?" Swannet interrupted. "Are there more coming?"

Oxen plodded down the towpath, and the craft carrying the Odés slid away. Noler shook his head. "The canal man said that was the last one."

Gillensa patted Swannet's hand again. "At least your mother and sisters got onto a barge too. Parhutni's only a couple of miles from our place at Tamanello. They'll join my mother and go there with her."

"But it's not just a couple of miles from *here*!" Swannet complained.

"It may take a while, but we'll get there," Gillensa assured her. "It's really a charming little place, and we have four guest rooms, two of them with their own breezy verandas. You can have a nice bath as soon as we arrive, and then Rigna and Trimlait will give us all supper."

"But what about brigands along the road?"

Noler slapped his bodkin in the palm of his hand. "Commander Macci said I could accompany you as military escort. We'll be fine."

Swannet regarded him. Noler was fit and stocky, but he was only one Cadet. "Where's your Harnishman gotten to?" she asked Gillensa.

"I think I see him—Samma! Over here!"

A tall man wearing dark lenses turned, but it wasn't Samma. He arched his eyebrows and strode away, dragging a pair of wailing children by their hands.

"Drat," said Gillensa in a small voice. "Where could he be? We really should be going."

"Yes, the sooner the better," said someone beside her.

Gillensa spun around. "Samma! When did you sneak up?"

He shrugged. "Did your mother and the kiddies get off?"

"Yes, on the last barge."

"I guess we walk then. But take a look at this. A couple of kids were running around back there passing them out."

He handed her a strip of paper. The type was smudged at the corner. Swannet and Noler joined them, looking over Gillensa's shoulder.

ATTENTION ALL!

CITIZENS OF HIN HOINA
and our
HONORED GUESTS!

The Reorganized Striving Lodge of Hin Hoina by the
Bay and associated municipal Authorities offer their
heartfelt Apologies for the late Disturbances!
The Aforesaid deeply regret any Inconvenience suffered
by either Residents or our valued Visitors!
An Attempt by a Gang of *desperate* and *subversive Criminals*
to upset and disturb the Peace of our magnificent Fair, as
well as the proper Governance of the City,

HAS BEEN THWARTED:
PEACE IS RESTORED!

However: It is with deep Regret that we must
declare, in the Interest of the public Safety,
the Fair to be at an End.
All Persons are required by the Authorities to return to
their Homes at once! Tune in to the Voice of Hoiin for

Important Announcements!

Those not possessed of an Æther-Receiver are instructed
to visit Neighbors, local Shops or Taverns so equipped!

~

Note Well: Anyone found committing *unlawful Acts* or
spreading about *seditious Rumors* will be
Summarily Dealt With under the Emergency Rules!

~

by the Hand of
M Ompito, Str 4°
for the Committee on Reorganization.

~

Word of Hoiin Printery, 25–29 Ymietsy Prospect.

"You see the 'Reorganized' bit, Gillensa?" Samma said. "Something
strange is happening. They put this out in an awful hurry, too. The ink's
still wet."

"Sounds like a coup!" said Noler.

"Hoiin doesn't indulge in coups," said Gillensa. "Parnala, maybe…
but I know that Micsin Ompito's only second degree, and this calls him
a fourth. Something funny *is* going on…I wonder where Father is, and
what he's doing."

Now it was Swannet's turn to provide comfort. "I'm sure he's with
my father, Glensy, and they're probably the men really responsible for
putting down the insurrection or whatever's happened. They must
have known something was going on, that something needed to be
dealt with at the Lodge, or they'd have been with us at the Fair."

Gillensa smiled. "I imagine you're right, Swanny. There's been an
awful lot of whispering, secret notes and late meetings this past week.
They must have been ready for whatever it was. But this is unprec-
edented. I can't understand what was so serious that the Strivers would
use violence against each other."

"Let's get out of here before we find out the hard way," Samma said.

"Oh, can't we just go home, like the handbill says?" Swannet said,
looking at the sky. "It looks like it's already raining out over the Bay."

Gillensa shook her head. "Rain or not, I don't think it would be a
good idea to get any closer to town right now."

❧

Noler said he would go downtown anyway to see if his help was needed to subdue the rebels or whomever had caused the trouble, but Swannet reminded him of his instructions from Commander Macci, and the four of them started down the tow path beside the canal.

Clouds filled the sky, flying in from the west, but they spent themselves over the Bay and city and only a few sprinkles fell here. There were other people behind and ahead of them on the path, all Fair-goers to judge by their clothes and their bags of trinkets, snacks and souvenirs. Swannet was complaining about the rough surface of the path ruining her slippers when a woman ahead of them shouted, pointing at the sky.

Everyone looked up, swiveling their heads. "What?" said Noler. "I don't see anything."

Samma called, waving his eye-glasses, "Over there! East of north!"

Everyone's heads turned again.

After a minute Gillensa said, "I didn't see anything but a little dark streak."

"I did too," said Noler. "But it's gone now."

"A falling star?" said Swannet.

"I don't think so," said Samma. "I didn't see any light. A meteor would be all made of fire even in the daylight, wouldn't it? "

Others along the path who had seen it agreed with this description. One man said it was an umiot, but most discounted that. Another had heard a high whining from it. The woman who had first called out said it must be a big skate pulled out of the Bay by a water spout. Others thought a piece of the moon had broken away and fallen into Wennoc; the moon was mostly green, but the inside must be dirt and stone, which had dull colors. One man who had observed the moon the night before said he thought to have noticed a notch in its disk.

They walked on, and the sun began to sink. Most of the others on the path seemed to be headed for Parhutni, which was on the south shore of Lake Oha. There were several large resorts there which would be mostly empty this early in the year.

Tamanello, the Odés' summer house, was situated on a smaller lake east of Oha. Gillensa persuaded them to cut across country, which she said would save them at least a couple of miles.

The lane she chose wandered off into a small wood. "But it can't have been from the moon," Swannet said, continuing their conversation. "It hasn't risen yet."

"Maybe it came off yesterday and flew along for a while before it fell," Noler suggested.

Samma nodded. "You might have a point. Wasn't there something in the paper a while back about a new star being sighted?"

"That was almost a month ago," said Noler. "But maybe so. Maybe it finally burned out and fell."

They came out of the trees and walked on.

"Gillensa," Samma said, pausing. "Where would you say your lake was from here? We can see a good stretch of country right now."

She climbed onto a stone gate post and looked into the gathering dusk. "I can't see anything of the lake yet, but I'm sure it's in this direction."

They walked another hour, and the others stopped bothering Gillensa about her knowledge of the countryside.

It was nearly dark when Samma suddenly stopped. "Do you see that over there? That broken willow?"

Gillensa turned and stared. "Over there? Yes, I think I see it…do you suppose that's where whatever it was came to earth?"

"Seemed like this general direction…there haven't been any severe storms lately, and that tree looks like it took quite a beating."

Noler said, "I think our first priority is to reach the Odé's place."

Gillensa got down from the post and joined Samma. "It's just a bit out of our way," she said. "Yes, I'm sure this time! And think of the adventure! We might bring a piece of the heavens back."

Swannet was almost in tears. "That might be wicked. Or dangerous!"

"If there's anything left the locals will probably have carried it off by tomorrow," Samma said. "I think it's our duty to see if that's the spot. The lecturers at the University would give their eye teeth to examine a piece of the moon, or even a flying sea beast. The newspaper will write us up. We'll probably be interviewed on the Voice! 'Despite being traumatized by events at the Fair, intrepid band of young folk makes important scientific discovery! Their story, related by Miss Olinom, commences below.'"

Swannet smiled weakly.

Noler raised his club. "I think you're right. There might be locals who'll mess with whatever came down. They'll probably try to break it up and sell souvenirs."

They set off across a fallow field and found a lane that seemed to lead in the right direction. Cottonwoods bordered it and their seed-fluffs floated in the air. They walked between the parapets of an old causeway, arching a hundred yards on into a bridge. The scent of shade-blooming flowers wafted up from dark water that flowed between the roots of the trees.

Beyond the bridge three farmhands stood by a stone wall, looking out at a water-meadow. They glanced at the newcomers, then back at the meadow.

The flooded expanse was narrow at this end, bounded on three sides by trees. The sun had set, but at the far end of the meadow the travelers could see the damaged tree, a huge willow, half its limbs on the ground. The wood of the broken trunk was bright, and its leaves looked fresh. A number of younger trees lay bent or broken behind the willow, and between them and the willow, a sprawling mound of raw earth.

They approached the farmhands, Noler going first. The three men wore gray smocks and yellow straw hats, the hired workers of some plantation; private farmers wore better boots and felt hats. One of them held a long-handled spade.

"Nice evening," said Noler.

"Ar. Moon, she augurs bright tonight," one of them replied in a heavy lake-country accent.

"Going after mudrunners, are you?" Noler asked him.

"That be not of your minding," the man said. "But mayhap *you* comes to dig after they mudrunners?"

"Ar, they do look to be diggers," said another.

"Ar, verily," laughed the third.

The first farmer smiled broadly at his companions. "The Cadet can surely dig well, what with all his mighty thews."

"But arly, I didn't know they little mudrunners hereabouts was of an importance for to send us a Cadet to help," said the second farmer.

"Cadet'll protect Honorable Siitala's meadow," said the first, raising his smock to urinate over the parapet.

Swannet gasped. Noler snapped down his visor. He stepped forward, knuckles white on his bodkin. "And maybe the Cadet will punish your impertinence."

Samma stepped in front of Noler, barring his way. He fumbled at Noler's tunic and pulled out a flat, silver-bound flask. He tasted its contents; a pallid essence of dandelion. He held it out to the first farmer.

The farmer looked suspiciously at it, then put it to his lips. After a sip he said, "Dainty drink, but this one's hospitable for a city boy."

The others tasted Noler's spirits, muttering, "Ar, ar."

The first picked up a heavy jug and handed it to Samma. "Since we has our Tuvimat, we brung some holy-day's tonic," the farmer said.

Samma had intended just a neighborly sip, but he decided to show them what he was made of, and swallowed a searing mouthful of raw Eynnish corn liquor.

He blinked, but didn't choke or gasp. The farmers nodded admiringly.

"So," Samma asked them. "If there are no mudrunners, what's so interesting in the meadow?"

The first farmer answered. "Just after the lunching time we be up nigh the north bean field taking of our Tuvimat jollities. Then comes a whistle, and a noise like a great blowing of peat."

Gillensa leaned near Samma. "He means a marsh-gas explosion under the ground."

The farmer continued. "Honorable, he sends me and Corn and Tosti out to check there wasn't no fire to burning under the meadow."

Now one of the other farmers spoke. "There's no fire to be sure; Honorable's no dirt-sense. But we sees yon stone…"

"Where was no stone before," the first went on. "We starts to dig round about it. Tosti here, he stands up, hears something under the stone, he says, but I'm thinking Tosti's senses be atook by they siintimin, up in the airy parts making ready for their night-flying. But then somewhat—well, somewhat moves under my hoof, you see. We'll be having a break, I tells the boys; we'll wait on the lane for a spell, says I."

"Ar!" said the one called Tosti. "You should see old Simpte jump and jig, like Sirrah Mudrunner clumb up his leg! Ha ha!"

Samma stood for a minute looking at the far end of the meadow. He took off his shoes and stockings and hung the shoes around his neck. "Can I borrow your shovel?" he asked Corn.

The farmer gave it to him. Samma waded out into the meadow.

"He'll be stung by mudrunners!" Swannet cried.

"Nar, there be too much fresh water for them hereabouts, now as I thinks more on't," said Simpte.

"If it was really a peat-blow, there might be gas hanging over the water," said Noler.

"You go a few steps after him then, and drag him back if he collapses," Gillensa said, waving him on.

Samma walked carefully, poking under the water with the spade, but the meadow was quite flat and the flood that covered it was only a few inches deep. He looked back to see the Cadet following him, carrying his boots but still wearing his greaves.

They crossed the middle of the water-meadow; if by chance there were mudrunners here, they'd be closer to the tree roots at its edges. But a skinny green and black snake glided over the water, and Samma stopped. "It isn't a noxious one," he heard Noler say from behind him.

"You mean there *are* noxious ones somewhere else?"

"Don't you have any in Harna?"

Samma shook his head. His curiosity reasserted itself, and he went on, walking out of the water beside the giant willow, or what was left of it.

Almost directly behind it and spreading out to one side was a heap of damp earth. Three or four smaller trees lay flat or tipping away from it. A flat ledge of stone emerged from the mound, angling up, out of the earth, almost two yards of it hanging free, pointing away from the willow.

Noler joined Samma. "That's no peat-blow," he said.

They both turned at a thin call from the direction of the lane. The three farmers were still there, watching from the lane as Gillensa splashed toward the willow. Swannet was some way behind, standing with her hands over her mouth. "Oh, what is that?" she cried.

Noler went out and guided them to the willow. Gillensa was fascinated by the ledge of stone. "It looks as though it was cut and polished, made by men."

Swannet stood beside the willow. "I don't think there are really people in the moon."

Samma scrambled up the pile of displaced earth. He tapped the stone with his spade; it rang like metal against stone, or almost like metal on stone. He touched it with his finger. "It's not hot. Not cool, either."

Noler furrowed his brows. "You know, after all I don't see how this fell from the sky. Things like that are more round, or like clinkers from a furnace. More likely it came up, not down. Over the years frost heave or bog gas under the meadow might have pushed it out."

Samma frowned. "If so, it came out mighty quickly."

"I wonder if there might have been a house, or even a town, here at one time, so long ago the earth has completely covered it up," Gillensa said thoughtfully. "It shows you how little we know, how much we forget. That little stream over there might have been a straight, bricked-in canal. This stone might have been the door of one of the Heresiarchs' grim fortresses."

"Don't mention them," Swannet said, looking askance at the rising moon. "It's bad luck!"

Gillensa also climbed onto the stone, ignoring Swannet's pleas for caution. "Let's see if there are any inscriptions — oh, wouldn't father love to see this! We'll have to bring him here as soon as things have settled down."

"It's getting later and later," Swannet cried. "We have to *go*!"

Samma started clearing dirt at the lower end of the stone. Gillensa bent with her hands on her knees, studying its surface. Samma heaved another spadeful of earth away. Something tickled his bare foot. He slowly stood upright, not moving otherwise. Then he felt a thin line described across the bottom of his left foot, like crawling sand, or a little puffing of air.

Samma leapt from the stone with a yelp and slid down the hill of earth. Gillensa scrambled off after him. They stood side by side, clutching each other's arms.

"Yar-o!" one of the farmers called from across the meadow. "What befalls?"

"What happened?" Noler demanded, clutching his bodkin. Swannet stood quaking behind the willow.

"I thought something moved," Samma said softly. He approached the stone but didn't climb onto it. He suddenly moved his head closer, hand to his ear.

He turned to Gillensa. "I can hear something."

Gillensa made a sign with her fingers and came a little closer.

A small voice, low and dismal, almost like the buzz of an insect, came out of the earth: "Get us out!"

They both retreated. "What do we do?" Samma whispered to Gillensa.

Swannet had seen enough to send her splashing across the meadow, Noler close behind. The farmers took notice of their flight and sprinted off down the lane.

Samma swallowed, and swallowed again. He bent an inch nearer the pile of earth. "What do you want?" he said. "Who are you?"

A sound came from where Samma had been digging, a repeating sequence of soft thumps and airy gasps.

"Get us out!" said the buzzing voice. "Is there dirt on top? Get the dirt away!"

After a minute Samma climbed on top of the stone again. He scraped more earth from the place he had felt the tickle on his foot. The rising moon helped him recognize a rectangle outlined on the flat surface. As he watched, grains of earth puffed away from the engraved line. The lines widened, and then a thick square canted silently up from the stone. A few clods of earth fell into the cavity under it, and warm light shone up from the hole in the stone.

A voice, different from the first, issued from the hole: "Don't open it! The fishes will eat us!"

"*Gangen io, ecomered!*" said another voice from the hole.

"Harnish?" Samma whispered, bewildered. He turned to Gillensa. "They sound human, but—"

Gillensa gave a little scream. The thing that boosted itself out of the stone was hardly human at all. A shout came from its faceless head: "eSamma!"

"Wennoc," Samma hissed. "I'm come for!"

Gillensa stood flattened against the trunk of the willow. Samma scrambled back, fell from the stone and lay on his back in the dirt.

The creature jumped after him. A fluid reflection of the rising moon crossed its body. It knelt, planting its knees on either side of Samma's chest, and seized both his arms. "I thought you were at the Fair, back in Hoiin!" it boomed.

"Let me go!" Samma croaked.

It stood, pulling Samma up at the same time. With a hiss and a pop, like a jar of preserves being opened, the thing pulled off its head.

Samma's eyes opened wide. "You—what are—how'd you get in there?"

His brother's grinning face regarded him from between unnaturally bulky shoulders. "The boat or the war-suit?"

"Boat?" Samma echoed.

"But how did *you* get *here*?" Micca asked. He blinked as though trying to clear his eyes, then squinted. "Where are we, anyway?"

"I, I—we're in the country...the Fair, there was trouble at the Fair. We were on the way to Tamanello. The Odés' cottage. We saw..."

"Don't I know you?" said Gillensa, coming slowly toward them. "Yes, it is, it's Micca Mora! *What* in the—"

Then she stepped back. Another thick, dully gleaming man rose out of the stone, this one unhelmeted, but strange to her. He sat with his legs over the edge of the stone and surveyed the dark meadow with a forlorn expression.

Gillensa turned at a gruff call from the water-meadow. "Ahoy! How now yonder?"

"Noler? Come back! Samma's brother from Harna was under the stone!"

The Cadet slogged through the water. He hung back, still in the water, staring at Micca and the other glass man squatting on the stone. "They came from Harna?" he said.

"From the city," said Micca. "From the harbor, at Hoiin."

Gillensa peered into the gloom. "Where is Swannet?"

"I told her to stay by the lane until I investigated," Noler said, staring in wonder at Micca and the alien. "That's pretty unusual gear you're wearing. How'd you get under there? Did those suits keep you from being crushed?"

"*In* there, not under there," Micca said, looking suspiciously at the

Cadet. He turned to Samma. "It's not a stone. It's a machine, a flying boat!"

They all gaped at him.

A cry came from the hatch in the stone. "Micca!" came a weak voice. "Where have you gotten to?"

Micca said something to Neffafinnegal, and they both dropped into the hatch. In a minute the Striver Neypo's head showed in the hatch. He stared at the dark trees, up at the stars. "Praise Wennoc!" he murmured. "I thought we were in the deeps of the sea."

He crawled shakily out and dropped to the ground, Neffafinnegal and Micca coming after him. Neypo stood for a moment, looking around, then went off to the willow and lay down on his back under it. He knit the grass in his fingers and closed his eyes. Gillensa ran to him and took his hand.

"The Striver's been drinking essence," Micca told Samma in a low voice.

Then he spoke in Harnish to the alien. "Finna, this is my brother and his friends. Come on down here."

"Don't call me that," said Neffafinnegal, but he shuffled up slowly and joined the others. He looked at Samma. "My name is Astin Neffafinnegal, Foreign Outreach Mission."

Samma stared back at him, then mumbled in awkward Harnish, "Heartily met to, uh… goodly to meet thee. I am hetting myself Samael Robigæn Mora."

"You don't speak as well as my comrade here."

Samma backed away from him, smiling and nodding. "How doest thou? Myself, I am so fine."

Gillensa leapt up and confronted them. "What in the world are you boys saying? What's this all about?"

Noler frowned. "Sounds a bit like the way the people talk out east."

Gillensa gave him a dismissive glance. "Rubbish."

"We were downtown, at the harbor," Micca told her. "We just barely got away from the rebel Officers, and then I flew us here."

"The insurgents were downtown too? And you *flew*? Where are your wings?"

Micca smiled broadly at her. "I don't need wings. We got here in about three minutes, and we took the long way. Must have been half way to the moon before we came down. We've been sitting in there all afternoon. But why are you all out here in the country?"

"We were on our way to our cottage, at Tamanello, and…"

Neypo's voice came faintly from under the tree. "I'm afraid this is no time for a holiday, daughter."

"But father, we *had* to leave, on official instructions from the Lodge. There was trouble in the city."

"Yes, yes," Neypo sighed in the dark. "I'll explain things later."

"I don't think he knows what happened at the Fair," Gillensa whispered to Samma.

"And I don't think he's in a condition to hear about it just now," Samma whispered back.

Micca set his helmet on the boat. "The Striver was pretty upset after we came down so hard out of the sky, and I think he hurt his shoulder. It was a lucky thing he had that flask with him. I guess Finna and I were rattled too, but we only had a few sips."

Gillensa tried to look at Neypo's wound, but he pushed her away.

Micca went on. "But it was lucky we got away. There were two boat-loads of thugs coming after us —"

"Micca," Neypo called. He was sitting up now. "Remember your vows… and look, see where your negligence has led!" He pointed a finger shakily at the alien.

Neffafinnegal stood beside the boat, holding Micca's helmet. He seemed to understand the cause of Neypo's upset and handed the helmet to Micca. "A weird bug tried to crawl into it," Neffafinnegal told him. "It looks like the original settlers' terraforming wasn't completely successful."

Micca didn't understand him, but the alien pointed to a flat gray teardrop as big as his thumb, a buzzing thing with many tiny legs. It swarmed down the side of the boat and wriggled into the damp earth. Noler hurried over and stamped on it.

"And the farmhands claimed there were no mudrunners here!" said Gillensa.

"It wasn't a very big one," Micca said, but he inspected the inside of his helmet and knocked it hard on the boat before he put it on.

Noler looked him over. "Where did you two get that armor, anyway? Do you need to wear it when you go inside the stone? But the Striver doesn't..."

"Did you get the war-suit from the Lodge's visitors in Hoiin?" Samma asked cannily. "Is your friend one of them? Why does he speak the old language? Doesn't he know Eynnish?"

"He's from another world, Sam! Actually, more than one, though he himself is just from one. Finna says—"

"Micca!" Neypo called. "Your vows!"

"What did you say?" Gillensa eagerly asked Micca. "Does anyone have a pencil? I'm going to sit you down right now and—"

"Daughter! I forbid it! Ask him no questions, not now and not later."

Just then Swannet came stepping through the water, holding up the hems of her dress and calling out uncertainly. "There are people in the lane, asking about the falling star."

Then she saw Micca and clapped her hands over her mouth.

Noler caught her and held her as her feet tried to propel her backwards. Samma said, "It's only my brother."

Helmeted, armor-clad Micca advanced, ready to shake hands. Swannet screamed.

Noler slapped her face. Swannet was abruptly silent. Noler told Micca, "You just be careful of how you frighten my lady!"

Swannet slowly raised her hand and touched her cheek. "I am *not* your lady, you brute!"

"I thought you were taking a fit," Noler said. "The Cadet's Manual says to do that."

"Cadet," Neypo murmured. "If there are curiosity seekers nearby, go warn them off. Tell them the Lodge has declared this area off-limits."

Noler ran off. In a minute they heard faint shouting: "You, clear out of here! Yes, I don't care who you are! Lodge orders! Be about your business!"

There were outraged demands and questions, but several dark shapes finally moved away down the lane.

Samma glanced at Neypo, then stood close to Micca. "Whatever delusions you're suffering from, I still want to hear what you know about the rebellion."

"Did you hear about the fighting at the fairgrounds when you were downtown?" Gillensa whispered.

Micca shook his head. "No!"

Noler rejoined them. "It wasn't those farmers. Two men and a woman, spoke like they were from Hoiin. One claimed to be a Mendicant. People running from the Fair, and I suppose they saw the thing come down like we did."

Neypo didn't appear to have heard him. He lay peacefully again under the tree, hand clutching a willow leaf.

Swannet, still angry, scowled at Noler as she approached Neypo. If she was surprised to see the Striver lying under a tree in the depths of rural Eynna and stinking of strong spirits, she didn't say so. She put her hands to her face and bowed politely to him. "Has my father gone on to the cottage then?" she inquired.

Neypo stirred. "Swannet? Is that you, lass? I must tell you something, my dear. The Striver Caihar has...your father has been called away, called away on Lodge business."

"How tiresome," Swannet said.

She looked around. Micca now showed her a human head and the kind of foolish grin she'd expect from a rustic simpleton. Another glass-clad young man sat cross-legged on the mysterious stone. He appeared to be dazed and lost, but somehow his expression conveyed an air of mysterious sophistication. Swannet said, "I think introductions are in order, Glensy."

17. NIGHT IN
THE MEADOW

Samma brought his brother to Swannet, who nodded to Micca with a formal smile. Samma turned doubtfully to Neffafinnegal. Micca told Swannet his name, and that he was with the Foreign Outreach. "He can't speak like we do."

Swannet looked curiously at the alien. "What an innovative hair style he has, with the little peak in front. And he's dumb? How sad!"

Neffafinnegal wandered off a couple of yards, stopping to examine something at the edge of the flooded meadow.

"He can talk," Micca said. "It's just that he doesn't know how to speak Eynnish."

"What is he, feeble minded?" Noler asked.

Micca said, "He's probably smarter than some around here."

Noler laughed. "You're right. It takes a lot of intelligence to make mud pies."

Micca frowned. But Neffafinnegal did indeed seem to be playing in the mud at the edge of the flooded meadow. "What are you doing?" Micca called.

Neffafinnegal held what appeared to be a bunch of muddy leaves. "Food."

The Striver roused himself. "What's the outlander doing, Micca?"

"I think he found some wild cress or something."

"He must be a botanist," Gillensa said. "I thought he looked like the scientific type."

Neypo raised himself on one elbow. "It seems that Neffafinnegal functioned as the outlanders' cook. Didn't he tell you as much, Micca?"

"A cook!" said Noler.

"Victual Procurement and Preparation Specialist is his actual title," said Micca.

"Well, in any case, he's showing some sense," Neypo said, sighing as he leaned back. "Why don't you help him and see if you can catch a fish or an eel, as well, and we can have some supper."

"Supper?" said Swannet in a frightened voice. "They'll give us supper at your cottage, won't they Striver?"

"The cottage?" said Neypo, propping himself up again. "Are we so near Tamanello? Well, I'm sure it would be pleasant enough there, but it's dark now, my dear, and I'm afraid we must stay here tonight. I don't want you wandering about unescorted, and it's essential that I guard the flying raft, and the outlander with it, until other arrangements can be made. Meanwhile life goes on, and just now we're in need of supper."

Swannet was distressed about spending the night in the meadow, but Neypo appeared to have made up his mind. He folded his hands over his belly and closed his eyes, apparently comfortable where he was for the time being.

Micca thought about starting to dig out the boat — there was a spade lying near the hill their abrupt landing had thrown up — but he decided that although he wasn't particularly hungry right now he would be eventually. Neffafinnegal had by now gathered a small heap of things he considered edible. Micca didn't want to eat fish, especially not eels, but some kind of meat would be good, and the trees around the meadow looked promising.

He spoke to Samma about it, who said that he was very hungry. Micca put his helmet on. He sifted through what he remembered of Neffafinnegal's instructions, and after some trial persuaded the helmet to exaggerate what light was available. It was also capable of displaying other qualities of the world outside that Micca didn't recall or care about right now.

Samma followed him as he crept along between the tress on the south side of the meadow. "How can you move so easily in such a thick, heavy looking thing?" he whispered.

"Quiet!" came faintly from Micca's helmet. He had also learned to control the volume it used to send out his voice.

He suddenly crouched, then lunged forward and caught a brown and white tree-hen with his hands. It battered his faceplate with its wings as it tried to escape, but Samma grabbed it and wrung its neck. Another hen squawked and flapped away. Micca sprang after it, falling flat on his belly, arms outstretched, and caught it too. He passed the bird to Samma, who dispatched it as efficiently as the first.

"You won't need a bow anymore," Samma said. "Besides moving like a mudrunner, that suit must have a pig's nose inside!"

"Well, they did more or less just stand there waiting for me. I suppose they don't get many people going after them over here in Eynna. And yes, I can see really well in here, but I can't smell anything at all."

"I can't see your eyes, I can't even see your face. How can you see out?"

Micca shrugged. "I don't know. But I can see out of it as if I had the best eye-glasses. And it magnifies the light somehow."

"Amazing. It doesn't look very comfortable, though. What do you do when you want to have a pee? Does it open up down there?"

Micca looked at his crotch. "Not that I know of. Neffafinnegal said you have to relax and let go, and it gets drawn off somewhere. I couldn't do it at first, but then I pretended I was in the water—you know, like when you're swimming in a lake."

Samma laughed uneasily. "I'd rather aim at a tree."

They walked back to the broken willow, and now Samma caught a hen. He said, "This reminds me of home, when we'd go up in the woods with grandpa. But our hunting leathers were nothing like that thing. I'll bet there's no wild pig that could gore you wearing that. And that stone! I can't believe your story, or your weird friend's story, but I can't come up with a better explanation."

"I can't really believe it either, but it's all here to see. There's nothing in Wennoc like any of it. Not now, anyway."

"What do you mean, not now?"

"You remember the Beyalmer stories?"

"Fairy tales."

"Like this?" Micca said, running his hand over the raised end of the boat as they walked by it. "Wait till I take you up in it."

"Isn't it wrecked?"

"Finna thinks it's fine. As soon as we get some more of the dirt moved away, it'll fly again."

"Aren't you afraid to try it again after it crashed?"

Micca wondered...no, he wasn't. "It doesn't scare me. I had time to do some practicing after we came down. There's a set of step-by-step instructional pictures built into it, and Finna found a way to make it seem like we were really in the air for a while. It's like play-acting, to train pilots. Yes, I definitely want to try it again, look down and see the world like a bird does."

When they returned with the birds Noler was kneeling on the ground on the other side of the boat, nursing a fire. Besides the cress, Neffafinnegal had collected some white-stemmed vegetables and a heap of young leeks. The Eynnish were happy at first to hear they had something to add to the vegetables, but no fish was forthcoming and they looked away as Samma used the Cadet's knife to gut and flay the hens; it would take too long to pluck and roast them.

Neffafinnegal, too, was repelled by the hens, but muttered something about 'When in Roma' and rapidly cut the meat into little pieces. Noler went to the lane to fill his helmet with clean water from the stream, intending to boil up a soup, as he had been taught at the Cadets' camp-outs, but Gillensa made him give it to the alien. Neffafinnegal poured out the water, gingerly took what fat he could find from the birds, threw it into the helmet and set it over the fire. The bits of meat followed, hissing and sizzling. Then he added the vegetables and a dollop of pungent liquid from a flask he'd found in the boat. Micca thought the food had been spoiled, but the Eynnish came sniffing and forgot whatever doubts they had about the tree-hens.

Neypo still lay in the dark under his tree, some distance from the fire. Gillensa brought him a portion of the meal in a leaf wrapper. She and the others ate morsels with their fingers. Micca thought the alien's confused hash was more like Eynnish food than Harnish, and the vegetables were the next thing to raw, but he had to admit that it was good after all, crunchy and juicy; the aromatic sauce gave it some welcome salt. Swannet sat to the side, eating only vegetables, but eventually she picked out a bit of meat with a twig. She complimented the uncomprehending alien on how he had been able to rid it of its bloody taste.

Micca slouched back against the mound, knees raised. There hadn't been much divided among seven people, but it was the first food he'd had since dinner at the Striver's house in Rose Pond. He felt like he ought to be tired, but his mind was restless. There was a lot to do, too many things unresolved.

Samma and Gillensa sat near him. Micca raised himself to a squat and suggested they help him dig the earth away from the boat.

"That would probably bring out mudrunners," cautioned Gillensa. "I don't like even small ones."

Micca climbed onto the boat, thinking to get them more interested in it. "Come on up here. You haven't seen the inside of it yet."

Samma and Gillensa hunched down inside the boat, Noler and Swannet peering in behind them, but they had soon seen enough. "I can see how father became uneasy, stuck inside this thing," said Gillensa.

"Looks like the inside of a radio set," Noler said.

"What were you thinking of doing with it?" Samma asked as they sat again before the fire. "Carry us to the Odés' summer house?"

"There wouldn't be much left of the house after you came down!" Noler said.

Micca ignored him. "Sure. I'm sure I can fly us to this summer house if you point me in the right direction. I practiced for hours."

Noler snorted, then went off to wash out his headgear in the stream. A few minutes later they thought they heard him shouting, probably ordering someone else away from the meadow.

"What's his name — Noler — what's he doing with the soldiery getup?" Micca asked Samma. "Was he involved in whatever was going on in Hoiin?"

"No," said Gillensa, "he's a Cadet. They wear uniforms on holidays. But there was fighting of some kind at the Fair, as I said." She glanced at the dark shape of her father. "So — what happened downtown?"

Swannet was looking at Neffafinnegal. "Did your friend have something to do with the troubles?"

Micca shook his head. "They don't fight unless somebody attacks them first. And Neffafinnegal isn't a soldier."

"I'll say he's not," said Noler, coming back into the firelight. "But hoy!" He showed them a stoneware jar. "Look at what I found. The farmhands must have forgotten it up on the road. Another bunch of tourists were going to take it, but I sent them off."

He drank and passed it to Samma. After he had a gulp Gillensa hefted it with both hands and took a cautious taste. Swannet found a hollow reed stem from which she sipped. Micca swallowed a quick, searing gulp, then held the jar out the alien.

"Try it," Micca said hoarsely. "It'll do you good."

Neffafinnegal sniffed suspiciously at it, but he muttered something about 'Roma' again and put the jug to his mouth. He squinted and scowled, but swallowed.

No one admired its flavor but all agreed to its potency. "Well, you're probably going to start talking about it again anyway, so tell me about this so-called flying machine," Samma said to Micca, eyes watering after another taste. "How was it able to fly?"

"Yes," said Gillensa. "Why did the visitors come in such a thing? From what I overheard here and there I understood there were at least eight of them, and they couldn't all have gotten inside that little crawl-hole. And Micca, how did Neyfigin…Neyfa—"

"Neffafinnegal," Micca said, pronouncing it slowly.

"What?" said the alien.

"Nothing, Finna," Micca said in Harnish, then to Gillensa, "It turns out they came down from a bigger ship a few at a time. It's still there, floating over the sky. But how did he what, Miss Odé?"

"Over the sky!" said Swannet.

"Why, that could mean — but never mind that for now," said Gillensa. "How did the outlander here come to be traveling with you and my father? And how did you all wind up in his boat or whatever you call it?"

"Well, they had Neffafinnegal detained for interrogation, I guess you could say. The Strivers wanted to sink the boat, but when we went down to the harbor we had to get away in a hurry—"

"Oh, I can't think Micca's friend did anything to deserve arrest," interrupted Swannet, putting down her hollow stem. "…He doesn't have those *dead eyes* that criminals are supposed to have."

"Why did you have to get away, Micca?" Gillensa asked. "Were there rebels downtown, too?"

Noler was frowning darkly at Neffafinnegal. "If the Lodge has someone interrogated, there must have been a good reason."

"And some people think they know it all," Swannet said. "He was traveling with the Striver Neypo and Samma's brother here, wasn't he? A Striver wouldn't associate with malefactors."

Gillensa was getting impatient. "But something very serious is going on, and no one but me seems to want to know what it is!"

"Of course we do," Samma said. "But we should get your father to —"

Swannet said, "Is it true, Micca, that you can understand the outlander's odd way of speaking?"

"For the most part. He speaks like we do sometimes in Harna."

"Huh," said Noler. "Likely he came from some lost mountain valley then."

Samma said, "I'd understand him better if he didn't slur and leave out half of every word."

"Well, ask him this," said Swannet, smiling at Neffafinnegal. "Ask him where he comes from, that he speaks so strangely, and travels in so clumsy a boat."

Micca began, "Neffafinnegal and his —"

"What?" said the alien. "Speak so I can understand you."

"I wasn't talking to you. Be quiet and have another drink."

Micca switched back to Eynnish. "He and his people belong to what they call the 'Foreign Outreach'. That's a group that goes around finding people who need their help. They go to places where people don't have the same advantages as they do."

"What advantages don't we have?" Noler asked.

"Lots of things," said Micca, wondering how anyone could help but be awed by the proofs of the visitors' potential right here in front of them. He pointed his thumb behind them. "Things like that, for instance, the air-boat! We have to walk, or have a team of pigs or oxen pull a wagon, or get somebody carry us if we want to go anywhere."

Micca tried to set his recollections of what Neffafinnegal had said in order, something not made easy by interruptions from the others. But he told them that the visitors' arrival in Wennoc had been a lucky accident. Several years ago a man called Sulawan had come across some old records during his studies, records which mentioned a settled world well beyond any currently known to the other planets. Sulawan was an antiquary, and he was eager to visit this world and further his researches. His wealthy family owned a star-ship but considered the expedition foolhardy, and wouldn't give him money for provisions and crew. He tried his academic associates, but couldn't interest them because he was unwilling to let them see his evidence. Finally a philanthropic society, the Foreign Outreach, heard rumors of his discovery and offered to provide a crew and help with the funding, provided they were allowed to send along counselors to help any people they found. Sulawan agreed. He commandeered the family ship and they set out for the lost planet whose location the records described. The world they found was covered by trackless jungle. There were no people.

"Was the jungle-world the moon?" Gillensa wondered.

"Hush!" said Swannet, and she tapped Micca's knee with a stick. "Go on, please."

The jungle world wasn't the moon, Micca told them, and Sulawan hadn't meant to cheat his sponsors. There was evdience that people had lived there long ago, but a few ruins on the floor of a shallow sea held little interest even for Sulawan, and he was as disappointed as the members of the Outreach team.

"So as long as they were out there, they decided to just try their luck, and opened their ship's ears wide. They didn't have any other records of the region they were in. Who knew what they might find? And almost right away they heard voices coming through the aether from a bunch of stars Finna calls the Ridge Pole — that's where Wennoc is, our sun is part of it. Then they had to fly for another week to get here."

"They heard our radio broadcasts!" Samma deduced, and Micca nodded.

"That must be how the person who spoke on the Voice of Hoiin learned our language," Gillensa added. "Why can't Neffafinnegal speak to us then?"

"They didn't pick up Eynnish over the radio," Micca said. "They had to learn firsthand." Neffafinnegal had said they 'opened a man's head' to get the Eynnish out of him, whatever that meant, and Micca didn't tell them this. "It sounds like it was pretty hard to do in a hurry, and only a few of them learned. So anyway, Sulawan started examining some ancient ruins up on the north shore so he could see what our history was, and the Outreach team went to Hoiin, since that was the closest big town."

Gillensa shook her head. "But to take any part of this story as true, we have to accept the idea of people living in many different stars!"

Micca shrugged. "I know. It's hard. I keep expecting to wake up from a weird dream, but I'm pretty sure I'm awake right now, and I have to believe what my eyes see."

"Let's assume you're right. What do these non-Wennoc charity people mean to do for us?" Samma asked, taking the jug from the Cadet.

Micca remembered his close call with the City's Service in Hannava. "One thing is they think anybody who can read and write and listens to his conscience should have a say in the government."

Gillensa shook her head. "That Adinna-whatever said something like that during his radio broadcast. What an idea! He must be some kind of religious zealot."

"So what happens now?" Samma asked.

"Yes," said Gillensa. "Where are these Foreign Outreach people now? It's almost certain they had something to do with the trouble at the Fair."

Micca looked to where Neypo lay under the willow tree. "You'd better ask your father if you want to know anything else. I've said too much already."

"Oh, he'll just put me off. What about this fighting at the harbor? Exactly who was fighting whom?"

Micca thought about Swannet, who didn't yet know her father had been drowned. "I really don't know the details. You'd better ask the Striver." He took another drink from the farmers' jar, avoiding Gillensa's irritated frown. But Micca's head was beginning to swim. Soon he'd be singing or babbling. He'd had enough to drink...

And so had Neffafinnegal, apparently. Despite his initial reluctance, the alien took a sip or two each time the jar made its way around the fire. He was watching Swannet, a twitching grin on his face.

Neffafinnegal looked back at Micca. "Do you think she fancies me?" he whispered loudly. "She keeps looking at me."

"You said Outreach volunteers had more important things to do than diddle with women."

Neffafinnegal shrugged theatrically, rubbing the back of his neck. "My conscience doesn't seem to mind. Ask her, comrade. Ask the lady if she wants to swive. I'm willing to try. I'd like to try."

Micca gaped, trying not to laugh. Samma had understood the alien well enough, and did laugh. Micca could see the alien blush, even in the dim light. "Learn Eynnish and ask her yourself," Micca said.

Neffafinnegal sat down and twisted uncomfortably in his armor. "I can't wait that long. You're my comrade now—ask her for me!"

Micca blew out his breath and spoke to Swannet. "Neffafinnegal says he'd like to, um…to get to know you better, Miss Olinom."

Swannet had been observing their exchange, head turning from Micca to Neffafinnegal as they spoke. Gillensa handed her the jar. Swannet put her hollow stem into it and sipped, smiling under her eyelashes at the alien. "How sweet! How shy he is, talking so that I can't understand him."

Noler lurched to his feet and pointed a shaking finger at Micca. "You tell that damned foreigner to keep his attentions to himself! You can tell him he smells like pig dung, and you can tell him who said it!"

Micca unthinkingly began a translation. "The soldier says you smell like shit, Finna."

"Impossible," said Neffafinnegal with a dismissive wave of his hand. "I'm wearing a 'casing."

Noler took up a threatening stance before the alien, but Swannet pushed him away. She knelt and took Neffafinnegal's gauntlet, looked into his eyes. "Neffafidginel, far, far from home! You must be lonely…"

Noler barked, "Stand away, wanton!"

Swannet jumped up and faced him, outraged to speechlessness. Thinking her chastened, Noler stepped forward as though to take her hand, caught his foot on a root and fell on his face. Swannet choked with laughter as Gillensa helped Noler to his feet.

Samma quickly said, "In any case, Micca, whatever plan the visitors have isn't going to work now, is it? Even if some of Hoiin's Lodge is with them, it's pretty clear not all of them are. Not if they started fighting, and what else could they have been fighting about?"

"I don't know. And I don't think it'll matter in the long run. Even if they get stuck here, or even if they're all killed, others will follow them."

"You make it sound like their success is predestined," said Gillensa, rasing her voice to be heard over Swannet and Noler.

Samma said, "But you said this Sulawing character kept his 'lost world' or whatever a secret. And even then you said they only found Wennoc by accident. How would someone else out there know where to come?"

"Finna said that if they can't go back up to their big ship for some reason, after a while it'll automatically go back to the other worlds by itself and tell them where it's been. Apparently they can do that on their own if something goes wrong," Micca said as Neypo walked slowly into the firelight. "So even if what they've already started here doesn't take hold, others like them will come. The world will change."

Neypo was staring balefully at him. "Are you quite through, Micca? Hey? Have you told them *everything* you know?"

Micca blinked at the Striver as Samma tried to pass him the farmers' jar.

Gillensa jumped up and caught Neypo's arm. "Did you hear what he said, Father? The outlanders from the stars will know where to find Wennoc again, even if the ones here never go back!"

Neypo looked at her, then at Micca. He grabbed Micca's arm, pulled him to his feet and led him off beyond the big willow. Micca repeated Neffafinnegal's story of the aliens' star-going ship eventually returning home with records of its travels even if its crew were lost. He added what he had heard Gillensa say about the troubles at the Fair.

Neypo shook his head. "I have a little well-deserved nap and wake to *more* bad news. Dire news, dire. The insurrection must be more advanced than I had feared. You should have told me this business about their larger, star-traveling ship sooner!"

Micca shrugged. "I didn't know. Finna told me about it this afternoon. I'd have told you then, but you were, ah, indisposed … what will you do? Can you do something about it?"

Neypo stared thoughtfully at the sky. "There's no avoiding it now," he muttered. "I'll simply have to ask for her cooperation."

"Whose?"

Neypo shook his head. "I'll explain it later, and I'll need your assistance!"

They walked back into the firelight. Micca sat down again and Neypo stood by the fire. He looked keenly at those around the fire, who regarded him in silence.

"Well," Neypo said finally. "We've all had a chance to enjoy a little rest and recuperation, despite an enormous and ongoing catastrophe. It's time to collect ourselves and do what must be done, because when the sun rises our holiday will be over."

"Holiday?" Swannet said sarcastically.

"You *act* like you're on a holiday," growled Noler. "A holiday from *decency*!"

"Why, you priggish, beastly—"

"Silence, please!" said Neypo. He took the jug from Samma, tasted the liquor and cleared his throat. "I've been forced to make some momentous decisions. As of this moment, my young friends, you are all under the Mandate of the Lodge, lawfully decreed by myself. Wennoc's enemies are abroad in the land and they must be subdued. I will now issue your instructions—

"Swannet and Gillensa: at first light you'll take yourselves to Tamanello and bide at the cottage there, giving succor to Winetra, Sellet and the children, helping whichever of our servants may be there with their chores, as well as providing reasonable hospitality to other poor refugees in the neighborhood who have fled the city."

The women gaped at him. Neypo spoke on. "Samma of Mora—I understand you've come into a certain civil authority of your own...if that is indeed Samma in there."

Samma had tried on Micca's helmet. He pulled it off and gave it back to Micca.

Neypo put his palms together and made a perfunctory bow. "I regard you as a visiting civil authority. I would be obliged if you would accept the office of 'Adjunct-Honorary to the Lodge', and remain here in this meadow until such time as you can be relieved, guarding the flying raft, and the Lodge's detainee, known as Neffafinnegal, against interference from, or communication of any kind with the local citizenry or anyone else. As Adjunct-Honorary you will arrange for any removal of earth necessary to ready the alien craft for movement, commandeer wagons or other overland transport from nearby agriculturalists — I'll compose an official edict once we find some paper — take the craft to the Bay, and with its hatch open, sink it in the sea."

Micca opened his mouth in horror. Before could speak, Neypo snapped his fingers. "Cadet Hunsacup!"

Noler staggered to his feet and made a formal salute.

"You have the benefit of military training," Neypo told him. "You will accompany me to a certain location in the south on a matter of urgent Lodge business, acting as my military aide."

"Hoy!" Noler barked.

"And last, Micca Mora. You hold a suit of alien fabrication in trust for the Lodge. I want you to travel with the Cadet and myself in your current sworn capacity as Adjunct-Military to the Lodge...and if you don't want to wear your casque, maybe you should turn it over to the Cadet."

In general, the Striver's instructions were not enthusiastically received. Being created an Adjunct to the Lodge, even an honorary one, made Samma both excited and uneasy, and though not sharing Micca's apparent awe of the stone boat, he didn't think the Striver's plan for it was practical. By now Noler decided it would be an insult to march with an untrained farmer from the woods of Harna, be he armored or not, especially since he had made no move to give him the glass helmet, as the Striver had ordered. Swannet was relieved to hear she was to go to the Striver's summer house after all, but she railed at the idea she would do 'chores' there, much less welcome rag-a-tag transients to her refuge, and she thought it a shame poor Neffafinnegal would have to stay behind in the damp meadow.

"All very tiresome!" she told Gillensa. "I can understand why your father wants Noler with him, but don't you think the two of us should have a male escort to Tamanello?"

Gillensa stared defiantly at Neypo while trying to compose irrefutably logical arguments against going to Tamanello, a task made difficult by liquor-inspired relaxation she felt.

The only aspect of the situation to Micca's liking was the others' complaints. He ignored Neypo's comments about his helmet and held it stubbornly under his arm. Did the Striver think he would drink no more spirits if he were wearing it? Neypo was behaving more like a drunk than he was. Micca spoke to his brother, not caring if the Striver heard him.

"I won't let that boat be sunk, Sam. And I'm not going off on some adventure with that jumped-up Cadet, either. A Striver can't tell me what to do."

Neypo was busy lecturing Gillensa; if he heard Micca's comments, he ignored them. Samma said, "If you're an Adjunct-Military he *can* tell you what to do. I think the rank's at least equivalent to a first-degree Mendicant—you're in the Lodge, boy! How did you wrangle that?"

A first-degree Mendicant. Micca hadn't known that. But what good was it? "It wasn't voluntary, I'll tell you that much. But what are you going to do?"

"Well, it could be that the Striver knows what he's doing," Samma whispered, his face serious. "At least partly. There's such a thing as Lodge Secrets, you know."

"I've already heard more Lodge Secrets than I ever wanted to."

Samma was taken aback. "What kind?"

Micca flippantly made a sign with his fingers that for all he knew might have meant 'I am a fishmonger who offers discounts to members of the Lodge'.

He turned and switched to Harnish. "What do you think, Finna? He wants to haul the boat off on a wagon and drown it in the sea. You and…you and Sulawan will never get out of Wennoc. That's what the Honorable Striver wants to do."

Neffafinnegal blinked. "If he wants to move the lighter, you'll have to do it for him."

Micca calmly put on his helmet. Despite the drinking, the alien's mind was functioning better than Micca's.

He waited until Gillensa had finished with Neypo, then got his attention. "You must realize the boat would crush any cart or wagon you put it on, Striver, even if you could find a way to lift it. You know Finna can't fly it. And if you thought *I'd* help sink it, you can just forget about it again."

Micca fell silent, feeling suddenly alarmed that he had spoken to a Striver in such a manner. Neypo stared at him, whether in anger or shocked by this betrayal, Micca couldn't decide. But the Striver's attention was quickly diverted. Gillensa started to speak to him, and Swannet and Noler had new complaints. Neypo dealt with them one by one, making a few pragmatic alterations to his orders. Noler was testily reminded of his oath to Hoiin's Lodge and promised a recommendation of early initiation into the ranks of the Hustlers; Neypo suggested that while at Tamanello Gillensa systematically interview refugees, collecting information on the insurrection which she could later personally submit to the Grand Fellow; he spoke soothingly to Swannet, describing the cottage's comfortable accommodations.

Feeling somewhat sorry for the Striver now, and in a little bit of awe at how expertly he handled all these complaining drunks while he himself must be severely hung over, Micca betrayed interest when Neypo stated his intention to visit the ruins of the ancient city of Mellatuno.

"There's a branch of the Office of Antiquities still active there," said Neypo, whispering now so as not to spark Gillensa's interest as well. "You seem keen on history, Micca. You'll be fascinated by the mementos of olden times they have there."

"But Striver, I really can't go without the boat."

Neypo's lips tightened. "Of course you can! You have two long legs, and the armor's boots will doubtless wear very well. And before you correct me, I do indeed recall that the raft will obey only a man in such armor."

This wasn't quite the case, but Micca wasn't going to correct the Striver's misapprehension.

Neypo went on. "I think I see a way to relieve you of the onerous responsibility to the raft you seem to have assigned yourself. Yes, and it's a solution which will ease my own mind, as well.

"Your brother Samma, since he'll be acting as guardian to the thing, can be clad just as you are—now calm down, Micca, you'll keep your own suit. What I want you to do is to ask Neffafinnegal to exchange *his* clothing, such as it is, for your brother's. Samma appears to have enough knowledge of your old language to allow the alien to teach him to move the raft the short distance required to reach to the sea. All you have to do just now is lend Samma your helmet in order to complete his costume." Neypo smiled encouragingly. "We'll find you another one, one made of good bronze, with a terrifying face on its visor, and your own bodkin as well." He slapped Micca's back. "I know a military man doesn't care to march without proper equipment."

It was a moment before Micca was able to speak. "I'm not a military man, and I don't want a terrifying visor!"

Neypo scowled at him. "But you *are* a military man now. You swore a sacred oath to the Lodge. I am its representative and your superior in rank. You'll give your brother your headgear as I instruct. Under this arrangement Samma will be able to deal with the raft, and our alien guest's identity will be less obvious to anyone sent out into the countryside by agents of the treasonous elements in Hoiin…

"Cadet!" Neypo called. "Hand me that jug."

Samma got Micca's attention now. He agreed that Micca shouldn't have to give up his helmet permanently, but promised he'd take good care of it and said that he wouldn't mind trying on a suit of armor, 'just for fun'. He guiltily shrugged off Micca's outraged refusal and spoke in awkward Harnish to the alien. After a few minutes of talking and gesturing he was understood.

Micca felt doubly betrayed when Neffafinnegal agreed to Neypo's orders and began to open his armor. He'd probably be willing to initialize Samma and teach him to drive the boat, too…

"I've been looking forward to getting out of the 'casing," Neffafinnegal told Micca, sounding apologetic. "And Honorable's the leader, isn't he?"

"I hope a mudrunner stings your tackle when you take off the armor," Micca muttered.

With some effort Samma made Neffafinnegal understand that people here did not disrobe in mixed company. Noler, too, became interested in the armor, and described a scheme in which he would take the suit and deal with the boat first thing in the morning, and then escort the women to Tamanello; Adjunct-Honorary Samma would go south with his brother and the Striver. Samma told him he was too short to fit into the armor, but Noler went along with Samma and Neffafinnegal to the verges of the meadow, where Swannet and Gillensa wouldn't see them.

🌿

They walked along the trees skirting the water and chose a spot below the lane. "Should we wash the suit first?" Samma tried to say in Harnish. He understood the alien's reply as 'it cleans selfly'.

Noler didn't understand them but said, "I'll put it on if you're afraid."

Shortly Neffafinnegal was standing naked, shoulders hunched and shivering. He gestured impatiently at Samma. Samma took off his clothes, sat down and got his legs into the armor, then stood and worked the rest of himself in. Neffafinnegal snapped the back closed.

"Oof," said Samma, standing straight.

"Ha ha!" said Noler. "You farted."

"I did not!" Samma moved around. "It's snug, but it seems like a good fit. See, Hunsacup? The legs *and* arms are too long for you."

Neffafinnegal had quickly put on Samma's clothes, which fit him well enough.

"Now," said Samma, "let's go back and talk Micca out of the helmet."

"What was that?" said Noler.

"Micca doesn't want to give me his —"

"No, up there! In the lane. More nosy tourists, I'll bet."

"If it's the farmers coming back for their jug, they're going to be disappointed."

"No, it's ... I don't know what it is." Noler made sure of his club and climbed up to the lane, Samma and Neffafinnegal coming behind.

A tall dark box floated down the track, seeming to roll on one wheel. It looked like an oversized sedan, but there was no one carrying it. Then, behind it, four men came into view, sitting on saddles, their legs pumping pedals between two wheels almost as tall as Noler.

"Halt!" came a thin voice from the box. The men ceased their pedaling, and an arm emerged from the side window to pull back a lever. The vehicle squeaked to a halt.

A door in the sedan opened, and an old woman climbed out, steadying herself with a stick. She wore a broad-brimmed red hat and a long coat. "Good evening, lads," she said. "What's the news? What brings you out here? Did you see that thing fall from the sky after lunch? I was told it came down somewhere around here."

Noler stepped forward. "You can't stop here, madam. This area is under Striving Mandate, off-limits to the public." He pointed to the men who had been pedaling. "You chaps there; remount the carriage."

The woman frowned at Noler, then got a better look at Samma. She stared in fascination, came forward and reached out to touch his glass-clad arm. "Was this suit made in another world, somewhere outside Wennoc?"

"Yes!" said Samma in surprise. "Supposedly. How did you know?"

She squinted at Noler and Neffafinnegal, then whispered earnestly to Samma, "Be of good cheer, my friend! Help has arrived."

Then she gazed out at the water-meadow. She turned to Noler. "Striving Mandate, hey? What's that fire, Cadet? Toasting information out of your prisoners?"

"I have no idea what you're on about, old woman, but you and your flunkies are going to leave…" He slapped his club in his hand. "Now."

The woman signaled her pedal-men. They quickly pulled some kind of hoods over their heads, as did the woman. One of the men stalked forward, carrying a head-sized bladder.

The Cadet slapped down his visor and walked backwards, running into Samma. Neffafinnegal scrambled over the wall bordering the lane and into the meadow.

The man with the bladder squeezed it between his hands. A cloud of dust puffed out and hung in the air. Noler and Samma coughed and squinted. Their eyelids fluttered, and they collapsed. On the other side of the parapet Neffafinnegal started to run, but he too fell.

The woman bent over Samma and gently touched his cheek. "I'm sorry. There was no time to protect you." She straightened and spoke to the men behind her. "Put him in the cabin. Hustle now!"

Micca sat by the fire, fuming. What would he do about the boat? Neypo stood in front of the fire, and began to chant the *All's Well in Wennoc* in a wavering voice. The women made response in two-part harmony. Micca kept silent.

The others began to talk about where they'd sleep, what they'd do for blankets. Micca muttered something about spending the night inside the boat. Swannet and Gillensa were doubtful, but Neypo finally decided that was the safest and even most comfortable option. "We can send the Cadet to some nearby farm to find food for breakfast in the morning," he said. "I'm not sure I trust Neffafinnegal, cook or not, to prepare a proper Eynnish breakfast. He might put fish-sauce into the oatmeal rather than honey!"

Swannet laughed and said, "But don't forget his marvelous supper. I'm sure he'll do very well with better material."

"Yes," said Gillensa. "We should think about capitalizing a restaurant for him when things have settled down, Father! Can you imagine how the stylish set would fight each other to get a table? What could possibly be more exotic — 'Cuisine of the Stars'!"

Neypo showed a small smile. "It would probably be a great success, but 'Cuisine of Far Harna' would be a safer name. If the Grand Hierophant and the Preceptors get wind of these events, any surviving aliens will be carried off to an uncertain fate in Mennedal…"

He looked into the dark. "But where have those boys gotten to? Micca, you'd better go check on them. I hope Samma hasn't been frightened by the armor. I remember the hair-raising shriek you made when you first donned it."

Micca sneered at the Striver. He hadn't 'shrieked'. But he got up and started into the meadow. After he had gone a few yards he found Neypo splashing along beside him. "It occurred to me they may be quarreling over the suit," he puffed. "The Cadet seemed very keen to try it on, and I'm afraid he's rather drunk."

They saw no one in the lane. "Cadet!" Neypo called.

"Samma!" yelled Micca. "eFinna!"

They heard a groan from the side of the lane. A dark shape rose in the weeds.

"Noler!" said Micca. "What happened? Where's Samma and Neffafinnegal?"

Neypo grabbed the Cadet's arm and hoisted him to his feet. Noler looked left and right, mouth moving without sound. Finally he found his voice. "Where is everybody?"

"Yes, where are they?" said Neypo. "Where are Samma and the outlander? Where is the glass armor?"

Noler rubbed his eyes, stooped to pick up his bronze helmet. "There was a … a weird sedan, never seen the like. And an old woman, she was riding in it. She had a gang of ruffians with her."

Micca shouted from the other side of the lane. "I found Finna!" He pulled the groggy alien to his feet and over the wall, into the lane.

The alien had little more information for them. Neypo examined the two, and found no sign of injury. But he put a finger to the dust on the Cadet's helmet, then touched it to his tongue. "Some kind of fungus, I think...oof, I feel a bit woozy. You two were drugged."

They searched and called, but there was no sign of Samma.

Finally Neypo dropped onto the wall beside the lane. "You said you saw a sedan or something of the sort, Cadet? Tell me precisely what it looked like."

Noler did so.

"You're sure about the glyph?" said Neypo, eyes narrowing.

"There was no light but the moon's, but I'm pretty sure. Never seen that one before."

Micca said, "And there were peddlers sitting between big wheels? I saw them the first night I was in Hoiin. They almost ran me down!"

Neypo nodded. "I, too, saw these people in the city, though not their sedan. Those who appear to have taken Samma are bound by law and oath to obey instruction from a Striver, and so they shall, once we catch up with them."

"We'll catch them," said Micca. "The boat will catch them. But where did they go?"

"There's no desperate need for haste, Micca. Samma is surely bound for the same place we are."

"Well, we'll follow then! But who were they? Who took him?"

"It's certain that Samma rides with someone from the Office of Antiquities. I met one of its Directors briefly in Hoiin. No one else, at least, would use the archaic glyph our Cadet has described: seven jots, representing the lamps, set over strokes representing the watchtowers of a city. The towers have probably long since fallen, and there are now only three lamps in the sky. But the glyph is that of Mellatuno, the home of those who are supposed to have set the lamps in the heavens."

18. LEAVING HANNAVA

In Hannava, Branna Mora sat in the common room of the Somnolent Repose, staring at a tepid quarter-inch of liquid in the bottom of his cup. The landlord's wife called from the bar, asking if he wanted more tea. He didn't answer, but she came and filled his cup.

Branna rubbed his temples. The tea, though brown and strong, hadn't done much to relieve his hangover, nor did the roomful of Toivo's boisterous customers, shouting, pounding on the tables and spilling their beer.

He braced himself as the musicians prepared to play again. Two of them tooted woodhorns and another one thrumped a drum, aggravating Branna's headache.

Branna looked up at the sound of braying, over-loud laughter at the next table. The barroom was almost full. Somebody sat down on the bench beside him — Fola Marstoc. "I thought you were going to an entertainment with Carny tonight."

Fola sighed. "She said she had to help her mother with something. I don't know if I believe her."

"How can we be sure Micca went to Hoiin?"

Fola grunted. "You told me yourself that's where he went, and that's where he said he'd go. I'm sure he spent yesterday at the Fair with Samma and his friends, and he's probably there again today."

"Unless the City's Service got him and he never went."

"How about this. Tomorrow we'll get a boat and go over to Hoiin. I have enough silver to cover it. We can see the end of the Fair and all come back together with Samma."

"Toivo said the Fair was closed. He heard something about it over the aether."

"The landlord doesn't know what he's talking about. Hoiin's Fair runs all week."

"What about the criminals I heard about? Or what if Micca and Sam are already on their way back?"

"Samma wouldn't let Micca go before the Fair was over! Do you want to go or not?"

"Well, sure! I suppose so."

"Good. I'll break the news to Carny. If I can find her."

The drum beat, and the horns honked an Eynnish quick-step. Two Eynnishmen at the other end of the table, trying to persuade the serving girls to join them, leapt up and performed the dance, feet shuffling rapidly, hands behind them holding their hats. They were obviously drunk and one of them sat down again after a few turns, but the other kept up the dance, musicians playing faster and faster. Toivo nodded to one of the servers, and she joined the dancer. Branna had to laugh in amazement at his agility.

Just as the second dancer fell to the floor there was a commotion at the door. Two bedraggled men with long hair and a sickly looking woman stumbled in. The music fell off and Toivo went to speak with them. Everyone watched.

"Are they from Eynna?" Branna asked Fola.

"They look to be," Fola said, eyebrows raised. The newcomers flopped into chairs the landlord set out for them. One of the men began sobbing.

"I'm going to see what's happening."

Branna made his way across the crowded room. When he came to the bar Toivo was gone and the Eynnish people were drinking soup. They looked so dazed Branna didn't think he'd learn much from them.

Toivo's son was tapping the beer. He pointed behind him when Branna asked him where his father was.

Branna found the landlord in his office. Toivo wore a bonnet with bulging ear-flaps. He sat before a large cabinet, adjusting a series of dials. Branna bent down and peered into Toivo's face.

Toivo looked up in surprise, then took off the bonnet. "What can I do for you, Mister Mora?"

"What's going on?"

Toivo shook his head. "I don't know, not exactly, but the Honorable Matco Opensei, the gentleman who just came in with his wife and retainer, says there's serious trouble in Hoiin. He asked me to see what the Voices have to say... Hoiin's got nothing but singing right now."

The landlord put the bonnet back on and adjusted his receiver's dials. Branna put his ear close to the bonnet, but couldn't hear much. Finally Toivo lifted one of the ear flaps. "Parnala's full of rumors and speculation," he said. "A large party of their citizens and merchants went to Hoiin for the Fair's opening. Some of them came back tonight, full of wild stories about fighting, and right at the fairgrounds! They said others had been assaulted by Officers of the Lodge. But I'd take the stories with caution. I'm afraid there are interests in Parnala that would like to see another conflict."

"Can I listen for a minute?"

Toivo gave him the bonnet. Over the hissing Branna heard a voice: "... of the Lodge of Parnala apologize again. Be assured that the Repwidoi Ensemble's rendition of Seillinin's 'How Placid and Reposeful Thou Art, O Summer Pond', originally scheduled for this hour, will be presented in its entirety at a later date...

"But I have just been handed a bulletin from Hin Hoina's Office of Public Information and will relay it to our listeners, but, note well, with no guarantee of accuracy: 'The Lodge of Hin Hoina assures its neighbors, East and West, North and South, that despite the recent but minor police problem, all is now well in the city. Our Fair, alas, has been closed for a day or two, but visitors to our community will receive the warm and peaceful welcome they are used to'."

Parnala's announcer paused. "Nevertheless, our own Lodge has not, I repeat, has *not*, withdrawn its proclamation that no citizen of Parnala or the surrounding area is advised to travel to Hin Hoina at this time. Your Strivers will go to whatever lengths are necessary to see to the safety of any relatives or loved ones who may now be in Hin Hoina and its environs... in general, calm is advised by the Lodge. The report heard last evening concerning the sighting of an umiot or some such creature over the Bay has now been determined to have been the fantasy of the victims of a mental illness..."

"An umiot!" Branna shouted. He pulled off the hat and looked with alarm at Toivo.

"What did you hear?"

Branna told him and Toivo shook his head. "I think the stories are only rumors spread for some political reason by Parnala, although Opensei says otherwise. I'm going to see if I can raise Rondoiin," Toivo said, taking the bonnet from Branna.

"I've got to go to Hoiin right away. I've got cousins over there!"

"Now wait a minute, young man. No boat is going to cross before this is cleared up, or none but those filled with men from the City's Service! As soon as the Directorate gets wind of the Strivers' troubles they'll be over there to see what advantage they can gain."

"Why would they send Hannava's guards to Hoiin?"

Toivo leaned forward, rubbing his nose. "That story has been told before, and it's a grim one. During the troubles in Lemmin a hundred and twenty-odd years ago, the Directorate took several hundred of Hannava's young men over there before it was all over. The mainlanders didn't kill many in their fighting, you see, but both sides tore up hedges and walls, burned farms and spoiled the fish pools. A very spiteful business. The Lodges paid Hannava to help them rebuild, since their own boys were still under arms and didn't care to exert themselves with such labor; either that or they were off hiding in Lointei or Midoi, and even here in Hannava. The Eynnish have little stomach for warfare, you know.

"But our conscripts were gone almost a year. They were given little to eat over there but watercorn and came back skinny as wands, their legs covered by welts from mudrunner stings. My great-great-grandfather had foreseen the troubles and came over here, but his son Timo was one of Hannava's conscripts, so the family didn't escape the troubles after all."

Branna hurried back to the barroom. He pulled Fola away from the merchant he had been talking to. Toivo, following Branna, intercepted them and took both their arms. "Now listen to old Toivo, boys!"

"What's going on here?" Fola complained, spilling a cup of spirits as he tried to free himself from Branna.

"They're having a war in Eynna!" Branna shouted at him. "We've got to rescue Micca and Sam. Come on! Let's get our stuff and go."

"What you're planning isn't wise," said Toivo.

Fola frowned uncertainly. A man standing at the bar said, "Wife told me dead Eynnish were washing up at Irnapta yesterday. She had it from the neighbor's cousin, who come up to town this morning. Just like when Hoiin tried to take Parnala's corn silos."

"Nonsense!" said Toivo. "It had nothing to do with corn. The factors in Parnala wanted Hoiin's sea-coal depot."

One of the newly arrived Eynnish looked up from his soup, his face like that of a ghost. "Not war, but I saw an umiot. I saw it myself. It was huge, and flew with booming farts."

This speech seemed to give everyone leave to gather around the refugees and question them. It came out that the party had been celebrating Tuvimat on a floating pavilion on the Bay south of Hoiin when the umiot had been sighted. Panicking, they had cast off their lines and drifted away, finally beaching on the western shore tonight. One of their servants had been taken by fish during the crossing.

Others in the barroom contributed rumors and speculations. Branna yanked on Fola's arm, frowning furiously at him. "Are you a man or not?"

"Well," said Fola, squaring his shoulders, "if Micca and Samma are in danger, we'd better see if we can find a boat. I'm sure the combatants won't bother foreigners. Come on, let's get our bags."

An hour later Fola stood in the street, not far from the harbor. He tried to pull his wrist from the meaty grip of the man behind him. Another was rooting through Fola's bag, while a third counted the silver from his purse. A fourth, the press gang's chief, stood in front of him, turned out like the others in the green uniform of Hannava's City Service. His hands were clasped behind his back, his head cocked to one side.

Fola shouted at him, "I'll tell you again, I'm Voling Marstoc, heir to the Marling's seat!"

The man behind twisted Fola's arm, eliciting a gasp of pain. The other members of the press gang laughed. "Do you want me to fit this draft dodger with a silencer, Chief?" said one of them.

Fola spoke again, with more dignity. "I have urgent business in Hoiin. I must meet my transportation. I'm sure you're a reasonable man, Bureau Chief. My father has important connections at the

Directorate."

The chief smiled at Fola. "I'm sure he does, your Honor, and we'll get you to Hoiin in quick order."

"I'm not going on *your* boat! Let me go!"

He examined Fola's stylish clothing. "You've had your holiday from duty, and among the Eynnish, it would seem. Well, maybe you'll meet some old friends over there who'll offer to take your place."

"I'll take you to law, you wretched shit!"

The chief snapped his fingers. "Piuling—the silencer."

Fola yelled, "Go to Hinnioc, you—"

Not far away, a large man with yellow hair jumped out from behind a fountain and sprinted toward the harbor.

"Down the street, boys, another one!" the chief yelled.

19. LEAVING MARSTOC

Standing beside a closed wagon, Monitor Smolic, Visiting Member of the County Commission on Invigoration, studied the great house at Marstoc. Rows of glazed doors on the ground floor flooded shrubberies and stretches of lawn with yellow light.

"Why isn't your man here yet?" Smolic hissed, chewing his knuckles. "Who was it you talked to?"

"Our dear brother Anlaf, a long-time resident here," whispered Deaconess Wamod of Mora. "You probably saw him with the ruffians who carried off our dear priest. But although he hides it from his kinfolk, Anlaf is well and truly Invigorated. He'll give us a sign when he has a way open."

Bacnod was also watching the house. "I know Anlaf good enough. He won't let us down. And that looks to be our sign yonder." The others looked to where he was pointing. Something moved slowly up and down beside the greenery at the far end of a row of low outbuildings.

"It's a branch, stirred by the wind," said Wilmar, an Invigorated man who had joined them during a brief stop at Topping.

"There's no wind, you fool," said Bacnod. "It's an arm."

"Oh, don't let us speak unkindly, one to the other," Binta pled.

"Quiet, boy!" Smolic hissed, rapping the top of Binta's head with his knuckles.

Bacnod briefly opened a lamp. The arm down at the other end of the house waved again.

"Wilmar, get them oxes moving, but slow-like," Bacnod said. "There's a field path down there. We'll swing 'round and come out by our man Anlaf. That'll give us a quick way out if there's any noise made."

Wilmar went forward, speaking in a low voice to the oxen. Wamod murmured to Bacnod, "It must be difficult for you, brother, to return to Marstoc, after its people treated you so unfairly."

"Shut up," Bacnod said.

"Well then, I'll not mention it again. And I'll be so thankful to quit this neighborhood of evil folk...and evil..." She glanced fearfully around her, then took a clay bottle from her pocket and sipped from it. "Binta?" she said. "Do you too still remember Goranstura?"

Binta choked back a relieved sob and reached out, but Bacnod grabbed the bottle. "If anybody gets to forget that place, it's going to be me."

"Yes, it's good you came here instead of Topping," said the Marling. "Though I think your mother is better off there. The opportunity for some private reflection at her home place and a candid discussion with your father is probably just what she needs. I'm sure recent events have upset her."

Ennesia sighed. "They've upset everyone."

The Marling leaned forward in his chair and smiled graciously. "You're very welcome to tarry in my house until things are more settled, or for as long as you like. My son and your friends Micael and Brannoc will no doubt be back soon from the north, and it's likely they'll come here first."

He held out a tray arranged with small slices of cheese and crispbread. Ennesia smiled and shook her head.

"How are you settling in, then? Are you content helping in the laundry?"

"Oh, I'm fine. The other girls in my room are cheerful enough. But Marling, are you sure some of the other Invigorationists shouldn't be locked up for a while too? At least the more radical ones?"

"Your own Priest Linto is under house arrest at Topping. Did someone tell you about that? Good. As far as the others go, I can't imagine them pulling any tricks with their leaders sequestered and humiliated. Let them suffer the stares and sharp questions of their family and housemates for a while, and you'll see their so-called Vigor lessen considerably."

"And you're holding Mora's priest here?"

The Marling nodded. "Wudego's a bit more influential than Linto. I'm sorry we didn't know you were still at Mora when we collected him. It might have pleased you to see us seize the priest and warn his followers."

Now the Marling smiled. "Would you like to see him? Make sure he's really here and not out stirring up more trouble? Frankly, I wouldn't try to dissuade you from a little gloating. Shame is often the best therapy for such people."

Ennesia smiled a little too. "His flunkies meant to lock *me* up, and wanted to cut off my hair, too. Maybe I would like to see him. Do you have him in chains, with an iron collar around his neck?"

The Marling stood and took her arm, laughing. "Nothing so traditional. But I'm sure his quarters ain't quite what he's used to."

The room was under a wing at one end of the house, half sunken in the earth. The Marling led Ennesia down a flight of stairs, then through a dark, empty room with a heavy door at the end. He took out a ring of keys. "I suppose we should announce our presence," he said with a wink. "There's only an open sump, and you never know, he may be using it."

He rapped three times on the door and called out, then turned the key. He frowned. "Doesn't seem to be locked. Someone's been scamping their duties."

Ennesia followed him down another flight of stairs and into a small room. In it was a table with a flickering lamp, a chair, and a water tap over a stone-curbed hole in the far corner. The walls were undressed stone, the floor packed earth. A horizontal window with three blue panes was set high in the outside wall. Priest Palmer sat on the edge of a narrow cot under the window, hands folded in his lap. He didn't look up at them.

The Marling took a wide stance before him, hands clasped behind his back. "So, Wudego. What occupies your meditations tonight?"

The priest didn't lift his head. "Just now I was wondering what the consequences will be if you don't leave this little hole."

The Marling frowned. "I can't say I know what you mean."

Palmer unfolded and refolded his hands. "My meaning is immediate, and possibly dire."

"Do you mean that as some sort of threat, priest?"

She didn't know why, but Ennesia looked at the window above the priest's bed. A young, pale face stared back at her through the dirty panes. "Binta?" she said in wonder.

"What?" said the Marling.

Ennesia pointed. "Binta, from Mora! He's gone now, but I saw him, out there."

From the dark space under the stair came a hiss of indrawn breath. A man jumped out, seized Ennesia's arm, struggled with her for a moment, then pricked her flesh with a needle. Ennesia dragged her fingernails across the man's face, but her eyelids fluttered and she slumped into his arms.

The Marling lurched forward. "Anlaf! What have you done? What are you —"

Now Bacnod came from under the stair, face empty, his eyes like knots in a plank.

"And you!" exclaimed the Marling. "I gave you clear warning at Mora. Do you understand you have both made yourselves criminals by this invasion?"

Bacnod came forward in two deliberate strides. His arm rose, a long, narrow blade in his hand.

The Marling's head jerked back and a short, high-pitched grunt came from his throat. Bacnod let go his blade. The Marling crumpled to sprawl on the floor. The blade, its pommel protruding from the Marling's right eye, caused his head to rest crookedly, as though he were twisting his neck to look up at Priest Palmer.

The priest rose slowly from his cot, his face twisted in horror. He watched as a small pool of blood formed under the Marling's head.

Anlaf bent down with his ear close to the Marling's head. He rose. "I think he's dead."

"Hinnioc take him," Bacnod said. "We'll go now."

"The girl saw us," said Anlaf. "But not what happened just now."

"We take her, figure it out later," said Bacnod. "The blade stays where I put it."

Anlaf rearranged his grip on Ennesia's body and carried her up the steps.

20. EVENING IN HOIIN

The day wore away. In most parts of Eynna, things went on as they always had. The sun sank, the moon rose, and the stars and the lamps waxed bright in the sky.

Seen from the roof garden of the Lodge that night, the city looked much as it had just a few days ago. Some of the villas in the hills were dark, abandoned by their inhabitants, but the courtyards of the old houses on either side of the river glowed with light. The street lamps were lit, mapping Hoiin with a glimmering web.

In the commercial district the streets were still busy, hours past suppertime; today the statutes forbidding commercial activity after sunset had been lifted, probably for good. Practicality had won this liberty for the harbor years ago, and since the expulsion of the Heresiarchs the Eynnish had been for the most part a practical people. They understood that the wind and the currents of the sea couldn't be legislated against, and neither could the energy that now pervaded the chief city of the west.

The wind touched his face, and Caihar again felt amazement at his own continued life, coupled intimately now with that of his people. There was much to do, years of work, but Caihar would devote whatever remained of his time in Wennoc to it.

He had no memory of being pulled from the Bay, and when he had come back to his senses, retching sea water, lungs burning, one of his toes bitten away, he wished they'd left the rest of him for the fish. And the torment he'd experienced following his awakening had been worse. He'd thought himself bound, unable to move. Intense physical pleasure was contrasted by soul-shattering dread and loathing; he experienced curiosity, boredom, heart-rending love and suicidal melancholy in rapid succession; a glimpse of unimaginable terror and nauseating disgust was followed by a half-second of perfect bliss.

At some point during the torment of his madness Caihar had noticed that someone was nearby, someone who promised hope. It was Adinnegram, the man Neypo's committee had spoken to, whose speech on the Voice of Hoiin had caused such consternation. Adinnegram caused beautiful voices to sing peace to him, but Caihar's eyes were filled with new tears as he was shown Wennoc as it really was: befouled, crawled over by a perversely eccentric, backward race, tragic in their ignorance and selfishness. Then he saw Adinnegram and his friends as though walking out of the sunrise, human and unassuming, but given grace by great wisdom. They examined Caihar and his people and reacted not with disgust or anger, but compassion. Even the shades of those visitors the Strivers had killed smiled at Caihar and held out their hands.

Though he knew he was unworthy, Caihar accepted them, and was in turn embraced by them. With his new understanding he became one of them, and proudly wore a blue arm band, which Neypo Odé's colleague Micsin had devised as an outward sign of fellowship with the Outreach. Together with the Outreach he would strive with all his might, sacrifice everything for the greater good. Together they would bring Wennoc into the brilliant sunrise Caihar had seen in his vision.

Caihar knew that all of Wennoc's children — all the people of all the worlds — were equally important, but the visitors had to be practical. Those who had been influential or had held important posts had the necessary experience and proven talents. It fell to them to become the Outreach's eyes, ears and hands. Caihar had been busy conferring with Reimi Rytalla, Micsin, Riino and others all day. There was little time for rest, less time to eat, no time at all to waste on a quiet cup of spirits. Things in town had been more or less stabilized, but the radio broadcasts from other cities were carrying wild stories. They must show Hoiin as a prosperous and peaceful city, a city to be visited. It was essential to show all the people, and at the moment especially their leaders, the Outreach's wonderful vision. Having felt it themselves, none would go away carrying their sorry old burdens of reactionary mistrust and self-interest.

But there were practical problems to overcome. In order to be personally convinced of the visitors' Blessed Vision, as Caihar thought of it, one must first undergo a special treatment 'to make fit the vessel', as Soliël had put it in her rough and often pithy Eynnish. Though Caihar had been only vaguely aware of his own treatment, Reimi Rytalla told him that it included one's neck being bitten by a little thread-like thing—whether insect, animal or something artificial Rytalla didn't know—which cleansed the mind and awakened one's better nature (Caihar did indeed carry a wound on his neck, though it was less sore tonight). After the bite came a brief course of counseling and instruction. There were plenty of threads, which multiplied quickly in a jar of honey, salt and water, but there were few people capable of doing the counseling. Soliël was busy training more operatives, but it took time. Adinnegram and his comrades probably hadn't expected Wennoc to present so great a crowd to be helped. Only so many citizens could be processed in a day, so the 'leadership class' must have precedence, or so Adinnegram had explained.

Caihar looked to the suburban hills, thinking regretfully of the absence of his colleague, Neypo Odé. As a commercial man Neypo had a knack for organization and would have been useful now. He had also been accustomed to long working days...Caihar was getting very tired, but there was much to be done. He had to emulate Neypo's devotion to duty (though Neypo had yet to be acquainted with his real duty). And Caihar wouldn't have turned down Adinnegram's invitation to visit him here on the roof of the Lodge building if it had come three hours before sunrise.

As if in answer to his thoughts, Adinnegram arrived now, smiling. "I hadn't intended to act quite so quickly or in so dramatic a manner, Caihar, but now that it's underway, I find it exciting. And in spite of our rocky start together, I think we could say the two of us have gotten a lot done in a short time."

Caihar beamed. Adinnegram was pleased now that Hoiin had begun its return to normalcy. Caihar hesitantly put his arm around the man's thick, glass-clad shoulder. The Harnish were said to favor physical demonstrations of affection; Adinnegram wasn't a Harnishman, but he could speak like one, and seemed to have a degree of cultural affinity with the people across the Bay. Caihar hadn't gone so far as to change his style of dress in emulation of the visitors as Micsin had, but Caihar had great admiration for everything about Adinnegram. "*You've* gotten a lot done," Caihar said. "I've only just begun."

Adinnegram shook his head. "We've *all* just begun. Still, we've made marvelous progress. You'd be surprised how many people resent and persecute those who mean them only good. We've never had the opportunity before to bring the better way of life to a whole people, all at once, as it appears we're going to do here." Adinnegram looked west, out to the Bay. "But I'm congratulating myself too much, and too soon. I still can hardly believe what you've told me about these Harnish, as you call them. They must have been almost completely submerged. You Eynnish folk must have been much more obstinate last time."

Caihar grimaced in shame. "The Heresiarchs. They had to have come in the time of the Heresiarchs. To think we might have been lifted up almost a thousand years ago, but for them! They were more evil than I had ever imagined, to have spurned the Outreach's gift and then condemned its representatives to such ignoble obscurity!"

Adinnegram patted Caihar's arm. "Well, comrade, I'm not at all sure they offered you what we have. Sulawan thinks they must have come during the days of the Welcome Congress. The Congress is long gone, and our knowledge of those times is spotty. But those mercenaries Lemwulin brought in—I can speak to some of them in the classic language, Caihar! It was an eerie experience in a place like this, like talking to someone out of an old drama. This trip has turned out to be a bigger adventure than I had imagined it would."

Something suddenly flared in the sky. A line of light shot out from between the stars. A bright bead grew at the nearer end of the bright streak, slowing its progress as it fell toward Hoiin. The light slowed and dimmed, then hovered for a moment before disappearing out in the harbor.

Adinnegram clapped his hands together, making a loud clack. "That's it! Sulawan and your radio people have done it." Adinnegram put on his helmet and walked rapidly through the shrubbery and flowers of the roof garden. Before going down the stairs he turned briefly to Caihar, his suit now reflecting the stars. "I'll be gone for a day or two," he said. "Keep up the good work. Talk to Soliël if you have any questions on procedure."

Caihar paused, basking in Adinnegram's compliment, but then he went after him. "May I ask where you're going? Could you use my help?"

Adinnegram stopped. "I suppose I could, now that you mention it. And you might be useful when we meet your comrade Odé."

"Neypo Odé will be my comrade again when he sees the light I have seen," Caihar said with earnest hope.

"He'll come around."

Tomwith Chowdry, one of Adinnegram's comrades, and fifteen young men met them outside the Lodge. The new recruits wore the blue armbands of the Outreach. Many were still in Harnish clothing and carried travel bags. They were among the first to have been processed of the boatload of young men that had arrived late the previous night, sent from Hannava along with three factors representing that city's Directorate. Members of the Reformed Lodge met with the factors and made an agreement for service from the draftees, who would assist Hoiin's Officers and Cadets and engage in other work yet to be finalized. Adinnegram appointed those who spoke Harnish to his personal squad of assistants.

Caihar knew the outlander they met here as Nial Sulawan, not one of the Outreach, but an associate of theirs. He wore armor like Adinnegram's, though he carried his helmet under his arm and clenched a pipe of sotweed between his teeth.

Adinnegram waved at the young men. "Do you think you could use a couple of them on your dig, Sula? Keep resentful locals off your back?"

Sulawan looked them over. "I wouldn't turn down some help. I'd like it better if you hadn't tricked them out with your cheap processing, though."

"You don't seem to appreciate how calmly and efficiently things can be with our method. No arguments or whining about conditions or wages, no jealously of your betters. It lets someone in a position of leadership perform with serenity and confidence."

"Well, the way they fawn over their 'serene leader' makes me a bit ill."

Caihar didn't understand their words—Indeduits, Harnish, whatever—but he saw surprise and anger in some of the Harnishmen's faces. Adinnegram patted one of them on his shoulder. "Don't pay too much attention to Sulawan, boys. Notice his accent? Even odder than yours! He comes from Holm, a barbarous place where they have no interest in right-living and the common good."

Sulawan picked a bit of weed from his mouth. "Yes, and unlike some other folk, who will go unmentioned, on Holm we don't allow self-appointed elites and plutocrats to ride the backs of dehumanized zombies who don't care what they're being paid for their labor or how they live." He turned to Adinnegram. "This conditioning destroys whatever imagination and initiative they once had—even Dikr Epimanter. I knew Epimanter at the Institute before he joined your cult, as you'll recall."

"Elites? And *plutocrats*? I don't know a sept on Sumacron that can afford to own its own starship."

"My great-great-grandfather started out a penniless immigrant from Terra, an orphan! He built his locating business from the ground up."

Adinnegram held up his hands as though he thought Sulawan were about to assault him physically. "All right! You earned your wealth, or at least your ancestor did, and don't think I'm not happy he did. But I'd like to see your old practical side again, Sula. If we hadn't processed the new men here they might have thrown you into the sea, as their countryman did yesterday. Think about that."

"Simple luck on his part, the great lout," Sulawan said. "I just forgot to reset the default prophylactics in the 'casing, that's what happened. Then the damn thing locked up on me when he got in a lucky punch. As if there's anyone to project a gut-spiller at me in a place like this! Otherwise my natural reflexes would have laid him out flat in a trice."

Sulawan peered at Adinnegram's helmet. "Speaking of 'casings, I see that one's taken on your face. Find it makes a more stylish impression?"

"I thought it was a good idea to personalize it. I've been suited up all day, and being able to see my expression helps the comrades understand what I want them to do. Otherwise they tend to take me too literally."

Sulawan frowned. "Yes. Sometimes your words can have unexpected results. Like getting the natives stirred up. If you were more careful of how you go about kidnapping the local notables I'd still have my lighter…"

He stared at the dark sea. "You *do* have somebody out waiting for the drop-case."

"Of course. How good was the signal to the ship? Can you contact it again? Will it be able locate the lighter for us?"

Sulawan shook his head. "The harmonics were off. The ship didn't want to accept an ave from such a strange source, but it agreed to send down the extra goods. I don't think it was fully awake yet. It's damn lucky I had Chowdry pack them up before we came down."

Adinnegram's helmet showed a smile. "Isn't it surprising what an initiative-lacking, dehumanized zombie can do?"

Sulawan snorted. "I'd say rather that some of Chowdry's native common sense miraculously survived his conditioning. To answer your question, no, the ship wasn't sure enough of me to be willing to locate anything for us, or probably even talk to me again until I can use the proper equipment and encoding to contact it. And something in the natives' equipment burned out before I could change the security or give the vale, so it's still awake, and more than a little suspicious."

"But the lighter will be able to give it an acceptable ave and whatnot, right?"

"Of course."

"We have to get the lighter back."

They all walked down to the harbor. Adinnegram and Sulawan discussed the upset caused by the excavations Sulawan had begun that morning in the nave of the Basilica of Saint Eon the Seer.

"I found some provocative artifacts there, and up north too," said Sulawan. "Nothing publishable yet, but intuition, benefited by experience, tells me this place was probably settled before Sumacron, or even Holm. An old story has it that in the early days of the diaspora, a certain degenerate clique on Old Earth were being investigated for crimes against the race. They scarpered off and founded their own colony, and were supposed to have kidnapped a couple of shiploads of people to use as servants and agricultural workers... I've been thinking that this may well explain the natives' subservient performance when greeting someone; an unction harkening back to unhappy days of slavery. And to top it off, they have legends of overthrowing a race of monsters who had ruled them."

"I rather like their hand-pressing and bowing," Adinnegram said. "Not very chummy, but respectful."

Caihar listened patiently, trying to gain a few more words of their odd but interesting language. If Neypo Odé were here...

But now they saw a light bobbing out on the Bay, and in ten minutes a boat rowed by four more young men moved slowly into an empty slip, towing a dark shape nearly larger than their boat.

Sulawan and three of the conscripts from Hannava waded out and pushed a long ovoid shape shoreward until its bottom ground into the sand between two piers. Adinnegram joined them and dismissed the Harnishmen. Sulawan tapped a pattern on the case's surface. Part of its top split slid and away, revealing a compactly ordered cargo.

Sulawan started digging into it. "I don't see any avefactors..."

"We brought all of them down on the second trip," said Adinnegram. "They were in our quarters here."

Sulawan glared at Caihar. "And your good comrade here had those thrown into the ocean. We ought to suit him up and make him look for them."

"The equipment may be fifty or sixty meters down. These old body-casings weren't designed for such depths."

"Let him hold his breath."

"That's hardly—"

"You know, for a man who smiles so much you have an amazingly atrophied sense of humor. Are you sure someone didn't slip a worm into your neck one day when you weren't looking?"

Adinnegram began stiffly, "Outreach policy requires the leadership class to remain in the basic, unenhanced state so that we can see good and evil side by side, recognize the—"

"All right, all right, I've heard it all before. But I'd probably take a worm myself if I could have the lighter back in one piece."

"Were you on long enough with the ship to ask whether it had heard from the lighter?"

"Of course I asked, and no, it hadn't heard a peep."

"I hope the lighter didn't take some damage. But I don't understand how they were able to move it in the first place. Finnegal's processing expressly forbids him from operating things like that."

"Then this Odé managed it, or that oaf with him who nicked the bodycasing. It's more likely than not that Neffafinnegal thinks the rest of you Outreachers are dead…would that free him up enough?"

"No."

"Well, I just hope to hell they didn't drift out to sea…or off into space."

Adinnegram shook his head. "We've had credible reports of sightings from the locals. One northeast of here, and then a couple more to the south. It's been moving."

"Well, why didn't you say so! That's splendid news. They may have locked themselves in somehow and are just drifting."

Sulawan returned his attention to the cargo. "What else did Chowdry lay away for us? Good heavens, a carton of hundred-amp Biht thrashers…a gross of food tubes…"

Sulawan opened the next section of the vessel. "Bodycasings… looks like the ship's whole stock!"

"Excellent."

"Chowdry had a lot of gall appropriating them. They're supposed to be part of the ship's stores."

"I wonder why your ship had that kind of equipment on it? Did the family locators tangle with a lot of pirates? Or perhaps a world or two that had already been claimed?"

"Are you suggesting my family are pirates? And if you're such a pacifist, why the thrashers?"

"I've been told with good authority that you never know what you'll run into out here. In any case, I thank you and your people for having the suits on hand."

Sulawan opened the last hatch. "My goodness, straddle-rides!"

"Those were my idea," Adinnegram said. "On Sumacron the field-comrades found them useful while proselytizing in the hinterland."

"I didn't even know they were onboard. But, yes, I suppose they had to make a quick getaway now and then." Sulawan pulled out a long, plank-like thing. "If the locals here don't break your legs, these might do the job. I had a Prairie Breezer when I was a kid. I don't know how many times I nearly killed myself on it."

He began to wade to shore with it, but Adinnegram took it from him. "You won't need a ride, Sula. You're staying here."

"The hell you say! What do you think you're going to do when you find the lighter? It's my property, and *you're* certainly no pilot."

Adinnegram gestured, and his conscripts pressed in. Sulawan fell silent. The new Outreach converts might have lost their imaginations and initiative, but Sulawan knew the strength of their loyalty. Adinnegram said, "If I can't make sense of the tutorial — it has one, right? — I'll send for you."

"Leave me with a thrasher, at least."

Adinnegram didn't answer. As his Harnishmen worked to pull the drop-case fully ashore, Adinnegram tapped on the plank he had taken. It rose, hanging unsupported in the damp air, and unfolded stirrups and handlebars. Adinnegram swung a leg over the saddle and hunched down. He tipped a boot back and forth in a stirrup, twisted the handgrips, and suddenly soared off into the dark with a startled whoop. In a moment he returned under better control.

"I haven't ridden one of these things since I was a boy either," Adinnegram laughed. He turned to the Harnishmen. "You, you... and you chaps there, yes. Get the suits out and lay them out on shore, then take off your clothes."

21. A PIG'S FUNERAL

After Samma had been kidnapped, the party from Hoiin left the water-meadow at first light. Cadet Noler Hunsacup trudged ahead of the boat, leading it southward. He held a length of black cord in his hand, the other end fixed to a stanchion inside. The great, softly humming slab glided along behind him a couple of feet over the surface of the lanes, snapping branches from the hedges that bounded the lane as it passed. Now and then the boat would unexpectedly dart forward, butting Noler and throwing off the rhythm of his march. At times it would rise to two or three times his height above the ground, pulling the cord out of his hand. Noler resented his assignment as foolish, unnecessary, and most importantly, humiliating; both for him, and for the Striver, whose idea it was, afraid that Micca would shoot them into the sky again.

But after they saw the unburning star come down in the northeast, very likely near Hoiin Noler thought, Neypo conceded that some speed was necessary.

He accepted Neffafinnegal's theory that the thing that had fallen could be a cargo of supplies — possibly including weapons — sent from the ship in orbit. Neypo admitted to Neffafinnegal, Micca translating, and with justifications for not telling him sooner, that some of his erstwhile colleagues had still been alive when they fled Hoiin in the lighter.

But if the Striver was correct in his declaration that all the portable broadcasters — 'avefactors', as Neffafinnegal called them — present in the city had been sunk in the sea, Neffafinnegal said his erstwhile comrades wouldn't have been able to contact the orbiting ship — not without an avefactor or the lighter.

How had they done so then? Micca suggested that they could have used Hoiin's radio tower. "I suppose it would have taken some jiggering, but they could have gotten the engineers to help."

With this Neypo gave up any hope that what they had seen in the sky was a natural event.

Neypo instructed Micca to drive at the height of two tall men, moving 'as quickly as our Cadet might sprint when well rested', or even a little more quickly where the road was straight. Neypo didn't want him to take off across the fields, being unfamiliar with the local countryside.

In the middle of the morning a light rain began to fall. Gillensa and Swannet, who had been enjoying the air on top of the boat, crowded inside.

They cruised southward, this part of Eynna a flat patchwork of pools, orchards and green fields under the dripping sky. Micca slowed when he saw people wading with nets in a pond; Neypo hoped to find someone on the road who had a radio at home and might give him news of any reports of how things went in Hoiin, but they ran away when the boat neared and Neypo decided the fish tenders would have nothing to tell him anyway.

Eventually the landscape grew hilly, spotted with trees and small woodlots. Neypo decided it was time to slow down and have a look outside with his own eyes.

Micca cracked the hatch. The rain had nearly stopped. "I see a house yonder, and what might be a sizable lake beyond it," Neypo called down, as Micca and the others looked at the same scene inside the boat. "The house must be some gentlefolk's freeholding, possibly the manse of a Hustler or Mendicant of modest means. This is probably the best we'll do. I want to hear the news, and it might be a suitable refuge for the ladies. Drive a little closer—whoa there, Micca!"

Neypo dropped back inside. The boat dropped, skimmed over a hedge and down a wet slope. Ahead was a green pond, bordered by higher ground and a line of ancient trees. Micca lost sight of the house by the lake, but he saw something colorful ahead.

He drove toward it, keeping a few inches between the boat and the earth. Under a red and green canvas awning four people sat on chairs of cane, tilted on the uneven turf. In the meadow before them, near a small heap of freshly turned earth, a slender woman leapt and pranced, drawing a bow over a fiddle. Micca could hear music over the boat's auditory pickups. Swannet said, "They must be taking in an entertainment."

The boat slid low behind the hill, swung a buzzing arc around a row of hoary black elms, then settled to earth under one of the trees, hidden from the people below, and offering some protection from the rain.

Micca crawled out the hatch after the others. Neypo tried to brush the wrinkles out of his coat. Gillensa adjusted the ribbons of his hat as best she could while expressing her doubts as to the suitability of these people as hosts for her and Swannet.

"We don't know yet, do we?" Neypo said. "Don't be so negative. Gillensa, Swannet, you'll accompany me. The rest you stay with the raft, and keep yourselves out of sight."

They climbed over the rim of the meadow, the women holding hands over their heads in an effort to avoid drips from the trees. Neypo raised his arm several times in a Striving salute as they approached the group. There were three men and a woman under the awning. The woman was imposing, and had a Harnish look to her. She stood up with her arms folded across a large bosom as she saw them coming down the slope. Her suspicious expression became welcoming as she identified Neypo's plaid, but the man standing next to her squinted and held up his hand. "Hold yourselves just there!" he called out.

"Elmo!" the large woman hissed. "The fellow is a Striver."

By his plaid, Neypo determined the man to be a low-ranking Mendicant. He introduced himself, then Gillensa and Swannet.

The Mendicant pulled a pair of lenses from a pocket and put them on his nose. "A Striver indeed!"

He bowed to Neypo and his young women, drawing down his hands. "Welcome, sir; welcome, young misses. Glad to see you here at old Hwistomellian. Elmo Ansitap, at your service."

The Mendicant waved them in under the awning. "You must wonder why we sit out here on such a day." He gestured at the pile of earth. "Munteen, our pet sow, has been Called Home. Today we bury her and say our farewells."

Neypo nodded. "I'm sure she meant much to your household."

"She was a good ratter." He gestured to a basket, in which sat a healthy looking pig. "Snyppe here will take up her duties...but must I ask you sir, by what means Wennoc has favored us with your august presence? You seem to have conjured yourselves out of the rain. Most remarkable."

A tall, athletic young man wearing a cap with a long bill rolled his eyes at Swannet, as if she shared a secret with him. "Maybe they were hill-walking, and were attracted by Aunty's dirge."

"Be still, Horemps," said the large woman.

Neypo ignored the youth and returned the Mendicant's bow. "I am engaged in an important mission for the Lodge, Brother Elmo. Mennedal may well hear of my efforts; how they were aided, how they were thwarted, and by whom. Need I detail the matter further?"

"Why no, Striver, certainly not. No need to tell us the particulars of your special mission. And if perchance I am possessed of any information which you might find useful, I say again, that I am at your service!"

"I have an information!" declared the third man, coming forward to glare at Neypo. "I heard the growl of a virvitat up yonder just now, behind Hwistomellian's ellums, whence you appeared."

The Mendicant frowned at the man, then bowed again to Neypo. "My wife's uncle, the Honorable Suto Cwannoc."

Neypo, Gillensa and Swannet pressed their hands together as the Mendicant Elmo introduced the others of his household. His son Horemps and his wife Iuléli bowed. Now Iuléli's sister Slimpia came in from the meadow. Slimpia stared blankly for a moment at the newcomers, then improvised a cheery little melody on her fiddle as a welcome for them.

The Mendicant's wife said, "You and your lovely young ladies must come up to the house, Striver, and have a beverage, and perhaps a light meal?"

"That would be most welcome," Neypo said. "And if you wouldn't mind the presumption on your hospitality, my young ladies have told me they would dearly like to tarry in the country hereabouts for a short while; do you have room for them at Hwistomellian? — Ah, excellent, that's fine then! You'll be doing us and the Lodge a great favor."

"Oh, joy! New friends!" exclaimed Slimpia. "We'll sing and dance the days away!" Neypo refused to meet Gillensa's eye.

Elmo Ansitap smiled, and suggested they be off. "I see the sun is peeking betwixt the clouds now, and my manse is just over the hill. We can sit on the veranda over the lake and take refreshments. And do your young people enjoy listening to radio presentations?"

"Indeed, as do I!" said Neypo. "I meant to inquire whether you had a set—that was, in fact, the principal reason I thought to stop..."

Snyppe the pig suddenly raised her head and squealed. She launched herself from her basket and charged up the slope toward the line of elms.

Everyone turned and watched her run. Something not quite hidden by the trunk of an elm flashed in a beam from the newly emerged sun. The pig reached the trees and made for the source of the flash—a polished bronze helmet.

Snyppe tried to seize the leg of the helmet's owner in her mouth, but the greaves he wore prevented her from getting a purchase. The pig squealed furiously and leapt up and down, targeting a bit of his anatomy less well protected. Before Snyppe could find it, she dropped to her feet, squealed once, and raced back down the slope.

The man with the bronze helmet had disappeared, but now a huge, floating rectangle of shimmering gray stone edged slowly out from behind the elms. When three or four feet of it was visible it stopped, then just as slowly withdrew. A faint, buzzing hum trailed behind it.

Snyppe came back under the awning, looked up at them all, and hopped into her basket.

For a moment everyone was speechless. Gillensa fixed a friendly smile on her face to show the Ansitaps. Neypo and Swannet followed her example.

"My, what verve, what élan!" Neypo said. "Does your pet often amuse you with such clever antics?"

The Ansitaps' son Horemps twist the cap on his head. "Not that I've noticed, but then she hasn't been here long..."

"Oh, it was a miracle, a calling of Wennoc!" Slimpia cried. "I *tingle* with magical inspiration—oh, siintimin fly all around me! Come, my new friends, dance with me!" She began sawing on her fiddle.

"It was a virvitat, you silly girl, sure as chicken-dirt!" cried Suto, squinting under his hand at the elms.

The Mendicant's wife was also still staring up the hill. Elmo Ansitap was watching Neypo.

Neypo bowed to him. "Well, it was a great pleasure to meet you all... and it's nice to see a bit of the sun again, isn't it?" He glanced up the hill. "But I think after all that the girls won't take advantage of your kind offer. Our heartiest thanks, just the same! We'll be on our way now."

The Mendicant watched the Striver and his ladies until they had disappeared behind the row of trees. "Uncle Suto," he said. "Find Pinset, and Trumpo too. I have errands for them."

"Huh," said Suto. "Likely they're in the must-house. I'll have to find my hat and muck-boots."

"Do so then, and do it now!"

Neypo, Swannet and Gillensa walked up to the elms, trying not to walk too quickly. Swannet glanced back once and murmured, "Good riddance."

"But Horemps was rather a darling, wasn't he?" Gillensa asked her.

Swannet nodded. "He was positively a piece of art, and so fit!"

"Ladies!" said Neypo. "Remember yourselves."

They found the boat more or less where they'd left it. Micca and the alien must be inside, but Noler stood on the turf outside. Neypo walked up to him and stood with his hands on his hips.

"Cadet Hunsacup. Why did you choose to ignore my instructions? Did you think those people wouldn't see you?"

"And you, Adjunct Mora." Micca's helmet had risen out of the boat's hatch. "Did you think they wouldn't see the raft? What were you two playing at? Thanks to you the women have lost their refuge, and you've lost me my chance to hear the news on the radio."

Noler started to speak, but Micca had boosted himself out of the hatch. "That mad piglet was about to make a meal out of the Cadet's bollocks. I nosed the boat up to scare if off. What did you want me to do? Sit in there and watch a mauling?"

Neypo bit his lip in frustration. He turned to Noler. "What were you doing lurking out here in the first place, Cadet?"

Noler looked at the ground. "I was worried. I was worried how Miss Olinom would get on at this forsaken place…and I wanted to *see* her, see her one last time!"

"Oh!" cried Swannet. She ran to Noler, took his head in her hands and pressed her cheek to his.

Micca said, "Did they see the boat then, Striver?"

"Of course they did. The old man and the girl thought it was supernatural, but the others didn't seem so fanciful, and they were already suspicious of us, wondering where we had come from. But get in, everyone get into the raft! I wouldn't wonder that they'll summon whatever passes for a constabulary in these parts."

They settled back into the boat and Micca slowly drove back the way they had come.

"You said those people had a radio you wanted to hear, right?" Micca asked Neypo. "You can do that right here now."

"What! You said that—"

"Finna turned off the part that hears and can reply back to what are like, ah, *personal* messages. I never thought to ask till now whether it could still act like one of our regular radios, but it can. I tried putting in climbing combinations of numbers. It found some music, then I heard somebody talking, and it was Reimi Rytalla on the Voice of Hoiin. Then I got the 'Tales and Tattlings' show from Midoi."

"What did you hear?"

"Well, not a lot, but Midoi said there were silver bandits riding around on broomsticks."

"Bandits on broomsticks!" said Neypo incredulously. Micca tapped and found one of the frequencies he had listened to earlier. The sounds buzzed, cleared again and grew louder: a children's choir, just finishing a song, and then came the unctuous voice of the broadcaster Reimi Rytalla:

"And there you have it, citizens. Were they not precious? You listen to the Voice of Hoiin. The hour is precisely the first past noon—" there was the sound of a bell being struck "—and now, from our studios in the penthouse of the Concord Prospect Massif, we shall next hear the Usuma Quartet, under the leadership of Mosco Ismetamoi Tingwe, perform Pycca's much beloved 'Variations on the All's Well in Wennoc', brought to the aether with a generous gift from the makers of Felmo's Favorite Oatmeal: a splendid bargain of wholesomeness, available at the central market. Look for the attractive red and yellow jar. And now, our heartfelt welcome, Master Tingwe! Before you begin, let me remind our listeners that at the supper hour this evening you will hear the comic dialogues of Snet and Snapsni, followed by..."

Neffafinnegal spoke in a mocking, sing-song voice: "Oyna moyna, snapsi tapsi. Find a signal with some music, comrade."

Gillensa threw him a puzzled look, then said, "Things sound too calm considering what happened at the Fair."

"Yes, but they're not going to broadcast alarming news other cities would hear," Neypo said. "They're trying to sound normal."

Micca worked the radio's controls and was able to raise Parnala.

"...regarding rumors concerning residents of our city who visited Hin Hoina's reportedly aborted Fair. Our Lodge recommends calm, but also suggests that folk in rural areas and on the outskirts of the city practice a watchful vigilance and remain indoors if possible. Officers have been dispatched to investigate these trouble makers and their alleged accomplices, and we will relay their findings as soon as they are made public."

Parnala's announcer had a deeper and more sedate voice than Rytalla. He sounded professionally bored, but also a little uneasy. After the sounds of shuffling papers, he went on: "This just received. This morning's reports from Sumniameiamisaillyn of a Hustler molested at his manse by oddly clad ruffians have, apparently, proven inaccurate. Said Hustler, the Honorable Hys Penmo, took luncheon with his brothers today at the sub-Lodge in Eiapi and has assured them of his good health and that of his family..."

Gillensa said, "The ruffians might be some of the outlanders. Do you think they bewitched or hypnotized this Penmo, father?"

"Perhaps." Neypo's voice rose. "But if things work out for us at Mellatuno, Adinnegram and his minions will find the tables turned. Drive on, Micca; on to Mellatuno!"

"Where is it?"

"Where indeed. Well, you have your magic mists there that have been showing what's outside. Can you make the raft's eyes show us what's underneath? — without tipping us over, that is! Yes? Good. Take us up high enough that we can see the world like a map."

Micca raised the boat. First they saw shadowed, wet grass, then rapidly dwindling trees, a tiny red-roofed manse by a blue lake, then a whole network of lakes and trackless green wetlands, growing smaller and smaller.

"How high are we?" Neypo whispered.

"The Indeduish measures are different...I'd say about two thousand yards, give or take."

"Good heavens! Take us down! I don't recognize anything...the face of the world looks nothing like a map." He pointed. "But I think that's north..."

Micca found the house with the red roof again, which seemed to be near their landing spot.

"Look," Gillensa said. "That surely must be the Ansitap house. He said it was on a lake...and isn't that him there, on the dock?"

Neypo squinted. "It may well be..."

The Mendicant, if it was him, was waving his hands at another man, who jumped into a narrow little boat, took up a two-bladed paddle and darted off across the water. Another boat was already some way off, traveling in the opposite direction.

"I hope they're going to fetch the lady of the house some cornmeal or a case of essence," Neypo said.

"And that the Mendicant hasn't been corrupted," Gillensa added.

22. THE SLOUGHS

"Take us a bit west of south, Micca. Keep an eye out for ancient looking buildings, either ruined or not, but especially any with signs of current habitation. Let us proceed at, let's say, half the speed at which a small melon would fall — but horizontally, of course."

After one failed attempt Neffafinnegal caused a compass to appear in a corner of the outside view, and Micca adjusted their course. Eynna moved under them, green water, green earth. They saw a few more tile-roofed villas beside the chains of lakes, small farms with barns and fish-drying racks, and then nothing much but sluggish streams connecting grassy lakes and ponds of every size and shape.

Neypo and Gillensa climbed out onto the boat's deck. Swannet made as though to join them, but Neypo muttered some discouragement and she came back inside. "The Striver must have taken Glensy into the Lodge!" she huffed.

Micca could hear the two of them whispering above. He did some tapping, and his helmet was able to bring him most of what they said. "...to hurry!" Gillensa was saying. "People besides Elmo Ansitap must have seen us, and even if he didn't see the flying raft, others like those fishers probably have, and they're not likely to have mistaken it for an ox cart. And people like to talk...or they can be *made* to talk! Why else would the outlanders have come as far south as Eiapi? Just to do missionary work among the fish-gatherers?"

Neypo whispered back, "As long as we're aloft they can't come upon us unawares, and what force they might send after us would be small."

"Why small? Who knows how many people they've bewitched? You said the visitors have some mysterious coercive power. And have you forgotten about the thing we saw fall from the sky last night? Our outlander said there might have been weapons in it, and 'silver bandits' or whatever it was they said hints at more glass armor, too — and flying broomsticks, who knows? They might be hiding behind a bush, looking up at us right now, aiming their weapons, plotting how they'll storm the boat when we're forced down."

"Daughter, I really—"

"And don't tell me they don't want Micca's raft back. All the Cadets and Officers from Hoiin and Parnala together would find it daunting, crewed with a gang of murdering pirates. Why, retaking the boat is probably the first thing on their agenda…"

Eyes on the view outside, hands on the rods before him, now Micca spoke to Neffafinnegal: "Could somebody get in here, into the lighter if I don't want them to? Can your people's weapons stop it or wreck it?"

"Not if you're in here to stop them. I told you about that. I think somebody could open it from outside if they knew how to and nobody was in here to countermand it. But I'm pretty sure no hand weapon can hurt it. Why? Is the Outreach coming after us?"

"What if they were? What would you do if your Adinnegram was outside right now, telling us to come out?"

"Micca!" Neypo said, waving off Gillensa. "What are you two chattering about?"

Blank faced, Neffafinnegal stared at Micca. "I'm not sure. Adinnegram was my mentor. But I thought he was gone, dead. I know he's not now, but maybe my conscience doesn't know…or more likely, I think, is that all this weird stuff going on lately *killed* my conscience." He touched the back of his neck. "I don't know what to do most of the time. It's confusing."

"What is this with your conscience all the time? I've got one too, everybody does. But it's just there; it doesn't come and go. Sometimes it's hard to listen to it, and if I don't I feel bad…usually too late."

"You're not using the word in the right way. Maybe the meaning changed over the years." Neffafinnegal nodded, as though he had solved a problem. "I know what it is. If you people came here long enough ago, you probably didn't have modern consciences. It's not something you're born with."

"How do you mean?"

"When you're ten or twelve they give you one —"

"Like getting initialized?"

"No. But some get one, others don't. If you have a trade or a job, if you're a regular person, you get one; but entrepreneurs, money handlers, politicians, most of them don't. Those people need to have wild brains, I suppose. Adinnegram doesn't have one. Sulawan doesn't."

"Can these consciences *make* you do things?"

"Micca!" Neypo said. "What's the news?"

"They counsel you to do things that are good and useful," Neffafinnegal said. "It was a big help to me in school. That was a different one, though. I got a new one when I joined the Outreach."

Micca said, "Conscience or not, let's make a pact to look out for each other, Finna. Are we real friends, not just comrades?"

After a moment Neffafinnegal stretched his arm over the hump between their couches and shook Micca's hand.

"Good," said Micca, nodding. "We've got to figure what we're going to do if there's trouble."

"Micca!" Neypo shouted. "What have you been talking about? Report at once!"

"We're talking about the, ah, security, Striver. Securing the boat."

"Oh! Good idea, yes."

Micca spoke to Neffafinnegal again. "The Honorable wants me to help him once we get to Mellatuno, and that probably means I'll have to leave the lighter. Can we lock the hatch? Is there any other way in?"

"As far as I've noticed, the main hatch can be opened from outside by anyone who knows how if there's no one inside to stop them. I could stay and do that, but I can't be sure what would happen if Adinnegram could speak to me…I could lock it and close off the pickups from outside, but then I wouldn't hear you when you wanted to get back in." Neffafinnegal paused. "Maybe it would be best if we all got out and then hid the lighter. With the guest access dead nobody could find it if they couldn't see it. Unless they had an avefactor, and they'd have found us by now if they had one of those."

"You mean we should bury the boat? That would be a lot of work, and what if we needed to get going again in a hurry?"

Neffafinnegal gestured. "There's a lot of water here. You don't need to dig that. And if you're close enough and wearing a 'casing, you can call it to come up again."

"It can go under water? But I'm stupid — if it can go outside Wennoc, I guess it wouldn't be bothered by a slough, or even a deep lake."

Most of the earth below was covered by water now, choked here and there by vast reed beds, open in other places and pocked by irregular, tree-bearing humps of land. The sun was well out now and pushed up the clouds in the west. There were ducks and hwerrits on the water, storks hunting in the reeds, but there were no signs of people or any habitations, ancient or modern.

But finally Neffafinnegal reached to the receptor and enlarged the view. They saw blocky lines now, sketched along under shallow water.

Neypo said, "Those look like ruins, or maybe a highway... right under us, are they?"

"I think so," said Micca.

Neffafinnegal's finger tapped again.

"Someone's out there," Gillensa said. Noler hunched forward. "There are at least two of them."

"Have they seen us?" Neypo asked.

"They don't act like they have," Noler said.

Neypo said, "Bring us down, Micca. Can you float us just where we are? We'll approach whomever it is on foot."

Micca let them drop until the boat's cushion of repulsion rippled the waters of the sloughs, disturbing a few birds, then let it slowly sink until its top was a couple of feet above the surface. Reeds and rushes, brown, gray and newly green, surrounded the boat, merging on one side into a bank of chokeberry bushes and stunted but luxuriously flowering thorn trees.

He opened the hatch and the Striver cautiously crawled outside. "From here I can see no one," he whispered down to the others, "but I think I hear voices."

Micca unfastened himself. "The rest of you'd better stay here," he said, crawling and twisting by the others. Noler offered him his bodkin. Micca waved him off and pulled himself out of the hatch and crouched down beside Neypo.

There were too many reeds to see far. Micca increased the sensitivity of his helmet's ears, but heard only a cacophony of bugs, birds, and rustling plants. He took off his helmet. As usual, he was disappointed and annoyed by the weakness of his naked eyes, and again surprised by the richness of Wennoc's unfiltered air. Under the rank green smell of fresh growth was the perfume of flowering plants and dead fish and mud.

Neypo said, "I'd almost forgotten what you look like, despite the strange glass face you sometimes display," he whispered. "But you should remain fully armored out here."

"I don't know about this glass face you go on about, but I'd like to get out of the whole thing off for a while. Before it grows onto me and I can't."

"I'm sure it's not what anyone would call comfortable. But soon now, if luck is with us, you can be rid of it. Maybe one day you'll set it up at your plantation as a memento of your — wait. Did you hear that?"

Micca pointed west. "Off that way."

Neypo stood up warily. "Don't you think they must have seen us come down? I wouldn't think they'll move before they've determined that we have gone as well. I'm going to send the Cadet to investigate."

"No, it should probably be me who goes," Micca said reluctantly.

"I'm afraid that as our vessel's pilot you are less…dispensable, let us say. I hate to make so unfeeling a judgment, but duty requires it. Let's go below."

Noler listened to the Striver's instructions bravely enough, Micca thought. "When you come upon the people we saw," Neypo said, "be sure to tell them you're an official representative of the Lodge. But be *friendly*, charming, don't try to overawe them, Noler! It's likely they can tell us how to find the Office of Antiquities and I don't want them to be frightened away."

Against everyone's advice Noler left his greaves on, and he arranged his kilt in a way that made it sort of a high-riding pair of short pants. He dropped off the boat with a splash and waded into the reeds, arms out before him. Micca nudged the boat ahead, slowly spreading and flattening the reeds as they moved ahead, some yards behind Noler, but still able to see where he was.

Noler raised his hand. Micca halted the boat. Noler crouched low in the water, studying something beyond the sight of the boat's eyes. Noler beckoned and Micca started forward again.

Through the boat's ears Micca heard a sudden, hoarse shout. He saw the Cadet's shoulders dip and twist, as though he were groping at something under the water. Noler fell backwards, then lurched up, flailing his arms. He seemed to be trying to run, and rose far enough out of the water to show his back.

Micca nosed the boat ahead. He could see Noler grow taller, vanishing and reappearing between the thick reeds. The boat shuddered slightly, plowing mud aside, and messages flashed under Micca's nose.

"Striver, we have to stop or go up in the air."

"Settle here then, Micca," Neypo replied. He got up and crawled cautiously out the hatch. A moment later he called down, "Micca! I think you'd better take us up again. I can't see the Cadet or anyone else out here now."

"I can't either," Micca called back, and raised them straight up to the height of two men. He still couldn't see anyone. He lifted to ten yards — when Neypo jumped back inside — then twenty, still seeing no one.

Micca descended, went forward a few yards and set down on a narrow, brushy island. Under a line of nearby willows was a small hut or shed thatched with reeds. Everyone got out. Almost immediately Gillensa found the Cadet's bodkin, half buried in muddy soil that had been trampled by a confusion of long, splayed footprints.

Gillensa said, "So he lost it, or more likely, it was taken from him."

"Cadet!" Neypo called. "Noler! Show yourself!"

The slough was silent but for the boat's low hum and the chirpings of a few bugs. Micca slowly approached the shed. It was made of gravelly poured stone, weathered and broken at the corners. There was a long, slot-like window under the eaves of the roof, a plank door next to it. Micca peeked in. There were half a dozen grimy cots, a low table with the remains of a meal, a chimney with a cooking fireplace in the corner, a number of pots and large ceramic jars.

Neffafinnegal and Neypo joined him. Neffafinnegal picked something up, a grotesquely long shoe made of green gum.

"Like the footprints outside," Micca said.

Neypo found a torn bag, also made of stretchy green stuff. There were a pair of glass disks cemented into it, and under them a snout with a long, upstanding tube. He turned the bag inside-out and found curving tabs at the end of the tube that could be taken into the wearer's mouth. "Things are beginning to make sense," he said. "The user could breathe under the water. It would make him sort of a human mudrunner, or a frog-man."

"I wonder what this stuff is?" said Micca. He had dipped a stick of firewood into one of the jars. A dark, viscous substance dripped to the floor. "I don't think it's cooking fat."

Neypo sniffed at it and wrinkled his nose. "But it is some kind of oil, and I would say that extracts from a number of herbs had been added to it. These frog-men may well smear it over their skin in an attempt to keep warm when the water is cold, or to make themselves unpalatable to water creatures, or perhaps both."

They heard Swannet calling. "What is it?" Neypo called back, running from the shed.

"I see something in the water!" She stood in the middle of the boat's deck, pointing to the west.

The sun was lowering in the sky, and the Striver squinted under his hand.

"I see them too," Gillensa said. "Little sticks, several of them, moving away."

Neypo became agitated. "Breathing tubes, snorkels. We've been wasting our time. This is my fault. The bandits or frog-men who live on this island must have him. Take us away, Micca! Everyone watch for breathing-tubes or movement in the water."

All got into the boat again and Micca lifted. Much of the water was open here, meandering between curving stands of small trees, many of them dead, their trunks half-drowned. There was no sign of the breathing-tubes as they coasted over the place Swannet had first seen them, but they found a shallow line of stone, a causeway or the top of a wall. It ran out into open water and vanished, hidden either by the depth of the water or the sun's glare. After three hundred yards it rose again and met an oblong green and white island, larger and rising farther out of the water than the one they had left. As they watched, three men emerged from the water over the causeway. Another one struggled between them; it looked as though his arms were bound.

Neypo signaled Micca to open the hatch, then he scrambled up into it. "Ahoy!" he shouted. "You there! Halt!"

"HALT!" Micca yelled through the boat's annunciator, his voice thundering over the slough.

The frog-men looked back, then hurried onto the island, pulling their captive, now recognizably the Cadet, with them. They disappeared between the tumbled stones.

Micca called the Striver back in. He shot the boat forward. They came down in the water next to the causeway. The island seemed to be a cluster of partially drowned, ancient buildings rather than a natural feature of the topography. Its edges were canted and fractured, spilling geometric chunks into the lake. In the center a series of blocky shapes rose up out of the grass and bushes. No one was in sight.

Neypo got up onto the deck again and the others joined him. "Hallo the island!" Neypo called. "Men of the water! I must speak with you! I Strive for the Holy Lodge, and command emergency authority over this district!"

Water lapped stone, a bird called.

Neypo called out again. "Come out at once! Deliver to me your prisoner or suffer the wrath of the law!"

Neypo's voice fled over the slough.

Gillensa stared at the island. "Is this Mellatuno?"

Neypo pulled his mustache. "I don't think so, no; not Mellatuno proper. Too small for one thing. It may be a bastion or an outpost, one the antiquaries haven't explored yet. Or these water-going bandits may keep them away. In any case, the frog-men came here and are probably hiding now in some bolt-hole or crevice." Neypo dropped to the causeway and trotted onto the island.

Micca, Neffafinnegal and Gillensa followed him, Swannet creeping after them, holding onto Gillensa's hand and watching for mudrunners.

They could see only a little of the island from where they stood. Neypo climbed onto a flat stone. "Here's the mark of a wet foot, and there, another. They lead to the upper hills — onward!"

Micca helped Swannet over a face of rock to the next level of the island and vaulted up after her. Gillensa quickly followed. The Striver, approaching the ascent with less fear of mudrunners or frog-men, but with more bulk, strained and puffed. Neffafinnegal pushed from behind and Micca pulled the Striver's arms.

They found another puddle of water on the stone, then came to an irregular path of grass that tipped up to meet a wall of white stone. If the footprints continued, no one found sign of them in the grass. A few little bushes mounded the top of the wall before them. Other green-shrouded hillocks were partially visible beyond it, but they saw no doors.

Neypo decided that he, Micca and the alien would each explore a section of the island, and one of them would find an entrance to the ancient structures. When a door was located, its discoverer was to immediately call for the others.

Gillensa wanted to join them, but Swannet refused to join the hunt, so Neypo said both of them would stay with the boat. "Be sure to call out at once if you see anyone," he cautioned. Micca quickly tutored Gillensa in how to close the hatch if the bandits should return to the shore, though that seemed unlikely.

Micca climbed to the south and quickly lost sight of the others. At close hand the little hills and outcroppings of stone didn't look so much like they had been built by hands. There were no doors or windows, though many were squarish, and not so natural looking after all.

He came to the highest point of the island. To the west were stretches of open water, fields of rushes, cattails and lily pads. Some distance beyond was a long, straggling ridge of stone, the same dirty white as this island, green bushes and trees sticking out of it here and there. The pattern of plant life and water before it included a straight, unnatural division, probably a continuation of the partly drowned causeway to the east, but he saw no one walking it, or swimming beside it.

Micca heard the rattle of falling stone. He spun to see Neypo clambering up behind him. "Did you find a door, Striver?"

Neypo shook his head. "I take it you haven't, either."

Micca pointed west. "Could that be Mellatuno?"

"It seems likely. I don't how much of the place remains; it was quite a large city in its heyday. But the sun is going down. We have to find some sign of the Cadet, or soon make other plans."

Then a woman's voice echoed among the rocks...Gillensa's?

"We'll be with you presently!" Neypo shouted. "The women are getting impatient. Or maybe they've found the Cadet!" His tone was hopeful, but not his expression.

They went down a twisting path, the sun making long shadows ahead of them. As they negotiated a narrow stretch of the path Neypo said, "I have some things to tell you, and this seems a good time...

"I know you think of the aliens as indomitable bullies, while Wennoc is a small, frightened child with no choice but to submit or be bludgeoned into — hoy! That would have been a nasty fall."

Neypo steadied himself on Micca's arm and spoke on. "But you see, although Wennoc is gentle in many ways, it is not weak. You've seen violent storms, cruel deaths in the forest. Wennoc is powerful and can be dangerous. I admit this fact had made me confident, not as anxious to reach Mellatuno as I might have been. But once aroused, I don't know how far Wennoc will go in its anger. I suppose I haven't wanted to face the responsibility of being its agent."

"What's going to happen? What are you talking about?"

Neypo answered in a low voice. "I think I mentioned to you earlier that I came upon certain records in the Lodge's Archives, Micca. When seen in the light of happenings both recent and ancient, this information is astounding. So far as I know I'm the only living man who understands these records' implications. The knowledge must be shared, and this is where I must trust you."

"I won't tell anybody."

"Well then, I am quite sure there are means to assure that the aliens never leave Wennoc, just as your own ancestors never left it. Most importantly, neither will the ship that brought them here, the one you described as 'in orbit'. You and I will see to that."

Micca stopped. "How? What have I got to do with it?"

"The archives mention a certain resource at Mellatuno, something lost a very long time ago, but recently rediscovered. As to your part in the plan, your recent experience with the —"

"Hello! Hello there!" Micca yelled, waving his hands. "I can see Swannet, Striver. What's she jumping around like that for?"

"You should have noticed by now that she's an excitable young woman, Micca. You can understand why I've withheld news of her father's tragic end—Swannet! I say, Swannet!" Neypo called. "We're coming as quickly as we might."

Micca and Neypo scrambled down the last drop to the causeway and splashed out to the boat.

"He's gone!" Swannet screamed at them.

Micca tapped on his wrist and his helmet swiveled.

Neypo looked sharply all around. "Neffafinnegal? Neffafinnegal is gone? But he went to search when we did—but where is Gillensa?"

"Glensy heard him call, and she hasn't come back!"

"Swannet: tell me what happened," Neypo said.

"He called! He called from the cliff over there. He said 'Find' or something of the sort. Glensy called for you. We heard you call back, and she went to meet you."

"Micca," Neypo said quickly. "Climb up yonder and investigate."

Swannet hugged her arms together as Micca returned to the island. He followed the path Swannet had indicated, a crumbling trail between the water and a nearly vertical wall of stone. There was a set of worn steps ahead, leading to the top of the wall.

He heard Swannet scream again and turned back to look at the boat. Neypo was trotting down the causeway toward him. Swannet crouched on the deck, pointing in Micca's direction.

Micca looked down. A glistening arm reached up from the water, groping for his ankle. Micca jumped and threw himself onto the steps, scrabbling up on his hands and knees. His hand found a fist-sized rock.

He turned to see a dripping man with a green, snouted head crouched at the foot of the stairs, two yards behind him. The frog-man grunted huskily and snorted a spray of water from his snorkel. Brandishing a club, he started up the steps.

Micca jumped to his feet. Remembering days on the ball field at Mora, he swung his arm and pitched his rock at the frog-man. The rock struck the man's shoulder. A tooting squeal came from his snorkel and he tumbled into the water.

Micca stumbled down the steps, shaking with excitement. Neypo ran up the path and met him. The Striver found a large stone and heaved it into the lake where the bandit had disappeared.

There was a tremendous spout of water. Several feet away the end of a snorkel appeared. It made a choofing sound, spitting water, then cut a line in the surface of the water, swimming away.

"So much for that one," Neypo said. "But come, come! We have to find the others before it gets any darker."

Swannet wailed from the boat. "We can't leave her here," said Micca, hanging back.

"Go fetch her. Quickly!"

Swannet met Micca at the edge of the island. Neypo called from somewhere out of sight. Micca jumped onto the boat and took Swannet's hand. She clung to his arm and they climbed the steps.

Beyond the top of the wall the surface of the island tipped into a narrow, grassy depression. Micca was afraid the Striver would have disappeared too, but they found him at the far end of the little valley. The ground rose in a tangle of flowering vines, small trees crowning the top of the slope. Neypo was studying the greenery below the trees. The sun had dropped behind the hill, but through a gap in the undergrowth Micca could see a rectangular, stone-framed cavity. Neypo turned and beckoned excitedly. "I've seen neither Gillensa nor Neffafinnegal, but they must have found this place too."

Micca started forward. "No!" Swannet cried hysterically. "Wights live under hills like that!" She turned and ran.

Micca followed her to the top of the steps and caught her arm. Swannet seemed to be afraid of him now as well as spirits and frog-men, so he took off his helmet. She smiled timidly at the sight of his face.

"Here," Micca said, giving her his helmet. "Hold it out if you see any ghosts. That'll drive them away. You know the power a looking-glass has over them."

Swannet gingerly took the helmet. She held it away from her body, as though it would burn or soil her. "It doesn't look like a mirror now that you're not wearing it," she observed sharply, but she let Micca take her hand and lead her back.

It was getting darker by the minute in the sloping valley. Neypo was nowhere in sight, but they heard him calling hoarsely. "A door, I've found a door! Hoy, Micca, hai! Are you there? Come help me get it open!"

Swannet stumbled backwards, shaking her head. "It isn't him! It's a sprite that's taken his voice!"

"Wait here then, wait just a minute," Micca told her, and ran to the gap in the bushes. The face that looked out of the gloom was grimy and scraped by branches, but it was Neypo Odé's.

"The door is stout, but we'll both try," Neypo told Micca. "Help me push!"

They heard a short cry. "I'll get Swannet up here first," said Micca.

"Yes, yes, but hurry!"

She wasn't where Micca had left her. She wasn't anywhere.

"Damnation!" Micca hissed. He started back for the door in the hill, stopped, turned around. "Swannet!" he yelled. "Gillensa!" Then, more weakly, "Finna!"

Micca ran back to the door. "Striver! Neypo! Swannet's gone!"

The hole between the bushes was empty. If there was a door here, it was closed.

The moon was coming up, full now, pale and translucent; there was still an orange flare over the hills in the west, but the little valley was dark. Micca began tapping an order to amplify his helmet's vision. He blinked, touched his naked, almost unfamiliar, nose and forehead. "Damnation!" he said again, with some desperation.

He walked as slowly as he could force himself to, scanning the ground. His foot hit something under a fern. Micca jerked back, then quickly squatted and grabbed his helmet, which Swannet must have dropped here. Just as he pushed it over his head he heard a muffled scream, then a metallic clunk.

He hadn't even looked before, but now he found a mess of footprints in the damp earth where Neypo had disappeared. A number of them were long and wedge-shaped. Micca hit the back wall with his fist, which returned a resonant boom. The metal door fit tightly into its stone frame. There was no handle.

Micca pounded again and shouted, increasing the volume to its maximum. The slough creatures fell silent.

He left the door, cursing himself and his companions for their carelessness and stupidity. He thudded his boot on the moss-covered earth under him. Would the others hear him, down in the bandits' hole?

Why would people choose to live in caves in the middle of a slough? Why would they kidnap people? If he could find one of the frog-men—

Something heavy smacked into his back. Micca went down, face first. A pair of wiry arms wrapped themselves around his chest. Frantically cursing himself again, Micca wrenched himself loose.

His assailant quickly reattached himself. Micca's vision was blocked by a flabby snout flattened against his faceplate. One of the bandit's glass eyes clicked on his faceplate, inches from his own.

Unbalanced, Micca fell, then staggered to his feet. The bandit hung to his neck. A flippered foot slapped hard at Micca's crotch. Unhurt but outraged, Micca seized the man's shoulders and brought up his knee to return the favor.

The bandit made a muffled howl. He let go of Micca and fell back, but got quickly to his feet. He dodged away before Micca could catch him and hobbled off at good speed, away from the door.

Micca went after him. The man flapped away into the gloom, arms swinging on either side of a swollen false belly. Suddenly he vanished, dropping straight into the earth.

Micca stood by a stone-curbed well, almost flush with the grass. He could see nothing in the depths.

He felt rage, humiliation. Before he could think better of it, he dropped feet-first into the well.

23. SUPPER INTERRUPTED

"Come in, come in. I can eat any time. Let's see how you look."

"I look like an idiot." On his feet were clumsy wood and leather sandals. He wore a gray barracks-shirt, a sort of double-flapped apron around his waist, and under it an ill-fitting groin strap. A hooded snorkel and a pair of long flippers hung from strings around his neck. He had washed, but the guards' soap wasn't much good; his skin bore an oily greenish tinge, remnants of what the guards called 'duty grease'. He passed a hand over the stubble of hair on his head, where more of the green stuff had clotted.

"You'll get used to it, and you look no different than the others. Haven't they given you one of the new re-breathing bladders?"

"No."

"Well, I'll put in a personal recommendation. You'll have fun with it, but of course you'll have to maintain it properly, too. There have been problems with fungus tainting them."

Samma stared at her for a second, then shouted. "I don't *want* a damned re-breathing bladder! What am I? A frog? A slave? I have responsibilities. I've got lectures to attend, a farm to put in order!"

His words seemed to offend Mercy-Ann. "Of course you're not a slave. What do you take us for? Outlaws, Heresiarchs? It's only a matter of time before your case comes up before the board. It's true I hold the Directorship here, but I don't have absolute power; far from it. Nevertheless I'm on your side, and I'm sure things will be settled expeditiously. Until then you don't want to just lie around, do you? I'll see if we can get you released from your duties with the guards and you can help for a while with a very interesting dig down in the fifth level. In fact your underwater training would be useful there, since most of the site is flooded. But at the moment we have other business."

Mercy-Ann grabbed a cane and got up from behind her desk, which bore the remnants of her supper. She spoke and looked like a Harnishwoman, though she was shorter than many Eynnish. Her hair was white, and curved in upturning wings under a broad-brimmed red straw hat. She had a long coat stenciled with a pattern of stylized green and yellow flowers, like that a Harnish farmwife might wear while gardening, and black slippers. Her face was dignified if wrinkled, with a long nose and highly arched eyebrows. Her white hair and cane made her seem old, and although she seemed to have trouble breathing, her voice was almost girlish, and she had a ready laugh.

There was another visitor in the high-ceilinged office: a thick, neckless Eynnishman with arms and legs like tree trunks. Mercy-Ann touched his shoulder with her cane. "This is Tumpo, Samma. He came here with news, from a local Lodgeman, for me in my capacity as a government official. Tumpo, tell Samma what you told me."

The man described the suspicious visitors who had come to a place called Cwistamelling or something of the sort; Samma barely understood his accent.

"What do you think, Samma?" said Mercy-Ann, waving her stick. "Two good-looking young women and a Striver with a fancy hat and coat came to visit them. Could that be the same Striver you told me of?"

"It might be them, I suppose." Samma tried to keep his face calm. Neypo Odé and the others must be on their way here to implement whatever the Striver's plan had been. Samma hoped that would now include rescuing him. But only the Striver, Gillensa and Swannet? If this man had seen Micca in his glass armor, he certainly would have mentioned it. Micca might have stayed with his strange boat, or even taken it to Harna in one of his fits of impetuousness... assuming the thing really could fly.

Mercy-Ann spoke on: "You told me that there were a couple of young women in the water-meadow with you as well as a Lodgeman, and a Cadet, and your brother from Harna. I believe I briefly met your brother and the rude Cadet on the roadside that night. But you also said there was another man with you, one of the strangers visiting Hoiin? Him I didn't meet."

She appeared to have confused Neffafinnegal, the outlander, for Micca. Samma couldn't remember all he had told the Director that night after he had recovered from his dose of whatever it was, or even precisely what had happened; at least he was pretty sure he had said nothing about Micca's stone boat, which would have lost him whatever credibility he had with this weird old harridan. "Well, that's who my brother claimed he was. He could only speak Harnish, so I didn't get to know him very well."

Mercy-Ann almost fell. She staggered back to her chair and dropped into it. "Harnish? You're not speaking of your brother now? You mean the visitor from Hoiin I mistook you for speaks Harnish?"

Samma wished she'd ask him to sit down and offer him something to eat. He realized that he must not have mentioned the alien's speech before. "Yes, him. Supposedly only a few of his people speak normally. Micca — my brother — is pretty fluent in the old language."

"Well, never mind your brother for now," Mercy-Ann poured a little greenish-yellow essence into a cup and drank it down. "I have too much to think about already. If what you say is true, the implications are truly enormous! Both for the Harnish *and* the wretched Eynnish!"

Samma asked Tumpo, "Why do you say the visitors were suspicious?"

Tumpo shrugged. "Those're Mendicant's sayings, not mine. But he tells me and Pinset he sees a haunt or somewhat a-hoover behind the ellums aft the doorcomers come down from there. That was in west meadow, I didn't see nothing, I was off, but the doorcomers are like as not bewitched. Mendicant, he knows of these things."

Mercy-Ann said aside to Samma, "These rural Eynnish see a sprite or rolloc under every stone."

Tumpo heard her. "Mendicant didn't send us off for nothing, never sent word to nobody afore," he said defiantly. "He sent to the Lodge, too. Pinset, he goes all the way to Hynnysoi for him."

"All right, my man. I meant no offence."

To Samma again, Mercy-Ann said, "The Lodgemen will probably dispatch a ghost-catcher. Hynnysoi is crawling with them."

"It is for a fact," said Tumpo solemnly, misapprehending her pronoun. "Hitchets, back-clutches, mosslings, roof-runners; oh, it's a place I'd never go after sun's gone. I hope poor Pin gets back with his right mind."

Mercy-Ann said, "I meant…oh, never mind. But Tumpo, did one of these visitors, one of the doorcomers you saw, speak strangely?"

"I never heard them nor seen them. I was in mash-house."

"But why would they come in this direction from the water-meadow north of Hoiin? Is it possible they mean to visit Mellatuno? There are few other attractions of note in this district."

Tumpo shrugged in bewilderment.

Samma brightened. "Maybe they're coming to find me."

The old woman snorted. "More likely this visitor to Wennoc wants his remarkable suit back…but, yes! That could be it!" She leaned forward. "You said the Lodgeman told him to give it to you?"

Samma nodded cautiously.

The network of wrinkles around Mercy-Ann's mouth became more pronounced as she frowned. "The visitor must have been coerced somehow. But I can only deduce that later the tables turned, and not long after you left them. This particular visitor, at least, must have overcome the Striver and his people. Perhaps he had a miracle weapon of some sort secreted about his person and was waiting only for the right moment to wield it, or maybe your absence evened the odds enough; your brother looked much weedier than you. Whatever the case, the visitor must have taken command one way or another, and now he's coming after the suit you appropriated. It would obviously be very valuable to him — or anyone of his stature, for that matter."

"I didn't steal it. He even told me how to —"

"I thought you couldn't speak to him."

"I could, a little! As I told you. When he spoke slowly I —"

"Perhaps I'll quiz you later, since I myself can speak our beautiful tongue. But never mind that for now —"

She looked past him. "What is it, Noma-Linda?"

A large, slab-faced woman stood at the door. She wore gum boots and a coat like Mercy-Ann's, and looked to have some Harnish blood too. "We've got more visitors; two young women and a middle-aged man, according to Hoscar. Seems they got as far as Hnyliats on their own, and then some of Hocsar's lads invited them downstairs."

Mercy-Ann got to her feet, excited again. "It may be the party from Hwistomellian! They must have been right on Tumpo's heels—but no young men among these new arrivals? Even one? None of them speaks Harnish?"

Noma-Linda frowned impatiently. "I haven't interviewed them or even seen them yet, Ann."

"Well, where are they?"

"Hoscar put them in the old almshouse."

Mercy-Ann pulled a cord, and somewhere a bell sounded. "I've sent for my carriage. We'll interview them at once…

"Tumpo, you're welcome to stay the night. I think they're serving fresh eel in the men's mess tonight."

"I best go back to old Hwistomelly," Tumpo said. "But I got to get by those greenies. You give me some writing to show, Mistress? They liked to take beating on me when I come hither, only I knew Sappi back when, and he vouched me."

Mercy-Ann pulled on a pair of boots. "Linda, give him a pass."

Noma-Linda made a note. Mercy-Ann took it from her, tapped a stamp on an ink pad and endorsed the paper. Tumpo took it, made a perfunctory bow and left the room. A moment later two skinny men in white coats arrived with a small, open sedan chair.

Samma said, "May I come along, Director?" Micca might have abandoned him, but the idea of seeing civilized people again—especially Gillensa—was a warm ray of sunshine, the chance of a return to sanity, even if they locked him up with them.

"No. I don't want you influencing the Lodgeman's testimony."

Samma dithered. "Can I at least have some of that cheese then? I haven't had supper, and eel doesn't agree with me."

Mercy-Ann stared at him, then laughed. "'*Eel* doesn't a*gree* with me'," she said, mimicking his rendition of Hoiin's accent. "Yes, you can have the cheese. Eat the bread, too, and have a drink. If Hoscar catches you with it, tell him I gave it to you…but come to think of it, don't go back to your barracks tonight. I think I'll want you to put on the suit again and perform some tests for me. Yes, stay up here for now."

Mercy-Ann climbed into the sedan. She used her cane to tap the men to action, and Noma-Linda followed them out of the office.

Samma stood alone at the door, looking down the corridor outside. He wouldn't see his friends just yet, but recognized the upturn in his fortunes and was grateful. He didn't have to go back to the stinking barracks and try to keep out of the guards' depraved games. And the Striver would show Mercy-Ann who was in charge...or so Samma hoped. After a few moments he closed the door, hunched down at Mercy-Ann's desk and tore off a piece of the bread with his teeth.

The Mendicant Elmo Ansitap strode back and forth across the parlor, hands behind his back. From time to time he looked out the windows or onto the veranda, then resumed his pacing.

His son Horemps had stormed off to his room after a sharp word from his father, leaving his tatting things strewn about the cushions, which aggravated the Mendicant further. Slimpia moped on the veranda, though Iuléli had warned her of the evening chill. Uncle Suto sat cross-legged at a table that supported a ponderous old copy of the Writs, occasionally raising a finger and reading aloud an obscure passage concerning malevolent wights and spirits. The staff were all downstairs in the buttery, probably drinking the Mendicant's beer and discussing the unusual events of the day.

The Mendicant looked outside again. The sky was still clear, the moon was bright. "Is supper ready?" called Slimpia from the veranda, where she slouched on a bench.

The Mendicant glanced at her and went back to his pacing.

Iuléli went to the kitchen. "Elmo," she said, coming back up the stairs after a few minutes; "Elmo, do you hear me?"

The Mendicant halted his progress and faced his wife with a smile he considered a miracle of self-restraint.

"Elmo, supper will be a little bit late," Iuléli declared. "Trippo and Addalora have been listening to Hydda's tales, but the fish is on the boil now. I think we'll eat in here, and have honey-cakes with our meal. That will bring you out of your sulk. Uncle will stoke the brazier and we'll all be toasty warm, won't we be, Uncle?"

Suto, head bent so that his nose almost touched the pages of his book, glanced sidelong at Iuléli. He got up slowly and went to the fuel box, muttering about pleasure-loving modern youth.

The Mendicant stared at the floor. Iuléli shook his arm. "Elmo, you must remember your dignity."

The Mendicant drew back, frowning. "'Dignity' is near the bottom of my list of worries, my dear. We had a Striver come to visit, possibly the only Striver who will ever visit Hwistomellian. And who should it be? A changeling, a rebel, at best a grubbing politician, an upstart who rejected my hospitality, who shat upon my honor!"

"Come now, Elmo!" insisted his wife. "You did nothing to provoke his rude behavior."

"I've failed my duty to the Lodge, to our people. Yes, I know I tried, but to what effect?"

"You sent Tumpo and Pinset off to alert the authorities. What more could you do? The Hoinish fellow ran off without explanation or a word of farewell!"

"And now I'm doubting the wisdom of doing even that. How do I know my colleagues in Hynnysoi haven't turned rebel too? And what then?"

Now Iuléli frowned too. "But what of Tumpo's errand? Mellatuno is also a seat of authority, and these rebels or whatever they are won't have gotten there yet."

"No, and they won't go there in any case. If they're out campaigning to subvert the Lodge, they'll head for Midoi or Slivotuno."

The staircase door opened and Trippo carried in a large, fuming platter. Addalóra came behind with the table service and Uncle Suto helped her spread a cloth on the table. At his wife's prodding, the Mendicant went off to get Horemps.

Finally they sat down to eat. The Mendicant served the fish while Iuléli cut up the cake. "Slimpia!" Uncle Suto shouted in the direction of the veranda. "You'll go to bed fishless!"

"What?" came a puzzled voice from the gallery. "What—oh my! Yes, yes, just a moment! Wait, oh do, and I'll get my instrument!"

"A fine time for fiddling," said Uncle Suto. "I'm eating, with or without her."

But the Mendicant jumped up and strode onto the veranda.

"Elmo, Slimpia, please!" Iuléli called. "The fish grows cold!"

The Mendicant returned but passed the table and hurried down the stairs. Slimpia came after him and raced off to the inner regions of the house.

Iuléli looked at Horemps and Suto. All three got up and followed the Mendicant.

In the ground-floor corridor near the water door, Hydda peeked from the kitchen door, backed by Trippo and Addalora.

"There are beans that need sorting!" Iuléli admonished them, coming down the steps.

The Mendicant had opened the water door, but stood away from it, hands raised before him, palms out.

The servants came out of the kitchen, but Iuléli said nothing to them now. Everyone pressed forward to join the Mendicant.

The moon shone over the lake. They saw a swarm of manlike figures, each sitting astride a beam that might have been taken from some drowned boat. The apparitions floated free in the air, thick bodies reflecting occasional oily glints of moonlight, like the water below. Glowing numerals were set into their chests and shoulders.

Suto pushed himself forward. "It's the silver hooligans, just as the radio-box warned!"

The apparitions eased up to hover over the manse's brick-built staithe. The people in the house were frozen in dread and indecision. One of the riders dismounted his beam and walked to the door. Unlike the others he wore no numeral, but some kind of drawing or glyph on his chest. An unnatural voice spoke: "A good evening to you all. Where are the people from the north who came here today?"

Elmo Ansitap opened his mouth, but no words came.

Horemps whispered, "Maybe we should offer them refreshments."

The silver man spoke again. "Did they have an unusual wagon, one without wheels?"

Outside, another man had climbed stiffly out of a sort of basket or partially enclosed chair attached to the side of one of the floating beams. This man was of normal appearance, shivering in a coat of Striving plaid.

"Another rebel Striver?" hissed Iuléli.

The new Striver's voice was cultivated and rather weak. "You're a Mendicant, are you not?" he asked Elmo Ansitap, fingering a sign. "I bring you fraternal greetings in the name of the Lodge's Committee on Reorganization at Hin Hoina. Where are your visitors? We spoke to your man near Hynnysoi, a fellow called Macsym Pinset; don't think to prevaricate."

"Pinset?" the Mendicant whispered. "Where is he? What have you done with him?"

Clutching her fiddle, Slimpia pushed by the others in the house and ran out onto the dock. She dodged past the Striver and threw her arms wide before the silvery man. "Take me to Tin-Nimarona, O shapely sprite!"

Another man sprang off his beam and swung his arm, hitting Slimpia in the jaw. She fell to the dock, and her fiddle splashed into the lake.

The man who had hit her tentatively prodded her flaccid body with his boot. "She shouldn't have attacked me."

The Mendicant lurched forward, shouting hoarsely. "Poltroon! She never attacked you!"

"I'm afraid appearances take precedence," the man dressed as a Striver said sadly. "My comrades are counseled to be especially cautious when on duty of this sort."

The rest of the men dismounted. The first confronted Elmo Ansi again. "What about your visitors?" He looked up at the lighted doors inside the veranda. "You can't hide them from us."

"If they're not still here they may well have gone east," the Striver told the first man. He asked the Mendicant, "Did they mention Yonoma? Rondoiin?"

"Find them yourself! I have no idea where they went, and I'd not tell you, *traitor*, or your hideous friends if I did!"

A sculpted face floated inside the first man's glassy head, and it smiled. He spoke to his companions. "Third, Fifth: take a ride around the site. I've described what you're to look for."

Another man, this one with '006' on his chest, came forward. He held a long, flexible tube; one end was connected to a large needle, the other to a jar squirming with pale strings.

The Striver touched Elmo Ansitap's arm. "Be brave, brother."

☙

"I found it disturbing to learn that he had heard some garbled description of our party from the radio," the Striver said some time later. "Perhaps we should be a bit more discrete in our operations from here on?"

"None of these people can tell us where he took the lighter?"

"No. They saw nothing but a dark shape behind a tree, and they didn't see it in the sky when their visitors left."

"What's your instinct, Caihar? Where will he go? What would seem good to him?"

Caihar clasped his hands earnestly. "Well. It seems clear that he kept both Mister Sulawan's flying ship and his encased Harnishman hidden during their stop here. They say he wanted to leave his female dependents, but became alarmed at something and fled with them. He can be overly imaginative, but at heart he's a realist, I think. He probably understands that his battle is lost, and now he's merely trying to find some out-of-the-way refuge, resigned to living out his days as a friendless outlaw."

Adinnegram smiled. "I agree he's probably looking for a safe haven, but I've worked it out better. You assume Odé is in command of his resources and able to go where he likes. But how could that be? Finnegal would be as useful to him as a bag of stones, and more likely a detriment. And the others, the natives? No, the evidence tells us they're lurching along, stumbling, almost crashing again every time they move. When they crack the hatch they have to ask the locals where the devil they are. Do you see now? Yes? Remember to process *all* the facts when I ask you for an analysis."

"I'm sorry, comrade. I'll do better in future."

Adinnegram punched Caihar's arm playfully. "I know you will. Tomorrow we'll ride in a widening spiral around this place. The people of this house can help too, ask their neighbors what they've seen, that sort of thing. Shouldn't take long. And then, comrade, you can look forward to somewhat more comfortable traveling...unless you've taken a liking to riding in Third's bug-along?"

Caihar returned a smile almost as glassy. "No, I haven't."

24. INSIDE

icca dropped down the well. His armor locked up imme-diately, anticipating an impact. The sound of a splash and a near halt to his descent told him he had hit water. As the armor loosened he felt cool air enter his nose and mouth, though he had to work to pull it in.

What had he done? He was suspended in an inky limbo, buried in a tomb of water. He groped and felt circular walls. The well was hardly a yard wide. There was no frog-man here; there wouldn't have been room for both of them.

But was he at the bottom of the well? He couldn't think the armor would float...when he touched the walls, he felt himself drifting downward.

He tried to make himself calm. With shaking fingers he touched his wrist, and when he remembered the right taps his faceplate brightened to chalky shades of gray. Other than sketchy outlines of bricks, there was nothing to see, but the water must be full of silt and the dissolved remains of animals that had fallen into the well, drowned and rotted. He put his hands on the walls of the well again. Bricks were slipping slowly past.

He groped and found what seemed to be a cleft between two courses of brick, one he could get his fingers into. Micca grabbed at it before it slipped by and tried to raise his leg to find a foothold.

Something pulled back at his foot—the frog-man? But he strained, and his foot came up, darkness clotting before his faceplate. His other leg was drawn down deeper, into the mud that must lie beneath him. Pulling with his arms, right boot nudging the bricks, he managed to raise himself.

A curving lip of dusky gray edged into view, a foot above. Micca threw his hand up and caught the lip, pulled himself belly-high, then got his knee up. He struggled into a horizontal cylinder of water that branched off the well.

Micca crawled but saw nothing ahead but more water. The frog-man's false belly must have carried a supply of air. He must have gone on, down this tunnel.

Now the tunnel slanted upward. Micca continued crawling, expecting to be attacked at any moment by the frog-man. He had been incredibly stupid to jump down the well after him. It hadn't been bravery. Brave Beyalmer had done such things, but Beyalmer never regretted his actions or got frightened. Micca's anger at being attacked and fear of being left alone had overwhelmed common sense. The others might have found their way back to the surface by now, and maybe they hadn't been taken by frog-men in the first place. The Striver had probably just gone around the other side of the hill to look for Swannet. Gillensa and Neffafinnegal would go after Micca and really be caught this time.

The tunnel seemed to close in. Micca wondered if the well behind him was closer to him than wherever it was he was crawling. He could find more cracks in the well's walls and climb out again.

Micca grunted, trying to turn around. His shoulders and hips scraped brick. He stopped, sucked in a breath, then twisted furiously. His heels and butt pressed one wall. His right shoulder and the top of his helmet ground the bricks of the other. Micca paused again, blinking at his vaguely seen knees, trying to slow his breathing.

"Unh!" he grunted, squirming frantically. He was no longer stuck, but still pointed away from the well. He lunged forward suddenly, kicking out his legs. Then he could kick no more, there wasn't room. He wriggled forward like a worm, pulling himself with outstretched arms, scraping his belly along the bottom of the tunnel. There was nothing in his head but a despairing memory of wind and sun.

Something in his helmet clicked. Micca exhaled and heard a watery snort. He drew in a breath, which came easily now.

For a few seconds he lay on his stomach, panting. Then he pushed out an elbow and was able to flop himself over onto his back. Above him was a dim space of ambiguous dimensions. He was out of the tunnel. Micca sat up, wrenched at his helmet, then remembered himself and performed the opening sequence.

Damp air, heavy with the odors of rotting vegetation, mold and ancient masonry entered his lungs. Dripping water plunked and echoed. Micca stood up in a shallow trough of water, which slanted down behind him into the drowned tunnel. There was a little light, its source not evident.

He took another deep breath, then scrambled to his feet and shoved his helmet back on. He looked rapidly around the chamber when the helmet had connected itself. There was a tunnel, a man-high, brick-lined passage, and two paces into it, rising steps.

The stair was slick with a glaze of mud and fungus, smeared by the passage of many feet. Micca slipped twice, and finished the climb on his hands and knees.

His helmet bumped into something with a dull metallic gong. He backed down a couple of steps and got carefully to his feet. He groped ahead and his hand caught something, a metal rod. Pulling it accomplished nothing, so he twisted and pushed.

A vertical line of night appeared, bright in comparison with the darkness at the top of the stair. Micca heard croaks, chirps and buzzes. He went out and knew where he was. He trotted down the valley to the steps that led to the island's shore. The sloughs spread out below him. The green-mottled moon hung over a line of haggard trees, its double rippling below in black water. Micca stared at the moon in wonder, at the speckling of stars around it.

The boat still lay by the shore of the island, more mysterious, and now, he thought, more beautiful than the night. Micca ran the rest of the way. He met no bandits, no frog-men. A welcoming glow of light shone under the open hatch.

He drifted high over the wetlands, driving slowly westward. A long line of ruins passed under the boat. A few glints of yellow light glimmered in the stony piles.

Micca was beset by confusion and fear, by a terrible sense of loss, and an almost unconquerable urge to fly across the Bay, to find Ennesia and Mora among the trees and hills. But the boat was haunted by the absence of the people who had been in it a few hours ago, and Samma, almost seeming a ghost now, must be down in those ruins somewhere.

The land below was empty now. A few lights still flared below, most likely swamp gas, but in the west everything was dark.

The boat floated in the water, steady despite the sluggish waves caused by its settling. Micca stared at the view to the world outside. He was sure he was looking at the same little island where the others had disappeared.

He crawled out of the hatch, walked over the deck and jumped through tall grasses and onto a muddy bank. He fingered his wrist carefully, and heard the boat answer him. The hatch swung down and became part of the deck. Dark water rippled out from the sides of the boat, glinting green in the light of the moon. The boat sunk slowly, water finally closing over it and covering it completely. In a few minutes Micca received a signal confirming it was at rest.

Micca began the climb up the sloping sides of the island, recognizing with relief places he had seen that afternoon. He located the door Neypo had found and he had come out of. It was still open. Something disturbed the grass, not far off. A frog-man? He wondered if it would be worthwhile trying to speak to one of them. As long as he kept his helmet on there wasn't much they could do to hurt him...as long as he was calm and sensible, as long as he kept his head. And kept 'his head on', as Neffafinnegal had said once...Micca felt woozy. He hadn't gotten a lot of sleep lately...

He could hear wind rising. Clouds billowed up, their edges glowing in the light of the moon—

Something pushed at the backs of Micca's knees and he sat down hard. A dark, smallish shape dashed by him and into the vine-shrouded door with a mocking squeal. The quick raps of a pig's trotters echoed down into the earth.

Anger at beasts was pointless. Micca followed it down. The pig was gone when he reached the bottom of the stair. He made a cautious circuit of the chamber, something he hadn't done before. A dim glow came from somewhere out of sight. At regular intervals sections of the walls bent to form inward-leaning buttresses that supported a dome. Doors opened between some of the buttresses. Two of them were bricked up. One was low, like a smooth hole in a pig house, but the damp sand and mud before it was undisturbed. He found the source of the light, an electric bulb hung from the arched ceiling of the last tunnel. Micca caught of a glimpse of the pig's rear end, disappearing down the passage.

Even the most intelligent pig couldn't speak, but it might show him where the frog-men lived, the place they would take their prisoners (and feed their pigs). Micca followed the pig, encouraged to see a second electric bulb around a curve in the tunnel.

After several hundred yards, the way descended a short flight of steps. It leveled again and became square in section. Here and there were round, basket-like cages of corroded metal set over holes in the floor. Micca thought he could hear a distant gurgling from them. He found them disquieting and kept well away.

But there were footprints, a lot of them, visible in the occasionally muddy stretches of the passage. Neypo and the others must have been taken away through such a tunnel. The frog-men, guards, whatever they were, probably swam in the sloughs only when they had to. He must have found Mellatuno, or be close to it.

At one point he saw the pig, but it disappeared again, and Micca came upon a little branching tunnel, a hole made of pottery cylinders like a sewer. He thought that the pig had gone through this hole, which was too small for Micca to get into.

He went on, walking at a relatively good pace considering his weariness. The wan glass bulbs continued, appearing every ten yards or so. Finally the walls broadened and he came into a large, low room. A crude hole had been hacked in the pebbly concrete at one end, and wires fastened to ceramic knobs looped away under the arched bricks of a curving tunnel. It looked as though the passage ahead had been built long after the subterranean structures of concrete. The Office of Antiquities must have spent years tunneling under the slough, digging from one ruin to the next in pursuit of their researches, though what they had thought to find here he couldn't imagine. There were no carvings or statues, no antiquities, unless they had been carried off.

Micca followed the new tunnel. The lights were spaced more widely now, and between them mudrunners clung to the walls; one of them was humped, slowly palpitating as it consumed whatever prey it had enveloped. Micca climbed and descended winding steps, sometimes slid down slopes of rubble. He saw no one, heard nothing.

Finally he came on a room that looked recently used. It had a light mounted on a short stick, held in turn by a green bronze arm sticking out of the wall, like the runner in a torch-race had collided with the bricks and been trapped, just his arm poking through. The place must have been some kind of office. There was no one here, but papers — lists, charts, maps covered with spidery notations — lay scattered on a long table near the light. A bottle and three dirty glasses held down the curling papers.

There was a bench opposite the table. Micca decided to sit down for a minute. One of the displays in the helmet counted numbers like a clock, but either it hadn't been set properly or it measured something other than Wennoc's hours. He should have asked Neffafinnegal about it when he'd had the chance, but there had been so many other things to learn about the suit...what day was it? It must have been a week, or a week and a day? since he left Mora. Dinner at the Striver's house had been Sunday, the day the Invigorationists had planned their nice wedding...

His mind fumbled stupidly, trying to sort out what time of day it was, and when they would bring him to his grave. The pendulum of the wooden clock in the Mora's little office behind the chimney of the oak parlor swung back and forth, but the clock's hand was poised at noon, and it just clicked right, then left, then right, without making any progress. But his grandfather's old couch was a comfy one, and it wasn't his job to fix the clock; he was a carpenter after all, and they'd have to send for Brunabur's clockwright to mend it. Then he heard Ennesia's voice: 'Forever and always...'

He tried to rub his eyes but his hand wouldn't quite meet his face. He clawed at his head and twisted in the armor, then woke completely and sat up. He was alone and lost under the sloughs, no stars to wink out here. And he was hungry. Was he breakfast-hungry or supper-hungry?

He left the room. Not far on was a hive of low chambers, heaped with moldering piles of junk. He thought he saw human bones among them but didn't stop to investigate. Narrow doors led from one room to the other through walls four or five feet thick. Moisture dripped from the ceilings. The place was forgotten, empty. There were more drains with cages over them in the floors. Micca again avoided them, thinking they must have been covered for a good reason. Possibly there were big mudrunners below.

He heard a mutter of voices. Ahead was a low, wide chamber, lit with a string of lamps hanging from a sagging wire. Half a dozen people wearing round, brimless hats, aprons, sleeve-protectors and gloves sat at a table, beheading and gutting small fish, tossing the resulting fillets into pots.

"Hello!" Micca called, trying for a friendly voice, though he thought it came out as a croak. "Can you tell me what time of day it is?"

The butchers looked up. All but one rose silently and left the room. The remaining butcher looked around absently. The way he did made Micca think he was blind.

"I'm not sure just what the time is," the man said. "Where have my mates got off to? Seemed to me like they thought the dinner gong sounded, but it didn't; my ears are as good as anyone's, you know."

"I don't know where they went. I might have startled them."

"Well, what do you want? We can't all of us sit about wittering all day." The butcher took up his filleting knife again and reached into a pan for a fish.

"Sorry. I, ah…can you tell me where I can find the Director of Antiquities?"

The butcher stopped his work and looked thoughtful. "Well, you'll want her office. Don't rightly know where her private rooms are. So from here you'd want to…no, let me recollect. Been a spell since I seen it, as it were. Ah yes. Go right out the far door here and up the straight stair of nineteen treads outside; you don't want the one with twenty-two treads. That'll take you to a place neath the guards' boss-room. The right one gives onto another one at your left, a hunnert and twelve treads, then you're in the Long Gallery. Director's office is at the far end of it."

"Thanks very much for your time, sir. I'll leave you to your work."

A gong clanged somewhere. The man stood. "I'm off for me victuals. You might want a visit with the surgeon. Your voice is odd. Maybe you got you a chest cold or nose complaint."

"Thanks. My nose has been kind of stuffy."

Talking to someone had lightened his mood considerably. But he must have taken the wrong stair. At the top of it he found not another hundred and twelve steps, but a room with no other door. There was no point in going back to the fish-room, at least not for while. He heard footsteps and voices coming fom overhead.

There was a hatch of woven wire in the ceiling, almost touching his head. He had some effort into getting himself up and through it, and thought he must be pretty desperate for more company. The voice was louder inside a horizontal shaft, a glow at its end.

Micca crawled toward the glow. Bars of yellow light shone on his faceplate. He saw the backs of a pair of gum-boots through a grille. Beyond these were another pair, pacing in and out of sight. There was a voice again, clear enough to understand now.

"…through the water door?" it said.

A different, coarser voice replied, and seemed to come from directly over the grille. "No, they were nice and dry, more or less. Chuppy and the Huskies brought them through the under-way, said they were trespassing on Hnyliats. One of them gave Fig a nasty bruise — hit him with a stone."

The boots above the first voice stopped pacing. "Interesting. It's been a while since we've had visitors. Any guard material among them?"

"There's a stout middle-aged chap, too old and stubborn I think, and a brace of tasty young breeders. And youngish lad, skinny. Seems like a mental case, can't hardly talk. But we'll try him out. Can't talk much in a guard's kit anyhow, hey?"

"Yes, I suppose it's difficult," the other voice said absently. "Wasn't there also a strong, stocky youth? A chap wearing the uniform favored by the Cadets?"

There was a laugh from the bench. "Your gossip collectors are good, Martin! Matter of fact there was a goodly-built lad, and another one too, a giant, some kind of sport or monster to go by Fig's word, but they didn't pinch him, and I don't believe Fig anyways; the laddies are always seeing oddiments out there."

"What's the disposition of these new detainees, then? Did you give them to her?"

"Didn't have much choice, did I? Too many saw them. The old fellow and the lassies anyways. She didn't get sight of the skinny one, he was already off to training. I'd as lief got the use of those dainty breeders though. Even with their tonic the lads get restless and tend to bother each other."

"And she's also unaware of the youth with the Cadet's outfitting?"

"Ayup. He's in storage for now, till he calms a bit. Right feisty he is. I reckon he'll make a daisy of a guard. You don't be telling her about him, right?"

"I'll keep it to myself, Hoscar."

The nearest boots shuffled, moved away, and Micca heard what may have been the slap of a hand on someone's back. "All this managing stuff makes me thirsty, Martin. Let's have us a drink. Then we go gymnasium and you can have a look."

"I won't argue with a chance to wet my throat, Hoscar."

The feet moved out of sight. Micca heard the sound of a cork coming out of a bottle. He moved closer to the grille, twisted his helmet and got a view of both the room's occupants. One of them, Hoscar it would seem, was heavy and stooped, wearing a gray tunic and part of a frog-man's hood, which he wore pushed back on his head like a cap. The other man, Martin, was tall with a sparse black chin-beard, his narrow frame mostly covered by a long, stained apron. They both drank from a stoneware jar, then walked out of sight, taking the jar with them.

Micca waited as long as he could make himself, then pushed the grille away and twisted out of the hole. He found himself in the space under a bench fixed to the wall; the hole he had been in was just under Hoscar's seat, the opening of a ventilation shaft he supposed.

Micca surveyed the room. A slab of slate had been set into one wall, covered with illegible scratchings in white chalk. Near the door were racks piled with various pieces of what he supposed was underwater equipment. There was little choice of routes outside the room. Micca went as quietly as he could down a relatively well lit passage, coming after a few yards to a wider corridor. He looked into it and saw Hoscar and Martin, speaking quietly, taking turns with the jar. Between them and Micca, in the mouth of an adjoining passage, was someone else: a large woman in a green and yellow coat, peeping around the corner, unseen by the other two; Micca could almost see her ears flare in Hoscar and Martin's direction.

The pair started off again. The woman turned and disappeared into the dark passage. Micca sidled around a corner and followed Hoscar and Martin down a staircase.

There was a landing at the bottom of the first flight, where the stair turned and continued downward. To the left a concrete stub-wall guarded the landing from the drop into a deep, narrow chamber. Its ceiling was crossed by a maze of drooping iron pipes. Lights hanging from long wires showed a two-yard-wide pool of black water set into the floor at one end of the lower space, its surface made uneasy by slow drips from the ceiling. Several large tubs stood to one side on the chamber's uneven concrete floor.

There were echoing calls from below. Micca crouched and looked over the landing's wall. Three men wearing groin straps and flippered shoes stalked out of a door in the lower chamber. Their heads were shaved, but the tallest of them was Neffafinnegal—no doubt Hoscar's 'skinny mental case'.

Hoscar and Martin appeared below Micca's landing. They watched as two of the men dipped handfuls of moss-colored stuff from the tubs and smeared it over their bodies, gesturing for Neffafinnegal to imitate them. When their skin was coated, they strapped bladders to their stomachs and pulled snouted hoods over their heads, connecting them to the bladders with hoses. They brought Neffafinnegal to a hissing pipe, made connections, and his bladder inflated. The other two filled their own bladders and flapped in a high-stepping gait to the pool at the end of the room, pulling Neffafinnegal with them, hooting in their snouts at his clumsiness with his flippers. Hoscar urged them into the water, shouting out instructions on what sort of exercises they were to perform. Snouts sunk, flippers waved briefly above the water, and they were gone.

Hoscar and Martin disappeared under the landing, discussing the new recruit and how he could be made useful.

The frog-men didn't come back; the pool must lead outside to the sloughs. It was a great relief to have seen Neffafinnegal, though the sight also left Micca feeling guilty. They had promised to look after each other. But there wasn't much he could do at the moment. At least he now knew where he was now, more or less, and had even seen a way out of this place, even if it was under water... and Noler must be nearby too. He wondered where Samma was, and if he too had been turned into a frog-man. He had to investigate.

Micca crept down the steps, peered around the corner; he heard muffled voices from behind a door under the landing, its upper panel filled with pebbly glass, lit from behind. With luck Martin and Hoscar would spend some more time with their jar. Across the chamber was the door from which the frog-men had emerged.

It led by way of a short tunnel into a broad but low-ceilinged room, poorly lit by a few electric globes. The floor was wet. Greenish soap scum and what might be feces floated in a water-filled gutter that ran along one wall. For once Micca was grateful his helmet removed odors from the air he breathed. Flippered shoes, groin-straps and other bits of clothing hung from pipes in the ceiling. Along the near wall was a long bench, a row of narrow cupboards behind it. On the bench was a bronze helmet with a visor like a snarling face. Noler must have held onto it all the way here, under the slough, until they took it from him.

There was no one in the room. But in a corner he saw several iron hoops set into the floor. A water-curled placard hung on the wall. On it was printed,

DISCIPLINE AREA.
See & Remember!

Micca approached the hoops, which surrounded holes in the floor. The holes had grilled lids, and seemed to be nearly full of water. Micca pulled out the hasp that secured one of the grilles and lifted it. He saw nothing but water, but thought the watery oubliettes were meant to hold people.

Beyond them Micca saw an arched opening that had been walled up; the wall was of a different kind of brick than the arch, and a low iron door had been set into it. Near the bottom of the door was a hinged, horizontal plate. Micca lifted it.

Suddenly a pair of blinking eyes showed in the slot. "Who's there?" said a hoarse voice.

"Noler?"

"Who wants to know?"

"Quiet," Micca hissed. He found a hasp similar to the one on the tank's lid and removed it. The door swung in a couple of inches, hit something; with a muttered curse Noler lowered his head and Micca opened the door fully. He grabbed Noler's hands and helped him climb out of the cell.

The Cadet stood unsteadily and looked around, shading his eyes against a dim bulb in the ceiling. "Micca Mora?" he exclaimed.

Micca almost embraced him; it was a great pleasure to see someone familiar and civilized. Noler grabbed Micca and put his arms around him.

"Thanks. I'll never forget this," he said when he let Micca go. Noler looked back at the little door. "I was about to go crazy. I think there are ghosts in this place. And the living people are all insane."

"Well, we'd better get out of here. I saw Neffafinnegal a few minutes ago, but he's off under water somewhere now. Is my brother here too?"

"I don't know! I haven't seen either one of them. Have you got your flying boat?"

"It's outside. I hid it under the water. Where are the women and the Striver?"

"Did these frog bastards catch them, too?" Noler exclaimed.

"Yes, and they tried to get me. Is this place really Mellatuno?"

"I heard one of them call it that."

"Then we'll have to find the Director or whoever the Striver was going to talk to. Maybe he's talking to him now. I think it would be best if we sneak out through the pool in the next room. I just saw some of them and Finna there, and I'm sure it goes outside — can you hold your breath very long?"

"I'll find one of those head-bags. Let's get going!" Noler saw his bronze helmet and picked it up.

In the short tunnel beyond the door they met Hoscar, Martin two paces behind him.

Hoscar yelled loud as he caught sight of Noler. He spread his arms to block the passage. "Interloper in locker room! Ai-yup! Chi-chi! All guards! To me!"

Noler jammed on his helmet. He crouched, ran ahead and butted his head into Hoscar's belly. Hoscar hit the wall with a cough of expelled breath and slid partway to the floor. Noler ran by the stunned man and into the chamber beyond, dodging Martin, who had flattened himself against the wall.

Martin peered after Noler, then scurried away. Micca started to follow, but Hoscar leapt up and threw himself in Micca's path, arms stretched wide. Micca shoved him hard in the chest, but Hoscar wasn't caught unaware this time and seized Micca's right wrist with both hands.

Micca struggled, but Hoscar's fingers were like oak roots. Micca pried one hand off, only to have it clamp his left arm. He tried to drag Hoscar with him, out of the tunnel. Hoscar backpedaled, howling. Finally Micca swung himself from the waist and with frantic effort jerked Hoscar off his feet and slammed him into the wall. The back of Hoscar's head hit the masonry and he slid to the floor.

Now Martin and five other men crowded the other end of the tunnel. Hoscar regained his feet, though blood oozed from the back of his head. Micca ran back into the low room. He pushed over a tall cupboard and it crashed to the floor before the door. Hoscar dodged it, mouth trembling in fury. Martin shouted at the men with him and beat them on with a stick. They shuffled forward, bearing clubs and a net of heavy rope.

Micca turned to run and fell over a bench. Martin shouted again. Micca got to his knees, but the guards ran forward and flung the heavy net over him. Two of them leapt at him, forcing his hands to the floor, then pushing him over so that he lay flat on his back. Micca thrashed, kicking violently, trying to hit their faces with his fists. One of his blows connected and a guard crawled away, bleeding from his mouth, but the others clung to him. They forced his legs together and wound the net tightly around them, then around his chest, pinning his arms.

"Put it away! Put it in the lock-hole!" Hoscar screamed.

The guards took hold of the ends of the net and dragged Micca over the floor. They approached the bricked up arch. One of the guards went forward in a scurrying hunch, knelt beside Micca and yanked at his feet as the others pushed his shoulders, and Micca tumbled into the cell just vacated by Noler. The door clanged shut.

25. OUTSIDE

An hour before sunset that evening, a small band of travelers stopped to rest on the remains of an old bridge. A stream flowed under a mossy brick arch, carrying waters from Harnish streams into a region of meandering waterways and fields of reeds. The stone-paved road the travelers had been following quickly vanished beyond the bridge, swallowed by the wetlands, but off to the east bits of it reappeared as a causeway, describing a broken line across a stretch of open water.

Ennesia pushed a few strands of hair back from her face. Bristly seed cases and burrs clung to her skirts, but she had given up trying to pick them off. She watched a long-legged bird stoop to pull a wriggling thing out of the mud with its bill.

"Well, where are we?" she asked Priest Palmer, who was cleaning his eye-glasses with a rag. "I don't see any sign of your stupid seminary."

Palmer put on his lenses and rubbed peeling skin from the back of his sunburned neck. "Please be quiet, Ennesia," he said.

Another member of the group, an adolescent boy whose once pale skin was now dirty and red from the sun, wrung his hands. "Oh, darling cousin! Don't speak so to our priest!"

Ennesia pushed Binta away as he tried to take her hands. He staggered backwards, eyes still fixed on her.

The Monitor Smolic, the fourth member of the party, took notice of the boy's lustful stare. "Bindig! Leave off your mooning. Wennoc prompts such thoughts for to engender children—naught else!"

Binta flushed. Ennesia looked at Smolic in disgust.

"Binta," said the priest, "have you gathered greens for our supper as

I asked? Ennesia, please see to the kindling. Monitor, the oxen want their oats."

Binta didn't reply, but he went down from the bridge to the side of the road and started pulling shoots from the mud. Ennesia found dry grass and bracken. Smolic ladled out oats for the beasts.

Ennesia took a few sticks of firewood from the back of their wagon. She watched Priest Palmer where he stood below the bridge, poised on the bank of the stream. He squinted, raised a sharpened stick and speared a fish. It was probably some bottom-feeder, with oily, muddy tasting flesh, but it was a big one, and better than nothing.

After cleaning the fish, Palmer lit a fire with his flint and steel. While it burned down he wove a little basket of broad-bladed grass and put the fish in it so that it could cook over the coals without being scorched.

Ennesia sat on the curb of the bridge and watched as Palmer tended the fish. She was surprised by the priest's outdoorsy skills, though they had been of little use helping him to hold onto his position at Mora.

She supposed the difficulties presented by their situation weren't entirely Wudego Palmer's fault. He might have been content to remain in the Marling's custody for a while and eventually talk his way out. Just what had happened after she lost her senses that night at Marstoc, Ennesia didn't know; she hadn't regained consciousness until some hours later. From what she'd overheard, she suspected they had assaulted the Marling, and even injured him. They had kidnapped her for fear she'd bear witness to their house-breaking and release of the priest.

Whatever influence Palmer had held over Bacnod, Wilmar and Anlaf decayed after they freed him. Ennesia inferred that Palmer had been more alarmed than pleased to see them, and then found Wamod, Binta and Wilmar waiting in a wagon outside. But he'd been willing to go away with his team of rescuers.

He persuaded them to stop at Dimning, a small farm in the woods south of Marstoc, to release Ennesia and ask for baths and food. But stories of dangerous cultists roving the countryside had reached Dimning—too small to merit its own Invigorated priest—before Palmer's party had, and the farmers there told them to come out of the wagon and give an account of themselves. They drove quickly back into the woods.

In the evening Bacnod stopped the wagon so they could relieve themselves. Anlaf went off on his own, and after an hour hadn't come back.

The next day they approached the market town of Stoard and stopped a half mile from its gate. Ennesia was locked inside the wagon, Binta left to watch it and tend the oxen. The others walked into town, thinking that if things seemed friendly they would find lodgings and arrange some speaking dates for Priest Palmer; his audience would surely leave them with offerings enough to pay for a couple of days of food and beds. But a few hours later Ennesia heard anxious voices outside, and the wagon bumped off. Binta later told her that Bacnod had gotten too talkative over beer in an inn, and he and Wilmar had been asked by the town's guards to help them with inquiries regarding crimes recently committed in the north. From the window of a tea room across the road, Palmer, Wamod and Smolic had seen Bacnod and Wilmar being frog-marched down the street. Wamod rushed out to plead for them and she too was taken. The Marling's arm was long, or so Ennesia supposed. Palmer and Smolic left the tea room by way of an alley, walked nonchalantly out of the town and back to the wagon without incident.

After this Palmer, fully back in charge now, decided the only haven for them was the Hermitage of Saint Unwey, an Invigorated seminary located on an island in the wetlands at the south end of the Bay. The priest described the place as lacking frills or luxuries, but its occupants were honest souls. Palmer would probably join its staff, and he said Binta might become an acolyte. Given his experience in the field, Smolic might win a position as a lecturer, and Ennesia could work in the scullery or fisheries until her situation was resolved.

Palmer pulled the smoking fish apart with his fingers and served them each a portion, which they accompanied with Binta's onion-like reed shoots. Palmer advised against drinking the water so close to the sloughs, though Ennesia didn't think it could taste worse than the combination of the sharp roots and muddy fish.

The day had begun bright, but soon a greyness on the horizon was climbing. Now masses of clouds turned bloody as they pressed the otherwise unseen sun behind the low, vaguely green mountains in the west.

"I don't think it will rain," Palmer said. "We'll try to reach the seminary yet today. We haven't taken my old route, but Unwey's shouldn't be far off." He smiled hopefully. "Maybe we'll encounter some of my old chums and instructors, out for an evening's ramble."

"I don't think anybody will be out tonight," said Ennesia, in no hurry to meet Palmer's teachers. "And I think it *will* rain."

"None of us will melt if it does," said Palmer. He told Smolic to harness the oxen. Palmer walked down to the slough-ward end of the bridge. "The way is a little damp here, but further on it looks sound enough," he called.

Smolic drove the wagon down from the bridge, Palmer wading ahead over the flooded roadway. Ennesia stood for a moment with her hands on her hips, but she couldn't gather enough courage to run off. She was also a little afraid of the water. Palmer and the others wore boots and leggings, and weren't worried about what might be swimming in the water. Ennesia had only the skirt and house-slippers she had been wearing when they stole her from Marstoc. Finally she scrambled onto the open gate of the wagon as its front wheels were entering the water, then climbed up to sit on the roof.

Ennesia could see the water over the tall reeds that hemmed the way. It wasn't altogether dark yet, but the night-bugs were already singing.

Something splashed somewhere. Water moved between the reeds. Kneeling atop the wagon, Ennesia examined the ground. She saw a mudrunner detach itself from a dead fish at the side of the causeway and ripple away.

Smolic and Binta walked through knee-deep water beside the wagon, then gradually up onto mossy stone. Palmer stopped and held up his hand and Smolic reined in the oxen. It was almost dark and the bugs were very noisy now. He stared to the east, tilting his glasses to sharpen his vision.

Ennesia followed his gaze. Beneath the gloomy sky a line of cliffs rose from the slough, almost like a group of buildings. "Is that your seminary?" she said in dismay.

"No," he said finally. "We're farther south than I had thought, and on a different road, but I have acquaintances here too. What you see is the ruins of Mellatuno, once a great city. Parts of it now house an archaeological research station, but an age ago the Eynnish Heresiarchs did dreadful things there."

Then Ennesia jumped down from the wagon and pointed. "Look! Over there. Someone's got a fire!" If they were Harnish fishermen, she might ask them for refuge.

Everyone looked. Out among the reeds, a dim light flickered and disappeared. Binta cried, "It's not a fire, but a virvitat!"

Palmer shook his head. "Such phenomena are commonplace in the wetlands. They're only swamp lights, gaseous belchings of the mud, given flame by lightning bugs."

But all the bugs suddenly fell silent. Somehow Ennesia thought this was ominous, and she ducked under the wagon. Binta trembled where he stood; Palmer and Smolic frowned at the slough.

Everything remained still. A moment later there was a splash, somewhere beyond the causeway's border of reeds. Binta joined Ennesia under the wagon.

Monitor Smolic's brows came together over his nose and he looked questioningly at Palmer. The priest stared intently at the road ahead. He whispered to Smolic. "Be very still. They may have extended the scope of their security."

"Who?" Smolic hissed.

Palmer stood silent for several minutes, and the bugs began singing again. "A false alarm," he decided, blowing out his breath. "Binta, Ennesia, you can come out."

Binta reluctantly crawled out from under the wagon. A slough bird made a shrill call. Binta, startled, gave a little yell and ran into the reeds beside the road.

"Get back here, boy!" Smolic called.

There was a ruckus where Binta had disappeared. Reeds thrashed back and forth and water splashed onto the stone road.

Then Smolic fell. Arms stuck out of the reeds, grasping his ankles. He managed to beat them off, and bounded away with a throaty howl.

Palmer started after him, but something touched his shoulder. Before he could turn a wet arm wrapped itself around his throat.

Four masked men came out of the slough and crouched around him, their wet skin glistening greenishly in the light of the wagon's lamps. The arm around Palmer's throat tightened. "Let me go! Let me speak!" he gasped.

The priest's wrists were bound and the pressure on his neck was relieved. Smolic was led back, his arms tied with cord, blinking wildly at his captors. Another frog-man pulled Binta out of the reeds by his arms, legs flailing up and down behind him.

Palmer shouted, "I am Wudego of Palma! I'm a graduate of Saint Unwey's, I have friends at Mellatuno!"

The frog-men ignored him. They pulled a long, runnered sledge out of the reeds and forced their captives into it. All three were fitted with hoods, and tubes from the hoods were connected in turn to a tall pipe. The frog-men pushed the sled and its passengers into the water.

One of them unharnessed the oxen and beat their flanks with a stick until the beasts lumbered off they way they had come. Returning to the others, the frog-man saw a face peek out from between the reeds.

"Wait!" he called. "Another one — a woman!"

The frog-men ran shouting into the slough.

Off to the east, on the shore of Lake Hwistemo, two members of Adinnegram's mounted squad chivvied a man out of the woods above the lake. He hunched on the beach and they rode slow circles around him.

"Leave go of me!" he cried. "I'm mashman at yon manse!"

"Then why were you hiding in the woods?" one of the riders asked, lightly kicking the man with his boot.

"Things look amiss when I come home. Things like you all. I was afeared."

"I can understand that," the other armored man said reasonably. "Where had you been? Off tattling about what you saw?"

"No, I swear on't! I didn't see naught of such things afore I come back from a sending to Mellatuny last night. It was late, almost morn…"

He fumbled desperately with the pouch at his waist, snatched out a paper. "See? Vouching from Director; Tumpo it says here — that's me, Tumpo! I just wait here, to see what happens…been all day here, naught to eat."

One rider said, "First will probably be back soon. I think he'll want to have a talk with our mashman here. They tell strange stories about Mellatuno in Hannava."

The other nodded. He dismounted, tied Tumpo's wrists and attached the other end of the line to his ride. They set off down the beach, Tumpo coming behind at a stumbling run.

26. OUT OF THE POT

Micca heard boots and flippers walking away, a few curses and horrid predictions as to his fate. He yelled and clawed with his fingers at the door, but there was no purchase for them. There was no handle or latch inside the little cell. The door was strong and opened inward, so it was fruitless to throw himself at it, and the hinges seemed to be concealed inside an iron door frame.

There was no light, and his helmet's amplification was able to show him only vague planes in slightly different shades of gray. He couldn't see or touch the ceiling, and to the side the floor dropped in regular sections, like a stairway. It must have been a stair at some time in the past, blocked up to make this little prison cell. When standing on the lowest step his shoulders were about even with the threshold of the door.

He turned and sat on the steps for a while. What would happen, what did they mean to do with him? What could he do? Impatience and fear worked on him. In a way this was worse than the well on the island, the drowned tunnel. He had been able to move around there, and had found a way out. Strange sights began to squirm behind his eyes.

He stood again, breathing deeply. If this had been a stair, it must have led somewhere once. He hit the lower wall with his shoulder. He was surprised to hear a dull gong. He explored the edges carefully with his fingers. The center area felt smooth, harder than the brick. Another door? His fingers told him there was brick around it, marking its edges. He threw himself against it again and his suit locked up for a few seconds. Micca tried to breathe more slowly. The door was no more willing to open than the one through which he had entered, but this one didn't seem to have a metal frame, and the bricks in which it was set didn't seem so obdurate. He used his fist to hammer at the side he guessed was opposite the hinges. After a while he began kicking at the lower portion.

One of the bricks finally moved, down near the floor. He squatted on the step and pounded with his fist. The brick crunched back and clunked into whatever space lay beyond.

For a moment he was still, listening; he had been making a lot of noise. But all he could hear was water dripping somewhere.

He aimed a new kick, but didn't move his leg. A dim yellow light now glowed in the hole left by the brick. It shifted and brightened as he watched, glinting from the toe of his boot.

And from above and behind, outside the door, came the sound of voices and footsteps. He thought he recognized Hoscar's growl.

Now there was a squeak, but from lower down, inside the cell. In addition to the light behind the missing brick, there was a vertical line of yellow parallel to the wall; the stubborn door, open just a crack. A snake, or a flexible tube, wriggled through the aperture. There was enough light now to see a little puff of dust come from its end. A red symbol blinked in his faceplate, there was click, and now his breath needed a little work to draw in.

He swung around again. Now the upper door opened partway, and two forked iron rods pushed in. They swayed back and forth, probing and jabbing.

"Pin him down good!" came a shout from outside. Then, "Ayuh! You in there! If you don't shuck out of your shell, we got a big pot of water coming to the boil, and we'll make soup out of you!"

Micca ducked away from the forked rods. The tube on the floor puffed out another gust of dust. He remembered the night in the water meadow, and the gas or spores that had knocked out Noler and Neffafinnegal. He took hold of the tube and pushed it through the outer door.

From the tube came a soft puffing. Outside there were coughs and cries of alarm, then the thumps of bodies hitting the floor. The forked rods clattered into the cell.

Micca didn't wait. He pushed at the lower door. With a sharp screech it opened fully. A large woman crouched on a lower step beyond, holding a lamp. She appeared frozen. The tube ran past her down the steps, leading to a large, flabby bag held by another figure, also unmoving. Both wore underwater masks and air-bellies, but their clothing was normal otherwise.

Micca had no time to think about his choice of which way to go. He went through the bottom inner door, pushed it home behind him and turned down its latch.

The masked people became alive and quickly descended the stair before him, where it gave onto a low, arched tunnel. Here they joined three more mask-wearers. They stood beside a narrow arm-chair, carrying-poles on either side, its arm-rests and legs fitted with straps. They shuffled slowly backwards as Micca approached.

The first, the woman, looked to be the same one he had seen eavesdropping on Martin and Hoscar. Her eyes were wide behind the glass circles of her mask but though muffled, her voice was calm. "I see we won't need this after all," she said, glancing at the chair. "Will you come with us, whoever you are? There is a man in there, correct?"

She turned and waved for him to follow.

Should he go? These people were as odd as people came, but they must be a better bet than Hoscar and his frog-men, or getting himself lost again.

The chair was left behind. Micca followed the group down the tunnel, looking back until the little door on the stair had vanished around a turn. The members of what he now regarded as his rescue party took off their masks.

"Who are you, anyway?" Micca asked as they walked. "Why did you get me out? Where are we going?"

"To see the Director," the woman answered. "Your participation in our project was unlooked for, but helpful."

"I shoved your tube out the other door. There were frog-men out there who wanted to boil me. But why did you mean to knock *me* out with the mushroom dust or whatever it was, and tie me in that chair?"

"We didn't know whether their prisoner would cooperate, did we? And we didn't know whether he'd be in his right mind. Martin is often reckless with drugs."

She stopped and looked back now, the men behind staggering to miss walking into her.

"But just who, or what, are you?" she said. "You're not the Cadet the guards' captain and the surgeon were heard taking about, the one I expected to find. You hardly look human, but you speak well enough, and with a distinctly Harnish accent. County Dod, maybe?"

"Why do you want a Cadet?"

She started walking again. "Because a Cadet was reported to have come here from Hoiin in the company of a Lodgeman...and some other interesting folk."

The walls of the tunnel squared. The floor tilted upward, then became a broad stair, several short, wandering corridors, then another stair. Finally they passed down an open arcade with delicate arches and columns of braided stone, water lapping below; stars were visible in the sky.

"So this *is* Mellatuno?" said Micca.

The woman nodded. "What's left of it."

Inside again, they walked down a long, straight corridor. The woman rapped perfunctorily at a door, then unlocked it with a large key. The room they entered was tall, the walls set with small chips of colored stone to represent an antique palace. Its towers rose beside a river, and people with strange clothing and faces looked out from gardens on its rooftops. A wide wheel set with electric bulbs hung from a chain. Above it was a lofty barrel vault, darkening to cobalt blue as it rose, its apex speckled with pointed stars and seven round lamps. High in the end wall were three arched windows. Again Micca could see the real sky, almost as dark a blue as the ceiling..

At the end of the chamber a little woman sat writing at a wide desk. She wore a coat patterned with yellow and green flowers, like Micca's guide, as well as a red, wide-brimmed straw hat. A third woman, thin, hatless, but wearing the same kind of coat, looked up from a table piled with books and floor plans and maps. She caught sight of Micca and let go an ear-splitting scream.

The woman with the red hat staggered to her feet behind her desk, mouth hanging open. She took a stick in her hand and walked up to

Micca. She looked him over, then turned to Micca's rescuer with a broad grin. "Another one, and complete this time! This one must be authentic. Wherever did you find him, Noma-Linda?"

"Somebody around here has to keep her eyes open, Ann," Noma-Linda said brusquely. "As you can see he's not a Cadet, but—"

"Yes, yes, we'll talk about that later." The little woman gave Micca her arm, though she could hardly walk steadily herself. She spoke a kind of Harnish:

"Some persons of here too much keen about ours safeness. But you thinks maybe we needs big safeness aft I shows you here what we has. But now please, you takes my sorries for unneighbor of treatments, will you?"

Micca stared at her. She took her breath in short gasps, like a habitual sot-weed smoker, but she spoke quickly, in a high, light voice that belied her wrinkles. Her Harnish was even more difficult to understand than Neffafinnegal's had been at first.

"Are you the Director Antiquities?" he asked, also using Harnish.

She smiled again and lifted her chin. "I am. Mercy-Ann Bird Turner, one time of Turnoc, County of Muln. Now is Chief Director of Mellatine Station Office Antiquities. I is so please of meets you." She let go of his arm and steadied herself on her stick. "Then you is, sirrah?"

"I'm…" He stopped, remembering what Neypo had said about the Director's attempt to visit Neffafinnegal's people in the city. "I'm the outlanders' pilot, those who are now visiting in the settlement of Hin Hoina, as it were, and so forth and so on…I am with the Indeduish Foreign Outreach."

"'Outlanders'?" Mercy-Ann looked at him keenly. "Is how you all calls yourselfs?"

"Sure. Certainly. Why not? That's what the locals call us," Micca said, trying to clip his words the way Neffafinnegal did. "We aim to fit in."

Noma-Linda was smiling sourly. "He also speaks Eynnish quite well."

Mercy-Ann frowned at Noma-Linda, then turned back to Micca, still frowning.

"What be your name?" she said.

"I *am* their air-boat's pilot," Micca said, still in Harnish. "I've been initialized and had training."

"I ken not all your meanings of. What het yourself?"

Micca gave up the pointless charade. He must be getting light headed again. "Micca Mora of County Wendum, if you have to know. And if you're really a Harnishwoman you'll give me my brother and show us how to get out of this terrible place." She must think he was another Samma now, a Harnishman masquerading as an alien. How was he going to get out of the room now that his brief period of grace had expired? Noma-Linda, large and blank-faced, stood at the door, holding the end of a pull-cord casually in one hand. It would probably summon a squad of frog-men.

"I see," said the Director in a dull voice, in Eynnish now. She sat down at her desk. "Another impostor, and from the same place. When will I find the real thing?"

"I'm not an impostor," Micca said angrily. "I've been initialized, and—"

"You say the visitors initiated you? You mean you were conscripted? And you were given permission to wear that equipment?"

"I was *initialized* to use their equipment and I wasn't conscripted. I was *asked* to wear the bodycasing."

"Where is the visitor who was with you in that water-meadow? How did you escape?"

Micca frowned. He was getting confused. "I didn't exactly escape. I had just busted open the door when this lady here, your colleague or whatever, showed up and brought me up here."

Noma-Linda said, "To be fair, he did give us a bit of help getting him out." She smiled. "Turned the gas on Hoscar."

"Be quiet, Linda! I meant escape the water-meadow near Hoiin. Tell me this then, Micca of County Wendum—where is the *real* visitor, the one the Striver had?"

"First tell me where my brother Samma is. That's why I came here, to find him."

Mercy-Ann drummed her fingers on the desk. "Yes, yes, he told me about you, how you speak Harnish and so forth. We'll look him up later, he's fine, but never mind that right now—what about the visitor from the outer worlds? It's imperative, absolutely imperative, that I speak with him."

Micca snorted in his helmet. "You tell *me*. You Mellatuno people took him and made him into a frog-man. He can't speak more than a few words of Eynnish, so he'd be hard to miss."

Mercy-Ann leaned forward. "Are you certain?" She scowled at Noma-Linda. "So there *was* another young man with the Lodgeman's party! One of these days I'll have the tongue out of Hoscar's disloyal, duplicitous head."

Noma-Linda frowned. "Hoscar and Martin are both consummate sneaks. You can't expect me to keep track of each and every one of their plots and mendacities."

Mercy-Ann tapped a pen on the desk. She turned to the woman at the table. "Frita, go down to the shop and listen in for a while, do some surveillance. We must find this Harnish-speaking man at once. Wennoc, what he must think of us…"

The woman called Frita frowned fretfully, but began to pull on a pair of gum-boots. "I don't like it down there. It's so damp and gloomy."

Mercy-Ann smiled. "You think there are ghosts down there too, don't you? But they don't frighten you as much as our new friend here, do they?"

'Friend'? Micca wondered.

"And why shouldn't I be frightened?" said Frita. "Gruesome hulks in bottles up here, howling spirits in the stones downstairs."

"Ah, you Eynnish. So superstitious. I haven't heard a howl down there in over a week."

Mercy-Ann cackled. Frita clucked her tongue and left the room.

Mercy-Ann looked at Micca and gave him a surprising, almost frightening, wink. "When we find him we'll get you reinstated with your other-worldly master. I'll apologize and stand up for you."

" 'Other-worldly master'?" said Micca.

Mercy-Ann clapped her hands together. "Yes, the visitors to Hoiin! I thought you knew. They're *not from Wennoc*. They came here from some other sphere all together—I'm sure of it!"

"Yes, I know that. And they're from three or four different worlds."

Mercy-Ann sat back. "Oh? Well, in any case, what do you call him? Commander? Captain? Chief?"

"His name is Astin Neffafinnegal. I didn't know at first that his personal name was Astin, so I call him Finna for short."

"Must be an egalitarian sort...tell me, does the suit pinch you when you fail to obey him quickly enough, or spark you with electricity?"

"No!" said Micca. It came to him that Neypo had asked him something like this when he had first put on the armor; he hadn't thought about it since, and now it gave him a turn. But Neffafinnegal ordering him around? "He's not my chief or boss or whatever. If anything, I tell *him* what to do."

Mercy-Ann smiled tolerantly. "Is that so. Well, I'm anxious to speak to him, and his people. Tell me all about them, Micca, while we wait for news from Frita. The Lodge fusspots wouldn't let me interview the visitors while I was in Hoiin...and why don't you take that kettle off your head? It's hard to hold a conversation with someone who shows no face."

"How soon can I see my brother?"

Mercy-Ann rolled her eyes at Noma-Linda. "Soon enough! And if you don't trust me, I'm sure Samma will vouch for me. I rescued him from Hoscar, you know. Are all you farm boys so uppity and disrespectful of your elders these days?"

"Probably thinks he's just the last word in that show-offy suit," Noma-Linda said with a smile. "He showed some spunk down in the guards' room, but out of it he's probably as skinny as a stick and has spots on his face." She put her face close to Micca. "Do you moon around all day writing odes to buttercups when everybody else is out plowing?" Then she boomed with laughter and slapped Micca hard on the back.

Mercy-Ann coughed out a laugh. "Ah, Linda! Such a card...but look, here's Malting with a snack for us."

She waved at a chair, and Micca slowly sat down. This and the glimpse of sky outside the window gave him some idea of the time, at least. A door behind the desk had opened and a bald old man pushed in a clattering cart bearing a number of dishes, plates and jars. He stopped short at seeing Micca and rapidly left the room.

Noma-Linda rolled the cart up to Mercy-Ann's desk. Micca saw round bread like that Merim made, a wedge of ivory cheese, preserved fruit, half a dozen crusty pastries; it was the first homey food he'd seen since leaving Mora. His mouth watered.

"If you're Harnish, Director," he asked, "how did you get your office? I wouldn't have thought the Lodge hired Harnish people for jobs like that."

Mercy-Ann laughed, breaking the bread. "They don't, usually! But the Lodgemen pay little attention to institutions like this one. I studied hard, did my work with diligence. My predecessor was Eynnish but he had an enlightened attitude, and when he laid down his office I was the logical successor." She and Noma-Linda flourished napkins and began to eat.

Micca looked at the food, and the cup of beer Noma-Linda had poured for him. There didn't seem to be any immediate danger. He decided to take off his helmet. If they were waiting for him to do so, if they were trying to trick and disable him, this would expose them.

They looked at him, apparently fascinated, as his helmet made its usual gasping sound. He held it cautiously above his head for a moment, held his breath, glanced behind, but no one tried to take it from him. There was no taint of fungus dust in the air.

Mercy-Ann studied his face. "No spots, Linda, or none I can see in this light. Relatively strong jaw line, round, slightly protuberant eyes... I hope you aren't trying to raise whiskers, Micca. I think young men look better without them. I don't believe they're in style with this generation anyway, even in Hoiin."

Micca said he'd been too busy the last few days to think about shaving his face. He put his helmet carefully between his legs and arranged some cheese on a piece of bread. There was a jar of pickled mushrooms, too, but he didn't try them, not recognizing the variety and fearing mental side effects. The pastries were stuffed with parsnips, potatoes, onions and bits of spiced pork, greasy, but very good. The beer was rich and dark as befitted the time of day, with a creamy head. His stomach, neglected for so long, woke up eagerly.

"Why did you try speaking Harnish to me at first, Director?" he asked.

"Isn't it obvious?" Mercy-Ann said, wiping her mouth. "If you've met the visitors, you must realize the importance our language will have in the future. We'll have to work closely with our cousins — for our cousins they must be — to restore Wennoc to its former high estate."

"I think they call it 'Roma'," Micca said absently. But evidently she had gotten a fair amount of information about the aliens out of Samma, and maybe the radio? Micca started to ask her again when he could see him, but there was a knock on the door. Noma-Linda went to answer.

A young man with a shaved head and green-stained skin peeked in. It wasn't Samma, and Micca fumbled with his helmet.

"Yes?" said Noma-Linda, using her substantial presence to shove the frog-man back from the door and closed it behind them. She came back after a few minutes.

"Matco, from the guard," she told the Director. "He said both his chief and the surgeon have been assaulted by a mad ruffian, that a trainee guard is absent without permission and is possibly deranged, and that a violent deviant has escaped rehabilitation, though Matco wasn't sure of how many individuals these complaints refer to. Hoscar wants urgently to discuss the situation with the Director. I told him we would pencil him in, but that right now that you were meeting with an important caller."

Mercy-Ann nodded. "Fine. Let them sort out their problems themselves." She smiled at Micca. "But thinking of missing guards, go and hunt up our guest's brother, Linda. He'll be nearer these parts here than to the guards' quarters if he took my advice to heart."

Noma-Linda nodded and strode from the room, carrying a couple of the pastries with her. Micca breathed deeply and emptied his cup. The Director must be on his side. At least she trusted him enough to sit here alone with him (though there must be other functionaries nearby). If she wanted to rescue Neffafinnegal from the frog-men, the Director might let the Eynnish go, too. Neffafinnegal would surely speak up for Neypo. The weight Micca had carried since Samma was taken from the water-meadow lifted…

Or it should have. He tried to relax. The Director seemed cranky and out-spoken enough for him to believe what friendliness she showed him was genuine. Despite that and her sympathy for Neffafinnegal's people, Micca decided he didn't feel much better.

He looked at her. "How did the frog-men, Hoscar, whoever, get hold of Samma, Director? You brought him here."

"Something of a monomaniac, aren't you? Well, when Samma proved

to be a Harnish national, the disposition of his case left my hands…
it's a complex situation, based on generations of legal precedent and
practice."

"Oh."

"But as I said, it's straightened out now. I pulled some strings and
he's a frog-man, as you say, no more! When he joins us we'll go upstairs
and have some more potent refreshments. What a jolly reunion, hey?
You can set out what you know of the visitors' agenda for us."

The door clicked and scraped, and Noma-Linda came into the room.
"I haven't found the Harnishman's brother, but Scaliny thought she saw
him skulking in an arcade south of the gazebo earlier."

"Good. Keep an ear open. Maybe leave a note for him up there," said
Mercy-Ann. She returned her attention to Micca.

"So what can you tell me? Have you met any visitors besides the
one?"

"No. But Neypo Odé has. He's talked to them officially, as a Striver.
He was on some committee or something at the Lodge. Have you
talked to him? You have him here too, right?"

The Director frowned. "Odé? Yes. I don't like him. So pushy and
imperious. He was the one who refused me access to the visitors after
my laborious trip to Hoiin, visitors who were probably about to be
locked up by Odé's criminal friends. The guards have him now. I doubt
they'd let us see him."

This didn't agree with what he'd heard Hoscar and the surgeon say.
Micca said, "I understood that the Lodge has authority over all you
people here."

Mercy-Ann was offended. "They might have some authority if they
troubled to fulfill their duties, or acknowledged our work or even our
very existence."

Then she leaned forward. "But it's due to Odé and his foolish Lodge
that we stumbled upon your brother. After my abortive trip to Hoiin I
was frustrated, my feelings hurt, I admit, by the off-hand, disrespectful
reception I had gotten from the Lodge. I *am* a government official, after
all, even though I'm of Harnish background and my office is relatively
obscure. But before leaving I paid a visit to Hoiin's dreadfully commer-
cialized spring fair. A childish impulse, I suppose, and I regretted it

immediately. There was an awful crush of people, and the food and drink were criminally overpriced. But just after we left I heard word of riots and fighting, and then the falling star! I didn't know what was happening, whether these remarkable events were connected, but a falling star was too good to ignore, so I chased off to see if I could find where it had come to earth."

Mercy-Ann wheezed for a moment. "You must know the rest of the story. I found what I thought was one of the visitors on a dark lane in the country, apparently held captive by Eynnish thugs. I bundled the visitor into my carriage, thinking to effect a rescue." She stopped and smile ruefully.

Micca returned her smile, impressed by her ability to rattle on at such a rate when she had so little wind. "Yes, you took my brother. One of your 'thugs' was Neffafinnegal."

"Really! This Neffathinna..."

"Neffafinnegal."

"Neffafinnegal then. Well then, I think I see where I made my misassumption. Samma's garbled account confused me, but yes, it fits with what you've told me—

"But say! While we wait for further developments you'll have to see my workshop, Micca. I've got a thing or two downstairs that even our cousins from the other world—other worlds! will be impressed with."

27. DOWNSTAIRS

She pulled a cord and a bell rang somewhere. She waved Micca to the door, and he opened it to two men carrying a small, coracle-like sedan. Mercy-Ann climbed in and her porters lifted it. "Come, come!" she called to Micca.

Micca put on his helmet and followed the sedan. They came into a square shaft floored by an iron grille. Micca walked slowly over the metal rods, hearing them creak under his weight. Between them he saw only blackness; the space above was as dark. In one corner of the chamber was a helix of woven iron, an insubstantial stair screwing up and down.

In the center of the space Mercy-Ann's porters put her sedan down beside an open-work basket suspended from a cable. She dismissed them and clambered into the basket. She told Micca, "Go down the winding stairs. Look for the lighted door."

Mercy-Ann pulled a lever. There was a clunk and a grinding from above. Her basket dropped through a hole in the floor. Micca started down the spiraling stair.

It twisted around and around in the darkness. There was a thumping sound echoing up from below between the clangs of Micca's footsteps. Checkered light penetrated the grillwork above. The walls of the lower shaft were pocked with holes and slots, some blocked by brick, others supporting the stumps of great iron beams. Micca wondered if there had been some huge mechanism here at one time. Maybe it had been broken up, mined for its metal. The chamber seemed to have no function now but add to the general gloom and mystery.

The stair ended and he felt soft earth under his boots. There was a wan glimmer of light ahead: the mouth of a tunnel. The thumping was louder here. Micca saw the outline of an enormous, turning wheel, and despite his helmet he noticed a smell like that of an impending thunderstorm. Numbers flickered under his nose.

Micca walked a narrow path between piles of broken bricks and drifts of mud, then negotiated a line of stepstones across a pool of black water. The tunnel ahead was short, lit by a dim electric lamp at its far end.

Micca heard something between the thumps of the engine, the sound of something heavy dragging slowly through the mud. There was a low chitter, as though mudrunners were flexing their mandibles. He hurried to the end of the tunnel and met a blank wall under the glowing bulb.

Not knowing what else to do, Micca hit the wall with his fist. It made a dull gong.

"Push it. Push on the right-hand side," came a voice from a horn near the light.

He put his shoulder to the metal wall. There was a brief screech, and then it moved easily, pivoting on the left. Micca followed it into a curving cavity. Another slab of iron came out behind him, pivoting on the same axis. It followed him, enclosing him in a black, triangular space. He continued pushing and was rewarded by a vertical line of yellow light. A rush of wind accompanied the light, and he stumbled into a larger space. Behind him, the following door-slab clunked home. The wind dropped to a whisper and fell still.

He found himself at the head of a broad, straight stone stair. At the bottom, under a heavy beam, he could see a series of low, crowded spaces that dodged off between heavy stone posts. Wires hung with glowing bulbs looped under rising and dipping ceilings, lighting cluttered work benches, piles of crates, rivet-studded rusting tanks.

The elevator basket sat under a pair of doors in the ceiling. Between two tall racks Micca saw a red-hatted figure in a high chair. The chair moved, large, spoked wheels rotating on either side, and it rolled toward Micca.

Mercy-Ann pulled the handle controling a valve. Trailing hoses bloated and wheezed. Her chair stopped an inch from Micca's boots. "What do you think of my workshop?"

"Very interesting!" Micca said, taking off his helmet.

"I'll give you a tour. Follow me — hustle on, now!"

Operating the valve again, air hissed into an engine under her chair, which caused the chair's wheels to revolve. Mercy-Ann rolled between two posts and down a ramp. Micca followed her into a further chamber.

Mercy-Ann's assistant Frita sat on a stool before a board studded with glass bulbs, some dark, some lit, others blinking on and off. She wore a listening bonnet, and jumped from her perch with a yelp when Mercy-Ann rolled up and poked her in the back with her stick.

Mercy-Ann laughed huskily. Frita glowered at her for a moment, then said, "It sounds like Hoscar and Martin have some grim plans for your friend here. 'A monster in a glass jar', they call him."

"Any word of a tall new recruit in the guard? Have you heard the name 'Neffafinnegal'?"

"Not that I could make out."

Micca said, "They think he's a half-wit."

"Nothing about a half-wit either," said Frita.

Mercy-Ann frowned, then waved at Frita. "You can go now. Take the lift if you'd like, but send it back down."

Frita looked at the Director as if she doubted her senses, remaining here with Micca, but she seemed happy to leave.

"This board, as you probably have deduced, lets me keep an ear, so to speak, on certain parties' private conversations. I had to be a bit unscrupulous when I first took the directorship. Imagine me, Harnish and a woman to boot, up against an old and entrenched work culture..."

"Where is your dynamo?" Micca asked her. "How do you get it turning? You've got lots of water around here, but it doesn't seem to move much."

Mercy-Ann smiled slyly. "We don't *need* a dynamo. We'll talk about that later."

Micca followed her into another chamber. "Here you see a model of an engine that makes air more compact," Mercy-Ann said, pushing down the fork of an electrical switch. A shaft spun between heavy windings of copper wire, in turn rotating a disk fitted at its perimeter with a rod. The rod moved rapidly up and down, operating a piston inside a cylinder. Valves opened and closed, and air hissed from a pipe into a balloon, which quickly puffed up.

Mercy-Ann opened the switch again. "We've found larger engines of this kind and use those that still work for a variety of duties, including driving my chair here, condensing essence of air for the water-guards' use, and more importantly, filling these lower levels with pressed air."

"To keep out the water that would leak in?"

She nodded. "How clever of you. Some of the lower places are no longer completely watertight, and the added pressure helps. We don't have our lodgings down here, but the lower regions is where we find the artifacts. And according to my predecessor there are ancient electrical wards against the waters, too.

"But never mind! The device you're wearing, your suit. Tell me how it works! All the little details, and in particular how you *operate* it. Samma said there were any number of things it will do for you, and that you pushed and picked at your arm, as though there were switches on it, to implement them."

"They're more like imaginary switches — nothing actually moves. You tap instead of talking to the armor; Finna said that's immoral, and dangerous too. You have to set your mind in the right way, or get into the right…mood? Sam didn't have time to learn about that…there aren't any wires or gears or normal machinery in —"

"Well, all that aside, would you say your finger work resembles, say, playing an organ or keyed fiddle?"

"I suppose it does, in a way."

"Ah, now you're talking! I'm familiar with keyboards. Come."

She rolled into another alcove. Micca saw the vehicle that had almost run him down that night in Hoiin, the one described by Noler on the road beside the water meadow.

"I saw you in the city," he said, wondering how they had gotten the thing down here. "In Hoiin. I was just off the boat from Hannava, it was at night. You hollered out the window, called me an Eynnish pig or something like that."

Mercy-Ann gaped at him. "You don't say! Well, I suppose I took you for an Eynnish bravo! You weren't the only one I yelled at there. I was in a sour mood after being dismissed so rudely by the Lodgemen." She shook her head in wonder. "And events have brought us together again, at a better time and place. But to my demonstration."

She lifted a panel on the side of the sedan to reveal a row of ten or twelve flat sticks, much like those on a string-organ. Mercy-Ann ran her fingers over them and Micca heard a series of beeps in different pitches.

"With this I can send instructions to the office here when I'm off on one of my rambles. It can broadcast a good distance. Frita and Noma-Linda have been trained to interpret these signals, which of course are meaningless to anyone else. And it's quite portable, since it requires only eight Number-Three battery pots to power it. So I understand keyboards, you see."

Mercy-Ann spoke now in almost wheedling tones. "Won't you tell me, Micca, about the tunes you play on your arm, and what they mean?"

"They're not tunes. It's more like writing and praying at the same time. But talking about Hoiin reminds me. The Striver Neypo said it was very important for him to talk to you about a machine or something you have here. He didn't tell me exactly what…it's a Lodge Secret."

"So the operator taps, or spells out his wishes in words then. Excellent! Just as I had hoped."

Micca was disappointed she wasn't interested in Lodge Secrets. But he explained that someone had to be wearing a bodycasing, helmeted, sealed up and initialized, for such commands to be effective.

"And you fit the bill! You'll perform the test I have in mind. You know all the proper words and so on, don't you? Good! Follow me, soldier of the new dawn!"

"I'm not a soldier."

"Well, you look like one. Follow me in any case!" Mercy-Ann rolled up a ramp and down another. "Yes, all sorts of new ideas are percolating in my head. This will be a day they'll long remember in the halls of Harna."

She got out of her chair. "This thing is convenient as far as it goes, which isn't far! More a plaything, really…roll it over there, would you?"

She disappeared into a lower part of the maze of chambers while Micca found a corner to put the chair. His boots clanged over a large disk of perforated brass as he went after her, and he heard water rushing underneath. He walked down a slime-covered wooden ramp and over another floor drain to a narrow crevice at the end of the tunnel. Inside the crevice, a light flashed on.

Micca entered, ducking his head. There were wires hanging from the ceiling, but the walls inside were roughly hacked out of older stuff. He saw strata of brick, concrete, hardened mud, gravel, fish bones and the carapaces of long-dead mudrunners as he passed. Nothing he had seen thus far here looked so ancient. It must have been ruined and forgotten, built over, ruined again, and rediscovered. Micca stopped to touch a rough brick. He thought he could see the marks of the fingers that had pressed clay into the mold. A little grass-kilted Eynnishman had made it, back in the very morning of the world. He could almost hear him murmuring, whispering…

The crevice widened abruptly, its walls now smooth stone or concrete; it was hard to tell which. The light he had seen grew brighter as he walked on, much brighter. Micca put on his helmet, wondering suddenly what Neffafinnegal had done with Samma's tinted lenses, and the helmet obligingly dimmed the light, and also warned him of unwholesome airs (or so he understood it). Glass pipes buzzed overhead, the source of the harsh light. The space reminded him vaguely of the aliens' boat, with its stingy, trough-like aisle, or of a certain pantry at Mora, one tucked in under a stairway, lined on either side by countertops. Here the counters were replaced by slightly canted shelves of polished stone, rows of glass-filled glyphs set flush into them.

On one of them lay a helmetless suit of glass armor, which must be Neffafinnegal's, the one Samma had worn. It was face down, the back flaps open. A large lens on an articulated arm was poised over it. Around it lay an array of tweezers, picks and priers, but the suit didn't appear to have been damaged.

Mercy-Ann called. Micca found her in an alcove down at the end of room. He had to duck through a rough hole to get through to where she sat. Her alcove had evidently been forcibly opened. A heavy looking metal door beside the irregular hole was intact, still locked into its casing.

Mercy-Ann was sitting with her back to him. "This vault was discovered while I was assistant to Inioi, my immediate predecessor in the Director's chair," she said quietly without turning. "It had been untouched, unopened, for many years. He knew it was an important find, and had me write up a report and send it to Hoiin and Midoi. They never bothered to reply or acknowledge it. Afterward Inioi lost interest in his duties, feeling he had nothing else worthwhile to accomplish. He often sat down here in a melancholy mood, musing and talking to himself, and finally passed on before his time. But I shared his fascination with the place. I have a telescope up on the roof for star-gazing, but I like to sit here too and watch the sky."

And she was right. There were stars here, down in the bowels of the ruins. The wall she was facing was made of polished black glass. But it wasn't a wall. It was a window that looked out on a deep night sky. A million stars glimmered in it, impossibly far away. Micca felt a spasm of vertigo.

He swallowed and looked again. The stars weren't distributed in as random a manner as they were in Wennoc's sky. Razor-thin lines of light connected some of them, and they burned in colors he'd never seen in the sky. And a sphere of watery blue with a greenish splotch the shape of a boiled seababy floated in the bottom of the starry window. Hanging over it was a widely spaced swarm of seven small blue spheres, each with its own glyph. They dropped yellow lines to globe below them, kindling scores of tiny glyphs — the names of cities, Micca supposed — on the surface of the planet.

After a moment he said, "The blue balls are the lamps, aren't they?"

Mercy-Ann turned. Her face was half hidden by a pair of dark blue lenses. She pushed them up onto her forehead and squinted under the bright tubes. "Very astute, Micca. They are indeed the lamps, and Wennoc below them. Do you recognize Harna, with its curling tail? Eynna and Lumien? And this large dun land here. I wonder if it's still above the waves."

"How can we see all this down here? Are there mirrors or something hanging up in the air?" Micca immediately regretted his question as stupid. The window must operate in the same way as the eyes of the boat.

"Amazing, isn't it?" said Mercy-Ann. "All done by the power of our Harnish ancestors, potent to this day."

"But didn't the Eynnish build this?" Micca leaned past her, pointing to the glyphs in the stone table. "I can't read it, but it sure looks like Eynnish writing."

Mercy-Ann pulled her blue lenses down again and pushed Micca away. "Don't touch. The symbols are switches, something like the spots you spoke of on your wrist, or so I believe. As for the Eynnish building this, we weren't sure at first. It seemed unlikely given the state of their science today; such skills wax over time, they don't diminish. And once I saw the sign in the heavens, once I heard Mister Adinnegram speak on the radio, it was clear to me that these visitors to Hoiin were not of Wennoc. And when I discovered they spoke Harnish, everything fell into place."

"Then why aren't these switches or whatever Harnish words?"

"Micca, use your powers of reason. When our ancestors, the *first* set of visitors, came into Wennoc, do you suppose the Eynnish could understand the Harnish language? Can they now? Of course not. Our ancestors, acting in the spirit of altruism, built this for the Eynnish to use and carved the instructions in the natives' language as it was at the time. The Eynnish brain just isn't capable of taking on a second tongue, you see."

"Oh...but what's it all for? Why did these ancestors build it?"

Mercy-Ann smiled broadly. "Where do you think my little research station gets its electricity? Where do Mennedal and Naen Tula get theirs?"

"So you mean they send down electricity, like they used to send it to Hoiin's sun-field. I heard that's where they hold their fairs now, but I didn't get a chance to see it."

"Where did you hear that story about Hoiin?"

Micca shrugged. "Oh, some book or other we have at home. 'Legends from Hut and Hedgerow in Eynnaland'. Or 'A Hundred and One Curious Tales', maybe. I don't remember."

"Hm. You have books written in Harnish? But where was I? Oh yes. We've seen what things were like ages ago. Now we'll have a look at Wennoc as it is tonight."

Mercy-Ann delicately held her hand over one of the shining glyphs, then another. "Only three of the original lamps have survived," she murmured. "Probably due to negligence of some kind on the part of the Eynnish—unless you know better? Did one of your farm's books tell you what happened to them? No? Well then, in any case, the lamps that still float above us are working."

The images in the wall swam and became uncertain. Now the portion of Wennoc's globe that bore Eynna and Harna was cloaked by night. Only three lamps remained, still connected by threads to Eynna, but only to three locations on the surface.

"So the yellow lines must be paths from the sky to the earth," Micca said, trying to read the cities' glyphs.

Mercy-Ann looked at him, perhaps expecting a more excited reaction. "No," she said. "I suppose Odé told you our cousins docked their vessel at the lamps and climbed down into Wennoc by way of ropes or long ladders!"

"I didn't mean that kind of path."

"My own theory, more scientifically sound," she said, holding up her finger, "is that our kinsmen have conveyances that float on the currents of aether that flow between the stars; they might use these currents the way a thistle's seeds use the breeze to carry them about. When they arrived here, they floated their craft on the top of our sky; the air clings to Wennoc like a rind or a cloak, you see, and doesn't go on forever."

She paused for breath. "They probably used a large basket, or more likely a closed barrel, well cushioned inside. They got into this barrel, somehow punctured the skin of air, and simply let the natural suction of Wennoc's surface to draw them down."

Micca's faceplate chose that moment to perform one of its imitations of his expression. Mercy-Ann started, then smiled thinly at him. "You balk at the workings of their science when it's set out in plain language, preferring to think in terms of colorful old legends. Ladders from the lamps, indeed! But I have empirical knowledge of these things, Micca. I've seen the evidence down here, and I've been watching the night sky directly from my observatorium ever since I sighted the new star. I knew it was an important sign."

She pointed to the great window. "You see this star, just here? I believe the yellow circle around it means it's new to the heavens. This, I'm sure, is their vessel, floating above us! It's made of bright metal, or possibly glass or crystal, as is your suit, which would catch the sun's light and appear as a star to us down here. Well, twenty-three days ago another star — their landing barrel — separated itself from this one and fell, a signal to the wise —"

"Did you see that their ship sent something else down too, just a couple of days ago?" Micca broke in. "But the first thing wasn't a barrel or a basket. They flew from the big ship down into Wennoc in a sort of boat; a lighter, Finna calls it. It looks like a barge, or a raft, but it flies, and you can steer it, it doesn't just fall. I suppose the boat might have looked like a falling star coming down … it's nothing like a barrel, though."

Mercy-Ann stared at him. After a moment she said, "Did the visitors tell you all this?"

Micca laughed. "Like I told you before, I'm the boat's pilot now. I drive it, fly it, so I know a thing or two about it. How do you think we all got down here from Hoiin? It's a little far to have walked so quick."

Mercy-Ann didn't respond at once, but continued to stare at him. Micca couldn't see her eyes through the dark glasses; was she offended, even hurt?

The Director smiled. "Well, start talking then, Micca! Everyone around here is so taciturn I've gotten used to filling in when the conversation lags, but I can be a good listener, too. I can see there's more in your head than I gave you credit for; I suppose I assumed you were as dull as your brother Samma."

Then she gave a loud laugh, almost a bark. "But they came down into Wennoc in a flying barge? Micca — I want to ride in it! I want to smell the upper airs, see the tops of the clouds. I want to sail beside the moon when it shines high over the dark world!"

Micca smiled to see her excitement. She was the first person he'd met who didn't react to the boat with boredom, fear, or disbelief; even Neffafinnegal didn't have much interest in it. "I haven't seen the moon up close yet, but I could … I can take you along!"

"Marvelous! Wonderful! Oh, what a day. And this makes my plan seem all the more promising. But I've been remiss. First tell me all about your adventures. How did you get in with the visitors? Just why did you come here, other than to find your brother?"

Micca gave her a brief account of his involvement with the Lodge and the aliens. He told her that besides having something important to talk to her about, Neypo had come to Mellatuno to rescue Samma, that he had felt guilty about losing him.

One way or another Mercy-Ann inferred that Micca had been responsible for freeing Neffafinnegal from the Strivers, and she congratulated him for it. But she wouldn't accept the idea that a Striver was capable of feeling guilt.

Micca didn't feel she had a good grasp of what he had told her. "Whatever reasons the Striver had, he was anxious to get here. He would have walked—I think he would rather have walked, actually, he was afraid of the boat, but he was in a hurry."

Mercy-Ann tapped her fingers absently on the panel before her, then snatched her hand away, which was near the glyphs. "I wonder if this boat or lighter of theirs isn't the 'important secret' Odé babbled about—where is it now?"

"Not that far from here. I hid it so the frog-men wouldn't bother it. But the boat was just a fast way for the Striver to travel, it wasn't what he was talking about. He said the secret was already here, at Mellatuno."

"He told you what his so-called secret was?"

Micca shook his head. "He meant to, but your guards got him before he could. But why ask me? Ask the Striver! He's an intelligent man. He knows a lot."

"Give me credit for realizing that much, young man. But whatever plan he has must by nature be opposed to mine, and he'd never give me an ounce of cooperation."

"What have you got in mind, exactly?"

Mercy-Ann put her finger tips together. "Well, at first I meant to offer my help to the visitors. We have a resource here that will give Wennoc an absolutely enormous head start on the climb back to where it should be. And the Eynnish, or certainly at least the wreched self-serving oligarchs in charge of the Lodge, are sure to resist any change, even if it means all our lives will be enriched and improved.

"But I think your presence here, and what you've learned about advanced machinery, changes that. You offer new and wonderful opportunities—yes, a raw youth from Harna, and the marvelous machines he's mastered. So rather than shuffling up meekly and putting myself at the disposal of our kinsmen, who, after all, might not necessarily believe that I can help them, we'll now *show* them instead. Yes, we'll show them that our world already has a great deal of potential for progress, that we won't have to start from nothing."

Mercy-Ann put her fingers to the glyphs before her. The view a high-flying bird might have, appeared in the great window, a broad landscape. The scene grew larger, and Micca saw a dark expanse of tiny domes and rooftops, lit only by the moon and a thousand pinpoints of yellow light. There seemed to be water nearby, a harbor, but he didn't think it was Hoiin.

"This is Mennedal," Mercy-Ann murmured. "I've been able to make the window here respond in pictures when I press certain glyphs on the panel —" she pointed "— and this one is Mennedal's. You may say the characters bear little resemblance to the modern ones, but a scholar of grammatology can recognize their origins here."

"The Striver would love to see this," Micca said softly. Just then he imagined he heard the voice of an ancient Eynnishman again; but it came from nowhere, everywhere... from his own head, he supposed. He wondered if he had eaten some kind of inspirational fungus upstairs without being aware of it.

"Would you please stop interrupting me?" said Mercy-Ann. "I was about to say that the lamps gather electrical essence in the emptiness beyond the world, where it grows like wild grass, and they send it down to us. That's their function. They weren't put there only to hear the sentimental entreaties of young lovers. In ancient times twenty or more cities received this bounty, and only three still do. The present recipients must use only a fraction of the power the lamps are capable of supplying. Mellatuno is one of the modern recipients. Naen Tula is another, but most of it is said to be in ruins and only a couple of hundred people live there now. The third of course is Mennedal, home of the Lodgemen's masters, an important and ancient city."

"Where does Mellatuno's come down?"

"A dry patch a couple of miles south of here. You can see it from the roofs; I'll point it out in the morning. It's not much to look at, just a featureless dish. But it never gets wet in the rain, and if a pig or a bird tries to cross it, too bad for them!

"Anyway, back to business. When we're a little more at home with the controls here, we'll show the visitors, *and* the Lodge, what the lowly Harnish, represented by a frail old woman from Turnoc and an unshaven farmer-boy from Mora, can do all on their own. I'm sure the sleights you use to control your suit are the missing link. I hope they are, at least."

She pointed to the window. "Look here. I'll make Mennedal's line prominent... so. Now this is what we'll do: when I press Mennedal's glyph, and then this one, you'll write on your armor's wrist — a confirmation, or a repetition of my order, depending on what happens. What I hope is that your armor will provide the missing link or activator we need, and that the equipment here will hear you; you'd better speak it aloud, too. Is there something you tell it when you want it to obey an order you've already given?"

"Yes. Ii, Na, Pe — inpoa."

"'Empwaw' I see, I see..."

"'In-po-ah.' It means 'Do it thus.' It's in the imperative case."

"Imperative, of course. Use that one." She touched Mennedal's glyph, which glowed yellow. "Are you ready?"

"What will it do?" Micca asked, staring at the next glyph under Mercy-Ann's finger. It was odd, but vaguely familiar. "Are you going to cut off Mennedal's electricity?"

"Only for a minute or two. My darkening the city, then lighting it again, should provide convincing, empirical proof to the visitors that the lamps' system is working and powerful. They'll be impressed with us and treat us with respect... Now, as far as I can tell, the view here is current, things as they are tonight, right this minute. We should see the lights go out."

Micca was almost certain now that this was the 'resource' at Mellatuno the Striver had spoken of. What had *he* meant to do with it? Cutting off someone's electric lamps or radio receivers didn't seem very threatening in the short run, though he supposed it could cause a big upset to the way they lived and did business in a pretty short time. But the more he could learn about this the better.

He bobbed his head once. Mercy-Ann's finger moved and light

shone from the glyph. He suddenly felt doubtful, but he ordered his mind as he was used to doing when dealing with the boat. He tapped three spots on his wrist, thinking 'inpoa' at the same time.

They waited breathlessly for several seconds, then a minute, staring at Mennedal in the window. Nothing happened. The yellow sparks of the city glowed as before.

"All right," Mercy-Ann said finally. "It was worth a try. We'll go on to Plan Two."

She reached into a slot in the wall and brought out a silver hoop. It was etched with tiny glyphs all the way around. "Take off your helm," she told him. "I want you to try this…don't worry, it doesn't hurt! I've worn it myself. But be careful! It's very ancient, an irreplaceable artifact."

Well, he wanted to learn. Micca removed his helmet again. The hoop seemed to contract as he lowered it over his head, hugging his temples and forehead. He squinted in the buzzing light.

"The words on the circlet you're wearing, as far as I can make them out, have something to do with communication and authority. It may be purely ceremonial since I haven't been able to actually implement any change I make to the pictures while wearing it, but maybe with your words, your accent? Or maybe this 'initializing' you spoke of? Anyway, let's try it."

The circlet felt almost warm now. Micca repeated his preparation, but before he could speak the word the wall before them went completely black. The tubes overhead flickered. The wall came back to life, showing them a complex pattern of orange, red, green and yellow lines, blocks and circles.

Mercy-Ann jerked forward and fingered the glyphs in a panicky fashion. "What did you do?" she cried. "Whatever is was, do the opposite!"

He didn't hear her. Other voices spoke in the vault, more substantial than the little whispers he had thought to hear before, a basso mumbling of many parts, half awake.

The mumbling raised in pitch and became words, though still unintelligible. But with them a thought edged into his mind, a thought not his own. It took on more substance; he saw nothing, but a presence seemed to turn and regard him. If there had been a face, Micca thought it would be smiling at him with solicitous expectation. He thought of someone bowing.

Micca pulled off the circlet. The voices left him, but the strange presence remained, waiting patiently.

Mercy-Ann poke earnestly at the glyphs. Finally the glass wall changed, again showing Mennedal. "Well," she said, panting, "we've accomplished *something* at least, and you didn't even need to speak! Let's start again."

Still bemused, Micca leaned over Mercy-Ann's shoulder and watched. She managed to bring back the image of the benighted face of Wennoc and told him now what she knew of the each of the glyphs' functions, or at least the effect they had on the images in the glass wall.

"And using the circlet in combination with your armor could be the answer," said Mercy-Ann. "The circlet is probably a signal of authority, a key of some kind perhaps, but useless alone. I knew as soon as you told me about writing on your arm that that must be what we were missing! In ancient times wearing such remote controlling machines must have been part of operating larger ones."

She was wrong. It had to have been only his mind the wall responded to, not his tapped command to the alien armor. The headband must be a counterpart to something similar in his helmet. The wall had recognized him, just as the armor and the boat did after he had been initialized; but the tone, or flavor, of its response was completely different than the boat's, as unlike as fish and fruit…

Mercy-Ann shook his arm. "Come now! We'll try it once more." She made him put on the circlet again and started tapping. Every time she put her finger on a glyph, Micca heard the voices chant in response.

A discordant gong interrupted the chants. In irritation Mercy-Ann threw a switch and spoke into a horn at the end of a bracket extending from the wall. "What is it?"

Noma-Linda's voice sounded from another horn. "Ann? Yet more visitors. A little after sunset Halter's squad caught them trespassing on the West Road and brought them in by the water door. One of them has run off."

"No one important would have come from the west," Mercy-Ann

said into the horn. "Put Hoscar on the job. That's what he's here for."

She pushed the horn away and returned her attention to Micca. "Now! Let's see if we can get something done before we're interrupted again."

But they heard another noise, a dull bonging, this time coming from the workshop outside. "Now what?" Mercy-Ann cried in frustration. "Frita? But she wouldn't come down here again for no reason. Come with me, Micca," she called over her shoulder, leaving the vault. "I don't want you damaging something."

Micca took off the circlet and laid it cautiously on the panel.

28. IN THE GAZEBO

Micca put on his helmet as he followed the Director. A line of writing appeared inside the faceplate, which he understood as a warning that he shouldn't remove the helmet again in such circumstances. The 'circumstances' weren't defined. Either the armor assumed Micca had knowledge he didn't, or it had sensed something unknown and potentially dangerous in the vault.

And Micca appreciated the armor's concern. He could still hear the voices...a mental echo, a soundless discussion behind the stone, brick and earth around him. He hurried after Mercy-Ann.

The noise of hissing wind came down the stair by which he had entered the Director's workshop. A tall man in damp, muddy clothes came down the steps. He set a pair of dirty eye-glasses on his nose and squinted at Mercy-Ann.

"Director! Ann, my old friend! I had hoped to find you here. The brutes you use as guards tried to lock me up in a dirty hole. I managed to get away from them but they hold two of my companions, and I'd be very grateful if you'd see to their release."

"Wudego!" said Mercy-Ann. "Calm down, calm down. It's fine to see you, but what ever are you doing here after all this time? Don't tell me you lost another post?"

"It's a long story, with few cheerful passages," Palmer said, trying to smile. He cleaned his lenses as well as he could and put them back on. "Sometimes I wonder..."

He gave up on the smile when he noticed Micca, standing in the shadows behind Mercy-Ann. "What in this blessèd orb is that thing? Some new horror to shock your visitors?"

He came dubiously forward. Micca took a step back. Palmer retreated in alarm when he saw the thing could move.

Mercy-Ann laughed delightedly. "Micca, take off your helm! Wudego, this is one of our countrymen, and in a sense a representative of those who are going to assist the rebirth of our society."

"What do you mean, the rebirth of—Micca? Micael Mora!"

Micca held his helmet under one arm. "I'm surprised to see you, too. Who's bossing things at the farm these days?"

"I take it you two know each other," Mercy-Ann said bemusedly.

The Director counseled them to friendship. A new day was dawning in Wennoc, she said. The misunderstandings of the past should be forgotten; bigger things were afoot. Palmer agreed, and complimented Micca on the importance he had apparently achieved since leaving the farm. Micca said little, but shook the priest's hands.

Rubbing the imprint of Micca's fingers on his flesh, Palmer asked Mercy-Ann again to see to freeing his companions.

"Who'd you bring with for company?" Micca asked. "Incseth? Bacnod?"

Palmer shook his head. "This trek south wasn't my idea. There was some trouble I wasn't responsible for, not directly at least, and my associates arranged a speaking tour for me. That didn't work out. The original party I accompanied dwindled, and at last there was only myself, Smolic, your cousin Binta..."

He looked away, as though trying to see through the stone around them. "And one other companion. Mercy-Ann, this person disappeared when your pirates captured us, but as far as I can tell they didn't catch her. She's on her own out there, lost in the wetlands."

"Wamod?" said Micca, but Palmer didn't answer.

Mercy-Ann was irritated. "I know, Wudego, I know. The guards have gotten completely out of hand. Even so, they're good at finding people. We'll send a squad out to search immediately."

"The sooner the better," Palmer said. "I fear for her safety..."

Mercy-Ann told Micca to go with Priest Palmer to her office; Palmer said he knew the way. She got into her basket and was carried off through a pair of air-tight flaps in the workshop's ceiling. Micca, Palmer following, pushed through the revolving door.

Palmer seemed impressed by Micca's armor though he asked few questions about it; maybe he assumed it came from Mellatuno's workshops. But the priest kept up a steady monologue as they climbed the winding stair, giving what Micca had to admit was an interesting account of his trip through the western marches of the Mellatine sloughs: what sort of animals he had seen there, which fish and plants they'd found to eat, his impressions of the ruins of Mellatuno as seen by setting sun, as well as a harrowing description of his trip under the waters as a captive of the frog-men. He said little about how he had come to leave Mora, but seemed more sad than resentful.

They disagreed about just where the Director's office was, but after a few detours they found it. Mercy-Ann wasn't there, but Noma-Linda sat at her desk making notes on a sheet of paper. She seemed to know Palmer. She told him his companions had been released, and that a squad of guards had been assembled to search for the missing one. Then she grinned at Micca. "You remember Hoscar, the guard's chief? Well, you should have seen his face when he heard that one of his recruits was a man from the stars!"

Micca couldn't help but smile back. Palmer cocked his head inquisitively at them, but Frita came into the office and beckoned to him. "I found some dry clothes for you," she said. "You smell like a feral pig."

Palmer stretched out his arms humbly, as if to say Wennoc was Wennoc, and who was he to say how it had been treating him lately? Frita showed him an inner room where he could wash and change.

When Palmer was ready (Micca smiled again at the priest's new clothes — huge barn boots, foppish brocaded trousers and a dairyman's smock that hung to his knees) Frita led them down a corridor and up a steep staircase. After twenty steps she stood aside, indicating that Micca should push up a slanted door, half of it in the ceiling. It banged open and Palmer and Frita climbed through. Micca came after them.

They were on a flat stone roof under the night sky. Further roofs stretched out in a staggering line to the south, some like stony hills supporting small trees and bushes; other roofs were broken, open to the wind and sky. Micca looked over an eroded parapet. There was enough light from the moon and iridescent growth in the waters of the slough for him to see steep, meandering brick steps leading down to a strip of dry land bordering the walls. Beyond, the causeway he had seen from the island stretched eastward, mostly above water at this end. He thought he could make out the island where Neypo, Neffafinnegal and the women had been stolen, surprisingly nearby considering how far he thought he had traveled underground. The Indeduish boat would be on the other side of it, sleeping under the slough. Directly below, the water flashed with small, luminous fish, revealing glimpses of a sunken world between the lily stems. He wondered how much further down the ancient vault was buried. The voices were still now.

Micca turned to follow Palmer and Frita. He crossed an arch of brick between two flat roofs and paused. The further roof was higher, with another roof above it, tent-like and made of wood, its vertical planks painted alternately red and white, supported by turned and bracketed posts. This aerial gazebo was lit by colored bulbs hung on strings of wire under its eaves, as if to advertise Mellatuno's wealth of electricity. To one side was a sort of protruding bay or oriel, roofed with a copper-sheathed dome. A long brass tube, Mercy-Ann's telescope no doubt, stuck out of a slot in its dome, pointed at the sky. Mercy-Ann's little retreat, perched on the top of the ruins.

The others had gone. Micca climbed steps, opened a little gate and entered the gazebo. Between the rafters at one end was a large pulley, Mercy-Ann's elevator basket hanging from cables under it; they must be directly above the cellar workshop. The Director herself sat in a chair beside the elevator, at one end of a long table. Palmer had taken a chair next to her, and he saluted Micca with a cup. His gesture and expression were feeble, almost pathetic.

Two others sat with their backs to Micca. He recognized Monitor Smolic's grating voice as he asked Wennoc to bless a cup of spirits. The boy Binta, perceiving a presence behind him, turned. "Micca? Oh, Micky! Is it really you?"

Before he could jump up and embrace him, Micca pushed Binta back into his chair and sat down at the empty side of the table. Binta stared at him resentfully for a moment, but then teared up and began mumbling about his 'lost love'. If this was the friend they had lost in the sloughs, it couldn't have been Deaconess Wamod.

Palmer pushed a cup and the jar over to Micca. Micca poured and tasted it, a good essence of rose-hip. Frita and a helper set out several cheeses, a ham, bowls of raisins and roasted nuts, a pickle of carrots, onions and pepper pods, a plate of toasted cakes. Smolic quickly blessed the food, and after a few minutes Binta wiped his eyes and joined the others in their snacking. Smolic forbade him tasting the rose-hip.

A tall, almost bald young man with a coat like Mercy-Ann's, bare knees and gum boots came doubtfully over the bridge from the next roof. Micca got out of his chair, hurried up to him, stopped short to look him over, and began to laugh. Samma gave Micca's shoulder a shove, then took his hands. He smiled broadly. "You found me, didn't you?"

"I guess I did." They stood in silence for a minute, then sat down at the table.

Samma took note of the Director's guests. Priest Palmer nodded politely. Binta rushed up and greeted Samma as the Mora, tears filling his eyes again; Micca thought the boy's experiences as an itinerant evangelist must have strengthened his sentimental nature. Monitor Smolic chastised Binta, saying that the New Vigor required no kow-towing to farm chiefs on the part of its adherents.

Samma glanced at Smolic, then grabbed Binta's arm to hold him still and with his other hand made the signs over his head that bestowed the Mora's blessing.

Binta bowed to Samma. The boy sat down and poured himself a cup of the distillation, smiling boldly at Smolic's minatory stare.

Samma sat again, next to Micca. "We have to get out of here!" he said from the corner of his mouth. "Did you know that Gillensa, the Striver and Swannet are here too? The guards told me."

Micca whispered back, pouring for them both. "I know. I've been trying to talk the Director into letting them go. I've got a lot to tell you. A lot's been happening. Neffafinnegal's here too—they made a frog-man out of him, too. Noler got away but I don't know where he is."

"How did you all get here? Don't tell me you came in your giant doorstone."

Micca nodded. "Flew all the way. It's not far from here. I hid it."

Mercy-Ann leaned out of her chair and rapped on the table with her cup. "Has everyone had refreshments? Well and fine! Micca, before we go any further, I'd like you to stand up and show yourself to everyone. Put on your helm, too, if you would. We want the effect to be complete."

Micca put his helmet on and stood. Seized by some perverse impulse, he imitated the heroic stance of the armor displayed in the hall at Marstoc: legs planted wide, fists clenched at his sides, chest thrust out, head titled back as though gazing at some challenge or vision of glory in the heavens. They all looked at him. Two or three clapped their hands. Micca sat down, suddenly embarrassed.

"Here you see the future of our world," Mercy-Ann declared with a proud smile. "Think of Micca as a model, a foreshadowing of things to come. He looks proud and bold, but purposeful and efficient, ready for whatever might present itself, just as we must be.

"For our cousins, our kinsmen, have come back from the outer worlds — the original home of the Harnish race! — and we must show them that not all of us have sunk into the mud, along with the Eynnish who spurned our help!"

"Other worlds?" Binta said in a worried tone. "But we were begotten by Essa, and issued from Essy into the bosom of Wennoc!"

Monitor Smolic started to speak, but Mercy-Ann rapped the table again. "Stuff and nonsense. The early Harnish invented that tale for their children in an effort to hide their failed stewardship."

"This doesn't sound far from the mark," said Palmer. Smolic looked at him in astonishment.

"But let's get back to Micca," Mercy-Ann said with a nod to the priest. "Just look at him — you may remove your headgear now, there's a good fellow. Before long all of Wennoc will be like that. A gleaming new semblance, fresh as the rain where there was untidiness and filth, a world without stain or idiosyncratic whims."

"Will we all go about in glass hides, then?" Binta wondered.

Mercy-Ann spoke patiently. "It's fine that you're interested in our discussion, lad, but if you want to join in, you must think before you speak. I said that thing Micca wears was a *model*, a metaphor. You weren't to take it literally."

She turned to Palmer. "We'll have to design a special course of study for the youngsters, Wudego. They'll never be able to cope with the new world otherwise."

"I imagine the Outreach has plans for that," Micca said.

Mercy-Ann raised her eyebrows. "Well, I suppose we'll have to take your word for it…did I tell you, Wudego, that Micca here has been in personal contact with our cousins from the hithermost stars?"

Smolic snorted, but Palmer looked intently at Micca. "Not that I disbelieve your story, Ann, but Micca, what do you say?"

"It's true."

Samma added, "I met one of them too."

The doors over the hatch on the next roof clattered open. Noma-Linda's flat white face appeared across the bridge.

"Have you got him?" Mercy-Ann called excitedly.

"As far as I can tell." Noma-Linda withdrew.

Mercy-Ann told Palmer, "Now you'll meet one of our visitors in the flesh."

A tall, skinny frog-man wearing all his equipment flapped into the gazebo, escorted by Noma-Linda. Binta slid down in his chair. The frog-man looked around the gazebo in a bewildered fashion. Noma-Linda tried to indicate by mime that he should remove his snorkel.

Micca jumped up and went to him. He peeled off Neffafinnegal's hood, tossed it away and led him to the table.

"Are you all right?" he asked in Harnish. "I did what I could to get you free."

Neffafinnegal looked at Micca reproachfully as he sat down beside him. Samma pushed over a cup.

"What's this?" said Neffafinnegal.

"A drink, made from sugar-root and yellow rose-hips," Micca said patiently.

"One of your poisons? Good. I hope it kills me." Neffafinnegal drank it off.

The others were staring at the newcomer. "It's one of those greasy hooligans who kidnapped us," Smolic whispered to Palmer.

"Is this him, then?" Mercy-Ann asked Micca.

"It is."

Mercy-Ann, remembering the name Micca had told her, introduced Neffafinnegal to the others. Noma-Linda sat down with a pen and paper at a little table to the side, ready to record what was said.

Mercy-Ann smiled expectantly at the alien. When he didn't say anything, she spoke slowly in her version of Harnish, greeting him in the name of all forward-looking citizens of Wennoc and made a long apology for the misunderstanding that had led to his conscription as a guard.

"Is she trying to speak Indeduits?" Neffafinnegal asked Micca. "The only thing I got was something about flowery bollocks and wicked fly catchers."

Mercy-Ann, frustrated, instructed Micca to speak for her. Micca recited a condensed version of her speech.

"So she's happy to have the Outreach here," the alien said. "Why? She hasn't been processed yet, has she?"

Mercy-Ann leaned forward, hand to her ear, but was again baffled by Neffafinnegal's speech. Smolic's knowledge of Harnish was limited mostly to the pre-Invigoration devotional phrases he had learned as a child, but he whispered to Palmer, who had no Harnish at all, "The chap for a fact has the old mountain tongue, or something much like it!"

Mercy-Ann asked Micca doubtfully, "Are you sure you understand him, and he understands you?"

Micca turned. "Of course. He's having trouble with your accent," he said, and continued in Harnish: "Tell them about the Outreach, Finna, the stuff you told me the afternoon after the crash."

Neffafinnegal took the bottle and filled his cup. He looked up, face blank, and spoke about the Foreign Outreach in rapid Indeduits, a piece he seemed have memorized, one Micca had heard bits of before.

Neffafinnegal fell silent and took up his cup.

"…and also very important," Micca said, finishing his translation, "the Greater Good Foreign Outreach Mission will provide you with helpful consciences, a sure and proven remedy to all slothful, disrespectful or quarrelsome behavior. Intelligent, prudent use of planetary resources will mean an improvement in everyday life, and full, rewarding employment will be assured for everyone. You will also know the satisfaction of being part of the fellowship of all right-thinking human communities, each ready to give her, his or its all for the masses," Micca finished.

He had stood up to translate, to befit the formal nature of the presentation, and Micca realized he had mimicked Mora's old Priest Crosfin as Crosfin had preached in his better days, speaking in a deep, portentous voice and rolling his Rs dramatically, a style unlike the more vernacular, emotional preaching favored by modern priests. He realized the liquor was making him show off again. Samma and Binta, and even Neffafinnegal, stared at him.

Mercy-Ann was very pleased. "And if that isn't enough for you, Wudego — and Smola, wasn't it? — Micca can give us a ride through the clouds in the visitors' flying boat!" she said. "I haven't seen it yet, but isn't that right, Micca?"

"There's only chairs for three besides the pilot."

Smolic was alarmed. "Flying boats! I have some Harnish, you know. Our Micca's word-turning probably lacks delicacy. If Mister Finnegal talks of such things, his words should be took in a spiritual sense, surely."

Palmer answered first. "I don't know, Monitor. Can you deny the evidence of your senses? The equipment Micca wears is one, isolated example, but I know of no hogs or kine who could give him such a hide. Notice how grotesque the form is, and yet it retains much of a man's shape, and even exaggerates it to fearsome ends. Do you know any Harnish or Eynnish wright who could produce such work?"

"None of us do," Mercy-Ann answered for Smolic, "but such wonders were common in our ancestors' time, and they will be again."

She spoke for several minutes, telling them of how she had tracked the ship of space and witnessed the descent of the alien visitors, what she had read and what she had heard on the Eynnish radio, and that both Micca and a highly placed Lodgeman from Hoiin had confirmed her conclusions.

Smolic finally raised his hands in praise of Wennoc's miracles. "Surely now, it was Wennoc who told me of the need for an era of New Vigor, and sent these outlandish messengers to help us." He put a finger to each temple and closed his eyes. "Yea, Wennoc tells me this is a divine intervention, indeed so."

Micca found his cup empty and Neffafinnegal poured for both of them. Palmer settled into a thoughtful study.

Smolic and Mercy-Ann got into a theological discussion. From time to time they sought confirmation of their points from Neffafinnegal by way of Micca. Neffafinnegal's answers were so obscure and Micca's translations so careless that each was able to find justification for their arguments.

Frita brought another bottle of spirits to the table. Micca put on his helmet again, thinking it might stop him from drinking any more, or at least make him think before he drank. The others were growing boisterous and stupid. Even Palmer, who had been saying little, roused himself and got into a heated discussion with Smolic.

Binta's head swiveled from one speaker to the other. It was hard to follow all this complicated talk. He got up, leaned over the railing and took in a breath of cool air.

It must have been very late, but the moon hadn't set yet. A light breeze moved its reflection on open water, far out beyond the tall grasses and reeds that fenced a stone road. Suddenly Binta jerked upright. He pointed out to the slough, yelling and flapping his other hand at the people behind him.

Frita joined him, expecting to see a large mudrunner or possibly a guard returning from the night watch.

There was indeed a guard below, and he too was pointing to the east.

"Director!" Frita cried.

29. AT MOONSET

The others got up from their chairs with varying degrees of dispatch and agility. Micca looked over the railing with them. When he understood what he was seeing, he was amazed, delighted. A line of men glided over the causeway, light from the setting moon sliding over the contours of their glassy armor. They weren't walking, but rode on long beam-like things, boots in stirrups, arms forward, their hands grasping horizontal rods. The beams coasted free in the air, a couple of yards over the causeway.

What wonderful machines. Micca thought that if they flew quickly enough, and he'd be surprised if they couldn't, they'd be perfect for hunting wild pigs. It might be hard to manage a bow riding one, but maybe you could use a pike or throw a spear, and if you missed, it would be easy to get away and circle back. Micca imagined zipping through the woods on one of the things, dodging branches and trees, or down a road like a winter wind out of the mountains.

These fancies were swept from his mind by a sudden, almost overwhelming urge to run, to find the boat and hide it and himself in a distant forest. Several questions he had up until now carelessly pushed out of consideration, things he had regarded as unlikely or distant possibilities, were staring him in the face. He was about to lose the boat, his armor, probably be condemned as a thief, as the Striver had warned.

Micca squatted down, still peering over the railing. There were eight of the flying beams, one of them with a sort of carriage attached, whose passenger seemed to have no armor, but was bundled in a cloak.

An excited yell came from nearer the walls of Mellatuno. Micca saw a frog-man crouched near the causeway, a club in his fist. Another one stood peering out behind him, also clutching a club.

The riders slowed and hovered over the ancient road. The first frog-man ran to meet them, yelling challenges, brandishing his club. One of the riders held out his arm, something in his hand. There was no apparent action, no sound Micca could hear, but the frog-man pitched backwards and tumbled into the reeds. The other one flung his club in the general direction of the rider and turned to run. His back arched, his arms flew out, and he hit the ground face down.

From behind him Micca heard startled cries. Someone nearer by murmured, "Is this the shape of the new Wennoc?"

He turned to find Palmer staring at him.

The faces of the others in the gazebo were drawn. "Are those water-men *dead*?" Smolic hissed. "They treated us monstrous, but still…"

Mercy-Ann, two yards down the railing, slowly shook her head. "I don't know. This is a tragedy. No doubt the guards looked aggressive, but are the visitors so timid they thought they were in real danger?"

Then she braced herself. "But they're strangers here. Maybe they didn't know… and it will be a strong lesson for Hoscar!"

The riders were looking up at the lighted gazebo, pointing as they drew nearer.

Those at the railing backed away. But Mercy-Ann called out, "Linda! They clearly mean to visit us, and it doesn't appear their miraculous mounts will float this high. Go down and show them the way up. You have no weapon and are no obvious threat to them. Smile and motion with your hands if they don't understand you."

"I'm not putting myself in the way of those murdering horrors!" Nome-Linda declared.

Mercy-Ann snorted. She came and grabbed at Micca's hand. "You go, Micca! Welcome them, offer them food and drink."

He retreated to the far end of the gazebo. Mercy-Ann hobbled after him, hitting him with her stick.

She spat in disgust, then spun around and seized Priest Palmer's arm. "Wudego, you and I will go down!"

Palmer freed himself carefully. "From here out I am only an observer, Ann."

Mercy-Ann stumbled to her chair at the table and dropped into it, face screwed up, almost weeping in frustration. The others milled around the gazebo anxiously. Both the inner and outer stair would probably lead straight down to the glass men.

"They're gone now!" Binta called, peeping over the railing. "They must have found a door and come in!"

Mercy-Ann roused herself again. She ordered Frita to lay out more food and drink. Frita nervously obeyed, taking pots, jars and bottles from a cupboard near the telescope. Mercy-Ann had Smolic turn her chair so that it faced the bridge over the roofs.

Samma and Neffafinnegal stood near Micca. "Shouldn't we be trying to get out of here?" Samma whispered. "Or are you friends with these people?"

Micca blinked stupidly inside his helmet. "No! I have no idea who they are!"

Samma said, "If they're inside now, there's an outside stairway just over…"

There was a bang as the door over the hatch on the roof below was thrown open. A glass helmet appeared, then another, swiveling left and right.

"All of you!" came a bark from one of them. "Stand where you are! Don't move!"

They rose slowly, armored figures identical to Micca but for large, illuminated numerals displayed on their chests and shoulders: 005 and 002. They came across the bridge, holding out stubby black tubes, waving them back and forth.

One looked back, made a signal with his hand. Another man in armor came up from the hatch. This one brandished no black tube, although there was one clipped to a bracket on his thigh. Rather than a number, his chest bore an illuminated image of two hands cupping a swarm of stars. And unlike the other two, a glass face floated below the surface of his helmet. It showed a broad, friendly smile.

Mercy-Ann smiled back at it, lips trembling a little. "Welcome," she said in Harnish, and was apparently understood.

"I thank you, mistress," the smiling glass man said in Eynnish. The movements of his sculpted mouth were synchronized fairly closely to his words, though no teeth or tongue showed between the lips. He looked around the gazebo. "Please everyone, relax! We're friends, not the bandits you probably take us for. I'm very sorry about those fellows outside. They'll be taken care of."

Then he froze. "Astin? Astin Neffafinnegal!" He came forward quickly, seized Neffafinnegal's arms, then hugged him close.

Neffafinnegal stared over the man's shoulder and said, "I thought you were dead, Dinna."

Adinnegram released him. He told Neffafinnegal that Soliël, Epimanter, Chowdry and Sulawan were also alive and well, busy with the work in the north. "But Cortina and Munzies are gone. I saw their poor savaged bodies. And I suppose you actually witnessed their assassinations — Finnegal, you don't know how badly I felt for you! You must have believed you were alone on this world, with no one to share your grief."

Adinnegram hugged him again, slowly patting his back. Then Adinnegram turned to stare at Micca, glass eyes blank and unblinking.

Neffafinnegal stepped up and put his hand on Micca's arm. "This is my friend Micca, from Harna. That's —" He waved vaguely. "I'm not sure where Harna is. But he got me away from the locals. They wanted to torture me…he found one of our bodycasings to use."

"Yours?" said Adinnegram.

"Mine? No. It's one from the house we were staying in."

Adinnegram said, "Where's the lighter, Finnegal?"

Neffafinnegal shook his head once. "I don't know."

"You must have come here in it."

Micca said in Harnish, "I learned how to fly it. I brought him here in it and then he got kidnapped by the frog-men, the guards."

The others swung their heads from one speaker to the next, though they understood none of their talk.

"Another Harna man," Adinnegram laughed in response to Micca's words. He beckoned to the other armored men. "Fifth, Second, this fellow is one of your kin."

They came forward to shake his hands, but didn't introduce themselves. Micca remembered the press gangs he'd heard about in Hannava. Could that be where they came from? Were they draftees from Harna?

Adinnegram motioned them back before Micca could ask them any questions.

Mercy-Ann came up with her stick and spoke, trying her Harnish again.

"A moment," said Adinnegram in Eynnish. Mercy-Ann retreated, lips pinched. Adinnegram returned his attention to Micca. "I'm impressed that you learned to operate the lighter. Where is it?"

Micca gestured at the night. "Out there. I hid it so the frog-men wouldn't get into it... I mean the guards here. Like the ones you people killed."

"You hid it? Where? In one of these ruins?"

"Under the water."

Adinnegram appeared surprised. "Sounds like something Sula would think of. Pretty clever. Maybe we'll take you on as our pilot."

Adinnegram looked around the gazebo, then took off his helmet. His real face was wide-mouthed, a little plump and and sagged, but relatively youthful, its skin darker than Neffafinnegal's. His eyes were wide and never still. His hair, like Neffafinnegal's before he became a guard, was dark and closely cropped but for a longer hank over his forehead. With a normal growth of hair, he might be a Harnish farmer.

Adinnegram sat down on a bench by the railing, leaned back and spread out long legs. He beckoned to Micca and slapped the bench beside him.

Micca looked around at the others, then sat where indicated. Adinnegram peered at him, eyebrows lifted, and motioned with his hands to either side of his head. Micca took off his helmet. Adinnegram took Micca's chin in his hand and turned his head, studying his face.

He let him go. "Not really a classic, but I think you could pass for an upper-class Presbyter on Sumacron if you got a decent haircut and some sun."

He turned to Neffafinnegal. "Don't you think he looks like a toff from Sumacron?"

"Sort of."

" 'Sort of.' When did you get so argumentative, Finnegal?"

Adinnegram laughed easily, then returned his attention to Micca. "Sumacron is where I'm from, where a million stars light the night sky.

Finnegal's from Sumarit, the next system over. Both settled about the same time and from the same places, according to what the historians can scratch out, and I'd say your ancestors were some of them. A lot of adventurers went off into the unknown ages ago and were never heard from again."

He bent closer. "As you've seen, I recruited some of your countrymen as my aides. I may be romantic and unscientific about this, but they seem to react well to the technics initialization. It's as though they had an ancestral memory of dealing with such things. And like you, some of them still speak the common language, more or less. I found that just fascinating, way out here."

"All the Harnish used to speak this way," Micca murmured. "We have books at home written in it."

"Is that so! We'll visit your home once things are organized, and bring our archaeologist along."

Then Adinnegram leaned closer, took one of Micca's hands and looked him in the eye. "I want to ask you something now, Micca. Why did you bring my lighter here?"

Micca ran his tongue over his lips. He didn't avert his eyes, which he wanted to do. "The Director here kidnapped my brother...but before that we were at the harbor at Hoiin. There were people who were trying to kill us. We had to get away quick. But once we—"

"All right. That agrees more or less with what one of the Lodge people told me."

Adinnegram turned and spoke to Neffafinnegal. "You must have used the 'casing to initialize him."

"It was in the tutorial. I had to do it, Dinna. I thought I was alone! And he's good with the lighter, he's interested in technics."

"Can you imagine how I felt when they told me my only way off this ball of muck and moss had flown off into an alien sky? The end of my mission, the end of my career—the end of all our careers!"

"I didn't know!" said Neffafinnegal. "Though I suppose I can cook anywhere," he muttered to himself, then looked up at Adinnegram in alarm.

But Adinnegram still had hold of Micca's hand, and his attention was on him now. "Why did you come here, to these ruins?"

Micca made a half shrug. "To find my brother...I had trouble controlling the boat, the lighter, at first, though. It fell out of the sky. We got partly buried. Then the Director here, she kidnapped my brother near where we came down. She thought he was one of *you* people, she wanted to get him away from the Strivers. She wants to help you."

"The old lame woman?"

Micca nodded.

Adinnegram dropped Micca's hand and smiled at Mercy-Ann. He said in Eynnish, "I understand you're our friend—Director? Is that the proper title? Good. I have a lot to talk to you about."

"Yes! And we to you! Isn't that right, Wudego?"

"I would certainly imagine so, Ann," Palmer said.

Mercy-Ann began speaking to Adinnegram, but he had turned away. "Go on," he told Micca.

"How did you find us here?" Micca asked him.

"What? Well, we happened across a fellow who'd been sent here by his employer to deliver a message, and he saw and heard some interesting things. But never mind that. Why did *you* come here?"

"Like I said, to find my brother."

"Who came with you? What about the Lodge member who was on the dock at Hin Hoina?"

Had Adinnegram seen Neypo there on the pier? Micca wasn't sure. But if not, someone would have told him. "There was a Striver with us for a while. I don't know exactly where he is now."

Micca glanced at Mercy-Ann and Smolic, but they appeared to understand little or nothing of what was being said. He wished Neypo were here, though he couldn't imagine what the Striver would say to these people now.

Adinnegram said, "Since *you're* not wearing it, where is Finnegal's bodycasing? I was told he was suited up when he was taken."

"My brother had it for a while. That's why the Director—"

"Where is he now?"

"There."

"That one?"

"Yes."

"Can he speak as we do? Has he been listening to us?"

"He's not that good at it. But better than the Director."

Adinnegram said in Eynnish, "You there, Micca's brother. You had control of a suit like ours?"

"Well, I wore it for a little while if that's what you mean," Samma said. "And without a helmet. Then, after they brought me—"

Adinnegram turned to Neffafinnegal: "Comrade, I'm curious. Why was this local wearing your 'casing? I can't understand why you took it off after what happened, and why did you give it to *him*? Did you feel so at home here, so secure, after what happened in the city? You must have seen Cortina and Munzies being beaten to death as they defended our mission."

"The Honorables forced me to take off the headpiece. They could have done anything to me!"

" 'Honorables'!" Adinnegram pronounced the Eynnish word with amazement. "Is that how you regard them? Where is your bodycasing now, Neffafinnegal? We have to retrieve it—immediately."

"I don't know where it is."

"You don't know much, do you?"

"I know where," Micca said. "Neffafinnegal's armor is down in the Director's workshop. It's a secret place though. She's not going to let us in there on our own."

Adinnegram grabbed Micca's hand again and squeezed it, or tried to. "Good lad. I was concerned with an unauthorized local getting hold of the suit. Despite his stupidity and punishable behavior, I think Finnegal had better don it again."

Micca wondered what harm an uninitiated 'local' could do with the armor, and he wondered how well Adinnegram had thought this out.

"First though," Adinnegram went on, "introduce me to your friends. I haven't been a very cordial guest so far."

Adinnegram and Micca stood, Adinnegram's hand on Micca's back as though he were a child to be guided. Despite his general unease, Micca found this repeated physical contact off-putting and presumptuous. It wasn't as if they were close friends or relatives. Neffafinnegal had never made such empty displays.

Micca went with him around the gazebo, reciting people's names. Adinnegram asked each a few questions about their homes and work, showing a relatively fluent command of colloquial Eynnish.

"Your office is that of a monitor?" he asked Smolic. "As in looking after people's conduct and moral welfare? I'm sure that's a demanding job. Let me assure you, it'll take a lot less effort once more people are gifted with true consciences…in fact, you may well have to look for other work!"

The smile Smolic returned was thin and pinched. "We had some talk of that term earlier," Smolic said. "I would like to take some discussion with you about these here consciences."

"That would be most welcome. In fact I can do better than that. We'll arrange a demonstration for you."

Palmer asked, "How do you mean?"

Adinnegram strode up to Binta and gestured to Palmer. "This young fellow said he was a student of the divine. But when there's opportunity I'll bet he's as much a hell-rasing rapscallion as any boy his age. Tell me this, young man: how would you like to have the sure knowledge and joy that you'll never sin again?"

Binta looked at him sidelong. "I'd as soon have one of those glass skins, like you and my cousin Micca. Then I could go fearless of toughs and buins."

"Buins?" Adinnegram muttered, then regained his train of thought. He slapped his leg and laughed. "Ah, the brash candor of youth! Well, my young friend, soon there will be no 'toughs' or 'buins' for you or anyone else to fear."

"Are you going to *kill* them all, like the water-men?" said Binta, facing him now and blinking.

"Good heavens, son, no. They too will become saints, living saints. We harm others only when the need is dire and immediate…and afterward we suffer terrible grief."

For a moment Adinnegram's face became a perfect model of remorse, but his smile snapped quickly back. He gave Binta a pat on the head, then strode over to Mercy-Ann. He pulled out a chair beside hers, sat down, hunched over and took her hands.

"Mistress Director," he said. "I've been saving you for last! Last but far from least. First, before we get started, please accept my apologies for bursting uninvited and so unceremoniously into your charming little eyrie, but we saw your lights, and this telescope…did you see my ship with it, or is my imagination running away with me?"

Micca thought he meant the raft, but Mercy-Ann had bigger ideas.

The lights overhead sparkled in her eyes. She held Adinnegram's hands tightly. "I *did* see it, mingled with the stars! And I heard your talk on the radio! I traveled all the way to Hoiin in hope of meeting you, but the wretched Lodgemen — I knew what you might mean for our race, and all of Wennoc — but may I call you Dinna? I feel I already know you like a —"

"Of course, call me anything you like. And I'll call you... Ann? Is that what your comrade here called you?"

"Yes, call me Ann! I'd be delighted."

Adinnegram smiled warmly, then sighed. "I can't tell you how refreshing, how wonderful it is to receive this warm welcome after what we've been through in the city, Ann. They're coming 'round now, but it was disheartening to arrive on this world, so far from home, so far over the sea of stars, offering the free gift of love, and be rejected with mistrust and brutality."

Mercy-Ann pinched her lips. "I know, I know. But you can count on us, Dinna. You have friends in Wennoc now... in Roma!"

Then she lurched upright and slapped her hands on the table. "But I've been terribly remiss! Pull up to the table, have a bite to eat! Frita! Pour for our guests. And Dinna, ask your colleagues to sit down, for pity's sake! They've been standing there like dead trees."

"They don't mind, Ann. They probably locked their joints and are having a nice rest." Adinnegram chuckled. The armored men at the gate shifted a little, but made no response.

Frita poured a cup of spirits for Adinnegram. Palmer handed over a plate of cheese. "Tell us, Mister Adinnegram," the priest said, "with what sort of weapons you killed those guards."

"Tell us about those incredible devices you appeared to be riding on!" said Mercy-Ann. "Needless to say, I've never seen their like."

Samma gave Adinnegram a dish of mushrooms. "Did your friends come in with you?" Samma asked. "I thought I saw a good number of men out there."

Adinnegram sniffed at a piece of cheese, nose working like a coney's. He put it down carefully and raised his cup. His head jerked back, and he put that down too. Finally he took a cake and a handful of salted nuts.

"Yes, there are a few more. Some of my Harnish helpers, and an official from the city who's signed on with us. They found a room down the stairs to set up in; I hope you don't mind us appropriating it, Ann. We prefer to bestow new consciences in a quiet, private setting."

"Make yourselves at home," Mercy-Ann said in a subdued tone, and then she brightened. "But we must send them some refreshments too. Frita, Linda, sort out a good supper and bring it down."

Adinnegram said, "I don't think they'll want to eat much of that... the tastes of men on this kind of duty are simple."

"Oh, let them have a little treat," said Mercy-Ann. "In honor of our meeting. Besides, the longer that stuff is on the table, the more *I'll* eat!"

Adinnegram shrugged. To Micca he murmured, "I'll be glad to have the smell of that decaying rubbish gone."

Noma-Linda put down her pen. She and Frita filled baskets with jars, bottles and pots, and wrapped what was left of the ham in a cloth.

Palmer emptied his cup, watching them lug the baskets over the bridge. He asked Adinnegram, "So there is some sort of ceremony involved in receiving this so-called new conscience?"

"Of a sort," Adinnegram replied. He waved at Binta. "This young fellow will soon be able to tell you about it."

Binta quailed. "Do you have to eat strong mushrooms or breathe in sot-weed smoke to get a new conscience? Because I can't do that, I just can't—I *know* I'd spew my supper!"

Adinnegram reached over and patted his hand. "Don't worry. We don't use toxic things like that. You won't remember anything but a glorious sunrise. You'll be eager to greet the coming new day—you'll want to run and dance, full of vigorous, joyous energy."

"*Vigorous* energy?" Smolic muttered, looking up. "But I reckon only Writ-scoffs and people of low 'Vigoration need this here new conscience you talk of."

Adinnegram was surprised, saddened. "But would you cheat yourself? I don't understand. Would you refuse a perfect life here on this earth, this Wennoc...or Roma, did you say? Whatever you call it, I regard this world as sacred, one of the precious few that can support our race. Are you willing to dishonor it and continue to stumble along in ignorance and unwitting moral filth while others prove the glory of their high estate, their duty to their people and to this wondrous orb itself? You'd turn your back on this heartfelt, loving call, cause your fellows sorrow and pain, even anger, by an ungrateful refusal of this freely given gift?"

He calmed himself. "My friends, some of you have heard of the material improvements we mean to gift you with, but the best of what we bring is hard to describe in words. See yourselves living in perfect confidence, sublime in the knowledge that you will never again know doubt, guilt or anxiety. All this will be yours."

Smolic blew out his breath. "I will surely study on this most prayerfully. Your words are fraught full with theological implications."

Frita and Noma-Linda returned, saying the guests downstairs had been happy to have a supper. She bent over and whispered to the Director: "And if I read my plaids right, they brought us another Lodgeman."

Mercy-Ann nodded absently and returned her attention to Adinnegram. He said that originally he had come south only to locate his lost transport, but now realized what a help Mellatuno could be to his project.

"We've won over the requisite numbers in Hoiin, but I've learned that the large settlements to the east are ruled by oligarchs even more reactionary than Hoiin's had been, and that they maintain companies of violent men they'd use against anyone who meant to lift the burden of exploitation and oppression from the shoulders of the populace.

"So, with your permission and aid, Director, I think that setting up our headquarters in an isolated locale like this would be very useful. A place of security and calm while the struggle for enlightenment outside proceeds, a place for training our outriders and planning the next steps."

Mercy-Ann clapped her hands in glee. Smolic suggested the proximity of Saint Unwey's and Harna also made Mellatuno a good choice, since those places held a stock of already Invigorated folk who should be eager to join in the work.

Micca's cup was empty. He reached for the nearest bottle. Adinnegram's hand took his wrist.

"Please, Micca," Adinnegram said quietly as he sat down beside him. "Don't pollute yourself any further. I don't want to offend the locals' folk-ways under present circumstances, but I think I can speak to you man to man. Once you're really our comrade, as young Binta will be shortly, you'll realize the damage such stuff can do. I'm surprised Finnegal hasn't mentioned it to you."

Hadn't he noticed that Neffafinnegal was drinking too? Micca wondered. No doubt Adinnegram had more important things on his mind. "Neffafinnegal calls it poison," Micca said.

Adinnegram nodded. "For the wise man, a word or two is enough," he said warmly. "I hope you didn't eat any of that animal limb they took away. Avoid those fungal growths, too, or whatever they are. I don't like their looks."

"Me neither."

"Good man."

Mercy-Ann and Smolic were now debating whether the morally needy among the Eynnish or the Harnish should have precedence in being given the visitors' consciences, or the new Vigorous Inwitting, as Smolic was now calling the concept. Adinnegram listened for a few minutes, then stood up and cracked his hands together.

Everyone's head jerked up to look at him. "I'm afraid that for tonight, at least, most of you here aren't... let's say, healthy enough, to take on a new 'inwit', vigorous or otherwise. Binta, however, appears to have kept himself unsullied —

"So! On your feet, comrade-to-be. Square your shoulders, loosen your collar. Fifth will take you to the processing area."

He waved his hand, and one of the armored men stirred himself and came forward to stand by Binta's chair. Binta peered up at him, hunching his shoulders. "I don't want a new conscience. I'll listen better to the one Wennoc gave me."

"Wants and wishes are whimsical, outdated notions in civilized society. Fifth, take him down and see to the preliminaries. I'll be there in a few minutes to do the counseling."

Adinnegram twitched his hand again. Fifth took Binta's arm and pulled him to his feet.

"Brave, be you," Neffafinnegal told Binta in Eynnish.

Adinnegram looked at Neffafinnegal, brows raised. Then he spoke to Micca in Indeduits. "Take Finnegal to wherever his 'casing is and get him suited up. Then he can join the boy; I think he could use a little booster treatment after what he's been through. When you come back you and I will go out and make an inspection of the lighter. Maybe we'll take it for a spin — call it an audition for the pilot's job, hey?"

Fifth took the trembling Binta's arm and led him off. Everyone fell silent as they watched them go. Adinnegram went to the man he called Second, who stood and listened to him for a moment; Micca didn't hear what was said.

Adinnegram turned to Micca. "Second will go along with you and Neffafinnegal. It'll good to have an extra comrade along in case you run into any difficulties."

Micca got to his feet, as did Neffafinnegal, and then Samma too.

"Where are you boys going?" said Mercy-Ann.

"I need to use the washroom," Samma said.

"Me and Neffafinnegal do too," Micca added, picking up his helmet. "Sam's going to show us where to find a toilet."

Mercy-Ann sniffed. "Well, if you're too shy to aim yourselves over the railing as Monitor Smolic has been finding it convenient to do, there's a slops-hopper ten yards beyond the foot of the stairs, off on the right — and lower the seat when you're finished!"

Adinnegram muttered to Micca, "Clever lad! Now the old woman won't suspect her work space is about to be violated. We may postpone your processing for a little while, see what other clever ideas you come up with."

30. THE VAULT

At the bottom of the stair they entered a wide, relatively high-ceilinged corridor, lit by standards on the wall. So far no one had spoken. Micca's and Second's boots thudded as they walked. Samma padded along in house-shoes he'd found somewhere, and Neffafinnegal's feet slapped the floor in the shoe portions of his frog-man's flippers; sometime during the supper he had cut off the long extensions with a knife from the table.

Samma sidled up next to Micca. "What did he tell you to do?" he hissed. "What's this other guy doing with us?"

"Making sure we do what we're supposed to, I suppose. Adinnegram wants Finna back in his armor, so we have to go down to the Director's shop."

"That's where she made me take it off."

Micca nodded. "Why did you say you wanted to pee? That was good timing."

"Because I need to pee." Samma glanced back at Second. "And I wanted to get out of there, of course."

Micca also looked at Second, then put on his helmet. Second said nothing, but nodded at him in what might have been a comradely way.

"You're all right with Finna taking it again?" Micca asked Samma.

"I don't want the damn thing! It was horrible."

Second said, "I don't only talk Harnish, you know, and my 'casing can hear whispers."

"Do you have a name besides 'Second'?" Samma asked him.

"I go by what First Comrade calls me."

"You sound like you're from Hannava or thereabouts."

He nodded. "Wittal Street, north of the market."

"Have the outlanders been over to Harna now?" Micca asked him.

"I don't know. We came and found *them*, in Hoiin. I was in the City's Service and I was just a week till the end of my time, then they hired us out to the Strivers. But I got a better job now…you too, by the looks of it. Seems like First took a shine to you."

Second got in front of Micca and pushed his helmet so close to his that they clicked together. "But don't be getting ideas, cousin. *I'm* Second, and I stay Second."

"Don't worry. I don't have any number at all."

"No," said Second. "I understand you haven't been processed. Yet."

They walked on. It was late, and the regions below the gazebo were quiet. They found a water closet and Samma and Neffafinnegal went in. Neffafinnegal also used a basin to wash as much frog-man's green from his head and hands as he could.

"When you're in a 'casing, it can wash, shit, *and* piss you," Second said proudly in Harnish. Neffafinnegal stared at him. "But probably you knew that."

Around a corner, light could be seen shining from an open door. They heard low conversation, forks clattering on plates, a belch. The others were walking, but curiosity drove Micca to trot down and look through the door. An armored back bearing the number '005' blocked most of the view, but a number of other people had gathered within. He didn't see Binta, but there was someone else, short, unarmored…

He heard Samma call him, and ran back to join them. Second told him, "That's where they set up the counseling room. You're not supposed to watch."

Samma looked at Micca as they walked on. "I saw sort of a face in your helmet," he said, whispering again. "It's gone now, but it looked like it had just seen a ghost."

"It had," Micca murmured. "A ghost from Hoiin."

"What about ghosts?" Second asked.

"This is a very ancient place," Samma said, with another curious glance at Micca. "Goes way back to the days of the Heresiarchs. Horrible things must have happened here."

"First Comrade says ghosts and sprites are nonsense."

"So you've never seen one yourself, or heard tell of one?" Samma asked sharply. "I saw one once, in the high woods. And you don't want to. Maybe there are none in other worlds, but..."

Second had no comment, and they found the stair that gave access to the Director's workshop.

"All right," said Samma. "Here's where I leave you."

"What?" Micca said.

"You weren't ordered to go along, but I think you're in my charge," Second told Samma.

"This is the hour I have to report to Chief Tamanello." Samma looked at Second, then at Micca. "Chief Tamanello is my commanding officer. Once I give him the news he'll be interested in these new consciences for all my comrade guards."

Micca said, "Is your chief the one with a daughter, name of Gillensa?"

Samma nodded.

Second said, "If he's your commander, I suppose you have to follow orders. Keep in mind your whole set up here will probably be changed by noon, though—but you'd better not tell him that, not yet."

"Right, I won't," said Samma, and he raised his hand. "I'll see you all a little later."

Micca, Neffafinnegal and Adinnegram's Second watched him go off at a half-trot.

Micca called out suddenly, "Sam! Tell him I think I found it."

Samma stopped and called back, "Found what?"

"Just tell Chief Tamanello—and bring him to the shop!"

"What's this Eynnish Chief guy got to do with *you*?" Second asked as the three of them went on. "Whether you know it or not, you guys are working for the Outreach now, not a bunch of Eynnish historians."

"It's like this...his name sounds Eynnish, but the Chief's Harnish, like us, like the Director. Yesterday me and him and the Director, we were doing some experiments, and a new condenser for an underwater breathing mask got lost. Won't work without it. Probably be very useful to the First Comrade if he's going to set up down here in the sloughs."

This seemed to be good enough for Second. Micca was sure the man had had nothing to drink upstairs, but he knocked his helmet hard on a low door lintel that Micca and Neffafinnegal had avoided; maybe he hadn't eaten recently either.

Second complained about the confusing layout of the place, its low ceilings and general gloom.

Neffafinnegal spoke a few words of agreement, and said it was even worse under the waters of the sloughs outside.

Second looked at him curiously, apparently able to understand his Indeduits well enough. "Why's that? I'd think it'd be fun to go under the water and see what all was down there."

"I wasn't there to have fun," said Neffafinnegal. "I was on guard duty. It was at night. The big green moon was the only light, but I saw people on the bottom of the lake. Dead people. Rows and rows of them. They were holding long knives and wearing ancient military equipment. Besides the knives, they had little lamps that glowed under the water. I was swimming along and then one of them, right under me, opened his eyes and stared at me…but there were no eyes under the lids. Just holes. Like…windows. They were like windows into the black empty space between the stars. Then all the dead people went white, like steam, and started swirling up at me. They grabbed out and tried to take hold of me. One of my comrade guards pulled me up out of the water. Later the other guards said the dead people in the lake were killed there in a battle thousands of years ago, when the lake was dry land. They said not to look under the water when the lamps were lit."

Second, though he made scoffing sounds, said nothing articulate. Micca didn't ask Neffafinnegal how many of Mellatuno's guards spoke Harnish.

They found the chamber above the workshops. He led the others over the clanging grille and down the twisting stair. Second's helmet turned uneasily in the chamber at the bottom. "There's too much of something in the air here, or not enough of something else," he muttered. "My 'casing says so…there's a strange sound, too, like something's crawling around."

"Through here, quick," Micca said.

One at a time, Micca going first, they turned through the rotating door and down into Mercy-Ann's workshop.

"Where is it?" Second said, helmet swiveling slowly back and forth.

"Where's what?" said Micca.

"The bodycasing! Give it to the comrade so we can get out of here and back with the others."

They went through the Director's shop. Neffafinnegal looked at Mercy-Ann's devices and inventions with the interest he might have shown in a pile of rocks.

Second asked, "Why aren't there any windows?" he asked.

"Didn't you notice how many steps we came down?" Micca said. "We're way down under the slough, I don't know how far. Open a window and all you'd see is mud or water."

Second's helmet tipped back to study the ceiling, which wasn't far from his faceplate. Micca led them on to the archway leading to the vault. Second halted and pointed to the perforated brass disk set in the floor, where running water could be heard. "What's that? What's under there?"

"I don't know," Micca said.

Second hung back until both Micca and Neffafinnegal had walked over it.

Neffafinnegal paused, pointing at something in the wall Micca had earlier taken for the ribs of a fish.

"Finger bones?" said Neffafinnegal. "It looks like a hand...see, there's part of a wrist."

The buzzing lights were still burning in the vault ahead. Second, turning from the ancient fingers, said, "My 'casing is telling me something again..."

Micca said, "What's it saying? Mine had some kind of message last time I was here, but I didn't understand it."

"I don't know, but something's not right. I'm waiting here. Now hurry up!"

Neffafinnegal had wandered on. Micca hurried after him. He glanced back, but couldn't see Second.

Neffafinnegal was at the shelf bearing the armor he'd worn in Hoiin, already stripping off his frog-man's gear. Micca swung the armor off the shelf and Neffafinnegal got into it. He reached back, closed the suit and stretched his arms. "I didn't think I'd be glad to be in a 'casing again, but right now it's great. I don't feel as vulnerable."

He passed a gauntlet over his shaved head and looked at Micca...or at his helmet?

"Say," Micca said. "Did you really see corpses in the slough? Were you trying to scare Adinnegram's man?"

"I didn't see anything but weeds and fish. The dead men was a scene I saw in an old story. I thought Mister Second needed something to think about besides how fine he is with a cheap military conscience and an old surplus 'casing."

"Huh."

"What are we going to do?"

"I don't know!...Is Adinnegram going to want me to get one of your consciences?"

"Didn't he say you'd be his comrade, like that nervous boy?"

Micca replied slowly. "That's Binta, my cousin. But I think...I'm sure I saw somebody else I recognized in that room they took him to. You remember Striver Caihar, the one in—"

"I remember him."

"He's there. I thought he had drowned, at the harbor."

"If you saw him here, he's not dead."

"If Caihar is here, he's cooperating with Adinnegram...the Striver Caihar! He must have been the Outreach's biggest enemy. And the other Lodge people Neypo said were hypnotized must not have just changed sides for their own gain or whatever. From what you said, there's more to the consciences than just stop you from doing things like robbing and swindling. Or flying a lighter if you're not a pilot, or eating meat. And they must be able to make you do things, too. Like fighting and killing. Bad things."

"Whatever's appropriate. I told you all about consciences."

"More or less," Micca conceded. "Well, come on."

They went further into the vault, to Mercy-Ann's window into space. Micca thought to hear the voices, muttering among themselves. "The Director said my people built this, but I think the Eynnish did."

"Well, it's like nothing I've ever seen. Can you read these marks?"

"Some of them. This here says Mennedal. This other one is where we are, Mellatuno."

Micca found the circlet Mercy-Ann had made him wear.

"Here, Finna. Put this on."

Neffafinnegal's eyes narrowed. "Why?"

"The Director made me try it earlier but you must be better with this stuff than I am. I want to see what can be done with it so we're ready when the Striver joins us."

"The Honorable Neypo? What's he going to do?"

"That's what I want to find out. He thinks he can take charge of things somehow. I'm afraid of your Adinnegram."

Neffafinnegal cocked his head speculatively. Finally he took the circlet and carefully lowered it over his head.

Immediately his eyes went wide. He blinked rapidly, hands poised to either side of his head, but he didn't take off the circlet or touch it again. Then he made a strange sound in his throat, fell back against the wall and slid slowly to the floor, fists clenched.

The window-wall had gone blank. Now the ghosts were speaking, wailing and singing, but not to him.

Neffafinnegal's eyes flicked blindly from side to side. Drool dripped from his mouth. Micca gingerly plucked the circlet from his head. Neffafinnegal gasped. His eyes slowly focused on Micca, then on the circlet in his hands.

"No!" Neffafinnegal croaked. He jumped to his feet and ran.

Micca trotted after him. Second stood outside the passage, watching as Neffafinnegal sprinted through the workshop. Second spared Micca a glance, then ran too, overtaking and passing Neffafinnegal.

Micca heard clunks and hisses of air as the workshop's door opened and closed. He must be alone now. He stood silent for a minute, looking at the circlet in his hand. Why had Neffafinnegal panicked? His own experience with the circlet had been very strange, but not overtly frightening. Maybe he was insensitive. Or was this machinery just so different from what Neffafinnegal was used to that he couldn't deal with it? Maybe Micca felt only a little of what the thing did, where Neffafinnegal had felt the full impact. Or were the ghosts — influences, memories, whatever they were — more fully awake, stronger now?

He walked slowly back into the vault. No voices now, but he could feel their presence like an itching under his scalp. The great window had come back to life, showing roaming geometric shapes, busy, interacting with each other. Micca looked into the workshop again. Had Samma found Neypo? Would they make it by Adinnegram and the guards?

Micca leaned over the glyph-studded panel, found Mellatuno's glyph, and recalling what Mercy-Ann had done, was able to brighten the line linking it to the lamps.

One of the glyphs he'd noticed before looked very much like a modern one, a barred rectangle under a stylized roof, used even in Harna to indicate a place that was closed or private, but he thought a verb, 'shut', or 'close', made more sense; it was the one Mercy-Ann had been ready to press when she meant to cut off Mennedal's power.

He thought he heard something from outside; another rush of air as the outer door cycled? Neffafinnegal? Samma and the Striver?

He went into the passage, looked out. He went a little farther and looked around a blocky column. Baggy barn boots, coming down the steps. Then brocaded trousers…Priest Palmer.

The priest trotted toward him. "Micca," he whispered. "Is that Micca? I see no number."

"It's me, right. What are you doing down here? Have you seen my brother, or a Striver?"

"No. Isn't Samma down here? I came to see what had happened to you. Your friend Adinnegram is angry now; he seems to have an uneven disposition."

"He's not my friend. Why is he angry?"

"Because you haven't come back with this Neffafinnegal and his glass suit. And I just crossed paths with one of the others, Number Two. What did you do to him? I didn't speak to him but he seemed very shaken."

"He's afraid of ghosts. Was there any talk about a Striver up there?"

"The official Adinnegram's brought from Hoiin? He's a Striver?"

"Yes, but I didn't mean that one." Micca looked around. "You'd better come in here."

Palmer followed him. He looked in awe at the window and the shining rows of ancient glyphs. "What is all this?" he asked. "Is this Mercy-Ann's great secret?"

"So she told you about it? What did she tell Adinnegram?"

"Hints and obscure boasts. Nothing of substance. I think she's beginning to suspect Adinnegram of condescension. She's also feeling the drink. But Micca, how is this picture in the wall made? I feel I could put my hand into it."

"How did you know where to find me?"

"I've also had more to drink than necessary, but not as much as the others, and I'm not an idiot. It was said that at some point your brother wore a set of this glass armor. When I met him he was no longer in the suit. So Mercy-Ann must have appropriated said suit, and where would she have put something like that but here, in her subterranean hobby shop? And, of course, you had been down here, and had probably seen it, and so knew where to bring Mister Neffafinnegal. So my conclusion is that you somehow frightened off Adinnegram's minion, and presumably Mister Neffafinnegal as well — and Samma?"

Micca shook his head. "Samma went to find Neypo Odé, a friend of mine, the Striver I asked about."

Palmer looked surprised, but not surprised enough.

"I joined the Holy Striving Lodge of Hoiin. I'm an Adjunct-Military," Micca said. "Same status as a Mendicant."

Now Palmer was surprised. "You, an honest builder from Wendum, in the Lodge?" Then he waved his hand. "But that's not important. What are we going to do?"

Micca paused. The voices had come back, chanting confusedly. He took off his helmet. Silence? Nearly so.

"What are we going to do about what?" he asked Palmer. "Adinnegram? Is he mad at you too?"

Palmer snorted. "He's not concerned with me. I went off with the same excuse your brother gave. But Micca, I am concerned about Adinnegram and his plans."

"You think his plans are competition for the Invigoration?"

"Please, don't waste our time mocking me. Do you agree with them? Are you going to help them? You haven't seen your cousin Binta after they worked on him. He pissed himself, and they must have been careless because he seems to be an imbecile now. It's horrible, but I suppose you've seen others they've taken."

"No, I haven't, not exactly," Micca said faintly. "What do *you* plan to do? Run off?"

"Hm. I had thought of doing that, but it won't do. I think *we* should do what we can to stop these people. If our ancestors were anything like this Adinnegram, I disown them here and now. You must see that if his plan succeeds it will be the end of life here as we know it. How can anyone be truly good if someone else rules their behavior? And worse, when this *other* judges what's good and what's bad? Neither word would mean anything. You'd be less than an animal, nothing more than fingers on your master's hand."

Micca answered slowly. "That speech sounds a little bit at odds with how things were going at the farm."

Palmer pressed his lips together. "Well, maybe so. These last days I've been examining my conscience — *mine*, not some man-made construction or drug. Despite Smolic's theatrics, Wennoc will speak if you listen closely, and it has spoken to me. I don't ask you to do anything but listen to *your* conscience."

They stood staring at each other. Micca turned away, grabbed his helmet, put it down again. He stared at the glyphs on the panel, then quickly looked back at Palmer.

"Priest, Wudego — did you see a frog-man's air-belly and mask out there, on the way in?"

"I did. Do you want them?"

"They're for you. Be ready to use them. Find Sam — no, find the Striver Neypo! Samma knew where he was. They're supposed to be on their way, but find them and tell them to come down here just as fast as they can."

"What's your plan?"

"I don't have a plan! That's the trouble. That's why I need the Striver. If there's a way out of this, he knows what it is. I'm sure he'd agree with what you just said. And find a light you can carry. I'm going to try to confuse things and give the Striver a chance." Micca turned. "Go now! Go!"

Palmer gave him a long look, then turned and left the vault.

Micca gingerly lowered the circlet over his head. The voices returned. There were more now. Groups of them chanted rhythmic harmonies to the right and left, others under his boots and above his head. They were busy with their own thoughts, but they recognized Micca's presence, and seemed to rebuke him for leaving them.

He wished he were any place else in the world. He felt queasy, sick. How long could he wait for Neypo? And the possibility of Neypo being able to come down here was, he understood, not very likely... the Eynnish voices seemed to quieten a little, listening to him, though he didn't speak.

His head jerked up. There was a sound outside, a human one, he was sure of it; a shout, a challenge?

Micca walked as softly as he was able out to the passage.

"What business do you have here?" he heard. It was Palmer's voice, some way off. "This is a forbidden area, open only to the Director of Antiquities and those authorized by her."

There was no immediate reply. Micca heard something crash to the floor.

"Stand where you are!" Palmer shouted. "You're damaging irreplaceable artifacts!"

Micca edged out of the passageway. Palmer was walking slowly backward, toward the vault. He held a length of iron pipe in his fist.

A man in armor stood a little way off. The chamber was dim where he stood, and the number on his chest cast a faint blue light on the floor. It was Second.

Another armored man was close behind him, and he leaned to look around Second's head. Adinnegram's face was in his helmet. There was a click as he snapped the black tube free of his thigh. He said, "Is Micca Mora down here? Micca! Finnegal? Show yourselves!"

Palmer stepped forward, brandishing his pipe. Adinnegram raised his arm. A rippling line of air linked his hand and Palmer's chest.

Palmer flew back, hit the wall and fell into a heap on the floor. He gasped, his breath rattled. "Wennoc," he exhaled, and a wet blackness spread under him.

Adinnegram pushed Second aside. He glanced at Palmer's body, looked up. "Micca! I'm sorry. I know this man was a member of your household. Second's thrasher was maladjusted."

Micca had heard him, but was already back in the vault, the circlet on his head. His head was filled with whispers, his eyes seemed to vibrate. Micca pressed a finger to Mellatuno's glyph, then that which meant 'close'.

The wall swam in black and gray, and then it showed Mellatuno, circled in red. A hundred ghosts wondered, "Yes?"

'Yes,' Micca thought back urgently. 'Do it.'

The buzzing tubes overhead went out, then reignited in a flickering, muddy blue. A low whine issued from the panel of glyphs, rose in pitch and passed beyond Micca's hearing. He trotted quickly to the entrance of the vault. Beyond was utter blackness. The muscular throb of pumps was gone. From several sources came the sound of dripping, trickling, streaming water.

He had managed to cut off the flow of power from the lamps to Mellatuno. What good had it done? Maybe he had given the others some time to get out during whatever confusion would result. Not for Palmer now, not for him.

Blue glowing hands holding a globe of stars bobbed out from behind a column. "Turn the lights on!" Adinnegram yelled. From some distance behind him came the sound of feet splashing away and a glimpse of jiggling, illuminated numerals: 002. At least he had scared off Adinnegram's recruit from Hannava. Micca ran back into the vault, water dragging at his feet.

The blue lights were still on. He wanted to put on his helmet but the voices hadn't finished with him. They sang to him, and strange odors invaded his sensorium: fresh, bitter, sweet; some he recognized: drying hay, bubbling must, flowering trees, rotting corn. Vines of colors he had no names for trembled at the perimeters of his vision. Somehow this told him he must ask a question, and after it, provide an answer. The voices were agitated now, impatient with growing wakefulness and suspicion. Micca whispered, "What do you need?"

The ghosts considered; now the ghosts remembered. A palpable spirit of watchfulness and dedication filled the vault: the world must remain inviolate, it must be protected.

The wall swam with shapes. The sense of watchfulness was quickly colored by alarm. A gust of danger chilled Micca's mind, waxing to a winter blast. The ghosts muttered urgently. The window showed stars, moon, three lamps, the world tonight. The new star, the Outreach's ship, was now circled in violet. A thickly stroked glyph Micca couldn't read burned beside it.

Sulawan's ship in orbit was a horror. It was a baleful eye — no, it was the mouth of a witless monster, an empty, bottomless chasm. It would devour him and everything he knew —

Micca started. Someone was coming. With his human ears he heard splashing steps, curses and threats. A helmeted Adinnegram walked cautiously into the inner vault. He held his black tube out before him. "Turn it off, eMicca!" he cried. "Whatever it is, turn it off... what *is* this place? What's that screen?"

The silent voices demanded Micca's attention. They required a decision. Two glyphs on the panel pulsed violet. One looked much like 'go', 'proceed', the other, 'protect'.

Had Samma found Neypo, Gillensa and Swannet? Where were Neffafinnegal and Noler? It didn't matter with Adinnegram here.

Adinnegram came forward. "I asked you, what is this place!" He stared at the window, the panel of glyphs. "What the hell is going on down here?"

A hundred unspeaking voices pressed a warning into the air:

YOU WILL NOT INTERFERE

Adinnegram dropped, water splashing. Grunting in an animal's voice, he crawled away.

Micca breathed rapidly. Water covered the tops of his boots. His stomach jerked and twisted, his hands shook. Had the dead voices bewitched him? Had they given him the horror with which he now regarded the ship above? Or had they simply made his eyes clear?

He tried to steady his hands and put a finger on each of the violet glyphs.

As before he felt a request for confirmation. "Do it," he gasped. "Do what you need to."

The wall flashed. Micca staggered back, hand over his eyes. The harmony of the voices broke into a multitude of different conversations, advising, questioning and answering one another. Micca squinted at the wall. It had retreated an age, and all seven of the lamps were present. There was also an alien star, circled like the one of today had been. Then everything moved in a blur, busily crosshatched with colored lines. The window redrew itself, and four of the lamps were gone. Below, the ancient alien star had been thrown into the Bay north of Mellatuno, where it sank and vanished.

A chord sounded in Micca's head, and the window returned to the present. The voices conferred briefly, came together in a grim chorus of agreement.

Threads linked the three lamps. They extended another to touch the alien ship, Sulawan's ship, which was now shown larger and with more definition: a plump, gleaming ovoid, a series of thin, bulb-tipped outriggers. The thread thickened and went red. A coursing pulse sprang down the thread and bathed the ship in a shimmering colorless nimbus. Thundering, defiant chords filled Micca's head.

The ship moved, lolled like a fat fish stirring in the mud. It tipped and started to fall. The outriggers were gone, the ovoid broken, but a bloom of threads sprouted from what was left, whipping, searching—

The images in the wall became flat and unreal. They were replaced by a spiral of tightly spaced glyphs, which spun into a central point and vanished as though down a drain.

The dim lights in the vault continued to burn but the Eynnish voices were gone, replaced by a low hum at Micca's temples.

What had he done? Micca felt like he had been dumped from a fever bed into a drift of snow. He threw off the circlet and put on his helmet. There were no voices in it, either.

The water had reached his ankles. He could see ripples on its surface as it flowed through the vault.

He sloshed slowly into the workshop...he saw the flat gray shape of the priest's body, arms out now, gently waving in the water. Adinnegram, with his glowing blue symbol, must have recovered from the fit that had taken him, and was crawling up the stair to the revolving door above. Second must be long gone.

Then the floor shifted. The movement was slight, but so strange and unexpected that Micca threw out his arms to balance himself. A new sound of rushing water came from several points, ahead and behind. Beside him, a tall iron tank creaked and tipped.

The flood reached his calves. He struggled through it past other tanks, racks, piles of junk. When he reached the stair the water was at his knees and rivulets were trickling down the steps from above. From behind came a grinding crumble, a vast splash. Micca started up the steps. Something rolled under his boot. He fell back to the landing and the armor locked up. Micca strained and yelled until it loosened. When he stood he saw the tube Adinnegram had used on Palmer roll down with the water.

The door was hard to turn, but he got through it and hurried through the now windless tunnel. There was no sign of anyone in the chamber outside. The fabric of Mellatuno trembled again. The great wheel he had seen below the winding stair no longer turned. No light came from the grilled floor above, but someone climbed out of a downward-leading tunnel: a masked frog-man, and two more behind him. They tore off their flippers and went quickly up the stair.

The floor heaved into a crease under Micca and dropped back with muffled, spreading rumble, and the frog-men's tunnel vomited a sluggish roll of black water. Overhead was a grinding and a tearing screech. A section of the grilled flooring hinged down and tore loose, catching the railing of the winding stair as it fell. The central pole of the stair writhed, squeaking loudly up and down its length. The last of the trio of frog-men caught the lip of the top stair with his hands and wrestled himself onto what was left of the grilled floor. The stair then slowly collapsed, each section breaking and crushing the one below.

Micca looked around frantically. Beyond the shape of the big silent wheel he saw a line of holes in the wall, chest-high, each perhaps a little better than a yard wide. Most were bricked up; one appeared open. Just under that hole, something low, broad, and larger than Micca was mincing toward him.

Micca gave a little cry. He ran to the thing, crouched, threw his arms out and vaulted onto its mucus-slick carapace. It vibrated angrily under his boots and rope-like tentacles whipped at his legs. Micca got hold of the horizontal flue in front of him. He threw himself into it, trying to shake the grasping branches from his boot.

31. A WALK IN THE REEDS

Ennesia climbed onto a hummock of dry land. She sat down, then discovered a tiny mudrunner climbing her ankle.

It buzzed as she crushed it between her finger and thumb. Ennesia had always considered herself at home out of doors, but she hadn't developed much love for these sloughs and marshlands. In comparison, the high woods above Topping were as tame as an Eynnish garden, or at least as tame as the articles in the *Hernespela* made them out to be. She didn't know where she was, either, but it seemed now that she must have gone east rather than west.

She groped around her and pulled up a plant that looked and smelled like some kind of leek. She wiped off the dirt with her skirts and bit into it. It was surprisingly sweet, almost like an apple. Ennesia stopped chewing when she noticed the stonework, just visible above the marsh growth.

Were the walls and broken roofs part of the seminary, or the archaeological station Palmer had spoken of?

It was hard to know whether they were the ruins they had seen at sunset, but she had walked so far that it must be the seminary. The priest had spoken as though the water-going bandits might be attached to it or to Mellatuno, and she had seen a snout like the ones they wore in his study at Mora. Why, then, had they treated him like a criminal or trespasser? It was possible, she supposed, that the seminarians at Saint Unwey's had replaced Invigorationist doctrine with something more — or less — reasonable, and wanted to apprehend and reeducate the old movement's leaders.

That was probably going too far, and it didn't matter. If she was going to get back to civilized country she had no option but to discover who burned the lights, but knew she'd be happier to find a party of antiquaries than a lot of priests and monitors, who would try to make her adopt some bizarre new creed, or stamp and wave her hands at the very least.

Ennesia groped around, found her walking stick and probed the ground, which suddenly seemed unsteady, almost quaking. Loose mud below? She'd better be careful. But ahead the water was only a few inches deep, and she walked on. The reeds rustled to either side, brushing her face.

The stars were fading to dim sparks. She could see now that the ruins were extensive, topped here and there by dark foliage. It must after all be Mellatuno. Areas of open water made this end of it look like an island. The feet of the walls were edged by narrow strips of unruly shrubbery and stone. She saw a red and white roof and heard voices from a platform under it. Other voices at last. But were they angry? Drunk? Ennesia moved as quietly as she could through the reeds and grasses.

When she looked up again she was close enough to see the people under the roof. Some moved around, others stood and gestured, but she couldn't make out what they were saying. Something was very strange, or some of the people were; one or two looked like statues, but of polished metal? No, it was more like mirroring, or glass. But they moved—

More shouts. She ducked behind a tall clump of cattails. She looked out and saw one of the statues leaping away over the roofs. And as if the thing had the weight of a giant, stone quaked and flaked away from the walls. The water around her ankles stirred.

Further down the way a figure moved down steps on the side of a wall, quickly followed by another. Were they running from bandits like those who had taken Palmer, Binta and Smolic?

With that realization she ducked down. These people escaping would bring the bandits out in force, threatening her own safety. Ennesia lowered her head and pushed through the tall growth.

When she looked out again there was no one in sight. A narrow path staggered along to the south, between the stone walls and the water. Ennesia used her stick to part the grasses before her and made her way around a jutting bastion.

There was a gap in the stones, and to her left the rim of the rising sun flashed. The water on the right was choked with vegetable growth, but further out, to the west, a lake full of lily pads glimmered brightly. Ennesia walked into the shadow of a taller block.

Not far along she saw a recess in the wall. A hand reached out to grasp the stone. Ennesia hung back. "Hello?" she said.

It was still dark between the stone door posts. Several shapes moved inside. A tall, thin woman in an apron dashed out and scuttled by her. Then a man masked like the bandits she'd seen and carrying an armload of soggy looking books, followed the woman out and ran after her. Ennesia hurried on, looking frequently behind her.

She came to another doorway. Ennesia raised her stick and approached it with caution. She moved to peek around the corner. A large, hard hand came out and touched her wrist.

It was another of the glass-statue men, but with the green head of a bandit. Her stick caught him in a false stomach strapped to his waist. His snout bulged and air farted out around his neck. Ennesia swung again, as hard as she could, and he backed away, muttering unintelligibly.

And now another man looked out, this one in a muddy kilt, a green bag hanging behind his head. Ennesia gave him a smart blow to his wrist with her stick.

He yelped and also retreated, but called out, "Miss! Have you seen a Striver, or some Eynnish gentlewomen?"

Ennesia ran from the door. How many freaks and monsters did this place harbor?

The grass grew higher as she went on. She could no longer see the open lake. The earth was soft, and trembled again from time to time. Soon she was wading through muddy water again.

Ennesia stopped. The roofscapes were lower here, rounder and covered with lichen, vines and little trees. To her left, the sun now hung almost clear of them.

Ennesia noticed she was sinking. Something touched her leg. A mudrunner? A noxious eel?

Using her stick for support, she got her feet out of the mud and stumbled backwards, into water. Something interrupted her progress:

a squat cylinder of mossy stone, like a wellhead, in the midst of the deepening water.

Ennesia leaned thankfully against it and picked a leech from her leg. She noticed a breath of dank air rising from the shaft behind her. Ennesia twisted herself and looked down. She saw lichen, hanging strands of moss…

There was noise from below: an echoing, rhythmic hissing, like someone panting.

Ennesia moved away from the well curb. The mud drew her down. She turned and reached for her stick, still lying on the curb of the well. As she grabbed it the sun dazzled her, reflected from the thing crawling out of the well. Ennesia gasped at a ghostly, astonished face, trapped inside a misshapen glass skull.

"No!" she cried in horror, and broke her stick over its head.

32. UPSTAIRS

Samma rattled the latch of another door. The others had been open; this one was held closed with a hasp and pin. He peered through a small, barred opening. "Anyone in there?"

There was a shuffling inside. "I demand to see the Director!" someone called.

Samma removed the pin and pushed the door in, almost knocking down Neypo Odé.

"Samma!" said the Striver.

Gillensa pushed by her father. She stopped and cried, "Oh, Samma, what's happened to your lovely hair?" Then she put her hands on either side of his face, pulled it down and kissed him.

Swannet crept out and looked down a narrow, canted alley between a lichen-covered stone wall and the row of connected huts where they had been penned. "Have you seen Noler?"

"And Micca? Is Micca here?" Neypo said. "What's happening? We felt tremors in the floor!"

"I did too. And all the lights are out, the electric's gone. Micca and Neffafinnegal went down below. Micca wants us to join him. I think I remember the way, but I don't know—and there are outlanders here! That man who spoke on the radio, and a bunch of others all wearing the glass armor. And they've got these flying—"

"Adinnegram? Adinnegram is here?"

"Last I saw, he was hobnobbing with the archeology Director and the priest from my farm, if you can believe it. At least some of his soldiers are Harnish, too."

"Did Adinnegram have their raft?"

"I don't think so. Not yet anyway. But he knows that Micca knows where it is."

"Where is the Director? I wonder if I can..."

The pavement under them shifted. A line opened in the wall behind them, fragments of mortar popping out.

But Swannet pointed at the sky. "Look!"

Dawn wasn't far off. Some stars were still visible, but one near the southern horizon, a bright spark, was moving, falling. And there were several long, crumpled plumes of smoke in the east, dirtying the pink rind of the morning sky.

Eyes on the heavens, Samma said, "Striver, Micca said I should tell you that he found it, whatever 'it' is."

The Striver was also looking at the sky. "But...no! How could he have?"

The hatch in the roof slammed open and Adinnegram, his armor blotched by mud, climbed up. Second followed. Adinnegram's face scowled glassily at him, and he smacked Second's helmet with the back of his hand. "Go to the processing area. Bring the others up here. Move!"

Second retreated. Adinnegram came into the gazebo. The face in his helmet now displayed vast alarm. "Director! Micca, he's gone rogue, he's insane. He..."

Adinnegram paused and looked around the gazebo. The strings of bulbs under the eaves were dark. Monitor Smolic sat holding a bottle tightly to his chest. He looked up. "Ah, Mister Adinnegram is back... have you seen my associate, Wudego Palmer? I need to talk with him."

Frita stood at the railing, staring at the sky. The Director was at her telescope under the copper dome. She wasn't looking into it, but sat with her hands limp in her lap. "Gone," she whispered.

Adinnegram, calmer now, strode up to her. "Where is Neffafinnegal?" He surveyed the gazebo again. "And Micca's brother hasn't come back either. I think there was some kind of conspiracy here."

"The end of an age," said Mercy-Ann, staring now out at the sloughs.

Adinnegram whacked his thigh with his fist. "What's the matter with you people? Are you all mentally ill? Is this the aftermath of the rotten stuff you ate and drank? I'm not sure you should be called human."

He slowed his breathing. A hopeful smile came into his helmet. "I'm sorry. I haven't had much peace or civilized company lately." He put a hand to the prow of his helmet. "I've been living in this thing for days. But I'll soon feel the wind in my hair again. In a few hours we'll all be comrades. Serenity will win out."

Now Mercy-Ann frowned at him. "You don't understand. They're gone. All three."

"You mean Finnegal and the two brothers?" He was angry again. "Or the priest? I'm sorry about that. As for the others—"

"Are you blind in that thing?" Mercy-Ann cried. She pointed at the sky. "Look! It's the lamps that are gone! They sent us our electrical essence. They were to be my gift, my bequest to the new world. They would have given Wennoc the means to climb back up the ladder of civilization."

"Wennoc's shining crown, cast down," Smolic whispered.

Adinnegram thought for a minute. "Interesting," he said finally. "Do you mean those old satellites? Sulawan said they were moribund. Only a trickle of power was being transmitted to the surface, barely enough to light one community on the east coast of this landmass. Sulawan thinks they were put in place primarily to compensate for the small number of stars in this region; a pretty display, an ornament to ease the original setters' homesickness."

Now he took off his helmet and placed it on the table. He looked compassionately at Mercy-Ann. "And you see, Ann, the kind of progress you speak of is only an outward symbol. Of course I appreciate your generous intentions, but not every world has to be transformed into a mechanized paradise, or as much hell as paradise, often as not. We'll make out. Your installation here will still function well as our headquarters."

For a long moment Mercy-Ann stared at him, eyes hooded. "It's not only the lamps, Comrade Compassion, Comrade Know-it-all. Your ship of space fell too."

Adinnegram shook his head. "There's nothing you people could do that would harm it."

She nodded slowly. "Ah, of course. Forgive my ignorance. The lamps were worn out old relics, decorative baubles. But evidently you woke them and reminded them of other duties."

Frita pointed. "I can still see the lines of smoke."

Adinnegram looked at the sky. "There could be many explanations for that. My ship is still in orbit. We have scientific ways to determine the facts, ways you people can't imagine. Once I have the lighter —"

"How wonderful!" Mercy-Ann shouted. "How very clever." She got to her feet, grabbing for her stick. "Yes, you have this Maestro Sulawan, a scientist, and other clever people, I'm sure. What of Neffafinnegal? What do you call him? Spy? Saboteur? Neffafinnegal, who must have come here at your instruction, slyly posing as an idiot. You sent him to my workshop, didn't you, and Micca as well, his conniving, two-faced subaltern, to subvert the mechanisms and destroy our heritage! Oh yes, I saw you plotting, giving them their orders, right here under my very roof, all the while pretending to welcome my hospitality. You'd destroy a world's hope for progress because you just couldn't tolerate any competition for leadership!"

Adinnegram's face was blank. "I have no idea what you're talking about, but you're soon going to learn to address me more respectfully. You can count on that."

A crack ran across the floor of the gazebo. Adinnegram put his hand on the railing. "Second!" he called. "Where is that idiot? Everyone, listen! We'd better get out of here. The water must be undercutting the foundations."

"What astonishing scientific insight! I'll undercut you, you supercilious poseur!" Mercy-Ann advanced on him, stick high.

Adinnegram's hand went to his thigh, but his black tube wasn't there. He pushed Mercy-Ann, who fell back into her chair.

"Peace!" someone bellowed from the bridge.

Heads turned.

"Odé!' wheezed Mercy-Ann. "Who let *you* out?"

Neypo entered the gazebo. He looked at Adinnegram. "In this world we consider it dishonorable to threaten and assault old women, or anyone else, for that matter."

"Wennoc deplores a violent man," Smolic added.

"You all —" Adinnegram began.

Mercy-Ann pointed at him with her stick and shouted, "Odé! This craven bastard, this fraud — he and his lickspittle minions have brought down the lamps!"

Now other heads showed in the hatch, and Samma, Gillensa and Swannet came over the bridge.

"Where's Micca?" Samma said.

"How should we know!" said Mercy-Ann. "Ask his master here."

"And Noler?" said Swannet. "And Neffafinnegal!"

"Away from here, Wennoc willing," Neypo said. "As we all should be."

"So you think we should just walk away, Lodgeman?" Mercy-Ann cried. "Our ancient heritage falls broken to the bottom of the sea and all you care about is keeping your feet dry?"

"Wennoc's sparkling diadem, drowned in the deeps," said Smolic.

"I wish it could have been otherwise," the Striver said. "It wasn't my intention they be lost, not again, not those last survivors."

"So you claim this was the result of *your* scheme?" Mercy-Ann pointed her stick again at Adinnegram. "Are you, too, in cahoots with this monster, Odé?"

"Please, madam! I count him our worst enemy," Neypo said. "My intention was to use the power of the lamps only to disable or destroy the outlanders' ship in the heavens."

"Insane fantasies, Odé," said Adinnegram. "Yes, I remember you. Capering, ignorant savage."

"And I remember you: sociopath, delusional fool, murderer of souls."

Mercy-Ann roused herself from a momentary fugue. "Look through my telescope before the sky is too bright, my good Comrade Dinna," she snapped. "See for yourself how savage we really are. As the Lodgeman says, the new star, your ship, is also gone."

Adinnegram looked at the telescope, but didn't use it. He kicked its support, and kicked it again until bolts broke free and the instrument crashed to the floor.

"You and your people will never leave Wennoc," Neypo told him. "Run if you will. You'll be caught sooner or later, and be made familiar with our penitential system. The less criminal members of your party may find new lives in Wennoc, just as the original Harnishmen did."

Adinnegram barked out a laugh. "You're incredible, Odé! I give you high marks for hubris. Don't expect me to do as well with mercy."

He strode to the bridge, pushing Swannet and Samma out of his way. "*Second!* Up here! Now!"

He turned back. "My weapon may be lost, but my comrades have theirs. But weapons aren't important in the long run. They'll be completely unnecessary in a few weeks or months. This will be *my* world. Those who cause others to stumble, who stand in the way of what's best for all the people—you're an example, Odé—yes, as soon as you have your consciences, you'll endure an hour of maximum correction every day and learn what agony and despair really mean. It'll cause me pain too, but I'll do my duty to right thinking. You can go first, Striver. And you, Micca's brother, you're next... so tell me, before you find yourselves begging for death: *where is my lighter?*"

Samma, Gillensa gripping his arm, said faintly, "I have no idea."

"Right. You'll go first."

Swannet screamed, but not for Samma's sake. An armored and helmeted man stood at the other end of the bridge. There were no numbers on his armor, but he had a black tube clipped to his leg.

"Micca?" said Adinnegram. "Finnegal?" Adinnegram held out his hand and spoke very slowly. "Take off that thrasher. Hand it to me."

The man laughed. "Merit Troavic, that's my name. You know *me*, First Comrade! Or maybe you only know numbers. How's about Fourth?"

Troavic came swaying over the bridge, arms out for balance. He leapt the last yard, fell against one of the gazebo's posts, righted himself, spread his arms again and said, "Ha! Made it!"

"What's the matter with you, Fourth! Where's your identifier?"

"Got rid of it, switched it off. Made me feel like a pig at the market."

Another glass man came over the bridge. His armor bore no numbers either, but on his chest was a simple rendering of a tree and a saw, and below, in regimented, glowing letters, 'BRAN-M'.

Samma stared at him. "It can't be."

"Samma!" the man said. "My old pal! His Honor the Mora! How'd *you* get here?" He disengaged his helmet, took it off and pulled his fingers through his hair.

"How did *you* get here?" Samma said.

Branna threw his arm around Samma's shoulders, leaned close and whispered loudly, "By way of Hannava, 'smatter of fact. Fola Marstoc, too." He straightened. "But that guy there, First Comrade? You know what? He bit our necks with worms; they didn't do that in Hannava... but don't be telling me that's old Smola Topping over there! And poor Binta said Micca was here too! Wait'll I get aholdst of him, scamping off like that and leaving me in Hannava."

Samma stood away from him. "Good grief, man, what have you been drinking? You smell like sump cleaner."

"Eynnish corn, mighty poor stuff too. Had some good rose-hip but we ran out." Then Branna walked slowly to where Frita stood cowering at the railing. Branna nodded politely to her, leaned over and retched a thin stream into the water below.

Adinnegram was nodding tensely. "You've been poisoned then, both of you. A good purge will..."

Yet another man in armor, this one bareheaded, came into the gazebo. He was blond, as big as Branna, but had Eynnish features. There was a freshly-scabbed wound on his neck, just visible above the collar of his suit.

Branna looked up, wiping his mouth. "Ansa, old son! Find any more?"

"Another jar, though I can't vouch for its quality." The man noticed Gillensa and Swannet and smiled broadly. "Have you forgotten me so soon? Horemps Ansitap! We met briefly at Hwistomellian! Or don't you recognize me like this? One of the chaps got tired of his suit and let me have it."

"You look very well," said Swannet.

Adinnegram slapped his hand on the railing. "All of you, shut up! Third, Fourth, snap to! Ansitap! Whose 'casing is that?"

Horemps looked mulish. "It's mine now."

Adinnegram drew a breath. He didn't manage a smile, and spoke earnestly. "Comrades. My good friends. Do you remember how happy you were? How meaningful your lives were? Remember riding down here, free as the breeze, laughing, talking till late about whatever came into our heads? We had some good times together, and we will again." He spread his arms. "Come on! All three of you. It's time for a good comradely hug."

Branna stood where he was. "You did most of the talking."

"You made fun of my accent," said Troavic. "That got some laughs."

"You might have laughed, First, but we didn't much," Branna said. "Besides, it was more like being stupid than happy. And that lady at Ansa's house, the one with the fiddle. I remember how dainty and beautiful she was now, but back then I didn't look at her twice."

Neypo spoke before Adinnegram could respond. "Tell me boys, how did you lose the feeling you had to obey him? I am correct in thinking that you have, yes?"

Branna snorted. "What do you think?"

"How?" Troavic said, then bowed to Frita. "Well, sir, the ladies—"

Adinnegram lurched at him, scrabbling for his black tube. Troavic lithely twisted away, seized his tube, and swinging his arm pitched it high into the air. A few seconds later there was a splash, far away. Adinnegram gaped after it.

"Hmph," said Mercy-Ann. " 'Ladies', you said. What did you mean? Where's Noma-Linda?"

"You mean the big one? Oh. She went to save papers from the water or something, I don't know."

Troavic looked suspiciously at Adinnegram, who, though red in the face, seemed paralyzed. Troavic went on, "Anyroad, the ladies come in and lay out a big supper for us. But what's good and what's not, we were wondering. What can we eat and not be sorry? Leave the ham, that's for sure. But mushrooms: are they veg, fruit, or what? Then the drink: how do you know what's in the jar without tasting it? So Third Comrade, old Branna-boy, he says 'I'm thirsty. We're not supposed to eat poison, but I never got poisoned from having a cup of this or that, and my Uncle Branna always says they don't know how to brew or 'still over in Eynnaland anyway.'"

Branna nodded approval. "That's what I said."

"So we start tasting this jar and that jar. A couple boys didn't want to, but we sloshed a cup or two down their gullets; fun-like, you know, and they came around. Pretty soon we went back like before we were comrades. First might have one or two good ideas, but I don't feel like I have to lick his horn anymore—sorry, ladies!"

Neypo said, "But you're sure you're no longer compelled to heed his commands?"

"I'm sure," Troavic said. "How 'bout you, Bran? Horemps?"

"Sure as shit."

"Indubitably."

Neypo raised his hands high. "Wennoc be praised!"

Smolic mimicked him. "Glory," he said.

"I suppose it was the drink," Troavic went on. "Some of them got sick from it though, and Bran's cousin had the worm crawl out of his neck again. Hadn't got far enough in yet, I guess."

Branna looked at his feet. "And I stomped it. Whatever else, the outlanders make a good boot."

Then he looked at Adinnegram. "Poor Binta, though. He's an idiot now. You were probably too busy listening to yourself talk to come and do the counseling after he got the bite."

Adinnegram came back to life, and spoke calmly. "Listen to me, fellows. Let's all go down to processing. It's for your own good. You'll thank me, I promise you will. No punishment. We'll give you a purge, and after a little lie-down you'll be back in shape in no time."

"Don't listen to him!" Neypo said.

Merit Troavic laughed. "I think you're the one who needs a purge, First Comrade. How about a pint or two of raw corn? We can find a funnel if you don't want to take it from a cup."

"I don't think he's really a comrade," Branna said grimly. "I bet he never got processed like he did to us. Ever see anybody telling *him* what to do?"

"Worm or not, I think a pint or two would do him good."

"His face is all red. You're right, I think he needs tonicking."

Troavic nodded and turned to Smolic. "Say, grandfather, can we borrow your jar there? Is it good strong stuff?"

Smolic blinked up at him. "Here, take it."

Adinnegram looked around, hands shaking a little. He saw his helmet where he had left it on the table and grabbed it.

Troavic snatched the bottle from Smolic. He swung and shattered it on Adinnegram's head, but his helmet had already made its connection.

Adinnegram gave a deep-throated yell. He pushed by Troavic and reached for the weapon clipped to Branna's leg. Branna threw out his arm and hit the prow of Adinnegram's helmet with his fist. Adinnegram fell back onto the table. The table went over, carrying Adinnegram with it. He slid over its top and sprawled onto the floor along with an avalanche of breaking crockery.

Neypo threw himself onto Adinnegram's chest. "Rope!" he called.

Samma yanked down a length of electrical wire from the eaves of the gazebo, bulbs of colored glass popping as it whipped to the floor. But Adinnegram had set his armor not to lock up at heavy impacts, and he threw off the Striver.

Adinnegram jumped to his feet, lowered his head, ran from the gazebo and over the bridge, arms pumping at his sides. From there he scrambled up to a further roof and disappeared behind a parapet.

"Should we go after him?" Troavic asked Branna. "Or you could try shooting him."

Branna looked at the weapon on his leg. "It would only bounce off."

33. BREAKFAST
OUT OF DOORS

Late in the morning Frita and a helper brought pots, jugs, platters and bowls to a table set up on trestles on the causeway near the main block of the ruins.

Neypo lifted a lid and sniffed at a smoking pile of hen's eggs scrambled and fried with onions, green herbs, pepper pods and something else...crinkled shreds of what was probably pig's flesh. He put bias aside and spooned out a good portion onto his plate, spread a slab of toasted bread with butter, filled a bowl with strawberries and poured on a measure of heavy cream.

Next to Neypo, Caihar nibbled at a piece of bread. Mercy-Ann sat alone at the other end of the table, morosely sipping a cup of tea.

Caihar sighed. "And Micca Mora told you that Adinnegram murdered his plantation's priest? Not his first victim. I hope he was the last."

"We must find Adinnegram," Neypo said. "He can't hope to go far—Noma-Linda, you are able to discriminate between our private conversation and what is meant for the letter, yes?"

She sat near the Strivers with paper and pen. "I *do* have a bit of experience in this kind of work," she said, and leaned forward to take a fillet of pickled fish from a jar.

Mercy-Ann snorted.

Caihar asked Neypo, "Are the straddle-rides well out of reach?"

He used an Indeduits term here, but Neypo took his meaning. "All but the one. The Director provided a hidden storage chamber for the others. The couriers will leave with our dispatch as soon as we finish it."

"I hope our brothers at Parnala will be able to absorb — and believe — our news, and react in a productive and determined way."

"From what I heard over the raft's radio the other day, I'd say they're well aware that things are not as they should be in Hoiin. Our letter should complement what they've seen and heard."

"If Parnala *has* been infected, the rot shouldn't have penetrated too deeply yet. Soliël had her hands full when we left…you're sure our couriers will be reliable?"

Neypo tasted the eggs. The bits of meat mixed in with them were unctuous and sweetly smoky, and with the onions offered a nice contrast in texture…"You know the Cadet well enough, and he was never compromised. He'll ride the carriage in which I understand you arrived, and Voling, heir to a Harnish plantation and an alumnus of the city University, will function as driver. He's been cleansed of alien influence, and he's had experience working the flying beam, whatever it is you called it. Voling is also more diplomatic than the Cadet, and is well spoken. And being a Harnishman, he won't be suspected of involvement in Lodge politics. This last point, I believe, is a significant advantage to us."

Caihar nodded absently. Then he roused himself and turned to Mercy-Ann. "Directoress Turner, does your facility here have a printery?"

Mercy-Ann grunted. "A small flat-bed press and a case or two of type, unless that's been drowned too."

"They tell me that end of the east range hasn't taken much damage," said Noma-Linda.

Caihar poured himself tea. "Good. Neypo, the straddle-rides aren't able to rise very far above the ground, but what if Micca Mora flew the lighter over Hoiin? Is he a competent pilot?"

"Good heavens. He could probably fly it edge-up between the trees of a dense forest, or claim he could. But to what end? A warning to the masses?"

Caihar leaned back and showed a slight smile. "Not exactly. The Diretoress's people will print some broadsides for us. They'll announce a festival of thanks for the 'new dawn' in Wennoc, something that sounds like it came from Adinnegram. It will be a drinking feast: 'All Officers,

Lodge members and other communicant citizens are instructed to show their loyalty and joy by…no, they're to toast the new age with their favorite brew, essence or other tipple.' And so on. The announcements would come to earth at random here and there, depending on the breeze. Many people would see them before they could be sequestered. The sight of the lighter itself would create a lot of gossip and interest in the announcement, and rattle Soliël's confidence."

"I like it!" Neypo said with a grin. "Something to set the ball rolling on the home front."

Noma-Linda fingered her chin. "Our cartographer could make a quick woodcut in imitation of the clumsy blue drawing we saw on the chief outlander's glass suit, and set it at the bottom of the sheet. Might give it an air of authenticity."

"Showing off again, Linda?" said Mercy-Ann.

Neypo raised his cup. "Perfect. Thank you, Noma-Linda. An excellent suggestion."

"I agree," said Caihar. "We—they, rather—have in fact been using that arrogant and condescending image on their printed edicts. But Neypo, what about the thrashers?"

Another grotesque Indeduits word. "The tube-weapons? Troavic has accounted for those here, other than Adinnegram's, which he threw into the slough, saving us from being murdered." Neypo leaned forward. "And this time we must not drown the rest. Not yet, at any rate."

Neypo was relieved to see Caihar nod acquiescence. The elder Striver looked ill and haggard, but he was tasting the eggs now, and his mind was certainly clearer than it had been an hour ago.

"What I meant," Caihar said, "is that there may also be thrashers in Hoiin. They didn't consider it feasible to look for those we threw into the harbor after the battle at the Guest Hall, but I don't know whether Adinnegram distributed all of the new ones that were sent down from their ship. I wouldn't wonder that Soliël, at least, has one."

"And there, of course, may lie a problem. Do you think Soliël will assume Adinnegram's role? What about Sulawan?"

"Sulawan isn't one of them. He seemed something of a dastard, though I think eventually we can make him useful in some way. I'm not as sure about Soliël. Her character is nothing like Adinnegram's. She may be more a true believer and less someone devoted to a monstrous ego. That would make her potentially more dangerous."

"And there are others who have been subverted to the Outreach's program," Neypo said. "If Soliël doesn't, there may be someone else who will seek to replace Adinnegram... and Voling Marstoc told me he heard rumors of Adinnegram sending some people to Hannava. If the infestation has gotten a foothold there, maybe we could make two or three of Adinnegram's erstwhile Harnish slaves Adjuncts-Military and send them over there in their armor, riding these flying planks. Assuming they can ride over deep water. Perhaps with a... 'tratser', to demonstrate their authority."

He took note of Caihar's expression. "Well, their frightening appearance may be sufficient. That and the Harnishman's fondness for strong drink!"

Mercy-Ann slammed her cup on the table. "You Eynnish consume far more than we do, and with little knowledge or discretion as to quality. *We* use beer or even water as our ordinary beverages, while you people toss down a pot of strong spirits before your servants have hoisted you out of bed in the morning."

Neypo spread peach preserves on another piece of toasted bread. "You exaggerate, madam. Do you see me tossing down anything but lukewarm tea this morning?"

"In any case," said Caihar, "strong distillations were clearly a part of Wennoc's plan in this matter."

Neypo nodded solemnly. "Noma-Linda, please add the following to our dispatch:

"When these 'facilitators', the parasitic brain-worms mentioned above, are used in combination with a form of malign hypnosis, the victim adopts the outlook of the invaders, and is transformed into a fawning, unquestioning slave to those who inflict this inhuman treatment upon him."

Caihar winced, but Neypo went on. "Recent evidence tells us that if ardent spirits are consumed by the victim, these brain-worms are damaged and the unnatural spell broken. Wennoc in its wisdom has concealed about its body certain instrumentalities we are usually unaware of. The would-be conquerors of our world were ignorant of, or arrogantly discounted, the effects Wennoc's yeasts have upon the juices of its growing things, and the effects of the resultant alcohols and oils have upon one's sensorium, or the unnatural things that may invade his corporeal mind. It may be that the outlanders have forbidden the consumption of such beverages for so long in their own worlds that they have forgotten their properties, or perhaps Wennoc's grain, fruits and yeasts produce something unique to our sacred world. Our good Wennish distillations, and a young Harnishman's seemingly accidental manipulation of an ancient artifact which destroyed the alien ship of space that would have carried news of our Wennoc back to the benighted outer worlds..."

Caihar raised his hand, thinking, not for the first time, that his colleague was sometimes prone to logorrhea. "Let's call it finished just after the bit about 'the spell being broken', Neypo. Our goal should be to present only the things in dire need of our Lodge brothers' immediate attention. We can fill in the details after we decide just how much our fellows in Parnala, not to mention those in Mennedal, really need to know of recent events. Hoiin has the right to its own Lodge Secrets."

Neypo bobbed his head, smiling. "My colleague is back on form. I thank him for his wise counsel."

Noma-Linda passed over her pen, ink bottle and the sheets she had written. Caihar scratched out lines here and there and made a few amendments, and Noma-Linda copied the letter onto clean sheets. The Strivers took it and drew their glyphs at the bottom.

Mercy-Ann held out her hand. "If I may?"

Neypo looked at her in surprise, but passed over the letter and pen. Mercy-Ann scanned what had been written, then jotted her name and office under the Strivers'.

"I have to be practical and look forward," she said huffily, as though someone had criticized her. "I *am* an official of the Lodge, and much of this involved my charge closely."

"Your endorsement of the letter will enhance our credibility," Caihar said with a gracious nod.

Neypo stood and took in the view. There was an acre or two of dry ground surrounding the causeway on this side of the ruins, grassy and speckled with dandelions and bluenoses. Most of Mellatuno's staff and dependents, those who hadn't fled or disappeared, had gone back into the regions that Bunter, the Director's architectural specialist, declared still structurally sound, though a mosaic restorationist had joked sourly that she wouldn't have to leave her studio now when she wanted to go fishing or have a bath.

Samma Mora was apparently anxious enough to bathe that he sat in a shallow pool of water under the branches of a straggling tree that grew out of a wall, scrubbing himself with a brush. Gillensa sat on a bank nearby, a towel ready for Samma. Meantime she tutored Branna Mora as he sketched a view of the ruins.

Neypo sighed, anticipating the decisions that would have to be made and the arguments that would inevitably occur between these two, and Neypo and his wife…Mora Farm, Rose Pond?

Down the causeway the Monitor Smolic was stumping after Binta Mora, who in turn was following a waddling water-hen, trying with simple lessons to restore the intellect he had lost. On higher ground, Adinnegram's former comrades stood talking and eating. A few of them had discarded their armor and put on clothes the Director's staff had found for them.

Neypo spotted Fola Marstoc among them. He called out, "Mister Marstoc! Are you ready?"

"I think so, your Honor," Fola yelled back. Still in armor, he put on his helmet and mounted one of the aliens' rides, which rose and glided up to the causeway. Stubby poles that extended from the side of the machine supported the half-enclosed chair Caihar had ridden in on the trip from Hoiin with Adinnegram's men.

Fola tapped on his wrist and called out in an amplified voice. "Noler! Time to go!"

Noler had acquired a set of glass armor. He and Swannet were sitting together on a low wall over the water, dangling their legs back and forth. Swannet leaned close to whisper something in his ear.

Neffafinnegal, standing nearby, looked away from them.

Fola called again. Now Noler waved, and he and Swannet came down to the Strivers' table. Neypo said, "Are you quite ready, Cadet?"

"Hoy!" said Noler. Eyes averted from Caihar, he and Swannet

embraced. Caihar grimaced. Noler attached his helmet, squirmed as the armor became fully active, then climbed carefully into the carriage attached to Fola's ride.

"You have an adequate command of your suit's operation?" Neypo asked him.

"I hope so."

"Neffafinnegal had his headcasing initialize him," Fola said. "I can finish telling him what I know about it on the way north."

Neypo sealed the letter to the Lodge of Parnala and handed it to him. "Talk to the Strivers Hwiet and Mullipenen at Parnala. They're said to be level-headed men. The fact that a Harnishman and a Hoinish Cadet are working together, and in control of such outlandish gear, should impress the gravity of the situation upon them."

He gave them another letter. "Remember to keep well away from Hoiin on your journey. Go first to Tamanello. This will introduce you to my wife Winetra, although I believe she and Dame Olinom have met you, Cadet. They'll likely still be at the cottage, and they may be able to tell you something of how things have been going up there before you enter Parnala. Remove your casques before you approach the cottage; call out as you walk, 'Do not be alarmed. We are only young human men, and bear news from your husbands and fathers'. Colleague, do you wish to add anything?"

Caihar stood and made a sign over each of their heads. "Wennoc be with you and guide you," he said. "I don't know whether the blessing will penetrate your bottles, but it's worth a try."

"So superstitious," Mercy-Ann muttered.

The riders raised their arms in farewell. Branna, who thought he was gaining skill as an illustrator, scratched his pen over a sheet of paper, taking down a view of the riders.

Caihar stirred himself and wrote out text for the papers to be scattered over Hoiin. Noma-Linda took it and went off to have it set in type.

The Strivers sat sipping their tea for a few moments. "I suppose we'll have to be getting back to the city soon," Neypo said. "Or should we wait for word from Parnala, and go there first?"

"At this stage I don't think there's any pressing need for haste…but it may be that I'm just feeling lazy, or suffering some kind of psychic hangover." Caihar glanced around. "But back to business, where is Micca Mora? I don't believe I've seen him."

Neypo squinted down the causeway. "Off to the island where he hid his—the *outlanders'* flying raft. He was so anxious to show it off to that mountain maiden who came wandering out of the fens that he barely allowed me a ten-minute interview this morning."

Frita had come to collect pots and dishes. "I don't know that this raft thing was their reason for sneaking off," she said, scraping up leftovers, which she threw to a group of water-hens that lingered nearby. "And I hardly think the girl was a maiden in the traditional sense. Didn't you see the way those two were smirking?"

Neypo spoke with dignity. "That is none of our affair."

Mercy-Ann came back. "Speaking of the flying boat, Odé, that villain from Mora promised me a ride through the clouds, and I'll have it or I'll bloody his nose for him."

"What is that you keep muttering?" Ennesia asked as they walked. They had to slosh through water in places, but one of Mellatuno's staff had found some leggings and boots for her to wear. She took a strawberry from a basket she carried and popped it into her mouth. "Some prayer you have to say as an Adjunct to the Lodge? Spells you learned from that so-called cousin of ours? You seem different since you got back into your jar. Always mumbling and playing with your wrist."

"Are you going to bust me over the head again?"

She'd found another stick, and she laughed, flourishing it. "For all the good it would do."

"It wasn't a nice way to say hello. Did you think I was a ghost?"

"I did! You're the last person I expected I'd see here, and I didn't recognize you inside that...why did you put it on again?"

"I told you. I need to find the boat. It's not exactly where I thought I left it. Besides, you said you liked the way it makes me look."

"I said it *flatters* you, in a sort of rude, physical way. And why weren't you wearing your eye-glasses? Isn't there room in there, or are you too vain now?"

"The Directorate in Hannava stole them when they tried to conscript me. I bought new ones, and I lost them in Hoina Bay. I can see really well through my helmet, but I'll have to get another set sooner or later…can't be wearing this *all* the time."

"You've got a lot more to tell me about what happened since you left Mora, I think."

"I don't think I've told you thanks for rescuing me."

Ennesia tilted her head. "It was you who rescued me…I wonder if you're laughing at me in there."

Micca stopped walking. "I didn't know up from down by the time I got out of that place. I was running from something down there, maybe a huge mudrunner, and it almost got me. Seeing you reminded me the real world was still here."

He spoke more slowly. "Until then the Eynnish ghosts were still in my head. Eynnishmen from the beginning of the world, Nessy. Heresiarchs, probably, who put themselves in the machinery. They used my hand to break the outlanders' ship of space. And before the ship died *it* broke the *lamps*, and they fell down and sunk in the sea."

Ennesia stared at him. After a moment she lightly slapped his shoulder with her stick. "The lamps fell into the sea, did they? Just like the song on the radio?"

"Forever and always," Micca sang in a weak voice. "Really, though, it was so weird it's hard to describe."

"I'll take your word for it." She looked up. "I suppose you're right about the lamps, but at least I'm pretty sure the stars haven't winked out, like the song has them doing…

"And what are those blue lights on your chest? They wasn't there before."

"Ah, that's a trick I just learned; I didn't know you could make the suit do that before Branna told me how. The three balls are the three lamps, and it says 'Our Rescuers' under…in Indeduits-Harnish, of course! Kind of a memorial for them."

He smiled at her, but Ennesia looked none the wiser, and maybe it was a stupid joke anyway.

They began walking again. Micca sang, "Even then, I'll be loving you."

Did Ennesia see a smile in his helmet? "Micca, are you making fun of me, or have you become a romantic?"

"You know, I think we're married now. Technically at least. Probably since before Midsomer."

Ennesia frowned. "I guess that's the way it was with the old farm-laws. If they caught you at it, anyway. But I think the couple is supposed to say some lines and throw salt on the fire; you know, to show they're not just casual fornicators like Branna, or some of those tarts you know at Marstoc."

"Maybe we should do that salt thing once we get back."

Ennesia stood still. "Micca, do you mean it? You're not just hysterical after your various frights?"

He took off his helmet so she could see his face, which was flushed and smiling. "Sure, and I'm not hysterical. You've had some frights too, and you don't seem hysterical. How about it?"

She smiled back and nodded slowly. "I'll want to move to Mora, then. When can we go back?"

"Pretty soon, I hope...are you going to eat all those strawberries yourself? I'm hungry."

Micca continued to signal the boat, listening and watching for a response. He was sure they were on the right side of the island now. When he'd heard about Adinnegram running off, he sweat with fear that the man would use his armor to find the boat. But one of the men conscripted from Hannava, out in a flat-bottomed boat with thoughts of fish for supper, had come across a pair of shining hands breaking the surface of the water in the middle of a shallow lake, splashing away like mad. Investigation revealed the erstwhile First Comrade under the hands, stuck in the mud at the bottom of the lake, waist-deep and continuing to sink.

The most popular theory was that Adinnegram had gone in search of the weapon Merit Troavic had thrown from the Director's gazebo; the First Comrade himself wasn't talking. He'd first been secured with ropes around his chest by a crew of frog-men interested in new careers, then with considerable effort pulled out of the mud. He was now presumably thinking things over in a relatively dry cellar at Mellatuno...

After another failed tapping, Micca moved on, and now he was answered.

"Rise!" Micca shouted joyfully, then tapped the command on his wrist. "Rise, three and a half measures: *inpoa!*"

Ennesia gaped at him. Smiling to himself, Micca spread his arms and slowly lifted them like a conjurer.

Ennesia took a step back as the water before them stirred. A long-legged bird standing near them squawked and flapped off. The surface of the water bulged, rippling, swirling. A great rectangular sheet of sun-struck water spread away to show patches of gleaming gray. The mass of the Indeduish lighter rose another yard, then rested in the water.

Ennesia came cautiously forward. "I thought you were out of your head, or fooling me." She threw up her arms and dropped them. "But there it is—whatever it is."

She turned to him with a worried smile. "But really, Micca. That thing can't…it's a, it's a big *rock*!"

Micca tapped and the hatch opened. He hopped onto the deck and held out his hand. "Come on. I want to see if I can find some clothes inside. I'm tired of going around either naked or bottled up."

The lighter floated now at the edge of a tree-lined pond south of Mellatuno. Tangled stems of yellow fen-rose hung over the deck. Micca held an ancient clay pot while Ennesia dropped blossoms into it.

"Are you sure this isn't more trouble than it's worth?" Micca said.

Ennesia shrugged. "There won't be any of these in flower yet at home, and this wedding talk has me feeling sentimental. I'd like a cup of bride's cordial to toast Midsummer—and tonight I wouldn't mind a sip or two of anything that's handy after the ride in this so-called boat…do you think your uncle knows what else goes into it?"

"The cordial? If Danna doesn't, Aunt Marfa will." He felt a breeze come up, and saw a few early stars sparking. He looked to the dimming blue uplands in the north and west, the hills of home. The sloughs would soon be a memory.

"He'll have to get them into the still pretty quick. They're not going to last long."

Colophon

This book was printed using 11,5 pt Adobe Arno Pro as the primary text font, with Brioso Pro used for titles.

Special thanks to Steve Sherman.

Book composition & Typesetting: Joel Anderson
Typographic design: Joel Anderson
Jacket blurb: Koen Vyverman
Management: John Vance, Koen Vyverman